BEEBE LIBRARY
345 MAIN STREET
WAKEFIELD, MA 01880

THE VIOLIN PLAYER
a novel of suspense

John Knoerle

THE VIOLIN PLAYER
a novel of suspense

John Knoerle

Mayhaven Publishing

This is a work of fiction.

Mayhaven Publishing
P O Box 557
Mahomet, IL 61853
USA

All rights reserved.
No part of this book may be reproduced or transmitted in any form or by any means without written permission from the publisher, except for the inclusion of brief quotations in a review.

Cover Art by Jo Kaczmarski. Photographed by Hank Kaczmarski
Copyright © 2004 John Knoerle

First Edition—First Printing 2004
1 2 3 4 5 6 7 8 9 10
Library of Congress Control Number: 2004112472
ISBN 1-932278-01-X

Printed in Canada

Dedicated to my grandfather, John F. Hazleton, Sr.

Also by John Knoerle

Crystal Meth Cowboys
Blue Steel Press - 2003

Acknowledgements

The author would like to express his appreciation to the following for their help and support: Anthony Earle, Richard Procter, Stan Corwin, Renee Raber, David Carmany, Jessica Jacobson, Susan Cohen, Gary Sieck, and the Staff at the Henry County Historical Society.

"The opposite of a great truth is also true."
—Niels Bohr

Chapter 1

I waited patiently. Imagine that. Waited in the dark chill of the lake breeze with only my inadequate impulse control to keep me warm while the Calvary Cemetery groundskeeper puttered about in his little three-wheel cart gathering up trash and stray tools, stopping to upright a vase of flowers. As the PoeT said, "Would a madman have been so wise as this?" It was quite touching really, the old gent tending to his flock, keeping house in the bone yard. Despite what you may have heard, I *can* feel tender emotion. I have the ability to put my feet in the other guy's moccasins—I didn't bust out crying, I'm not a fag—but I thought it was kind of sweet.

When the old fart finally locked up and drove off in his pole truck I waited some more. I didn't have to do this, you understand. I was not under any suspicion, did not suffer from paranoid delusions, did not hear the silken, sad, uncertain surf whispering *beware, Be-ware, Beeee-Warreee*!

Not at all. I just wanted to make sure I was alone.

Climbing the wrought iron fence with the gold-tipped spearpoints was a challenge, I will admit. The front gate was flanked on either side by scalable rough stone posts but where's the sport in *that*? I could have used the floor mats in my Volvo to blunt the spearpoints, but same question. Climbing the fence was easy. It was balancing on the thin upper rail that was tricky. I got my feet underneath me and crouched for a delicious minute with my arms outstretched like a hawk cruising on thermals before I flexed my quads and vaulted up and over. *N.B. I had rolled up my pants cuffs so as not to snag them on the spearpoints.*

The Sumner family plot was arrayed in front of Henry Senior's granite obelisk. I paused to inhale the peaty aroma of Virginia's just-turned grave. The floral arrangements shivered in the cold, saying, 'No fair! Why should we be here in this dark lonely graveyard freezing our pistils off? We didn't even know the woman!'

Well, they *seemed* to be saying that.

I plucked a long stemmed rose from a bouquet and plunged it into the soft soil above Virginia's heart.

Hell of a send-off Virginia. They were hangin' from the rafters. And that eulogy—whoo! I almost lost it when dipshit read the poem. Although it wasn't *strictly* true that you *died alone*, I figured why bring that up and spoil the moment? Anyway, sleep well.

Then I sidled over to her husband's grassy mound and unsheathed my sword. 'Sorry I missed you,' I murmured as I urinated on his grave. I zipped up and admired the empty plots set aside for the other family members. It was all so wonderfully convenient. Just fill in the blanks.

Walter J. Sumner sat at the head of the black walnut refectory table in the dining room of the three-story Cape Cod on Hamilton Street and stared at his hands. He had never sat at the head of this table before, not even as a kid. He hadn't dared. The previous

The Violin Player

occupants had been Henry Sumner Sr., Henry Sumner Jr. and Virginia Hanes Sumner. Walter did not want to be seated at the head of this table at forty-four years old.

Esmerelda went around the table with a tray of cordial glasses. Silvia followed with a half empty bottle of Port. Chairs scraped on the tile floor, throats cleared. The sounds echoed in the high-ceilinged room. Get up Walter, he told himself. Get up and do what you're supposed to do. You've already done the hard part, eulogizing your mother in front of the packed First Presbyterian Church, concluding with a verse from her favorite poet, Elizabeth Barrett Browning.

> *If God compels thee to this destiny,*
> *To die alone, with none beside thy bed*
> *To ruffle round with sobs thy last word said*
> *And mark with tears the pulses ebb from thee,*
> *Pray then alone, 'O Christ come tenderly!'*
> *No earthly friend being near me, interpose*
> *No deathly angel, twixt my face and thine*
> *But stoop Thyself to gather my life's rose,*
> *And smile away my mortal to Divine.*

When Walter stepped down from the podium there wasn't a dry eye in the house. He had felt a rush of exhilaration, a sense of scores settled. Granddad's funeral had featured a fill-in-the-blanks eulogy by a young minister who knew less about the great man than anyone in attendance. Henry Jr's memorial service had taken place in a half-empty downtown church chosen so his former business associates wouldn't have to drive the tedious twenty miles to Evanston. Walter had said a few halting words of tribute to a congregation stealing looks at their Patek Phillipes. But Virginia Sumner's commemorative service had been worthy of the name.

Esmerelda and Silvia returned with a tray of ripe apricots, strawberries, champagne grapes and a board of Stilton. Walt's wife, his two sisters and their husbands remained silent, waiting for him to speak. He told himself this was the easy part. But it was not. This was family. Virginia Hanes Sumner was a powerful woman who kept her clan together by sheer force of gravity, planets circling round the sun. How did one commemorate the passing of the sun?

Laura prodded Walt's ankle with the toe of her shoe. Twice. He climbed to his feet. The others rose with him. Walt picked up his dram of Port and said, "These Lalique glasses were a gift from Granddad and Grandma to Mom and Dad on their wedding day." He looked at the empty bottle of Port on the sideboard. "This Port is what remains from the bottle Mother was drinking on the night she died."

Walter raised his glass to the vaulted ceiling. "To the memory of Virginia Hanes Sumner, a great lady, a wonderful mother and, if I may say so—God knows she'd agree with me—one hell of a powerhouse broad."

The family returned a chorus of 'oh yeah's' and 'got that right's'. They were all tired of the long day's sanctimony. Walt released a laugh that became a sob, choked it off, and tossed back the dram of Port which went down the wrong way and came right back up. He pressed a linen napkin to his mouth, spilling fat tears down his cheeks. Walter shook his head as his wife Laura stepped toward him. He coughed and sputtered into the napkin, turned the napkin over and used the other side to dry his cheeks. The other members of the family regarded him warily, unaccustomed to what they were seeing at the head of the table. The Sumner family were pioneer empire

The Violin Player

builders and stoical Midwest Presbyterians. Sumners didn't cry.

Walt took a breath, folded the napkin, placed it on the table and resumed his seat. The late night wake commenced.

Laura and sister Kay paged through a photo album. Younger sister Chrissie, whose latest diet had something to do with her blood type, issued urgent instructions to Esmerelda. Husband Chris, a recovering alcoholic, stared at his untouched glass of Port. Kay's husband Ted attacked the chunk of Stilton with both hands. Walt surveyed them and smiled at a recollection. When he had asked Laura for her hand in marriage she'd said, "I'm not sure I'd measure up. Your family is just so…perfect." His family was far from perfect, but good enough and better than most.

Twyla, Virginia's overfed Siamese, wandered in looking for treats. If cats went through a mourning period Twyla was showing no signs of it. Walt bent down and hefted her to his lap, grunting with the exertion. Silvia set a cup of black coffee in front of him and added a dollop from the cream pitcher. Walt watched it swirl.

In that final phone conversation with his mother he had heard a sharp crashing sound. Virginia had gone to investigate. She reported that Twyla had jumped up on the stove and knocked over a pot. His mother had a massive old Tappan double oven and gas range that stood at least forty inches high. Twyla couldn't jump a foot. Walt supposed she could have clawed her way up a ladder of open drawers but why bother? She was served a dinner of boiled shrimp and raw kidney every evening at six.

The cat mewled for a crumb of cheese. Walt shushed her and she bounded off his lap with surprising agility. Worry about something important, Walter. Worry about your role as executor of the estate. No one, not even Ted, had been so crass as to mention the twelve million dollar trust fund that passed to the 'remaindermen' upon the death of Virginia Sumner.

"Mom was healthy as a horse," said Chrissie, stirring her nondairy decaf with a splash of kirsch. "She was in the tenth percentile of body fat for her age group and she had me gasping for air trying to keep up with her for a day. And she dies of a *heart attack*?"

Walt sipped his coffee. He agreed with his baby sister. Their father had been glum and withdrawn his last few years. Like Granddad in his hospital bed, Henry Jr. had seemed to await the end impatiently. Virginia Hanes Sumner on the other hand had been having the time of her life. While growing up during the Depression had taught many the virtue of thrift, his mother seemed to have drawn a different lesson. She spent a portion of her wealth on charitable causes and a much greater portion on herself. There was scarcely a foreign land she hadn't visited. Chrissie was right. This was a woman destined for ripe old age.

"It was certainly unexpected," said Walt.

"Seventy-two is not old anymore, not for a woman," said Chrissie. "I read that if a woman reaches fifty-five without getting breast cancer her life expectancy is ninety-two or something."

Walt completed her sentence to himself. "That's twenty years I've been cheated out of." Chrissie always took everything personally.

"We all miss her terribly," said Kay. "But Doctor Cleary said she'd had some trouble with arrhythmia. Maybe you're angry that she didn't—"

"Did *you* know?" demanded Chrissie.

Kay paused before she said a rather unconvincing no.

"I still say it bites," said Chrissie.

"It does," said Kay. "It bites the big one." This response from the famously proper Kay brought barks of laughter from around the table.

"So why are you all *laughing*?" said Chrissie in a voice that chased the cat out of the room. "Seems like you're all just sitting around here going through the motions and talking in low voices while *really* you're fantasizing about your villas in Tuscany and your sixty-foot yawls, or whatever you call them, and all the ways you're going to spend Mom's bazillions of dollars!"

The silence in the room was glacial. Kay stared, Ted stopped chewing. Laura shot her husband a look. Say something! Walt wanted to. He had plenty he wanted to say to and about his baby sister but said only, "It's been a long day."

The rest of the table rose with Walter. It was not a sign of deference to the new head of the family so much as a desire to get out before the dam burst. They scattered to the living room and the glassed-in porch, spouses muttering to each other in code. Laura said something Walt understood as "How can you just walk away?"

Walter muttered something Laura understood as "This is not the time or place." They passed through the kitchen and pushed through the swinging doors to the sitting room where Virginia had writhed and gasped and breathed her last.

"*Posole*," said Laura, inhaling the aroma from the serving kitchen, her face flushed. "That's definitely *posole*."

"I'll be in the study," said Walt. He didn't want to reminisce with Silvia and Esmerelda, whose family had worked for his family for two generations, sample their delicious hominy stew and then hand them their severance pay. He had a long list of such tasks and no idea where to start.

Walt entered the mahogany paneled study that had been his father's smoking room before he had been banished to the porch in warm weather and the garage in cold. He assumed the walnut armchair in front of the oak roll-top desk. His mother would miss the gallery opening this evening. A sticky note read *Bill & Jean, P.T. Gal'ry, 7P.*

Walt choked back a clutch of grief. He wiped his leaky eyes furiously and tried to concentrate on the task at hand. He opened desk drawers bursting with unfiled bills and receipts. The hell with it. Not now. He moved over to the computer table and called up the GenealoG website where he had posted the family tree.

His mother had been dubious when Walt began his research on the Sumner family shortly after his Dad's death. "They were just a bunch of dirt farmers," she had said. Her side of the family were the true aristocrats, her grandfather the mayor of New Castle and her father a Superior Court judge. But Mom had been very pleasantly surprised when Walt's research of the paternal line uncovered John Sumner Sr., his gr.gr.gr.gr.grandfather who fought the British as a member of the Westmoreland County Militia in the Revolutionary War. And she had ooh'ed and ahh'ed like a schoolgirl when he'd rolled out the complete eight-generation family tree on the dining room table.

Walter began to receive inquiries and contributions of material once he posted his research on the website. Some were breathless emails. "Great News! I think I have found the wedding date of your gr.gr.uncle—" Others sniffed, "This is not a branch of the family I am particularly interested in, however—" Almost all were from women. Walt assumed they were little old ladies with little else to do.

Then a treasure trove arrived from cyberspace. A complete report on the descendants of John Sumner Sr., including a copy of his will, a concise account of the family's migration west, a portion of a journal

The Violin Player

kept by John's wife, and an article about a distant uncle who was killed at Gettysburg. The sender, Alice Langley, wrote: "I hope this is of interest to you." It was that. Walt replied with profuse thank you's and requested her address so he could send a gift basket. "No basket gift is necessary," Alice Langley e-mailed in return. "I have already this information here and am please to share."

Alice Langley's data served to graft flesh onto the skeleton of names and dates. The Sumner family had been true American pioneers, on the first wave of the great migration west, already settled on the far side of the Cumberland Pass and the daunting Allegheny Ridge when John Sr. was born in 1760. They had founded Saltlick Township in the Ohio Valley in 1814, and bred like fruit flies. Every generation prior to his grandfather's had a minimum of eight children. If a wife died in childbirth the husband buried her, waited a year, married again and sired more. The Sumners fought the nation's wars, tamed its wilderness, raised its crops and schooled its children. They made Walter feel proud—and insignificant by comparison.

Walt typed in the family name and clicked SEARCH. He intended to enter his mother's date of death on the family page and write a tribute in the profile section. The morbid protocol of genealogy forbade such biographical details until the subject was deceased. The computer screen painted the familiar parchment yellow family webpage with its dates of birth, death, marriage and list of offspring in a separate box below. Walter loved the ruthless simplicity of it. This was what counted and could be verified.

He clicked through the generations to arrive at the family page of his parents, Henry and Virginia Sumner, married in New Castle, IN, 10 June, 1953. He scrolled down and positioned the cursor to enter his mother's date of death.

It was already there. 12 September, 1999.

John Knoerle

Odd. He hadn't posted a note on the website bulletin board, but Virginia's obituary had been published in local newspapers. Someone must have seen it and entered her D.O.D. as a tribute. Or some cyberghoul just had to be the first to document her death. It didn't mean anything. Still, no one had ever made an addition to his family tree before.

Walt felt himself growing angry. Entering his mother's date of death was *his* ceremonial prerogative. Did these people have nothing better to do? He meandered around the multilayered site in hopes of finding a visitor's log or some other means of tracing the unbidden contributor. There was nothing.

Driving down Lake Shore an hour later Walt told Laura what he had found. She agreed that it was rude. At least she said she did. Walt suspected Laura feigned interest in his family research the way other wives pretended fascination with fly fishing lures. They passed between the winking high-rises and the darkness of Lincoln Park in companionable silence.

"I thought the funeral went very well," said Walt, fishing for a compliment. "I think Mother would have been very pleased." He glanced over at his wife. She was asleep.

Walt piloted his Jaguar XJR down North Avenue and turned right on Paulina. Young couples were still out enjoying the Indian summer evening, returning from a late dinner at Club Lucky or Café Absinthe, drinks at the Mad Bar, or music at the Double Door. There was always something doing in Bucktown. Laura came to as they rumbled over the cobblestones of Bloomingdale. She reached up and pressed the remote control clipped to the sun visor and Walt pulled into the garage of their four-story, Frank Lloyd Wright inspired, red brick trimmed in white marble home.

Chapter 2

Walt hung his suit jacket on the cherrywood coat rack that matched the desk and credenza in his corner office on LaSalle. Henry Sumner Jr. had labored downtown for many years as a VP of CanneCo, an international food conglomerate. He had advised his son against locating his business in the Loop. "Nobody makes anything downtown anymore," he had said. "Downtown is just a place where a bunch of lawyers, bankers and executives pay too much rent to sit around and stare at each other." But Walt was able to negotiate a long-term lease on favorable terms before the downtown renaissance began in the early 90's. The LaSalle Street address gave him instant cachet and helped attract the bright indefatigable youngsters he needed to work the brutal hours required by a round the clock international dairy exchange.

Walt resisted the urge to look over the printout of the overnight sales figures. Once he started his daily routine he would look up five minutes later and find it was eight p.m. He searched the GenealoG brochure for a corporate ID but the lawyers had been there before him. GenealoG existed only as an 800 number and a website both of which, Walt suspected, were outsourced. There was no point in wandering through a phone tree to speak to a minimum wage employee in a boiler room somewhere in North Dakota.

Walt dialed Marcy's extension. When in doubt, delegate. He knew it was foolish of him to get so worked up about this but, dammit, it wasn't right.

Marcy burst in about thirty seconds later. She was wearing a pair of parachute pants and a puffy-sleeved peasant blouse that she must have had since high school and which looked as if she had slept in, which she probably had since she more or less lived in the offices of Sumner International.

"Took your sweet time," said Walt sternly.

"What? Oh sorry, I stopped to splash some water on my face and—you're teasing me again, aren't you?"

Walt grinned. No one on the staff of Sumner International could resist teasing their perpetually frazzled systems analyst. "Yes I am. But I promise never to tease you again if you can work your magic and penetrate this corporate shell."

Marcy took the brochure, parked her glasses on her curly mop, squinted and looked up. "You're teasing about the teasing, aren't you?"

"Of course. But I need you to do this. It concerns the death of my mother."

Marcy's expression darkened. The boss never discussed family matters at work. Walt explained about his mother's D.O.D.

"I'll do it on my lunch hour," said Marcy.

"No, go ahead and do it now." Walt looked up a moment later. Marcy was still standing there. "You're free to go, Ms. Huber."

The Violin Player

Walt's chest swelled as he strode the trading floor of Sumner International, a sea of glowing computer terminals under a twelve-by-twenty-foot black and white photo of his grandfather's creamery in New Castle. Sumner International bought great quantities of butter, cheese, and dry milk powder and sold it to traders overseas. Most of his customers were in Asia. Walt had foreseen the dairy revolution in Asia and been among the first to cultivate personal relationships with several key traders and trade ministers in Japan, China, Korea, and Singapore. Initial sales had been slow. Most Asian adults were lactose intolerant. But the next generation, weaned on baby formula, had no such problem. Young Japanese had acquired a taste for American cheese. Koreans favored yogurt and yogurt drinks. And the Chinese were consuming ice cream at a rate that would make them the world's number one market in ten to fifteen years.

If only his grandfather could see him now. "Make your own way," had been Granddad's simple creed. And that he had, rising before dawn to drive a milk wagon during high school. After graduation he pulled double shifts at the creamery, worked his way up to foreman, saved every nickel and bought the place from its ailing owner a few years later. He promoted the Dairy Dream brand through the new medium of radio, built a chain of regional creameries throughout the Midwest and sold out to CanneCo during the conglomerate craze of the 1960's.

Walt's father signed on in the early 50's, a few years after college. He started as a sales rep and graduated to sales manager of the seven-state territory. In a negotiated provision of Granddad's sale, Henry Jr. became VP of Sales at CanneCo. He prospered for many years, was promoted to Executive VP and transferred from corporate headquarters in Chicago to Paris where he oversaw

European sales. His central function was to wine and dine government officials and food distributors and "don't spare the horses." It was, Walt's father often said, "a long way from taking grocery-store rack jobbers out for pork fritters and fried pie."

The bubble burst in 1985. A group of New York investment bankers took advantage of CanneCo's undervalued stock and seized control in a leveraged buyout. Henry Jr. returned to Chicago to receive the golden handshake and get shown the door at the ripe old age of fifty-four. There were not, he soon discovered, many other $600,000 a year jobs available to him.

Walt loved and respected his father. But he idolized his grandfather. They shared that special bond between old and young, allied in opposition to the middle generation in charge. Their conversations were always the same, sitting in the glassed-in porch in the house on Hamilton, Walt jumping up from time to time to refill Granddad's glass. Walt would ask a question, Granddad would say "Oh I don't know," puff on his expensive corona, sip his cheap Scotch and, a minute or so later, render his considered opinion.

In retrospect he had been wrong about many things. "National advertising be damned, brand loyalty is regional." Enter McDonalds. "No one's going to pay a dollar for a quart of ice cream just to get a little more butterfat." Haagen Daz came along a few years later. But Granddad had anticipated Henry Jr.'s fate by many years, telling Walt, "Don't go to work for a Fortune 50. You're a thoroughbred, not a dray horse." Several puffs and a swig of Green Stripe later he added, "They'll ship you off to the glue factory just about the time you hit your stride."

At the time Walt thought his grandfather had been speaking about himself, about hearing the thundering hooves of the multinationals and having to sell out before he was trampled underfoot.

The Violin Player

But Granddad had not been bitter about his fate. He had done well. It was his grandson he was concerned about. How would Walt manage to continue the Sumner legacy of roll up your sleeves business building in a world dominated by corporate behemoths? Henry Jr. had plainly been a disappointment in this regard. He was a *yee*, Granddad's disdainful shorthand for an employee, not a *yer*. And it would never have occurred to Henry Sr. that his granddaughters could be entrepreneurs. So it fell to Walt to carry the mantle. This was never overtly stated—didn't need to be. Walter knew it as certainly as he knew his own name.

Trading basic commodities was a low-margin business. The real profits lay in buying product—not directly from dairy co-ops in Wisconsin and California, but via futures contracts on the Chicago Mercantile Exchange. The plan was to make major purchases when the quoted futures of butter, cheese, and dry milk powder dipped, take delivery when the prices rebounded and pocket the difference. Walt devised a complex risk management program that required constant input of climatological and agricultural production data, a program designed to give Sumner International a window into the future and a subsequent competitive advantage in commodities speculation. That was the theory. In 1991 Walt set about applying his risk management program on a daily basis. Incredibly, it worked.

"I think it breaks left then right," said Walt standing behind one of his e-traders who was lining up a putt on his computer screen. The young man arched his back and froze. He had a quarter-sized bald spot on the crown of his skull. Walt tried to think of something else to say. He was no good at banter. And he didn't play golf. Keyboards stopped tapping, heads swung in his direction. The moment expanded. Marcy, waving and gesticulating from the door of his office, rescued him. "Carry on," said Walt lamely and hurried off.

Marcy looked fit to burst as Walt closed the door behind him. "Were you able to penetrate the website?" Marcy nodded. "Did you find out who posted my mother's date of death?" Marcy nodded. "Who was it?"

Marcy looked at a piece of paper she was holding, coughed and said, "Alice Langley at truenet.com."

Walt felt disappointed. He couldn't very well flame the little old lady who had contributed three long lost generations to his family tree. She had said she lived in Lima, Ohio. How had she heard about his mother's death in Illinois?

Marcy continued to look at the piece of paper. "Your mother died Thursday night didn't she?"

"Yes. I called you Friday morning."

"I'm not insane, that's good," said Marcy. "I used a packet sniffer to hack in. Totally cheeseball security but I guess they figure, what's there to steal? I searched the contributor's log from Thursday night on and got zero hits on your page. This did not compute." Marcy ran a hand over her tightly curled copper hair. "So I did the only other thing I could think of to do, searched the log for contributions to your page *prior* to Thursday night and, guess what, got a hit from Thursday afternoon."

Walt stared at Marcy. Her glasses were so thick it was difficult to make precise eye contact.

Marcy handed Walt the piece of paper. "I printed it off. Alice Langley at truenet.com entered your mother's date of death approximately six hours before it occurred."

Chapter 3

Walt had expected Evanston police detectives to wear blazers and bow ties, but the taut young man who sat across the desk from him wore a windbreaker over a purple Northwestern t-shirt. He had sandy hair and ghostly white eyebrows. His unblinking gaze made Walt squirm in the battered metal chair. The police scanner squawked and squelched from a speaker on the wall. Someone requested backup on a traffic stop.

"So Alice Langley doesn't exist," said Detective Lieutenant Chris Bjork.

"Not so far as I can determine. I called 411 in Lima, Ohio, also the police department there, the county registrar. No record of her anywhere."

Bjork ran his hand over his mouth, across a pale wispy mustache Walt hadn't noticed before. His look said what did you expect, dimwad, entrusting personal information to some phantom on the internet. "And say again about the cat."

"I was on the phone to my mother, as I mentioned, at the time of her...attack. She heard a crash in the kitchen. I heard it too, and she went in, she has...had a cordless phone, and said her cat had knocked a pot off the stove. But her stove is about four feet high and her cat, who is, uh, quite stout I'd guess you'd say, couldn't jump a foot."

Bjork jotted a note and said, "Was your tech expert able to determine where the email posting came from?"

Walt pointed to Marcy's printout on the desk. "Well—"

"Not the internet service provider, the actual physical location from which the message was sent."

"Uh, no. That is, actually, I didn't think to ask her that."

Bjork waved him off. "We have a computer crimes unit that can pin that down if it comes to that."

"*Comes* to that? My mother's date of death was posted before she died, what more do you need?"

Bjork surveyed Walter with lupine blue eyes. He seemed to be listening to the unfolding drama on the police scanner. The dispatcher reported that the motorist had an outstanding felony warrant. "An autopsy," said Bjork. "We need to exhume your mother's remains and conduct a forensic autopsy to determine if she died of unnatural causes."

"Oh," said Walt. Until that moment it hadn't seemed quite real, the absurd notion that someone had set out to purposely murder a harmless life-loving seventy-two-year-old woman. The image of latex-gloved lab techs probing his mother's ashen carcass brought it home in a hurry.

"You okay? Want some coffee?"

Walt shook his head. "Wouldn't the coroner's report tell you what you need to know?"

"Case like this, elderly person, heart seizure, they just check for signs of trauma and sign it off. They'd need to examine her stomach contents and work up a tox report."

The Violin Player

"To see if she was, what, poisoned?"

Bjork shrugged.

Walt gripped the cold steel arms of his chair. Poisoned. He felt a scrim of sweat forming on his brow. Christ Almighty, it had been his idea to serve the bottle of Port his mother had been drinking on the night she died. He might have killed off half the family! Walt took a shallow breath and said, "Whatever you need to do."

Bjork nodded and stood up. When Walt got to his feet he felt better. Detective Bjork was several inches shorter. "I ask only that you don't announce this to the media. I don't want to stir up speculation in the local press."

Bjork held up a finger, listening. An officer radioed that the motorist had been hooked and booked. Walt heard the suspect protesting his innocence from the back of the squad car. Detective Bjork smiled a thin smile and said, "I hate the media with a passion."

Laura checked her watch when she heard the doorbell ring. 5:35. She set her glass down and peered through the fan window in the front door. Two men stood outside the wrought iron gate. The detective hadn't said anything about a partner. She pressed the intercom. "Who is it?"

"Detectives Bjork and Hernandez."

"Your appointment was for six."

"We're early," came the reply.

Laura ran her hands through her hair and buzzed them in, happy she had dropped the girls off at the cineplex at five.

They were quite handsome, the two detectives, one a Nordic blonde, the other a beefy Hispanic with big eyes and piano key teeth. Laura ushered them upstairs to the living room and ducked into the bathroom to freshen her breath. When she returned the detectives had their backs to her, admiring the view.

"You believe these fucking *palacios*?" said Hernandez. "In this neighborhood?"

"My old man grew up four blocks from here," said Bjork. "Used to run with the Insane Unknowns."

"That's a Rican gang."

"Is now. Forty years ago it was a bunch of badass Swedes."

Laura cleared her throat. "Why don't I make some coffee," she said, hoping to stall until her husband got home.

Bjork turned to face her. "That won't be necessary." The detectives settled into the white twill couch. Laura took a seat in the Queen Anne chair, thinking the cops looked supremely silly amidst the potted mums and the French café posters.

"First off," said Hernandez, extracting a throw pillow from behind his back, "Let me apologize for the press leak. It wasn't our doing. We think someone in the medical examiners office went public and we're looking into that. I'm guessing your husband was upset."

Laura remembered Walt's howling fury when they learned the results of the prominent Evanston socialite's autopsy on the ten o'clock news. The medical examiner had found traces of a sophisticated drug cocktail in her system that could induce cardiac arrest.

"You could say that. He should be here soon by the way."

"Great," said a grinning Hernandez as a grim Bjork flipped open a notepad. "In the meantime maybe you can help us fill in some background." Bjork uncapped his pen with his teeth. "Was your mother-in-law a happy person?"

"Yes. Very happy."

"No violent mood swings, prolonged depressions?"

The Violin Player

Laura considered. Did chronic impatience count as a violent mood swing? "No, not to my knowledge."

Bjork made a note. Hernandez continued. "Did she have any enemies, cheese anyone off enough to want to do her harm?" Bjork sat with his pen poised.

"No, not to my knowledge."

"How did your husband and his mother get along?"

"Fine."

"Always?"

Laura looked at Bjork, at his poised pen. "Always."

"Maybe I should explain what's going on," said Detective Hernandez, unzipping a blinding smile that Laura did not return.

"Case of poisoning, first thing we have to decide is if it's suicide. You don't seem to think so and we don't either. No note, no serious health problems, plenty of dough." Hernandez made the slightest nod in the direction of his partner. "Which leaves us with an unsolved homicide. At the Academy they teach that a homicide investigation is simple as ABC. *A*libi. Who could've been at the murder scene and who couldn't've. Gonna be tough in this case 'cause the poison could've been planted anytime really. *B*ystanders, a.k.a. eyewitnesses, none of which we have so far. And *C*ircumstantial evidence. Forensics, motivation. Nothing there either, other than the unusual poison. No sign of forced entry. We did take some prints but—" Hernandez shook his head. "Can you think of anyone with a motive to kill Virginia Sumner?"

"No," said Laura emphatically. "And what did you mean about the poison, that it could have been planted at any time?"

Hernandez hesitated, looked to his partner, said, "Well—" Laura said, "Whoever poisoned Virginia Sumner knew when she was going to die."

John Knoerle

Detective Bjork finally spoke. "We'll get to that. Right now we'd like to concentrate on motive."

"Meaning money, I suppose," said Laura.

"Mrs. Sumner did leave a substantial estate," said Bjork.

"Really?" said Laura. "How much is it?"

"Over a million dollars."

"Our net worth is considerably greater than that and, considering Virginia's estate will be divided between her three children and various charities, I think your implication that we murdered her for money seems pretty poorly thought out." Laura added, "Do your homework" and immediately regretted it.

Detective Bjork flipped back pages in his notepad.

"Upon the death of Virginia Sumner the twelve million dollar trust of Henry Sumner Senior passes to your husband and his sisters, with your husband to receive 50% according to the terms of the instrument. Walter Sumner met recently with officers of Chicago Trust to encourage them to sell off a substantial portion of the T-bills and municipal bonds in the trust and invest the proceeds in more aggressive stocks and mutual funds in order to grow the principal that he and his sisters would inherit." Bjork closed his notepad and looked up. "The officers at Chicago Trust unanimously declined this request, saying it was 'inappropriate'."

Laura sat with her hands in her lap. This was all news to her. Bjork asked if her husband had discussed this request to alter the trust with her. She said her husband handled all the finances. Was this why the detectives had arrived early? To divide and conquer?

Bjork made a note. Hernandez cranked up another grin. "We're not trying to pin anyone to the wall this early in the investigation, Mrs. Sumner, we're just—" He splayed out his long brown fingers and skittered them about. "Picking up the pieces."

The Violin Player

Hernandez sat back and stretched out his legs. A black leather ankle holster protruded from his pants leg. Laura looked away, out the window at the crumbling, yellow train trestle that bridged Paulina. The tracks were empty, too early at twilight for the late night psychos who occasionally raged outside their bedroom window. Where the hell was Walter?

"How did Virginia get along with her daughters?" said Hernandez. "So far as you know?"

"Okay. So far as I know."

"And their husbands?"

"Well, she didn't suffer fools gladly."

"She was rude to them?"

"No, no. Just very, very polite." Laura stood up at the sound of an opening door. "That's my husband. I'll let him know you're here."

The detectives stood as one. "I'm sure he can find us," said Detective Hernandez.

They remained standing until Laura resumed her seat. They waited in silence for Walt to climb the stairs.

"Sorry I'm late," he said a moment later. "Have you been waiting long?"

Laura didn't answer. Poor dumb loveable oblivious Walt assumed they had been making idle chitchat while awaiting his arrival. He hadn't always been this dim. He had even been funny once upon a time. And touchingly vulnerable in his younger years as he floundered about trying to find his way in the world. But with every new level of accomplishment, he became a little more sealed off and not quite there. If he achieved any greater success Laura feared the Walter Sumner she'd married would disappear altogether.

"I was ambushed by a TV camera crew at work this morning," said Walt. "Wanting me to cry on cue."

Hernandez repeated his apology about the press leak. Walt nodded grudgingly. He looked distracted, holding his briefcase and a FedEx package in one hand and patting his pockets with the other. Laura tried to catch his eye. "So what progress do you gentlemen have to report?"

"Only one thing definitive so far, other than you were right about Mrs. Sumner being poisoned," said Bjork.

They waited as Walt searched himself. You would think he would pay more attention to news about his mother's murder but Walter Sumner, Laura had learned, could only concentrate on one thing at a time. He pulled a wadded up memo from his breast pocket and turned to the officers. "*I* was right?"

Bjork flipped pages in his book. "In my office. You asked if your mother was poisoned."

"Yes, but you said they were going to pump her stomach." Bjork shrugged. Walt caught his wife's be-careful glance. He crossed the room and perched on the arm of her chair. "You said you had something definitive."

"Yes. The email, the premature posting to the website of your mother's date of death," said Detective Bjork. "It was sent from Ground Zero, a cyber café half a block from your office."

Laura watched her husband's face.

"That's my coffee shop," he said.

"Ground Zero?" said Hernandez.

"Yes," said Walter, barely audible.

Detective Bjork made a note.

Laura said, "Walter, they think you had an ulterior motive for telling the bank officers to juice up your Grandfather's trust."

Walter came to, back on solid ground. He explained that he'd had his mother's best interests at heart, that he fully expected her to live another twenty years and for her to do so in comfort and still have plenty left over for her children they needed to grow the principal.

"Did your mother agree with your suggestion about the trust?" said Hernandez.

"Well, it would have reduced her monthly income."

"Is that a no?"

"This is ridiculous," said Walt. "I wouldn't kill my mother over an asset allocation dispute!"

"No?" said Detective Bjork. "We had a moke down on Howard Street who killed his mother over an asset allocation dispute. I believe it was twenty bucks."

Detectives Bjork and Hernandez sat back on the white twill couch and grinned at one another like smartass kids.

Laura stood up and said, "Get out of my house. Both of you."

Chapter 4

There is another pervasive, pernicious myth about us that I would like to take this occasion to dispel—that we're somehow superhuman and as infallible as the Pontiff when he's on the throne, speaking *ex cathedra*. I am also on the throne at the moment, in ze bunker, the bottom apartment of a four-flat owned by a grotesquely porculent Ukrainian with diabetes who can only shuffle from his first floor apartment to the front stoop and back again. *I do repairs and maintenance.* Ralph has been a neighborhood fixture for years, greeting one and all from his stoop chair, the back legs sawed off so it fits the steps, while his fuzzy little dog spins and yaps, and I am considered something of a saint for looking after him—the neighbors don't know I don't pay rent. If I'm ever called before the bar of justice I'll have plenty of character witnesses.

But I digress.

I was reflecting on my encounter with Virginia Sumner. While the result was perfect, the execution, pun intended, was less so. Too easy. Old money makes you soft. While your typical *nouveau riche* social climber would have had an alarm system or a Rottweiler, or both, sweet Virginia had been swimming in it so long she had lost

The Violin Player

all sensation in her extremities. The back door was *unlocked* and the only attack dog was a fat Siamese who rubbed up against my leg and purred. Ho Mama! I thought to myself, I am *off* to Yokohama!

My plan was to inject my syringe into one of Virginia's chosen late night comestibles and get the hell out. *Her garbage told me Virginia favored Harriman's Port, Bosch pears and Eli's cheesecake.* But once inside, the spent adrenaline puddling in my shoes, I felt tremendously relaxed. I could hear Virginia talking and laughing on the other side of the swinging doors. Had I missed it? Was he, in fact, *here*?

An open bottle of Port sat on the kitchen counter. I could have dosed it and been gone. But I am not a mass murderer. I am a *sequential* murderer—and that's an important distinction. And I was so enjoying my stay in Virginia's cozy kitchen. She had rows of mason jars filled with exotic pastas as well as yellow metal canisters with brown lids that were labeled Flour, Sugar, Lard. *Didn't lard need to be refrigerated?* No. Moms always kept a can of Crisco in the cupboard next to the jumbo bag of popcorn which was dinner more nights than not. Feeling sorry for me? Don't. You haven't lived till you've gorged yourself on Uncle Bub's Authentic Hoosier Popping Corn cooked in a cast iron pot greased with lard.

I bided my time. I knew from her easy tone and the frequent interruptions that Virginia was speaking to a close relative or intimate acquaintance. This would make things easier in the short term and more difficult in the long. "Walter!" she said, laughing loudly. "Walter don't you dare!"

Walter! It was Walter! *Jesu Christi qui tole peccata mundi*! Walter Sumner could *listen in* as his mother made strangled sounds over the telephone! *But how to engineer it in a timely manner?*

John Knoerle

The *cat*. I would kick the cat through the swinging doors whereupon she would yowl, whereupon Virginia would think she was hungry and carry her back into the kitchen, whereupon she would set down her glass while she rummaged in the refrigerator—whereupon I would do the deed.

I'm off the throne now, you'll be glad to know. Anointing myself with holy water.

I imagine Virginia would have done as she was bidden had I not, bending down to scoop up the cat, *stupidly* caught the sleeve of my pea coat on a long-handled pot and knocked it clattering to the floor! I considered bolting out the back door, the job undone. I considered bolting through the swinging doors to beg forgiveness on bended knee. But, thankfully, sanity prevailed. I grabbed up the cat and put her on the stove, then backed into the pantry and got small.

Virginia flew through those swinging doors shouting, 'Get *down* from there you bad girl!' She set down her wine glass in order to pick up the pot. The glass was close to empty. *Merde.* My elixir was almost tasteless. I know, I tasted it. But dissolved in such a small solution it would be noticed. I waited, my telltale eye watching from behind the pantry door, my telltale heart jackhammering away.

I pictured, *fantasized* about, and ENCAPSULATED in supercharged psychic energy a piece of cheesecake. It was rich and creamy, a microscopic film of condensation *silvering* its puckered surface. I sent this image to Virginia as she rattled away on the telephone to her only son. She stuck her head inside the refrigerator less than a minute later. *She did, I swear!* My thinking was that a slice of sickly sweet cheesecake required a fresh glass of sickly sour Port. I crept from the shadows and dosed her glass, swirling it like a sommelier. The cat kept quiet. Cats understand skullduggery.

Virginia decided against the cheesecake but—*phew*! She did

The Violin Player

refill her glass.

Diatolphetathine causes a dramatic acceleration of the heartbeat. Atriothreynathil constricts the vascular system. The result is akin to connecting a soda straw to a fire hydrant. The blood vessels simply explode.

I listened to Virginia die from the other side of the swinging doors. When she was quiet, I pushed through and damned if the old ho-bag wasn't still alive. Lying on the floor staring up at me, her mouth moving soundlessly, blood spurting from her nose, Walter bellowing *'mom, mom, mom, mom'* on the other end of the line.

I stood there until her eyes grew opaque and her breathing ceased. I wanted to say a little prayer—I had thoughtfully memorized a passage from the Dead Sea Scrolls—but the phone was still on so I picked up the wine glass with my gloved hand, rinsed it out thoroughly in the kitchen sink, petted the kitty and left by the back door, *making a solemn pledge to do a better job the next time.*

Chapter 5

"So where does everybody want to eat?" said Walt as the Jaguar XJR wheeled away from the cineplex on Webster.

"Chuck E. Cheese, Chuck E. Cheese!" sang six-year-old Irene. "Oh vomit," said ten-year-old Thea.

Laura said, "Did you go to the Pokemon movie like you promised?" Silence from the back seat. "Thea?"

"Chuck E. Cheese it is," said Walt, passing the Gutman Tannery, crossing the Chicago River and signaling for a right hand turn on Ashland Avenue.

The girls followed their parents to the table after Walt ordered a pizza at the counter. "You don't have to sit," said Walt. "Not at Chuck E. Cheese." They were gone in a blink, Thea to play skee ball, Irene to ride the kiddie cars. Walt looked across the table at his wife.

"Why didn't you tell me you talked to the trust officers?"

"I didn't think it was that important," said Walter. "I mean, I've currently got a nine hundred thousand dollar position in November dry milk futures which, if the market doesn't rebound in the next few weeks, is going to put me in a world of trouble."

"And you didn't tell me that either."

The Violin Player

"I didn't want to worry you."

"Nine hundred? Why so much?"

"We haven't had a great year. I got greedy and tried to make it up on one trade."

"Could the police know about that? Think you're desperate for money?"

"They couldn't possibly," said Walt, still toting it up in his head. The cops didn't like it that he was on the phone to his mother at the time of her death. Too convenient. Same for his recollection of a loud crash in her kitchen. "But if I supposedly went to all this trouble to cover my tracks why would I post the email from a place right next door to my office?"

Laura placed her hand behind her ear. Walt repeated what he had said, adding, "And if I did place some poison somewhere in the house how would I know when she would, you know, what her date of death would be?"

"I've been puzzling on that a bit," said Laura. "Either her date of death was entered after the fact and pre-dated by some computer hocus pocus—"

"Marcy checked that. It wasn't."

"Or...Reenie, the pizza's not here yet, hon. Go see what your sister's up to, 'kay? Or...well, the cops asked if you had a key to her house—"

"To which I said yes!"

"Yes." Laura reached across the table to squeeze her husband's hand. "Of course you did. Why wouldn't you have a key to your own mother's house? What I think, what I *fear* is that the cops are thinking *I* called your mother to generate a phone record and create a distraction while you used your key to slip in and—" Walt buried his face in his hands.

"I was supposed to be there that night," said Walter after a time. "Remember? Mother wanted to discuss her finances for some reason. She called later to reschedule. Do you remember that?"

"I think so," said Laura.

"Could that mean something?"

"I'm not sure," said Laura. She tugged on his hand, pulling him closer. "Walter, I think the fact that the email was sent from next door to your office means someone has it in for you, not your mother. They killed her to get to you. Who in the world could possibly hate you that much?"

Walt shook his head very slowly. Laura turned to see Thea and Irene standing together at the head of the table, bored with the Chuck E. Cheese experience and frightened by the anxious and sorrowful faces of their parents.

Walt squared his shoulders in front of the double doors of Sumner International. He had used his pass key to enter through a fire door in order to avoid the camera crews laying in wait at the front of the building. His previous day in the office had been bad enough. After the media reported that his mother had been poisoned, Walt had been faced with clammy-handed employees expressing their sympathies at every turn. Today would be worse. The ten o'clock news had reported that dairy magnate Walter Sumner was now the prime suspect in the murder of his mother, wealthy Evanston socialite Virginia Hanes Sumner. No cops would say this on camera. The reporter cited reliable sources inside the department. Walt put his head down and entered the office.

He returned the receptionist's greeting cheerfully and marched down the corridor towards his office. Some of the administrative

The Violin Player

staff were chatting in the doorways. They fell silent as he approached. Jeffrey, his young operations manager, stepped forward to say something. "Did we ever get those supplier invoices figured out?" said Walt. He had been so preoccupied he'd lost track of the accounts, but there were always supplier invoices that needed figuring out.

"I'm working on it—"

"Good," said Walt and walked on, bracing himself for his encounter with round-faced, African-American Hyrametta, his secretary, his Gorgon at the door. Would she be arch? Sympathetic? Arm's length polite? Hyrametta always set the emotional tone for the rest of the office. She shuffled papers around her desk as Walt approached. He could feel the staff watching them. He began with his customary, "What's on the docket, Hyrametta?"

She examined his schedule, rattled off his list of appointments and conference calls, looked up and smiled from here to eternity. "And that's all you have to deal with today," she said. Walt thanked her, entered his office and closed the door.

He scanned the printout of the overnight sales figures, got on his desktop and checked the Chicago Mercantile Exchange site. Shit. The settle price of the November dry milk contract was down to 9.69 cents per pound, approaching a five-year low. What else could go wrong?

Marcy, arms wide, a tear trickling down her tallowed cheek, appeared moments after Walt buzzed her extension. "It's just so unfair!" she said as she rushed forward. Her arms didn't reach so Walt had to stand up and lean his head across the desk. Her hair was scratchy.

"I'm at a loss Marcy. I can't even begin to figure it. The only thing that comes to mind is to trace this phantom e-mailer somehow, find out who had that truenet address. Is that something you could do?"

Marcy chewed a thumbnail and looked sad. "I *could*. I could try hacking into truenet's accounts, but that's their bread and butter so they'll be seriously encrypted. And even if I do get through I can't picture that this...*person*, whoever did this, would have given their real name and address. Most likely he pinched someone else's credit card number to pay for the account."

"But he, or she, has been sending me stuff for three months. If it was a pirated credit card number the card holder would've noticed by now."

Marcy screwed up her face. "Ummmmmmm, not necessarily. If the e-mailer used a corporate account it might not get flagged for months."

"I guess that's possible," said Walter and, "Oh Christ."

Chapter 6

Laura set a bottle of cognac on the black walnut refectory table in the dining room of the house on Hamilton. "Remy Martin anyone?" There was silence around the table. "No, it's not from Virginia's liquor locker." Walter, Chrissie, Kay and husband Ted accepted a tumbler. Chris said nothing and wet his lips.

The forensics team had finished their work and unsealed the crime scene. Walt had been pouring over papers in the study most of the day. When Laura arrived he showed her a check stub. Virginia had written Chrissie a check for ten thousand dollars on the day she died, a check that was not in the stack of ready to be mailed correspondence on her roll-top desk. It appeared Chrissie had come calling on that fateful day.

Kay said, "Walt, I think I speak for everyone here when I say these reports, these press leaks painting you as a suspect are just completely obscene!"

Walt acknowledged the huzzahs from around the table. "The truth is that we're all suspects. Cops see a suspicious death and a big pile of dough and they assume the shortest distance between two points is a straight line. But let's get this tawdry money changing out of the way first shall we?" No one objected to this suggestion. "The trust is set up to self-liquidate upon Mother's death and pass to the descendants of Henry Sumner Senior. Kay, Chrissie and myself."

"In equal shares?"

"No, Chrissie, as you would know if you read your copy, you and Kay receive twenty-five percent apiece."

"Well that sincerely sucks."

"I agree. Which is why I've agreed in principle to divide my extra three million equally between the three of us."

"Thank you, Walter," said Kay. "That's very generous."

"It's only fair," replied Walter.

Chrissie said, "What does 'in principle' mean?"

"The trust tax exemption no longer applies once we receive the money but the law permits us, Laura and I, to gift up to forty grand per annum tax free to each couple."

"You're joking, right?"

"No, Chrissie, I'm not. As you've pointed out many times I have no sense of humor. I'm simply trying to—"

"Keep your little sisters on the string for the next thirty years."

Walter exhaled from the bottom of his diaphragm. "Chrissie, I understand that you're upset with Granddad for favoring me. He probably figured I'd need the extra money to help capitalize my business and that you girls would be taken care of by your husbands." Walt added quickly, "Not that you aren't, but you know."

"So fork over the extra million and let us worry about the damn taxes," said Chrissie.

"Fine," said Walt. "Though it will be more like nine hundred thousand once trust and legal fees are deducted. Then the feds and the state will want another forty-eight per cent."

Chrissie grimaced, sat up, slumped down, ran her fingers

The Violin Player

through her recently-auburned hair. Husband Chris whispered in her ear. Ted dug down in his briefcase and came up with a package of peanut butter crackers. "So how much of the extra million do we actually get to *keep*?" demanded Chrissie.

"Almost half," said Walter with a shrug. Silence around the table. "Mother's will, you'll be glad to know, is more equitable." Walt passed around copies of the brief document. Laura took a drink of cognac and kept the swallow on her tongue as she watched her husband turn a page filled with figures and smooth it out on the table. She smiled. He was in his element. They were interrupted at that moment by a plaintive yowl.

"Twyla," said Walt. "We forgot about Twyla."

Walt and his sisters rushed into the kitchen to admit the pampered Siamese. The neighbors must have been feeding her. She looked as plump as ever. Walt stooped to pick her up but Twyla hissed and darted away. "Who wants her?"

"Not me," said Chrissie. "She's way too spoiled." Walt gave her a half-lidded look. "Well she is!"

Walt turned to Kay who was bent over making kitty kitty noises. She stood up and smiled her upside down smile. "I'd love to but Ted's terribly allergic." Walt nodded, accepting his fate.

They reconvened in the dining room. Walt continued, "Mother had about a half million in stocks and bonds plus this house which will bring only about nine-fifty in its present condition." He paused to consult the figures. "Unfortunately Mother's combined credit card and home loan debt just about cancel out her liquid assets and her will mandates thirty percent of the net total to various charities."

"Translation?" said Chrissie.

"We sell our ancestral home now and realize, after taxes, commissions and legal fees, roughly a hundred and twenty-five thou-

John Knoerle

sand dollars per couple."

There was another silence around the table. Much louder this time. Kay asked if there were any alternative. "We could all sell our homes and move in here together." No one realized this was a joke so Walt added, "Just like the extended families of our forebears."

Laura chuckled warmly but glum silence prevailed. Someone muttered something about a lawyer and even Kay turned away. Laura wished Walt would blame his mother, say that Virginia Sumner's affinity for charitable causes and posh resorts is the reason you're all sitting here pouting and muttering so pathetically. But he would not. Walt had some crazy notion that his mother was entitled to spend her own money in any way she pleased. Laura polished off her cognac and said what she was thinking, "What a gloomy group of new millionaires you are."

"Yeah really," said Ted, dusting orange cracker crumbs from his chin. "Let's get a grip here. Let's not look a gift horse in the mouth." These remarks served only to deepen the gloom around the table.

"Well, on a more cheery note," said Walt, "I assume you have all been interviewed by the police." Yes they had. "Did they ask if you had visited Hamilton Street in the days before Mother's death?" Yes they had. "What did you tell them?"

"We told them no," said Kay.

"So did we," said Chrissie.

"And was that the truth?" asked Walt.

"Of course," said Kay.

"What the hell is this?" said Chrissie.

Walt pulled the check stub from his jacket pocket. "I'm only trying to anticipate what the police will—"

"I was here, that day," said Chris in his soft, uninflected voice. Chrissie smacked him on the shoulder as all eyes turned. Chris

The Violin Player

studied his fingers on the table for a long moment. "Christina called Virginia for a loan. Our mortgage was three months overdue. We didn't have time to wait for the mail and Christina didn't want to face her mother so I drove in to Evanston to pick up the check. She was quite pleasant about it. No lectures or anything." Chris returned his hands to his lap and stared at the maple sideboard. "I didn't kill her."

Walt pried open the glass display cabinet in the living room and picked up the ebony elephant with the ivory tusks that his parents had brought back from Thailand twenty years earlier. "You want this?"

"You take it," said Kay. "I would like a couple of those Royal Dalton balloon dolls though."

"Take 'em. Give one to Chrissie so she won't feel completely hosed." Walt sat down heavily on the green leather ottoman, drunk with exhaustion and one glass of cognac. Chrissie had stormed out following a top-of-her-lungs screed against her cruel and rapacious brother, dragging her terribly wronged husband behind her. Walt handed the balloon dolls to his sister one by one.

"Why did you put us all on the spot like that?" asked Kay.

"I wanted to shake the tree and see what fell out."

"But that check stub. You couldn't possibly think Chrissie killed Mom."

"Of course not."

Kay leaned forward.

"Yes, I did consider Chris a possibility."

Kay waited, her eyes doing the talking.

"Laura thinks the killer hated me, not Mom, which is why he posted the email around the corner from my office and paid his internet service provider with one of Sumner International's credit card accounts."

Kay reared back.

"Yes, I just discovered that little tidbit," said Walt. He hefted the ebony elephant in his hand, as if estimating its weight. "*Actually* I think the using of my company's credit card is a good thing. I'm tempted to go tell the Evanston P.D. because it's so ham-handed—so *obvious*."

"I wouldn't do that," said Kay.

"Why not?"

"Well, Ted has a favorite saying that I agree with. Never volunteer any bad news." Kay squinted. "Why would you suspect Chris?"

"He fits the profile, doesn't he? Polite, quiet, keeps to himself. He has access to family information, accounts. He's in financial difficulty." These last few words came out as one long wet syllable.

Kay asked if he wanted some coffee.

"I'm fine."

"But why would Chris *hate* you?"

"Because Chrissie does," said Walt. He looked down at the Persian carpet. As kids, their mother told them the weavers included a flawed stitch as an acknowledgement to Allah of their human imperfection. Walt and Kay had spent many quiet, happy hours trying to find it. They had, in fact, spent many happy and quiet hours playing Parcheesi and Scrabble and reading the funny papers to one another before Chrissie arrived and all hell broke loose.

"Walt, as you know, I'm not one to speak ill of my fellow man but I feel like I have no choice."

Walt looked up. Was dear charitable Kay going to cinch the noose around Chris' neck? Walt waited as her lips sought the proper words.

"Chrissie may resent your wealth and your first borness but she doesn't *hate* you. And, in my opinion, Chris is too ineffectual to kill anyone much less his mother-in-law who scared him to death."

Walt nodded, knowing she was right.

"You're not going to throw Chris to the wolves are you?" said Kay. "If the police didn't take that check stub as evidence, they probably overlooked it."

Walt blinked his sister's face back into focus. He missed her pudgy countenance. The adult Kay had a crimped look. How she maintained her slim figure while married to Ted, the human threshing machine, Walt had no idea. He fished around for his string of thought.

"The cops didn't overlook the check stub. They just didn't need it. What they need, needed, is the cancelled check, which I'm sure they have, you know—"

"Subpoenaed?"

"Right. If the check was cashed or deposited on the day it was written they know that Chris or Chrissie were here, or at least saw Mom on the day she died."

"The day she was murdered."

"Yes. Still can't bring myself to say that word." Walt put his hands on his knees and leveraged himself to his feet. He felt dizzy and sat back down.

"Walt let me get you—"

"In a minute. I think the cops, that albino looking one in particular, did you meet him?"

Kay said that she had.

"I think he orchestrated those press leaks to put pressure on me. Then he left the check stub here for me to find so I'd accuse Chris and Chrissie, and they'd accuse me in turn, and he'd just walk in and pick up the pieces."

John Knoerle

Walter was proud of his well reasoned theory. But Kay seemed dubious. Walt had long ago accepted his mother's judgement that, while he possessed brilliant analytical abilities and Chrissie was a drama queen who could wrap a crowd around her little finger, their middle sister was the only one of the them who had a lick of sense.

"I suppose that's possible," said Kay. "But I think it may miss the point." Kay looked away, not wanting to contradict her older brother to his face. "It doesn't feel to me like this is about hate. It feels more like envy. Someone on the outside looking in, you know, like you do when you're walking at night in a strange town. You might pass a window where a family is dining by candlelight or sitting by the fire and you're all alone and chilled to the bone and you so *yearn* to be a part of that warm and cozy scene." said Kay. "Or, if you're a sicko, to smash it to pieces."

Walt nodded dumbly. He fought back the urge to describe what it had been like to hear their mother die, to explain that he was supposed to be with her that evening but was on the phone instead, making his apologies, laughing at her unsparing wit, listening to her death agonies on the far end of the telephone.

Kay had suffered enough. It was his burden to bear.

Chapter 7

We're not so different, you and me. We're not! Don't tell me you have never in your lonely bed late at night fantasized about murdering your wife or husband or boss or neighbor, and not so quick and painless either, taking your sweet time, promising you'll stop if they will just utter those magic words. *Mea culpa, mea culpa, mea maxima culpa*. It's all my fault and none of yours. But they never do, do they? Oh, they'll *say* it. A filet knife dipped in lye is a stellar negotiating tool. But you can tell they don't really mean it.

My wife, my former ex-wife, was not like you and me. Butter wouldn't melt in her mouth and she excreted only rose petals and mountain spring water. She *freaked* when I used a post hole digger to decapitate a squirrel who was digging up her tulip bulbs, a squirrel against which she had hurled the most *vile* imprecations in *my* presence on *several* occasions. She didn't witness the decapitation, and I admit my antic wit may have gotten the better of me in this instance, but she went absolutely *batshit* when she saw that bushy tail sticking up in the middle of her row of just-planted bulbs.

I was doing her a *favor*! *I had nothing against the little rodent, had, in fact, come to admire his unapologetically larcenous little soul*. So I act on her spoken desire and she calls *me* deeply conflicted.

Well now. Umm ummmm ummmmm. I'm in the Mad Bar drinking coffee and the handsome dark-haired couple next to me who have been dipping and wooing all evening have just begun to kiss. Very nicely done.

Our relationship went downhill after that. It's a cryin' shame when you think about it. I had a good paying job, a little money on the side, we had a condo with a two-car garage and two cars to fill it. God was in his heaven and all was right with the world. Could be it was animals. I have never gotten on well with animals. Naw. *The fault lies not in our pets but in ourselves*. I would have understood her rejecting me for myself. I wouldn't have *liked* it but I would have understood. *I am not, you'll be surprised to learn, the easiest guy on the planet to get along with*. But *I* was not the problem. *I* have some potentially life-saving advice to share with you at this time. Pencils ready?

Never lie to a psychopath! We are not unreasonable people, despite what you may have heard. Intemperate if lied to or betrayed, *yes*. Unreasonable, *no*. Just don't lie to us.

Just don't.

My former ex-wife left a Dear John letter propped up on her pillow. In it she assured me she wasn't leaving me for anyone else but I have doubts. *Had* doubts. Had a wife, but couldn't keep her.

She said I was *emotionally unavailable*—and she was right. *Not such a bad thing in my case, doncha know*. After she dumped me, I got in touch with my true feelings. I tracked her down, of course. She and her non-existent boyfriend. As I mentioned previously, I am not a mass murderer. *He's* still alive—though not at all well.

Ironic, in'it? The faster I go the behinder I get. Meanwhile, back

The Violin Player

at Paulina and Bloomingdale, the pretender to the throne dandles his precious daughters on his knee while his devoted wife prepares a delicious dinner, they eat a lot of seafood, and his wealth replicates itself logarithmically. It borders on the unfair.

Oh, almost forgot. As Alice Langley would say, *I have on computer enter date of death for Laura Sumner in time of two weeks.*

I imagine it's created quite a stir.

Chapter 8

"Yes, we're aware of that," said Evanston Chief of Police Franklin H. Reeder after Walter Sumner made his stunning revelation about the posting of Laura's date of death. "We've been monitoring the website."

Walt said. "Oh."

He hadn't expected that the cops would know. Reeder, a trim, muscular man with cottony tufts around his temples and a face so black it was almost blue, looked across his desk to the office door.

"Do you know where it came from?" asked Walt. "The latest posting?" Reeder remained silent. "My technical expert tells me it was sent from a Kinko's three blocks from my home." Reeder did not respond. The whispers were that he was strictly a figurehead appointed as a sop to the black community. If so Reeder seemed to be taking the role literally. "My sister says you should never volunteer any bad news, but I think this demonstrates a clear and obvious pattern."

The Chief of Police checked his watch and said, "Did you ever go to this Kinko's three blocks from your home?"

"Yes of course. That's entirely the point."

The Violin Player

The door opened. A short-waisted white man with unkempt hair and a tie spilling down below his belt breezed in, introduced himself as Captain Davidson, head of the homicide division, and seated himself in a casement window.

Chief Reeder said, "Mr. Sumner here says the death threat against his wife came from a Kinko's he frequently visits."

Walt said, "As I mentioned to Chief Reeder, my sister advised me to never volunteer any bad news—"

"Smart lady."

"But I thought, given the obviousness, this thing about Kinko's *wasn't* bad news."

"But the use of your company's credit card was bad news," said Davidson.

"No, I was going to tell you about that," said Walt. "Don't you see, it's all part of a pattern."

"Pattern of what?" said Davidson, snuffling, running a handkerchief around his nose.

"Of someone going out of their way to implicate me!"

"Ohhh, a frame job you mean."

Walter had deliberately refrained from using the f-word, flaccid and risible from overuse on a million TV cop shows. Still, there it was, hanging in the recirculated air of the office like an unfortunate body odor.

"We can send someone to interview the Kinko's staff, but I wouldn't hold my breath. They get a lot of bodies in and out," said Davidson. "And my crack staff of pimple-faced propeller heads tells me this last date of death entry was from another ISP – Internet Service Provider—can't believe I know that—registered to Alice Langley, no fixed address, nowhere USA."

"But it's another potential lead," said Walt, leaning forward, hands on his knees. "Another chance to trace the ISP account back to the subscriber."

Captain Davidson sat back on the window sill, his head grazing the mini-blinds. He yanked up the blinds and resumed his perch. "It would be if we were dealing with an idiot."

Walt slumped in his chair, triangulated by the implacable stares of officialdom. "I assume, at least, this latest development removes me from suspicion," he said. "I have no financial incentive to kill my wife."

"Well, it clears your sister and brother-in-law," said Davidson, indicating the cops had indeed found the cancelled check. "Assuming the date of death posting isn't a prank."

"What, my wife has to die to clear them!"

"I wouldn't put it in those terms, Mr. Sumner," said the Chief of Police. "We'll do our utmost to see she isn't harmed."

Davidson honked loudly into his handkerchief. "Sorry," he said. "I got a touch of sniffilis."

"So I'm still a *suspect*?"

"The first thing they teach you in cop school is look at who gets happy," said Davidson. "You the primary breadwinner in the family?" Walter nodded. "Me too," said Davidson. "Thing I'm wondering is why a million zops in life insurance."

Walt cursed softly to himself. He had forgotten about that stupid life insurance policy Laura had talked him into. "The policy covers both of us equally. I couldn't—it would have been insulting to her to do it any other way."

The Chief of Police cleared his throat. "Have you consulted an attorney, Mr. Sumner?"

"None of your business, but no."

"I would strongly recommend it."

The Violin Player

"I'm innocent!"

Davidson snorted. "Plenty of innocent men on death row. Haven't you been reading that series in the *Trib*?"

"I came to you, remember?" said Walt. "Your coroner said my mother died of natural causes. *I* told your detective about the date of death thing. *I* came to *you*!"

"True enough," said Davidson. "But criminals incriminate themselves every day around here." He crossed an ankle over a knee. "Lemme give you the birdseye lowdown on this caper, Mr. Sumner. Your mother did a lot of charity work, she was a much-loved figure in Evanston. Her murder's our biggest homicide in my twelve years on the job and absent another workable suspect, you're it."

Davidson hacked some sputum into his handkerchief and examined it briefly. "We're investigating, don't get me wrong. I got half my detectives working it, but so far every stone they turn over's got your name on it. If your mother'd been murdered inside the city limits that employer of last resort, otherwise known as the Chicago PD, would've rounded up some Humboldt homie by now and took turns with him till he copped. But that's not the way it works here in Evanston. No suh. In this high-minded little university town you're worse than a Humboldt homie, you're a hated downtown capitalist." Captain Davidson held up his hand. "Understand, I'm just givin' you the lay of the land, the pressures that are brought to bear."

Walt looked to the Chief of Police to countermand this outrage, to reassure him, to chastise his subordinate. But the Chief seemed to be observing them both from a great distance. Walt said, "The poisons, the drugs that were used to—can't you trace them back somehow? Surely they're not available over the counter."

"No but they're available on the internet. A money order and a PO Box is all you need," said Davidson. "And don't call me Shirley."

Davidson's grin withered under a toxic look from his superior.

"So, uh, *subpoena* their records, the companies that sell this stuff," urged Walt.

"Can't," said Davidson. "They're all offshore."

"Jesus H. Christ. Is there anything you people *can* do?"

"Just keep turnin' over stones," said Davidson, sniffling. "It might help if you gave us something to go on."

Walt slammed the door to the Franklin Reeder's office and strode down the long fluorescent-bleached corridor thinking grim and bitter thoughts. Pressures that are brought to bear? What a load of crap. He knew about pressure. His lenders had dunned him mercilessly in his first year of business when he had to scramble just to keep the door open and the lights on. But he had toughed it out and kept to his plan and those same lenders now called him every other week with specially packaged loans at or below prime. You had to stay the course, not roll over to the first payday loan operator who came along. He knew about pressure. These goddamn brainless bureaucrats wouldn't last ten minutes in the private sector.

Bjork! The white-eyebrowed little prick was in his office, he had walked right past him. Walt turned on his heel and flung open the door without any idea of what he was going to say or do. Bjork was sitting on the corner of his desk, talking on the telephone. He held up a finger. Walt cooled his heels and collected his thoughts as Bjork said something in a low voice before he rang off.

"Mr. Sumner, what can I do for you?"

Walt took a cue from the Chief of Police and remained silent. If the cops really thought he was a stone-cold killer, this, Walt figured, should strike fear in the young detective's heart. And damned if it

The Violin Player

did not! Bjork tried smiling, standing up, backing away. Walt followed him step for step.

"Had any luck in tracking down those press leaks?"

"No, unfortunately. Not yet."

The Chicago media had grown bored with the Sumner family due to lack of new developments. If and when they stumbled upon the website-date-of-death angle, however, Walt knew his family would be spread-eagled on the network news for all to see.

"That is unfortunate," said Walt, husking his voice. "What will be even more unfortunate is if news of the posting of my wife's date of death should leak out—" Walt pressed his face to within six inches of Bjork's pearly blue-veined mug. "Exposing her to intense press scrutiny at a time when knowledge of her whereabouts could be a matter of life and death."

Bjork did not call for help or run screaming from the room. He did, however, stop chewing his cinnamon-flavored gum.

"If that were to happen," whispered Walt to Bjork's left ear, "The Evanston Police Department *will* be able to charge me with homicide!"

Walt clenched Bjork's dainty white hands in his big strong mitts and squeezed for all he was worth.

Chapter 9

Walt craned his neck and stared up at the eighty-story Amoco building on Randolph, startling in its monolithic simplicity. A "skyscratcher" Thea would call it. It looked slightly darker now. Its Italian marble skin had deteriorated under the assault of lake winds and prairie winters and had to be replaced, slab by slab, with hardier New Hampshire granite. The project had been completed in less than two years. Only in Chicago.

Walt checked his watch. Laura was fifteen minutes late. Probably having trouble rounding up a neighbor to babysit on short notice. Unlike Winnetka, Bucktown did not appear to have any stay-at-home moms. A driver down the block screeched to a halt and leaned on his horn. Walt flinched. He was not used to dealing with fear. The Sumner family had been spared the hit and run accidents, the rapists, the child molesters, the home invasion torturers and psycho killers that other unfortunates fell victim to. Those things happened to other people, not the Sumner family. Someone tapped him on the shoulder and he jumped about a foot.

"Been a snake I wouldda bit ya," said Laura.

"You're here, thank God."

The Violin Player

"I thought I was going to have to bring the kids, but the girls from two doors down pulled up at the last minute."

"The lesbians?"

"They're lovely people," said Laura. "C'mon."

Walt wondered how best to proceed as they rode the brass-fitted express elevator to the eightieth floor. Perhaps performing this most unpleasant task in his favorite place in all the world wasn't such a hot idea. The Central City Club, where the future is plotted at lunch and celebrated at dinner, would now hold a bitter memory for both of them. And Laura would certainly be unprepared for any bad news at the site of so many happy occasions, including their *wedding reception*. Walt worked his jaw up and down to clear the pressure in his ears. What had he been thinking?

The elevator eased to a stop. The doors parted with a whisper and Mr. and Mrs. Walter Sumner stepped into the reception area. Walt steadied his wife as the deep pile carpeting swallowed her high heels. Hans, the maitre'd, rushed forward and escorted them to a south-facing window table, "Your grandfazzer's favorite," his signal that he was aware of the accusations against Walter and the inquisitive looks of the other diners and that he considered it all beneath contempt. Third generation members of the Central City Club did not murder their mothers.

Walter and Laura settled into their seats beneath the thirty-foot cathedral windows and waited for their drinks to appear. The original Central City Club had been located next door atop the Prudential Building, at forty-two stories the tallest building in town until 1970. Now you had to stand up against the glass and peer downward just to glimpse the blinking tip of its antenna mast.

The new location was far more spacious. But the original Central City Club was where twelve-year-old Walt Sumner had been introduced to the power and majesty of big business, taking men-only luncheon with Granddad and his associates. Young Walt had studied them hungrily, watching for the headbutting and sly gamesmanship he read about in *Fortune*. He had been disappointed. All the discussions he witnessed were remarkably candid and thoughtful.

"What's the occasion?" asked Laura.

She wore a red suit with gold trim and a gold braid necklace. The diamond pendant Walt had given her for their tenth anniversary lay nestled in the hollow of her throat. She looked great, bright eyed, and ready to be pleased. Walt watched the sun cast orange on the black windows of the Harbor Point Tower, thinking Hans had lost a step. Grandfather's martini had always been waiting for him by the time he reached his table.

"A sad one actually," said Walt. He studied the floodlit columns of the Field Museum. Their drinks appeared. Walt gripped his cut glass tumbler. "Laura, your date of death has been posted on the GenealoG website, in two week's time, Friday, October 15th."

Laura chased a fleck of mascara on her eyelash with her little finger. "Oh that. Detective what's-his-name, the albino, called me about that this afternoon."

"He did?"

"He said he thought I should know."

"Yes, you should. But it wasn't his place to tell you," said Walt, biting off his words.

Laura said, "Well, it's probably just some stupid copycat prank," with convincing nonchalance.

"I hope you're right," said Walt, knowing she was not. No one but the family and the cops knew Virginia Sumner's D.O.D. had been posted before her death. "But we have to act as if it's real. Monitor our food and drink, medications, water supply, maybe hire a bodyguard."

The Violin Player

"*Whoaa* there, big fella," laughed Laura, patting his hand, sipping her Greyhound. "Maybe I should hire a taster like Marie Antoinette?"

Walt waited for her mirth to settle. "Laura, I believe this to be a serious threat. Detective Bjork must as well or he wouldn't have phoned."

Laura worried her diamond pendant between thumb and forefinger. "So let's throw caution to the wind and share a blood rare Chateaubriand, shall we? With a gravy boat of Bernaise on the side."

A waiter appeared from the shadows. Walt placed the order, adding a Caesar salad and a bottle of Roederer Cristal.

"What fun!" said Laura. "I should be sentenced to death every month."

Walt sucked on an ice cube. Though he hadn't smoked for many years, he longed for a cigarette. "It could be a trick," he said. "Who's to say he'll abide by the date of death."

"I don't think so," said Laura. "I was a psych major, remember? This guy's an obsessive-compulsive if ever there was. He invented this game, and he doesn't win if he breaks his own rules." Laura picked up her drink, looked at it and set it down. Her face darkened. "That he gave us a two week's notice this time means he's increasing the degree of difficulty to demonstrate his godlike powers. These types always have delusions of grandeur."

"Or he just wants us to twist slowly in the wind for fourteen days," said Walt.

"That too," said Laura. "And if he does attack it won't necessarily be poison. A true sociopath will alter his routine to achieve an important goal. Ted Bundy preferred a crowbar but he also used a gun and strangled some of his victims with his bare hands."

"And you remember all this from college?"

Laura met a stare from another table until the starer turned away. "I've been reading up," she said.

"So you don't really think this D.O.D. posting is just a prank."

Laura's brave smile quivered at the corners. "Probably not. No."

They fell into an uneasy silence. Walt eyed the waiter who was chilling the bottle of champagne. "Where's the relish tray? Didn't they used to have a relish tray?"

"About twenty years ago," said Laura. "Any luck coming up with anyone who might have it in for you?"

"No," said Walt. "And I'm not so sure it's just me. Kay thinks it's someone who hates *us*, *envies* us, our family, our...contentedness."

Laura made a noncommittal sound and looked out the window. "Interesting. Because, well…most poisoners are female. Hell hath no fury and so forth and—"

"I haven't had an affair, Laura."

"Oh, hon, I didn't mean…it's just that—"

"It's a logical question under the circumstances."

"Logical, yes," said Laura. "But not right. We've got to trust each other. We are all we've got," said Laura, her eyes brimming.

Walt met her eyes and reached his hand across the table, willing himself not to say something banal and spoil the moment. She entwined his fingers in her warm, delicately tapered hand. The champagne cork popped. Laura yelped and dug her nails in hard.

The waiter poured from the linen-wrapped bottle with his thumb in the bottom, Laura apologized profusely, and Walt ran an ice cube over the tiny precise punctures in the back of his hand.

Two hours later Walt half-carried Laura from the garage to the kitchen where she sniffed, straightened up and said, "Son of a

The Violin Player

bitch!" She stalked over to the cat dish. "Fuckin' cat did it again!" Walt threw the switch for the overhead can lights to get a better look. Twyla had urinated prodigiously on and about her recently-filled dish. "I'm gonna stuff that little fucker in the microwave, I *am*," said Laura, high-heeling back and forth on the tiled floor.

"Lore, sweetie, my mother fed her nothing but raw kidney and boiled shrimp. I explained that. Twyla's not going to eat anything out of a can."

"I bought her Fancy Feast for shit's sake!" Laura brushed Walt's hand off her elbow, declaring she was not going to live in a household where the pets ate better than their masters, and clickety-clacked out of the kitchen. Walt unwound a wad of paper towels and bent to his task.

When he was done, Walt climbed the stairs to the third-floor family room. He found his lesbian neighbors cozied up under an afghan at one end of the black leather couch. Thea was at the other end, her tattered blankie tented over her knees. Laura was describing their delightful dinner with expansive gestures while shifting her weight from heel to heel as if buffeted by gusts of wind. The TV droned away in the corner—something child inappropriate on HBO. A bowl of popcorn, two highball glasses and a blender filled with bright blue liquid sat on the coffee table.

Walter's neighbors separated and sat up. Thea rested her chin on her knees and looked up through her long eyelashes. Walt placed his hand in the crook of Laura's arm.

"They're drinking *blue* margaritas, blue—what do you call it?"

"Agave," said the younger, feminine-looking neighbor whose name Walt could not recall.

"A-*gav*-e, that's so cool," said Laura moistly.

"We've plenty left," said the neighbor with the bowl haircut whose name Walt thought might be Terry.

"Thanks, I'd love to," said Laura, "But my husband is squeezing my elbow so I think I'll say goodnight." Walt braced Laura as she slipped off her shoes. She wove her way across the room, her high heels dangling from the fingers of her left hand, her right hand brushing the top of Thea's submerged head.

"I guess we had a little too much fun tonight," said Walt. His neighbors didn't smile. Perhaps they wondered why a man suspected of matricide was out having fun. "Irene go to bed without too much trouble?"

"She was fine," said the younger neighbor.

Thea's extravagant eye rolling said otherwise. Walt thanked his neighbors for coming to the rescue, walked them down the stairs to the front door and agreed that they should get together more often. He took the ascending stairs two at a time and found Thea still snuggled into her corner of the couch, her oversized feet protruding from her blanket.

"How'd it go?" said Walt, gulping air.

"Okay," said Thea, shifting her head to see the television. Her father turned around and shut it off.

"Let's get you to bed."

Thea trudged up the stairs in her flannel nightgown. Walt followed. Her room was immaculate, bed made, pillows plumped. She unfolded the covers to a precise triangle and climbed in. Walt stood over her. "How bad was it?" he asked.

Thea bugged her eyes and blew out a breath. She always enjoyed telling tales on her baby sister. "She kept saying 'I wanna blue drink, I wanna blue drink' and then at bedtime she just totally freaked and ran around and around. She's really fast, and we were all trying to catch her but then she locked herself in the bathroom."

The Violin Player

Walter groaned. "They like begged her, which never works, to open the door and she would-ent. And then I told her to, kinda mean, and she still would-ent. So then Terry and Gina promised she could have a blue drink if she came out—and then she did."

"Did they? Give her a drink?" Thea turned her head away. "Never mind. You don't have to tell me." Walt looked around for a chair. His daughter shifted over to make room. Children are the barometers of family tension. He remembered reading that somewhere. "Everything else go okay?"

"Yes, yes," said Thea sounding like a long-suffering spouse. "Dad, I know Terry and Gina are lesbians. It's cool. They did-ent, like, try and kiss me or anything."

Walt laughed, a repressed rolling rumble that went on and on.

"Do we have to keep that stupid cat?" said Thea, sitting up, bouncing her head off the headboard. "She was Grandmom's, I know, but *gawd* she hisses at you if you even get near her and I found her scratching her claws on the bottom of my quilt you gave me from Aunt Belle. I tried to chase her out and then she turned and scratched me!"

Thea showed him a tiny scratch on the back of her hand. While Irene could run smack into a door, bounce back up and laugh, Thea was fragile as spun glass.

"It doesn't look too bad."

"It hurt!" said Thea, pouting, pretty as a primrose.

"Honey, Twyla lost her home. We have to take her in. That's what families do."

"The aunties didn't take her in," said Thea.

"No, because, as the oldest, it was my responsib...no, my *privilege* to look after my Mother's beloved pet." Thea sniffed. "Let me tell you a story," said Walt. Thea showed a flicker of interest despite herself. She loved stories. "It concerns your great great great uncle Travis Sumner and your great great grandfather William Sumner. When they moved their families from Pennsylvania to Ohio they had adjoining plats—"

"What's a plat?"

"It's a tract, a piece of land you farm. They were pioneers, Travis and William. When they arrived in Ohio there were still wild Indians and mountain lions, and wolverines, and wolf packs that howled at the moon."

Thea squinted up at him. "Is this a true story?"

"Absolutely. I got it from one of my family researchers on the web." Walt froze. Was it from Alice Langley? He couldn't remember, but he felt queasy, felt as if that nameless psychopath was hiding in the closet of his daughter's room.

"Daddy?"

"Sorry, snowflake. I'm having trouble remembering all the details. Wait a sec, I'll go see if I can find it."

Walt returned with a printed page scanned from *A History of Perry County*. It had *not* been sent by Alice Langley. "Ready? Here we go."

In the spring of 1821 Travis Sumner, his brother William and their families settled near the banks of Raccoon Creek and set about clearing the land. Some months later, from some cause unknown, Travis Sumner became a stranger to reason. So much so that he had to be confined and handcuffed and guarded by his brother to keep him from doing damage to himself or others. On one occasion it was necessary to change his linen, and to make that change William had to remove the handcuffs after which, while he was in the act of turning round to reach for a shirt that was airing by the fire, Travis took advantage of the attitude William was in by

The Violin Player

throwing a small wooden table with great force at William's head, just grazing it. After which assault William was careful at such times to leave nothing in the crazy man's way by which means he could do any one of his keepers or himself any harm.

At length the physician recommended that they should seek out a waterfall in some of the mountain regions, where a small cold stream of water fell over rocks several feet with some weight and force. The rill having been sought out the family built a small house close to the waterfall and divided it off with a partition of logs, keeping Travis Sumner confined in one end while the other served as a place of lodging and shelter for those who waited on him. And it was made the duty of William and his eldest son each morning to place Mr. Sumner under the waterfall, in such position as that the descending stream fell upon his head. And thus once a day was he treated to a cold bath with its influence direct upon his head. And the process was continued daily until unmistakable signs of returning sanity had made their appearance, and was continued once a day until it had the desired effect. Mr. Sumner was thereby restored to reason and remained a man of sound mind to the day of his death.

"Could we do that with Twyla? Put her in the shower or something?"

Walt laughed. "I was hoping you would take a more inspirational message."

"You mean like how his family helped out when he was crazy?"

"Yeah," said Walt. "Like that."

Thea slid down and pulled the covers up to her chin. "Okay," she said between yawns.

"Because I have to go out of town for a few days on a business trip and your mother's pretty upset. I'd like you, as the eldest, to look after her." Walt smoothed his daughter's brow. "Will you do that for

John Knoerle

me?" Thea nodded twice. "Will you miss me when I'm gone?"

This was the set up to their favorite joke. Thea held up her thumb and forefinger, half an inch apart.

Chapter 10

Guess where I am now. I'll give you a hint. *Food* is *served*. And there are *no prices* on the menu.

Have you been reading all the toplofty retrospectives in the weekly newsmags now that the millennial chasm yawns before us? *Time* is soliciting nominations for its Person of the Century. I'm guardedly optimistic.

You want to know my considered opinion? We are more confused and uncertain about the things that matter at the end of this century than we were at the beginning. The universe of Newton and Copernicus remained harmonious and well-reasoned on January 1, 1900. One hundred years later all that has been sucked down into a cosmic latrine of a black hole filled with anti-matter. The only constant in our new universe is the speed of light and, podner, I yam hear to tell ya, *that ain't much to hang your existential hat on*!

Space is no longer space but space-time, bent by gravity no less. The atom is no longer the basic building block of the physical world, it's now the quark, *which comes in four delicious flavors*. Run real fast, time slows down, so sayeth Albert Einstein. Look real close, you don't wanna know, so sayeth Niels Bohr. It's called 'quantum foam' because space *abandons* Einstein's theories at subatomic scales. Particles move from point A to point B without traversing the space in between. Electrons behave differently depending upon whether or not they are observed by a lab tech, *proving that even subatomic particles have a sense of humor.*

Contemporary physicists are attempting to bridge this gap with something called String Theory, which posits nine categories of subatomic particles and seven or eight dimensions beyond width, height, depth, and time, all linked by vibrating loops that no one has ever seen. *How pathetic is that*!

I propose we rewind and replay this sad century until we get it right.

Time to get back to work. I'm taking my fifteen minute break in the Club Room of the Central City Club where hard-charging yups swill microbrews and put their Rockports up on casual Fridays. I enjoyed Laura's overheard comment while I was chilling the Cristal. "These types always have delusions of grandeur."

Know your victim is my motto since I have elected to become one of 'these types'. I knew the Sumner's were a Central City legacy. Thanks to my college-age experience as a waiter at the Henry County Country Club, I got the gig.

Funny story I heard from another waiter at the Club. Henry Sumner Jr. arrived one night with a passel of hot-snot clients and asked for the wine list. The waiter disappeared and returned empty handed several minutes later. He couldn't find it!

A delusion of grandeur is only a delusion if it is untrue. Who were the two worst Presidents in recent memory? Lyndon Baines Johnson and Richard Milhous Nixon. Why is that, you ask? Because they were sweaty, insecure over-achievers who knew in their lonely beds late at night that they were rank *poseurs*. Who were the two best

The Violin Player

Presidents in recent memory? Franklin Delano Roosevelt and John Fitzgerald Kennedy. Why is that, you ask? Because they had no delusions. They *knew* they deserved to be the most powerful man on earth.

I could have done Mr. and Mrs. Sumner right there and then. *I always carry a little something.* But, despite my maladaptive personality structure, the worst I did was hock a loog into the mustard before I prepared their Caesar salad tableside. *Added a certain piquancy, doncha know.* Would Ted Bundy have been so circumspect, Mrs. Sumner? *I don't think so!* T.B. may have done his vics by different means but he used that same lame-o phony arm cast to inveigle them. And once he was roped and wrangled he couldn't stop gaming the shrinks even though they could have had him declared insane and spared him a hot date with Ol' Sparky down in Tallahassee.

Uh oh. I'm two minutes late. Ol' Hans'll be ripping me a new one but I want to get this down.

In the sorry ass attempt to explain *every element of the physical reality*—Einstein's words, not mine—someone in this sad century discovered neutrinos, ghostly particles expelled from the sun that pass through our bodies by the billions every day. A neutrino can penetrate a million miles of solid lead without mussing its hair and it rarely interacts with other matter.

Sound like anyone you know?

Chapter 11

Walter felt a guilty rush of exhilaration as he sped over and above the abandoned US Steel Southworks on the Skyway. He was a free man for five days. The mill, whose smoke-belching stack had served as his first thrilling Chicago landmark when he visited as a boy, now sat by the lake like a ghost ship at anchor. Downtown and points north had survived the shuttering of the smokestack industries and the stockyards, converting tool and die plants into upscale lofts. But the South Side was still in shock. Walt glanced down at the dispirited row houses and three flats rushing by and wondered how their occupants were keeping body and soul together.

A good question for New Castle too. Granddad's creamery was New Castle's second largest employer when it closed in 1985. The auto parts plant went down a short time later. Walt, who had not visited New Castle in many years, was afraid of what he might find. He eased back the driver's seat and settled in for the long drive. The XJR's instrument panel glowed like a starship. Exterior temperature, 53 degrees, time, 7:12 a.m., range, 412 miles.

'Give us something to go on' Captain Davidson had said, give us a 'workable suspect'. Well, Alice Langley was a workable suspect.

The Violin Player

Alice Langley had posted both dates of death. The only problem was that Alice Langley didn't exist.

Laura said the killer was playing a game. Good. A game has rules and either player can win. But how? The only potential clues Walt had were the family research documents that Alice Langley had e-mailed him. There were dozens. U.S. Census tracts, military records, birth, marriage and death registers amassed by the Mormon Church, Social Security rosters and cemetery directories compiled by retirees who made their peace with death by visiting abandoned graveyards with a can of acid wash to coax inscriptions from weathered headstones. These documents were available from a variety of sources. Walt removed these from the pile. The remaining documents represented Alice Langley's independent research. Walter spent the better part of two nights sifting through them. Two showed promise.

A copy of his gr.gr.gr.gr.grandfather's will bore a very faint imprint of a rubber stamp, too faint to read. Walt took it to Kinko's to have it enlarged. After adjusting the darkness and resolution the stamp came clear. *Perry County Genealogy Center*. He called to learn they did not conduct research via mail, you had to visit in person.

The other clue was a copy of handwritten birth records of his grandfather and some of his sibs. Someone had gone to the Henry County Department of Health to make them. They were Xeroxed directly from the bound ledgers. Alice Langley might have found copies of both the will and the birth records elsewhere but Walt didn't think so. And they were all he had.

Welcome to Indiana, the Crossroads of America. The Skyway descended over the gritty confines of Hammond. Walt set the XJR's cruise control to 72 mph as he wove in and out of the tractor trailers that seemed the only other vehicles on the road this brisk autumn morning. On the lake side of the Expressway two men climbed out of a station wagon with rods and reels and a beer cooler, laughing and joking, looking forward to a day of fishing the most polluted waterway this side of the Love Canal. Walt passed a flatbed semi doing sixty in the fast lane.

Had the fastidious Alice Langley left these vague clues intentionally? Hard to believe he or she had made two sloppy mistakes. It didn't much matter. Unless the clues were left deliberately in hopes of luring him away from his wife. He had been right to hire a security firm despite Laura's objections. He selected Irving Park Investigations—Security, Surveillance, Secrecy—and thought of what his wife had said when the hulking man in the gray raincoat met him in a back booth at Biasetti's Steak House. 'I don't want some guy with a twenty inch neck following me around all day. What would I say to him?'

The man introduced himself as Tony Sobczak and slid in across the table. Walt wondered how he could perform the covert surveillance promised in the Yellow Pages. Tony Sobczak might as well have been wearing a sandwich board with EX-COP printed in sixty point type.

Walt had explained that his wife had received a death threat on a date certain. If Tony Sobczak was familiar with their case he made no sign. Walt said he wanted twenty-four hour coverage of his house while he was gone and protection for his wife whenever she went out. Anyone casing the house or following his wife should be questioned if possible and photographed if not. 'What about the media?' Tony asked, indicating he knew all about Walt Sumner and the Evanston Socialite murder. 'What do you want us to do if they show up?'

'I don't know. What can you do?'

'Not much. We can run 'em off if they get too close. But then

The Violin Player

you've got a security situation not a surveillance. And the camera crews have something for the five o'clock news that makes you look guilty as hell.' Tony Sobczak had drawn a paw across his massive brow and grunted. 'Media's like a case of piles. The more you scratch 'em the worse they get.'

Walt smiled at the recollection. The media were the least of his worries. Walt slowed before a sea of brake lights and thought about why he was making this trip.

He hated being falsely accused. As the eldest child his parents held him accountable for his sisters' misbehavior. 'You're the manager of the junior division,' his father would say with a wink. As if Kay and Chrissie paid him any heed. Being held accountable for something you didn't do was infuriating. Infuriating but selfish in the present circumstance. Laura had been leery of leaving Winnetka and moving to the city from day one. Now she was trapped inside a four story prison struggling to maintain a cheery facade for the children while she waited for the axe to fall in twelve days time.

Walter considered turning around and heading home, but the XJR continued south on the I-90 Expressway.

Chapter 12

Walt felt a bittersweet tug when he saw the exit for Spiceland Road. He shooshed across the Big Blue River bridge in a light rain, remembering Boy Scout canoe trips and catching crawfish in the feeder creeks. The birches and maples along the river banks were just beginning to turn.

Walt fished out his cell phone and dialed his wife. "Network not found" said the readout. Didn't matter. He would call her from his motel room once he got settled. He scanned the radio band for something pleasing as he turned north on Highway 3. You would never know that New Castle was a hundred miles north of the Mason-Dixon line. The radio stations that weren't country-western were fundamentalist Christian. Walt inserted the soundtrack from *Amadeus* into his CD player and set sail across the verdant prairie of Henry County, the birthplace of Wilbur Wright.

There was a new Best Western south of town. A new Super 8 across the road. Both said No Vacancy. The signboard on the Best Western read 'Welcome NASCAR'. Walt cursed his luck. Hoosiers loved two things in equal measure – basketball and road racing. The motels would be booked solid. He watched for familiar landmarks

The Violin Player

but nothing clicked, just the standard issue franchise restaurants and cake box retail. They were, at least, pretty busy for a rainy Monday afternoon. He stopped at a red light and felt watched, conspicuous in his Jaguar.

Walt turned right on Indiana Avenue after passing the Southmound Cemetery. If he had time he would lay flowers and double-check dates of birth and death and see just what it was about graveyards that got genealogists so excited. The illusion of New Castle's prosperity dissipated as the XJR climbed. His fondly remembered Queen Anne Victorians were barely standing. The Ice House Tavern was still in business though. The whistles at the creamery and the auto parts plant used to blow at three-thirty. Walt checked his dashboard clock. The parking lot of the Ice House Tavern was full at ten minutes past two.

Walt fueled up at a gas station by the train tracks that advertised the world's greatest coffee. It wasn't. A young woman, looking marsupial with an infant strapped to her belly, exited the store and gave his car a surprised once over. "It's the pace car," said Walt with a smile. "For the big race." The woman clutched her infant and hurried on. He was no good at banter.

Walt drove to the city square on empty streets. He parked next to the County Courthouse and asked directions to the Department of Health. Right around the corner. He climbed an absurdly long steep staircase where he found an office divided into two sections. To the left sat two women with young children. To the right a sign on the counter read 'Vital Statistics'. Walt got in line behind two hard freckled sixty-year-olds. The man wore a tractor cap and a sleeveless tank top. The woman wore stretch pants and a floral print blouse. A fleck of silver gum wrapper clung to the back of her hairdo.

"Be with you as quickly as I can, sir. This could take a while," said the crisp, bespectacled woman behind the counter. Or 'bespeckled' as Thea would say. Walt eavesdropped. The man and woman were attempting to obtain a new birth certificate for a boy they had adopted. Complicating factors were that the child's mother had reassumed her maiden name after divorcing the child's father. That child's mother changed her name again when she remarried. That child was then dumped by his mother when she got divorced and was adopted by his grandmother—the woman in the stretch pants. And that grandma now had a new husband, which changed the child's name for a fourth time.

The bespeckled woman listened intently, took copious notes and said she would need twenty-four hours to conduct a document search. The man and woman nodded and shuffled off.

Walter stepped forward. The woman behind the counter appraised him with cool green eyes. "Now, how may I help you sir?"

Walt, accustomed to Chicago's bored and surly civil servants, was momentarily speechless. He had it all planned. He would say he was doing research on the Sumner family and ask to see their birth records. Perusing the books he would offhandedly inquire if anyone else had been doing similar Sumner research. But the lady behind the counter didn't look as if she was easily gulled. Walter used his real name.

It was well he did. She had seen his photo on WGN and was familiar with the case. "It's been written up here as well. People my age, which is most of the population anymore, still remember your grandfather."

Walt showed her the Henry County birth records he had received from Alice Langley. The woman, Mrs. Cantwell was her name, agreed that they had been copied there but had no idea when. The department kept no log of inquiries and did not charge for

The Violin Player

copies. Walt asked if anyone else might have fielded the request.

Mrs. Cantwell said, "I teach a genealogy class at the Senior Center every Friday afternoon. A lady by the name of Rita fills in. It's possible she might know something. Give me your local number and I'll have her call you."

Walt explained that he had yet to secure a motel room and that his cell phone didn't work in New Castle. He and Mrs. Cantwell faced each other across the counter. "And you are Henry Sumner's grandson, is that right?"

"Yes. You said you saw me on TV."

Mrs. Cantwell dismissed this with a flickering of fingers, as if to say that's all conjuring and sleight of hand. "What was your father's nickname in high school?"

"The uh…hold on, I know this…the…Emperor."

Mrs. Cantwell flashed a grin as she wrote down Rita's phone number on an index card. "The Emperor, those were the days. My sister had such a crush on him. Is he still with us?"

"No. He passed away five years ago."

"I'm sorry to hear that. He cut a very dashing figure around here. I remember seeing him walking down the church steps with his parents one Sunday. He was in his dress blues, just back from the front. When he winked at us I thought Peg was going to faint dead away."

Walt thanked Mrs. Cantwell and made his way back down the absurdly steep staircase. How did ill or disabled people access the Department of Health? There were no elevators that he could see. Well. That was one way to save taxpayer dollars.

Driving down New Castle's main drag was profoundly depressing. J.J. Newberry's was gone, a gaping hole in its place. The Chew Chew diner had been converted to a tire shop that was closed for

John Knoerle

repairs and had been for some time. Hannigan's Ice Cream Parlor, famous for their delicious hot fudge sundaes and idiotic radio jingle, was nowhere to be seen. Walt thought about what Mrs. Cantwell had said, her recollection of his father. The closest Dad ever got to the front was the ROTC program at Ball State. Not his fault, Henry Junior turned eighteen in May of 1945 and wasn't needed. But he should not have been parading around town in his dress blues.

Walt descended the hill and turned south on Highway 3, hunting a motel. He slowed for a stoplight. Set back from the road, sandwiched between a Ponderosa Steak House and a Taco Bell, was the New Castle Lodge. Walt pulled down the drive and parked in a carport next to the office.

The first thing he noticed was the ice machine. It wasn't often you saw an ice machine in a motel office. Walt supposed it was there to discourage guests from helping themselves too often. Then again maybe not. Looking closer he saw that it was coin operated

"You here for the stock car race?" asked an emaciated old gent behind the counter. Walt said he was. The old gent nodded and said, for some reason, "God bless us both." He said 108 was free, hesitated, cleaned his trifocals on the tail of his shirt and said no, the commode was backed up. Walt thought about making his excuses and driving the fifty minutes north to Muncie for a night of clean sheets and cable TV. But the old gent was studying the ledger so diligently.

"One eleven. Yeah, I can give you one eleven. That's a nice room," he said and slid the signature card across the counter. One eleven had a nice ring to it, thought Walt. Yeah, one eleven with the featherbed and the jacuzzi and—

"That your car out there?" Walt said that it was. "Be safer if you parked it on the street." Walt nodded dumbly. "That'll be twenty-five dollars. Cash." Walt paid. The man handed him a key and a remote

The Violin Player

control device for the TV. "Free coffee in the morning."

Walt pulled the XJR up to room one eleven and parked next to a rusted Plymouth Reliant with a plastic sheet for a back window. Room one eleven was small but reasonably clean. A crude water color of rainbows clashed with the bright orange bedspread. There was no telephone. Walt set down his suitcase and walked back to the pay phone by the office. He was pleasantly surprised to find that it still had a handset. He inserted a quarter and called the number that Mrs. Cantwell had given him. "This is Rita," said an out-of-breath female on the second ring.

"Rita, my name is Walter Sumner. I talked to Mrs. Cantwell at the Department of Health this afternoon—"

"And she gave you my number."

"Yes. I was wondering if—"

"I already know. Mrs. Cantwell already called me."

"Oh." In the pause that followed Walt heard a children's TV program in the background. "And did someone, when you were filling in for Mrs. Cantwell, come looking for vital statistics about the Sumner family?"

"Oh yeah. Big time."

"Can you tell me about it?" said Walt, struggling to keep the urgency out of his voice.

"I'd rather not," said Rita. "Not on the phone."

"Someplace else then? Is there someplace we could meet for coffee?" Rita did not respond. "A drink?" Rita made an ambivalent mewling sound. "How about dinner?"

"Well," said Rita coyly, "There's always Chi Chi's."

John Knoerle

Walt was waiting at the bar when a large young woman entered the restaurant and looked around. She wore an aquamarine dress with a lot of frills around the bodice and her blonde hair was piled up high on her head, the overflow spilling down forlornly on both sides. "Rita?"

"Are you Mr. Sumner? I realized after we hung up that I had no idea what you looked like and you had no idea what I looked like but I didn't have a number to call you back so I figured I'd just show up and, you know, we'd find each other somehow or another and sooner or later."

"Pleasure to meet you," said Walt, extending his hand. Hers was moist. Walt indicated the dining room. "Shall we?"

"No rush," said Rita, casting her eyes about. "I can join you at the bar. Is that vodka you're drinking? At Chi Chi's?"

"Just water. I didn't want to start without you."

"Well I'm here now," said Rita, ordering a grande margarita made with Sauza Anejo. Walt said make it two. "Then let's get a pitcher, it's cheaper," said Rita. Walt smiled and nodded. "The nachos supreme are killer too."

Walt tendered the order. He'd had his heart set on a heaping portion of chicken-n-dumplings and homemade slaw, sugar cream pie for dessert. But Chew Chew's Diner was now a tire repair shop. Rita chattered on about her life—she was divorced, lived with her mother, was studying to be a court reporter—as she scanned the room and looked over her shoulder every time the door opened. Walt asked about the person who had requested the Sumner family records.

"Ohhh," said Rita. "He was a weird one. Made my skin crawl."

"What did he look like?"

"Not so tall as you, 'bout six foot or so, bone skinny, wearing

The Violin Player

some outfit right out of Banana Republic, and a hairpiece, had to be."

"What was it about him that made your skin crawl?"

"Hmmm, dunno exactly. Something though." Rita sent her glass back for salt. "He was too polite, like that guy on Leave it to Beaver, you know—"

"Eddie Haskell?"

"Right. Like him. And he made these little jokes that weren't funny. Like, 'Isn't it creepy being stuck in here with all these human remains?' Like we were a funeral home or something!"

"Did he identify himself? Say why he wanted the records?"

"No. I'm not sure. Department records are open to the public anyway. Torrie! Denise! What are you guys doing here?"

Torrie and Denise rushed over to the bar amidst a great deal of squealing glee, sneaking peeks at Rita's well-dressed male companion. Walter asked the bartender for two more glasses and told himself he could ask follow up questions when he and Rita sat down to dinner.

"Torrie, Denise, this is my friend Walter Sumner." This did not spark any sign of recognition so Rita added, "He's the grandson of *Henry* Sumner. The guy who owned the creamery."

"Oh yeah," said Denise or Torrie, Walt wasn't sure which was which. "My uncle Lou used to work there. What happened?"

Walt was about to explain that the plant closing was a decision made by the New York LBO raiders when Rita said, "Ever wonder why they call it *Henry* County?"

Torrie and Denise were so agog and Rita so pleased with herself that Walt didn't have the heart to tell them that the county was in fact named for Patrick Henry. He poured margaritas instead. 'Mexican milkshakes' Rita called them.

The evening slid downhill from there. Torie and Denise joined them for dinner, sizzling platters of something or other smothered in cheese and tepid salsa. The women used their forks like a backhoe, tines down, and smoked all through dinner. Walt sipped a succession of Mexican milkshakes as the conversation whorled around him. Rita gave his hand a little squeeze whenever she thought a remark particularly funny. Walt did manage to ask his follow up questions once Torrie and Denise departed, their eyebrows arched. Rita had admirable recall and a way of illustrating her comments with elaborate facial expressions that Walt enjoyed. He wrote down her responses on a wet cocktail napkin.

Rita grew flustered when the check came, flailing around for her purse which had fallen to the floor. Walt gave the waitress his credit card while Rita pored through her wallet. "Rita, stop, it's on me. You've been a great help."

"Have I? Are you sure? I didn't know Torrie and Denise were gonna horn in on dinner though, knowing them, I'm not surprised and I didn't want to—"

Walter put his finger to her lips. She grew silent. They listened to a salsa song on the sound system as a high school boy in a hairnet bussed the table. Rita gently kissed the tip of Walt's finger. He did not pull his hand away. She took his finger deep inside her mouth and his loins responded instantly, shocking him. Walt half stood, sat back down, said he had to leave. Rita folded her hands in her lap and hung her head like a shamefaced kid.

Walt drove down Highway 3 at thirty miles an hour. He pulled to a stop at a traffic light. A squad car pulled to a stop next to him. Walt felt the cop's eyes on the side of his face and forced himself to look over and smile. Hell, he was a well-dressed man in an XJR.

The Violin Player

A NASCAR official if anyone asked. The cop gave him a friendly nod and roared ahead at the green. Walt saw the sign for his motel and parked his car on the street as instructed.

The New Castle Lodge was hopping. A group of young men in windbreakers, a few in shirt sleeves, stood around a glimmering barbecue pit in the parking lot, drinks in hand. Walt was surprised he knew the song blaring from the open doors of a half-ton pickup. The Allman Brothers' *Tied to the Whipping Post*. When he reached the pay phone by the office he stopped. Laura had not wanted him to go on this trip in the first place. She would be worried. He had to call. One of the shirt-sleeved boys let out a war whoop at the conclusion of the guitar solo.

Walt punched zero plus his home number and waited for the familiar tone. He tried it again before he noticed that the pay phone was privately operated. Access number. There was an access number he could dial. He dug in his wallet for the calling card and wondered what in the holy hell he'd been *thinking* when he kept his finger pressed against Rita's lips. The rest of it, the instant arousal, the warm hug and the rough kiss at the door of her Corsica, was beyond his comprehension at the moment. He was relieved to find that he couldn't find the card.

The barbecue pit, a jig-cut boiler laid sideways, was in front of room number one ten. Did one of these young men live there? Walt strode manfully across the parking lot. The boys got quiet at his approaching figure. Walt found his room key, got the key in the lock on the second try and waved goodnight.

He groped around for the wall switch, tried the other wall, found the switch and flicked it on. The walls moved, undulating sickeningly as hundreds of cockroaches skittered for cover. Walt flopped down on top of the orange bedspread and fell asleep with his coat on.

Chapter 13

"Jesus, Walt, I've been worried sick," said Laura. The pay phone was located in between the restrooms of the Bob Evans restaurant. It was nine a.m.

"I'm terribly sorry, Laura. Forgive me."

"What happened?"

Walt explained about his telephonic difficulties, told her that he had taken a clerk from the Department of Health out to Chi Chi's, that two of her girlfriends had joined them and that he'd had one too many margaritas.

"You? Did you behave yourself?" Laura chuckled when she said it which Walt found annoying. "Well, did you?"

He still couldn't make sense of it. Despite the occasional overtures from big-eyed women at work he had never cheated on his wife in fifteen years of marriage. He loved Laura with all his heart. That she was threatened with death made his transgression all the more incomprehensible. He yearned to confess his sins and beg her forgiveness.

"Yes," he said. "Stodgy old Walt behaved himself as always."

"Did you find out anything?"

The Violin Player

Walt told her what Rita had said, that their suspect was male, probably wore a hairpiece, seemed creepy. He searched his pockets in a panic, found the cocktail napkin and added, "Anywhere from thirty-five to forty-five years old, she couldn't tell."

Laura suggested that he take Rita to the local police and have their sketch artist put together a composite of the suspect. Walt said he doubted that the New Castle PD had a sketch artist and that he hoped to amass more evidence before going to the police.

"So how are you doing? The girls okay?"

"I'm fine. The girls are fine. How are you doing?"

"Well, save for this rusty knife lodged in my skull and a motel room bathroom so vile that I had to strip off my shirt and wash up in the Bob Evans men's room, I'm doing fine."

Laura laughed and told Walt that she loved him. Walter returned the sentiment.

Welcome to Ohio, the heart of it all! read the tri-colored sign on the steel mesh archway above Interstate 70. Walt slowed when he saw the trooper in his Smokey Bear hat parked on the shoulder. A mist of rain dotted the windshield heralding the black thunderheads on the horizon that mirrored Walt's mood.

He had called his office from the Bob Evans pay phone to speak to Marcy. Hyrametta said she was home sick with a cold. In Walt's last conversation with Marcy before he left she had seemed woozy. Walt told her to take lots of vitamin C. What he should have told her was to make sure that Jeffrey the operations manager kept the purchase of any futures contracts within the parameters of their risk management program. He *had* said that to Jeffrey, adding 'except in an emergency'. The opportunity to purchase a five hundred thousand dollar December contract on dry milk futures at 9.65 did not qualify as an emergency.

Rain pelted down in fat drops. The XJR's rain sensor increased the velocity of the windshield wipers. 'A bohunk from Cicero' his Grandfather would have said of Jeffrey Lezak, a fiercely ambitious young man from a blue collar background who often importuned Walt for the secret of his success. Walt never told him. Jeffrey would not have been interested. Jeffrey would not want to hear that the secret of success was to come up with a reasonably good idea then work eighty hours a week for ten to fifteen years to implement it.

Walter had chastised Jeffrey for the unauthorized purchase in a voice filled with cold fury, reminding him that Sumner International already had a nine hundred thousand dollar contract on dry milk at 9.96 cents per pound that looked like a serious loser with less than three weeks to go before the expiration date. Jeffrey said he had called and e-mailed Walt for approval without success. He had a gut feeling that the price of dry milk had hit bottom and was about to bounce. 'It had better' said Walter before hanging up.

Christ Almighty, one day on the road and the inmates had already taken over the asylum. Granddad was right. A sole proprietor cannot afford the luxury of a private life.

A thunderbolt rent the sky and the rain came down in sheets. A triple trailer semi threw back spray like a fire hose. Walt moved into the number one lane to pass as the XJR cranked its windshield wipers up to hyper drive. The cloudburst and the truck spray turned the windshield into an impressionist painting. Walt gripped the wheel and corrected right as the truck wash pushed him toward the grassy median. He nudged the speedometer up to seventy-five and hoped to God there was no RV poking along in the fast lane dead ahead. The triple trailer swayed and bucked like a runaway circus train.

The Violin Player

Walt pushed the Jag to eighty-five and signaled for a lane change. He corrected left when he felt the rumblestrips and decelerated to seventy. The XJR's speed sensitive steering adjusted the handling ratio accordingly.

Another tractor trailer was churning the rough seas up ahead. Time to pull over to the shoulder and park? Not now. He'd be roadkill if one of these CB cowboys strayed a few feet to the right. Best to maintain speed and look for an exit.

Walt turned off his wipers to see if that would help. It did not. He turned them on again at half speed. The road remained a gray-blue study in pointillism. An orange *road construction ahead* sign flashed by. Great. The XJR hydroplaned down the highway as Walt pined for the more orderly chaos of Sumner International. His hands damp with perspiration, his back stiff from the rocky motel bed, his lower intestine groaning with greasy food, Walter Sumner understood why his father had been so happy to get off the road and into a corner office.

Zanesville, Ohio looked to be in worse shape than New Castle, thought Walt as he cruised up Ridge Avenue behind a chrome three-wheeler flying the Stars and Bars. He passed vintage Georgian brick buildings housing consignment stores and pawn shops. And Sam's Sweeper Mart, Repairs and Rentals. Who rents a vacuum cleaner? Walt stopped at a stop sign. There was a bar on the corner. At least it looked like a bar though there was no sign over the door and the neon beer sign in the window was unlit. Just an open door above an unswept sidewalk. Walt drove on. He was famished after five hours on the road and hoping to find a locally owned and operated sit down restaurant. But even the fast food chains seemed to have turned their backs on Zanesville.

The XJR thudded across an iron bridge that spanned the Muskingum River. Walt wondered what had happened here. From the looks of it it wasn't the Chicagos, the Pittsburghs and the Clevelands that bore the brunt of the decline in heavy manufacturing. It was the smaller downriver communities that supplied their pig iron and car parts, the New Castles and the Zanesvilles, that took it in the neck. A battered station wagon passed him on the right. *If you think no one cares about you try missing a couple of payments*, read the bumper sticker.

Concentrate, Walt told himself, concentrate on the task at hand. This is not a sightseeing tour. You have a description of a possible suspect. The person who murdered your mother and is now threatening your wife. Does that description fit anyone you know? Walt had been through this drill before without success. Rita did not report any distinguishing marks or scars. No accent that she could recall. And forget the hairpiece, what color were his eyebrows? That's right, he had asked her that. Rita remembered light brown.

Walt stopped at a stop sign next to a drive-thru beer store and waited for a young boy in a braided rat tail to cross the street. The boy eyeballed the Jaguar as if it were an alien landing craft. Walt drove on, climbing the hill to the I-70 overpass.

Jeffrey Lezak had light brown eyebrows. He was younger than the age range Rita had indicated but he was slender and about six foot and Eddie Haskell polite in the presence of authority figures. He knew that Walt frequented Ground Zero and he had access to the company credit card accounts. But if Jeffrey Lezak had some delusional designs on taking over Sumner International why not just poison the boss? Well, if Walt were to die the company would be liquidated and the assets added to his estate. If Walter were behind bars, however, Jeffrey Lezak would be the leading candidate to move in to the corner office.

Walt crested the hill and saw a thirty foot pole sign for The Royal Coach Inn. He checked into third floor room and exhaled deeply. It was palatial. Working telephone, wall hangings that matched the bedspread, even a clothes closet. Walt shed his clothes and jumped in the shower. Refreshed, wrapped in a fluffy towel, he seated himself in an upholstered chair and burned up the phone lines.

He left a message for his wife informing her of his whereabouts. He called his office and spoke to Marcy who was back at work and sounded better. She seemed unaware of his dispute with Jeffrey. Walt said only that she should not process any large transactions authorized by Mr. Lezak. He spoke to Hyrametta and asked her to FedEx a copy of their annual report to his motel. He called Tony Sobczak's pager and got a return call twenty seconds later.

"Your family's fine. Your wife's been takin' the kids to school and doin' her daily shopping and layin' low."

"Great."

"You may wanna tell someone at your office to say you're on a business trip or somethin' cause I heard a report on WBBM where they asked a guy where you were at and he said 'I have no idea' which is not what you want the boys in blue to hear."

"Tony, I haven't been indicted. No judge has told me not to leave town."

"Not yet."

"Why in the hell should I have to get permission from the Evanston Police Department to lead my life? If they think I'm guilty they should arrest me. Tony!"

"I'm here."

Walt heard pink noise in the background. A TV, a police scanner?

"Stay off your cell phone." ordered Tony. "And reach out to the Evanston PD. You give the cops the juice before they hear it from some blow-dried haircut and you're that much further up the greasy pole. Bottom line, you don't want 'em to think you're on the lam."

Walter J. Sumner *on the lam*. "So I should contact them?"

"Might as well. Udderwise they look stupid in front of the reporters and they hate that worse than anything."

Walt called Hyrametta back. He asked her to call Evanston Chief of Police Franklin H. Reeder and patch him in on a conference line. The Chief greeted him with, "Back at work I see."

"Actually, no," said Walt. "I'm on the road for a few days. I understand that the media have been asking questions and I just wanted to assure you that I haven't flown the coop."

"I appreciate that. When will you return to Chicago?"

"End of the week at the latest."

"Okay." Walt waited for the Chief to ask him for his present location. He did not. Walt got nervous. Was the Chief stalling while they traced the call? "I've got to go," said Walt.

"All right," said the Chief, which annoyed Walt no end. Was he the subject of a massive nationwide manhunt or wasn't he?

"By the way, I'm developing a lead, a possible 'workable suspect' which, if it pans out, could break this case wide open."

"We don't consider you a flight risk Mr. Sumner. And if you have any new information we would welcome it."

Walt said goodbye and hung up. Well. Good news, he was a free man after all. Odd that he felt so ticked off.

Walt followed the phone wire to the wall. It was hard wired into the jack. He took his laptop downstairs to the Business Center, a glassed-in room with a computer, printer and fax machine. He connected his modem to the phone jack and clicked his desktop icon

The Violin Player

for wizz.net, the internet service provider Marcy had recommended when she discovered to her horror that Walt subscribed to AOL. It could not access his access number. Of course. The Royal Coach Inn was not going to permit long distance calls from their Business Center. Walt scrolled through the access number file in search of a local number but Zanesville was apparently too unhip for wizz.net to bother with. Walt asked the lady behind the front desk if she could bill his room for a long distance connection from the Business Center. She said that they were not set up for that.

"Then how do people send long distance faxes?"

"Oh that machine is just for receiving. If you need to *send* a fax we do it from the office and bill your room."

"Then could I possibly connect my laptop to the phone jack in the office and bill that to my room?" The lady behind the desk regarded Walt with both confusion and vague terror. "I've been on the road for days and it's very important that I check my email."

Fifteen minutes later, following extensive consultation with the manager and the assistant manager, Walt found himself seated in front of a typewriter table in the back office trying to sort through dozens of email messages while a radio announcer read the crop report and the manager and the assistant manager debated the merits of the Cincinnati Bengals' rookie running back. There were orders from his traders in Tokyo, Seoul and Singapore. And one forward of *You Know You're Getting Old When* jokes from sister Kay. Nothing from Sung Yee in Shanghai. Nothing in over three weeks.

Walt checked his watch. 4:35 p.m. 6:35 a.m. in Shanghai. He pictured the portly sharp-dressing Communist party trade minister sleeping off a champagne soaked twelve course dinner at the Shanghai Garden Hotel hosted by a retinue of French or Dutch ring-kissers. Could his European competitors be aware of Walt's distress? Possibly. The world of international dairy trading was a small one. Would they take advantage of a fellow trader who was fighting to clear his name and defend his family? In the words of the Chinese proverb, before a hummingbird's heart beat twice.

One thing left to do. One terrifying, pulse-pounding thing. Visit GenealoG.com. The manager and the assistant manager slid him sideways glances. "Almost done," said Walt with a wave.

The familiar parchment yellow home page with the sepia toned 19th Century family photo filled the screen. Walt opened his family tree page. John Sumner Sr., born 1760, Westmoreland County, PA, died 1844, Perry County, OH. He clicked through six generations to arrive at Walter John Sumner, born 1954, Henry County, IN and Laura Jennifer Sumner, born 1957, Lake County, IL. Both their dates of death were blank. Walt checked his children's pages. He checked his siblings' pages. Nothing new, thank the dear Lord.

Walt had deleted his wife's D.O.D. when he first saw it. Did it mean anything that the killer had not re-entered it? He might be afraid to, fearing the cops had put a trap on the website. Or maybe he thought he had already made his point or…Walt closed his eyes and ran his hand over his face. He was confident in his ability to negotiate his way through any conflict so that both parties came out the other end with their primary interests substantially intact. But a Northwestern MBA and years of experience in the world of hardball international capitalism had not prepared him for this. How do you cobble together an agreement with another party whose primary interest is killing your family?

Walt logged off and unplugged his laptop. "Get what you need?" said the manager, clapping his hands together. Walt nodded, thanked him and returned to his room.

Chapter 14

Walt drove the streets of Somerset, Ohio the following morning, admiring the shingled antique shops and the white clapboard cottages, Phanny's Phudge Shop and the Towne & Country Inn, gliding past silver-haired residents in teal and scarlet jogging suits. No one gave his Jaguar a second look. Walt understood why New Castle was in better shape than Zanesville. New Castle's neighboring towns were as lacking in charm as it was. There was no nearby Somerset nestled in the rolling hills for retirees with their bi-monthly Social Security and private pension checks to retire to. So they stayed in New Castle and kept the local economy afloat.

The XJR meandered through the dappled sunlight, then jumped up Highway 13 at the far end of town. Walt opened the sunroof. Sunlight buttered his windshield as the Jag surfed the last breaking waves of the Allegheny mountains.

Walt thought about the picture that FedEx had delivered to the Royal Coach Inn. Coming upon the boyishly grinning photo of Jeffrey Lezak in the Sumner International Annual Report he had been struck with the far-fetchedness of his suspicion. Jeffrey Lezak might well be a conniving two-faced slimeball but that hardly made him unique on LaSalle Street. Did he possess the bloodless cunning necessary for premeditated murder?

Laura was an excellent judge of character. What would Laura say if Walt told her he suspected Jeffrey Lezak? That was easy. She would laugh.

The Jag rounded a bend and sailed down the hill. Both sides of the road were thickly wooded. Walt had read about Perry County in his research, knew it to be a forbidding place full of wildlife but hadn't realized how poorly suited it was to farming. It must have been a grave disappointment to John Sumner Sr., uprooting his clan at age fifty-three and making the arduous journey from Westmoreland County only to find that the promised agrarian paradise looked much like southern Pennsylvania. No wonder future generations migrated to the treeless Indiana prairie.

The Jag was climbing the next hill when Walt saw an approaching truck with a camper shell swerve and screech to a halt. He slowed to a crawl. A squat furry creature squirmed out under from the truck's undercarriage, shook itself violently and loped across the highway on three legs. A wolverine.

New Lexington was a town of some five thousand souls built atop a steep hill, the old downtown on the summit, the franchise latecomers scattered about down below. The Perry County Genealogy Center was located in a restored gingerbread Victorian on a side street overlooking the valley. Walt parked at the curb, and climbed the front steps, telling himself to be patient with the dotty old dear he expected to find puttering about the place, straightening doilies and talking to her cats. It would be fine. Older women always liked him.

The Violin Player

The front door had an old fashioned pull cord. Quaint. When no one responded Walt knocked. He knocked louder. "All right already!" said a female voice before the door shot open. Walt entered to see a young woman stalking back to the parlor, calling over her shoulder, "Come in, come in."

The parlor was a hive. Researchers of all descriptions worked the books on six library tables flanked by wall to ceiling bookshelves, a bank of file cabinets and two computer monitors. The young docent was attempting to answer overlapping questions while hunting volumes in the stacks. Walt held his briefcase handle in both hands and waited to be noticed.

"Are you a member?" said the young woman after a time.

"I'm afraid not," said Walt.

"Then I'll need ten dollars and fill out this card." She was gone before Walt could respond. He filled out the card and felt disappointed. No way in hell would this woman recall a stray researcher from months before.

"What's a yeoman anyway?" said a researcher. "I'm not sure," said the docent. "Leo!"

A bearded troll of an old man in overalls and a plaid shirt emerged from a back room, his fingers dark with ink. He explained to the researcher that yeoman was a British term for a specific class of freeholders, lower than gentry but superior to peasants.

Walt stepped forward, directing his remarks at the young woman and the old man.

"Excuse me. I'm attempting to find someone who was here a few months ago, doing research on the Sumner family." Walt showed them the stamped copy of John Sumner's will. "The only description I can give you is that he's about forty, slender, six foot tall and has an overly polite manner."

John Knoerle

Leo looked up from the document with rheumy eyes. "Why do you want to find him?"

Walt had tried concocting yarns to answer this question. A fellow researcher with whom he had lost contact? A long lost relative who had suddenly vanished? Then why didn't he know the guy's name? The truth seemed to be the most effective ruse in this situation. Walt backed up a few steps, toward the foyer. Leo and the young woman followed. Walt lowered his voice. "I believe he may have murdered my mother."

This got their attention. Leo pointed toward the back room. The crowd of researchers studied Walt in silent envy as he, the young docent and the old troll filed past.

Leo's office had once been a trophy room. A moth-eaten twelve point stag, a one-eyed razorback hog, a toothless mountain lion and a massive full-antlered moosehead were mounted on the plaster above the wainscoting. Leo closed the door behind him and gestured to two red leather club chairs. Walt sat down amidst a cloud of dust. The young docent stood and hugged her arms.

Leo chewed his beard and leaned against his desk. "Why would you think this researcher murdered your mother?" he said in a voice as cracked and dusty as the room.

"I can't tell you that at the present time," said Walter.

"You a lawyer?" said Leo. Walt assured him that he was not. "You talk like one. And I should know. I was a silver-tongued devil myself once upon a time. That's why I started up this place, to make amends for my life of sin. Family research is the Lord's work. Only now were startin' to git money changers in the temple. Lawyers, and second cousins once removed lookin' to contest a will."

"I'm *not* a lawyer," said Walter.

"I had premonitions something like this was gonna happen and

The Violin Player

maybe in some screwed-up way it's my fault. You want something to drink?"

"A coke would be great," said Walt. "And it's not your fault."

Walt drove Highway 93 in a fog though the afternoon sky was clear. Leo had produced a can of warm coke and a crystal decanter of 125 proof Booker's bourbon. Walt had stopped at two which now felt like one too many. He hadn't spent so much time sloshed since his last trip to Shanghai. The Jaguar proceeded down the two lane road at a stately pace as Walt watched for County Seven road. It was supposed to be adjacent to a tar pit.

Both the young docent and Leo remembered the man who had spent two full days poring through records of the Sumner family. His registration card read Al Langley from Lima, Ohio in large block letters. They described a man who fit the general description given by Rita in New Castle though with a shaved head and tinted aviator glasses. The docent said his manner was more brusque than overly polite. Leo disagreed, calling him a real-ass-kisser. Neither one of them recognized the picture of Jeffrey Lezak that Walt had used his nail scissors to snip from the Sumner International Annual report.

The XJR glided past a herd of Guernsey's grazing in a veldt. The hilly terrain was smoothing down. Walt felt a tickle of anticipation. This was Sumner country. He'd hoped to have time to track down the Sumner family plat but Leo told him it was just a field of soybeans now and that the Saltlick Township that the Sumner's founded in 1814 no longer existed. Walt had been sorely disappointed until Leo mentioned the Sumner family cemetery. 'Your guy, the one you're after, he got real big eyed when I told him about it.'

Leo had produced a two page report that listed those interred and gave rudimentary directions on how to get there. 'This's about forty years old so good luck. Couple other researchers tried but no one's set eyes on the cemetery since the report was written so far's I know.' Walt asked Leo if Al Langley had ever said why he was so interested in the Sumner family. 'Never did and I never asked,' replied Leo. 'I assumed he was progeny.'

Walt slowed at an intersecting road. The post said Meeks Road. He drove on. Odd. Until Leo said 'progeny' Walt had not considered the possibility that the killer was a blood relative. Alice Langley's initial email said that she had been married to a distant Sumner Uncle, now deceased.

Ct. 7 said the road post that Walt sailed by, catching a glimpse of a dump truck idling by a tar pit. The Jag eased onto the soft shoulder and swung a U-turn. Heckfire, this was going to be easy.

Two hours later Walt returned to his car and removed the flashlight from the trunk. He opened the five gallon jug of emergency radiator water, drank deeply, washed his hands and arms and splashed the stale water on his face. The directions said the cemetery was located up an old ag road and not more than half a mile from County Seven and Highway 93. While there were two rutted old roads that burrowed through the wooded hills neither one led to a cemetery. Walt had wandered off the roads and carved a half mile circle through the underbrush. He had even asked the hardbitten tar pit workers for help. They had betrayed no surprise at the sudden appearance of a middle aged man in pleated khakis and topsiders, bloody bramble scratches on his forearms. But they could offer no assistance.

The October sun shot burnt red through the treetops. Walt took a breath, rolled down his sleeves and buttoned the cuffs. He knew his wife considered him monomaniacal when he set his sights. While that could be more of a weakness than a strength in some cir-

The Violin Player

cumstances, this was not one of those circumstances.

Walt marched up the second road. The directions said the road 'climbed'. The first road had been largely flat. Walt vaulted the same fallen tree and followed the same road that he knew dead ended two hundred yards ahead. Perhaps it branched off, perhaps he had been so intent on following the beaten path that he had missed the crucial turn. He walked on, looking off to his right where the terrain steepened. He found a spur of rutted wagon tracks just past a copse of trees. Walt clambered down a muddy creek bed, scrambled up the other side on hands and knees and climbed the mossy path. The trail snaked up the side of the hill then doubled back. The thick brush thinned as he ascended. Walter reached the crown of the hill and held his breath as he beheld, in the glimmering dusk, a clearing sown with the sepulchral bones of his ancestors.

The grave sites were widely scattered. Some had proudly erect stones and obelisks with legible engravings, some of the markers were at odd angles and weathered bare, others had toppled over and were wreathed in vines. A quick tour revealed several Parks, Evans and Drexels. The Sumners were clustered in one corner. Walt crept about on the balls of his feet. He lit his torch against the fading light to make certain he had just seen what he thought he saw. Yes. A tiny American flag planted in front of a gravestone as wobbly as a loose tooth.

Lieutenant James A. Sumner, Born 1829, Died 1863 in the service of his beloved nation.

Walt felt cold dread spider step up his spine. He moved over to a well-preserved obelisk in memory of Elisabeth Sumner, born 1822, died 1838.

She slumbers till the angels call.

The flashlight beam caught an extruding white corner at the base of the monument. Walt crouched down and rooted around in

Knoerle / John

the moist soil. He dislodged a laminated card and wiped it off.

She died of syphilis, the slut.

Walt stood up and looked around, shining his flashlight at the slender trees that fringed the cemetery. He felt watched but saw no one. He set about examining all the headstones in the Sumner corner. He found his gr.gr.gr.grandparents William and Jane. Their names were legible, their birth and death dates were not. Walter gently touched their grave markers.

The next slab over was Hannah Sumner, born July the 12th 1848, died April the 7th 1869. A tiny slab immediately adjoining read Infant Sumner and had the same date of death. Walt remembered Hannah. She was the daughter of James A. Sumner and had married the son of William Sumner. Walt did not have to dig in the soft soil this time. The laminated card was glued to the base of Hannah's headstone, partially obscured by fallen leaves. He brushed them away. The card read, *Cousin Fucker*.

Walt tore it off with both hands and scrambled through the remaining markers—Jacob, Samuel, Phebe, Joel—so angry his eyes watered and made it hard to see. He didn't find any other cards.

Walter stood up and stretched his back. Night had descended. Not the domed incandescent night of Chicago but the plummy black of rural Perry County. He hoped that his flashlight batteries would hold out. He made his way back toward the rutted cart path and cursed loudly when he banged his shin on a fallen headstone. Something skittered away in the deep brush. Walt limped on, stopped, turned.

The fallen headstone, toppled over on its face, lay alone in the very center of the graveyard.

Walt limped back and squatted in front and pushed the marker up slowly with both hands. *In Memoriam* was the only part of the

The Violin Player

inscription still legible. Unlike the other stones it was engraved in an ornate script. He shined his torch on the matted soil underneath. It was alive with slugs. He scooped them away and dug deeply, forcing his hands into the soil like a grave robber, terrified.

Walter felt something. He dug down deeper and removed a tiny ziploc bag, the kind a jeweler might use. He brushed it off and held it up to his flashlight's pale beam.

It contained a small black bead joined at top and bottom by a fine short silver chain.

Chapter 15

Oh, hello! Nice to see you! Thanks for stopping by!

I was just washing my hands in the kitchen sink—*no*, I'm not a compulsive hand washer—when a shaft of sun burst through the window and stabbed my forearm, burnishing my arm hairs to a lovely reddish gold. 'Look at how beautiful you are' my mother used to say when toweling me off after a bath. And I suppose I was. *Still am if the light hits just so, right profile, an insouciant smile playing about my thin red lips.* Mom's never slipped into my bed at night if that's what you're thinking. Nor I hers. She did breast feed me till junior high but, hey, we were poor! *Just kidding.* I do remember being old enough to climb up on the couch and unbutton her blouse.

Let's not mince words, shall we? *Motherhood is a form of mental illness!* Sperm fertilizes egg and even the most intelligent woman is reduced to a two-legged glandular secretion. The maternal instinct may be necessary for the propagation of the species but, Mein Got, it's not pretty. How many times have you seen the mother of an accused killer on TV saying 'Oh my son never couldda did that murder. He's a good boy, I *knows* dat.'

No, Mom, you don't. In fact, you don't have a fucking *clue*!

The Violin Player

And have you been reading that death row series in the Trib, all those cases overturned on new evidence? What's all that noise? I agree with that state official down in Florida, let's strap 'em to the gurney and rock-n-roll. If you're stoopid enough to get convicted for a murder you did not commit then your services *are no longer required on this planet*!

I imagine Walter Sumner has found my little clues by now. *I did everything but leave a trail of bread crumbs.* I have scoped out the Missus and have that situation well in hand. This little Sumner scenario is actually the least complicated part of my life at the present time—assuming there is such a thing. Ralph the fatass Ukrainian has decided that I'm his personal manservant and pounds the floor three times with a broomstick like the Black Rod heralding the arrival of the British regent to the House of Lords whenever he needs help opening a window or pulling on his socks. *That's why I was washing my hands.* Ol' Hans at the Central City summarily fired my butt for my 'supercilious attitude' and my current female, well, to misquote Niels Bohr, YOU DON"T WANNA KNOW.

Hey, cats and kittens, listen up. *Event horizon* is today's phrase that pays! Yes…hold on. Is that the broomstick of doom? No. Fat Ralph just dropped something. I like this dank mother-in-law apartment at the bottom of Ralph's four flat. Walter Sumner may have a downtown skyline panorama from his fourth floor master bedroom but I like my turn-of-the-century street level view—the city fathers decided it was easier to lay sewer pipes on top of the existing streets and fill them over rather than dig down into the swampy morass. *That's so Chicago, in'it?* 'Youse could jack up yer house if ya don't like it!' *Thousands did*—I like the nonexistent rent. But Ralph had better ease up on that broomstick. He might succeed in trying my legendary patience.

John Knoerle

Where was I? Oh yeah. The seriously misguided new generation of physicists say it is possible to time travel. S'true. All you need is a *slick*-smoking, *nitro*-fueled *jet dragster* capable of approaching the speed of light. Don't have one? Then logroll on the *event horizon* of a black hole. But watch out! Get too close and you're sucked down into an abyss of clockless gravity. What you need to do is tippy toe around the edge and ten thousand years will pass before you celebrate another birthday. Picture it. You, shootin' the breeze in esperanto with a bunch of huge-headed hairless humanoids in the year 12,000.

Not what I have in mind. I'm more interested in proceeding in the opposite direction.

Chapter 16

Walt pondered his phone conversation with his wife as he soaked in a tub in his room in the Royal Coach Inn. Laura had sounded oddly remote when he told her what he'd found out. She was scared, what else? The anonymous evildoer who had threatened her life was now a flesh and blood killer with a shaved head and a sick sense of humor.

His conversation with his Great Aunt Belle had been more pleasant. She had been happy to hear from him after all these years, knew all about his family's travail and was thrilled to hear that he planned to come visit. She gave him the address of her apartment complex in Muncie. Walt promised to arrive about six.

Walt had searched the family tree for candidates. Aunt Belle, Granddad's baby sister, gave birth late in life to a son, William, born 1949. A little older than the described suspect but close enough. Walt remembered Billy from New Castle as a wild, bullying kid who drove his churchgoing parents crazy. He had not amounted to much. Was Billy the lonely figure outside the firelit tableaux, driven mad with envy?

Walt climbed out of the tub and toweled off. He knew he should call the office to see if he still had a functioning company. He knew he should call Sung Yee in Shanghai and attempt to sweet talk him back into the fold. He knew he should call Tony Sobczak and get an update on his surveillance. And what he knew he really should most definitely do was check out of the Inn and drive all night to Chicago so that he could comfort his wife and children in this time of trial. Walt stretched out on the bedspread for a moment and fell instantly asleep.

The XJR sped across the prairie on Highway 38 the following morning and slowed at the sign announcing Hagerstown, Northern terminus of the Whitewater Canal. Walt knew the story. Some of his ancestors had been employed in the grueling task of dredging a canal system that sought to emulate the success of the Erie Canal by linking the Great Lakes in the north with the Ohio River in the south. Poor Indiana. Always a day late and a dollar short. After many stops and starts the Whitewater Canal had been completed in 1843, just in time for the railroads to make it obsolete.

The Jag picked up speed at the other end of the one traffic light town. Highway 38 would become Broad Street in about twenty miles, New Castle's main drag. Walt felt as if he should have turned right at the traffic light, taken Highway 1 to Highway 35 for a more direct route to Muncie. But the Jaguar seemed to have a mind of its own.

The cornfields looked haunted with their bleached stalks knotted over in the wind. A county spray truck crawled along the shoulder, killing ditchweeds. He had to see her again. Rita. Whether he liked it or not. She had made that clear when he called from the Royal Coach Inn and asked her to find a local artist to sketch her description of the suspect and send him the bill. 'Not by myself I won't.' Walt had wanted to scold her, tell her that this was a matter of life

The Violin Player

and death for God's sakes. But he had swallowed his words. Self-righteousness was not a luxury that he could presently afford.

A few hours later, Walt entered Muncie from the south, through the warehouse district. Muncie, Indiana, the town the Ball Brothers built. He knew that the Ball Corporation had spun off their container manufacturing operations and moved their corporate headquarters to Colorado so he shouldn't have been as surprised as he was at the broken windows and shuttered buildings. Had all of small town Mid America gone to seed? He continued north on Macedonia Avenue and stopped at a red light. A man sat on a bus bench at the corner, staring off sightlessly, mouth open. He had a heavily ridged brow that looked as if it belonged on a shelf in an anthropology department somewhere and a fresh knife scar from ear to chin. A little boy sat next to him on the bench. Walt looked away and drove on.

Things improved a few miles north. One-story homes with mowed lawns and tended flower beds sat primly on tree-lined streets. The Ball Brothers had left behind Ball Hospital, a major medical center, and Ball State, a small teacher's college that had grown to an enrollment of 18,000. Muncie had that all important secret of success in the modern American economy. A service sector.

Walt signaled for a left turn. His get together with Rita had gone better than expected. He had been prepared to treat her as he would a restive client, to bow and scrape, to make vague promises that could be interpreted as the listener was so inclined. But Rita seemed to want nothing more than for Walt to show up, pay the sketch artist and take her out to lunch. She made no mention of their drunken fumblings at Chi Chi's. Walt had steeled himself for an awkward scene in the parking lot of the Bob Evans restaurant. Expecting 'When will I see you again?' he got 'You and your family are in my prayers.' Hoosiers really were wonderful people.

Walt paused before he rang the bell to Great Aunt Belle's apartment in the gated complex. He twisted the bottle of sherry inside its brown paper bag as he listened to loud voices behind the door. It didn't sound like an argument exactly, more like free-form pandemonium. Cripes. Aunt Belle must have invited Bill and his brood to greet their esteemed visitor from the north.

Walt had not seen Bill since Granddad's funeral. He knew that Bill had married Winifred Grolier in 1982 and had three children, Miranda, born 1986, Melissa, born 1988, and Bradley, born 1992. The only other thing Walt knew about Bill for certain is that he had never liked him. He stepped forward and pressed the doorbell. A brief tumult ensued, followed by violent shushing. The door swung open and Bill said, "Well there he is, the man himself."

Walt shook hands and scratched another potential suspect off the list. Bill looked older than his fifty years and had grown a belly you could set a drink on. Shit!

Walt introduced himself to the flush-faced kids and Bill's pert pinched wife, Winnie. "Good looking youngsters you've got there."

"Do you really think so?" she asked earnestly.

"Yes. Of course. Where's the *grande dame*?"

"The who-who?"

"Aunt Belle."

"Here I am stranger," said his Granddad's baby sister, making a dramatic entrance from the corridor in a beaded midnight blue cocktail dress and black pearl choker, matching combs holding up her snow white hair. Her shoulders were stooped but she regarded Walt with gray-blue eyes undimmed by age. "Right on time, just

The Violin Player

like his grandpa" she said and "Sherry? That's an old lady's drink" and "Give me a good hug, I won't break." Walt did as he was told.

Bill took Walt by the elbow and dragged him to the kitchen as the women and children piled into coats. Were they going somewhere? Walt had visions of Aunt Belle's famous fried chicken and mashed potatoes, maybe even a candlelight salad for starters—a banana standing inside a ring of pineapple atop a scoop of cottage cheese, the top of the banana smeared with mayonnaise and sprinkled with paprika. But Aunt Belle was eighty-two years old and the kitchen was undisturbed.

"Damn shame about your mother, Walter, shocking frankly. She was a class act," said Bill. Walt agreed with him. "We heard all about these bullshit accusations against you o' course. I'll tell you what you need to do." Bill handed Walt a glass containing four ounces of scotch and two ice cubes. "Credit card receipts. I know she liked to travel so maybe—I'm just saying it's possible—single woman traveling by herself she might've met up with some good lookin' gigolo in Paris or Cancun or wherever and he lifts her credit card and is having a gay old time till she called him on the carpet and he, you know, slips her a mickey."

"I hadn't considered that possibility," said Walt dryly.

"It's a thought," said Bill. He had fang-like eye teeth that made his every comment seem threatening. "Winnie thinks it's just some passing psycho."

"What does your mother think?"

"That you're guilty as sin," said Bill, nicely deadpan. Walt braced himself for a backslapping guffaw that didn't come. "Naw, I dunno what she thinks. You'll have to ask her for yourself."

John Knoerle

The sommelier presented Walt with a wine list the size of a small town phone book. "Bill, why don't you do the honors?"

"Naw," said Bill from across the table. "I can't drink that stuff. Gives me a headache."

The restaurant was Foxfire on the north side, surprisingly elegant in muted earth tones, upholstered banquettes and indirect lighting. The only jarring note were the tapestries on the walls. Though pale and understated, they unmistakably depicted a popular cartoon character. A cat.

"That's Garfield, dear," said Aunt Belle at Walt's side. "Jim Davis still has his studio here. He opened this place so he could get a decent meal in town. David Letterman stops by on occasion. He graduated Ball State you know."

Walt did not. The concept of Muncie as a celebrity playground had not previously occurred to him. He surveyed the table. The girls were squabbling over a make-up mirror that one had and the other wanted, little Bradley was nibbling a pat of butter, Bill was craning his neck for the cocktail waitress, Winnie was telling Bradley to put the butter back on the plate and Aunt Belle was studying the dinner menu as if it were a liturgical text.

Walt felt like his father. Granddad would pick up a tab when he had to but he hailed from a generation that expected all ceremonial occasions to be celebrated at home. And no one knew how much money Henry Senior really made. To listen to his grumblings about greedy unions and grocery chains was to conclude that Dairy Dream was just scraping by. Henry Junior's salary as Executive VP of CanneCo, however, was a point of family pride. Let him pay. He can put it on the expense account. Not even Aunt Belle had asked Walt if he cared to pay for dinner for seven at the most expensive restaurant in town. He had not expected her to.

The Violin Player

The kids got quiet when the wine steward presented Walt his '76 Bordeaux. Walt swirled it, sniffed it quickly three times and trilled it on his tongue as the older girl, Miranda, studied him intently. Walt winked at her, swallowed and told the wine steward, "This is swill, take it away."

Miranda's girlish giggle reminded Walt of how much he missed his daughters. He would find a quiet moment to ask Aunt Belle what he needed to ask and then drive home tonight. Chicago was only five hours away.

Walt let the sommelier in on the joke. Wine was poured, food was served. Unlike Chicago restaurants that were all clamorous as a skating rink, Foxfire was too damn quiet. Walt had to wait until he drove Aunt Belle home to have a private conversation.

"Bill and Winnie seem pretty happy."

"I suppose they are," said Belle.

Walt made a left turn on the green arrow at McGalliard Road. "Their kids are nice."

"Oh sure. Great kids." Walt slowed for another traffic light. Traffic was thick on the north side of town.

"Aunt Belle I guess you know what I'm up against with all that's happened. I was wondering, hoping, that you might have some idea of who might bear such a terrible grudge against my family."

"James T. Farley," said Belle without a moment's hesitation. "Landsakes it could be anyone really, people will forgive you anything but success, but Jimmer Farley—you need to turn left at this corner—Jimmer was my sister Martha's boy."

"I know," said Walt.

"Daddy Red gave him a job loading trucks at the creamery but Jimmer, well, he was a cocky kid. They say he never did a lick of work, just lollygagged about, bragging on his uncle the boss man."

John Knoerle

Walt half listened as he waited for a break in the traffic. James T. Farley was an old man.

"It's hard for you to picture I imagine, but Daddy Red was a banty rooster in those days, quick on his feet and whip strong from loading skids all those years. When word reached him he called Jimmer up to his office, hitched that boy up under his belt and collar, marched him down the stairs, down through the plant and pitched him right off the loading dock. To great applause from one and all."

"Goodness," said Walt. "Was he hurt?"

"Scraped up some is all."

Walt took his foot off the accelerator and glided up to the guard gate. The gate remained closed until he lowered his window and Aunt Belle waved to the attendant. Walt said, "The man that we suspect of killing mother is no more than forty-five years old."

"Well, Jimmer was the butt of jokes in New Castle for many years. Moved to Mooreland and bought a farm. But I suppose it's perfectly ridiculous to think that anyone would nurse a grudge since, when was it, 1946?"

"Seems unlikely," said Walt.

"He does have a son about forty," said Belle as the Jaguar found a slot. "Would you care to join me in a glass of sherry?"

Walt learned that thirty-five dollar a night motel rooms were far superior to twenty-five dollar a night motel rooms. The additional ten dollars bought you a closet with hangars, a telephone, and a well-scrubbed bathroom with bright pink tile. And no cockroaches. He had called his wife to explain himself at 11:30 PM, gotten voice mail and made his apologies to a machine. Walt put two quarters into the Magic Fingers, kicked off his shoes, lay down on the

The Violin Player

vibrating bed and thought about what Aunt Belle had said.

'Your grandfather was a great man but I think my husband had a better life. Daddy Red never had time for anything. Times he wasn't working he was thinking about it. I remember he graced our table one Thanksgiving holiday, said the blessing, took two bites and started scribbling figures on my good linen napkin. Lord! Floyd was a fine provider and still had time to read his history books, volunteer at the Grange and sneak off on a fishing trip from time to time.'

Walt remembered Floyd as a knobby kneed old geezer in bermuda shorts and dark socks watering the flowers from his porch. Still, he was very tolerant of kids and always listened to everything you had to say.

"When Floyd sold the hardware store he just kept right on going till the day he died," said Aunt Belle. "I didn't see Henry often in those last years but it seemed to me, when he retired, he just stopped."

Stopped and waited to die is what she meant. Just as Henry Junior had done after a few years of frantic globe trotting. At least Henry Junior had a passion for tennis. Walt's parents had attended all the Grand Slam finals for three years running and visited tennis resorts on four continents until Dad blew out a knee. He came home to Hamilton Street not long after and repaired to the garage to smoke himself to death. Walter hadn't understood it then and the passing years hadn't made it any clearer. His handsome charming well-liked father rendered suicidal by a sports injury?

The bed stopped vibrating. Walt's extremities tingled. His eyelids weighed a ton. Why was it, he wondered drowsily, he couldn't manage to climb under the motel bedcovers before he fell asleep?

John Knoerle

Walt pulled up to the corner of Paulina and Bloomingdale in the dead of night. The house was dark, even the porch light was out. The front door stood wide open. He tore up the steps and threw on the lights. A dog was baying, long wolf-like howls that froze the blood. A tea kettle whistled feverishly from the kitchen. He raced upstairs, taking the steps two and three at a time but the faster he ran the slower he went, the stairs elongating, stretching upward into forever. Then, suddenly, he reached the top. The fourth floor was still as well water. He searched, bedrooms, bathrooms, broom closets, searching, calling, finding nothing, finding no one. He worked his way back down to the ground floor, searching, calling, searching, calling. The baying dog grew silent. Walt pushed through the kitchen door to still the shrieking tea kettle. It took forever to spit and sputter down, unmasking another sound. A ravenous feeding, somewhere close. The corner, the corner of the kitchen. The cat dish. He stepped around the slate-topped kitchen island on the balls of his feet. It took days. When he cleared the edge he saw Twyla bent to her dish, jaws working. He approached. Twyla turned on him, swelled to twice her size, hissed and bared bloody fangs. Walt advanced, fists raised, screaming defiance. Twyla bolted, claws skittering across the tile floor. He crouched down to examine the cat dish. He recognized the curled toes. It was Irene's foot. Small, white and well-gnawed.

Walt awoke and sat bolt upright. He reached for the phone. He had not talked to his wife in over thirty-six hours.

"'Lo," said a yawning Laura.

Walt resumed breathing. "Hons, it's me. Is everything okay?" Laura muttered something. "Is that a yes?"

"Yes, yes, a thousand times yes," she said dreamily.

"Are the girls okay?"

The Violin Player

"Sure, sure. Why not?"

"I got worried about them."

Laura made drowsy sounds for a time before she said "Then come home" and hung up.

Chapter 17

James T. Farley had a big farm. Walt drove a good quarter mile up the gravel driveway before he reached the house, passing withered corn stalks and fields of flowering soybeans. The two-story house with dormer windows was old, the barn and the outbuildings were new. A tractor labored in some field he couldn't see.

An attractive woman with close-cropped gray hair opened the front door before Walt was two steps up the mud porch. She gave Walt a crinkley-eyed smile.

"Good morning, ma'am. I'm Walter Sumner, a distant relative of James Farley. I was in the area and thought I'd stop by."

The woman invited him in without hesitation, poured coffee and called upstairs to her husband. Her name was April. James T. Farley shuffled down in his bathrobe a minute later.

The cocky kid Aunt Belle had described was still in evidence. Walt saw it in the way James Farley held his head, angled away in a 'so what' posture. They sat in the sunny breakfast nook over mugs of coffee and sugar doughnuts. When Walt said he was the grandson of Henry Sumner the old man's face got sly. "You're here about the money, ain't ya?"

The Violin Player

"What money?" James Farley angled away and smirked. Walt said, "I have no idea what you are referring to."

Farley swiveled his head back and said, "The loan."

"What loan?"

"You don't know about the loan?"

"No! I don't know anything about any loan."

James Farley angled away for a good long look. "Your granddaddy loaned me the money to buy this place."

"This is the first I've heard of it," said Walt.

James Farley took a drink of coffee and set down the mug, his eyes never leaving Walt's face. "Well," he said. "Here's the deal. We had some rough years at first but we kept our heads down and slogged through drought, plague and pestilence to where we could finally pay back the principal. Henry Senior forgave the interest. Don't have anything in writing to prove it though."

"I'm not interested in collecting any interest, Mr. Farley."

"Jim." They shook hands across the table. Farley's hand felt like a grappling hook. So much for the embittered-poor-relation-exacting-revenge-on-the-Sumners theory. "I'm surprised about the loan. I heard you and my granddad had a falling out."

James Farley coughed a laugh out his nose. "In a manner of speaking." His smile faded. "You don't know, do you?"

"Know what?"

"Let's have a walk." They got up from the table and crossed to the front door.

"Put some clothes on for God's sakes," April called from the kitchen.

"Who's gonna see me?" said her husband and stepped outside in his bathrobe and slippers.

The sun was working its way up a corner of the pale sky, burning off the mist that hung above the bean fields. Though his family had amassed its fortune on the backs of their labor Walt had not spent much time with farmers. He was pleased that the Sumner clan still claimed one as its own.

"Do you have any livestock?"

"Not anymore. Used to run some hogs but Iowa's got that deal cornered. Scale is everything in today's market."

James T. Farley crunched across the gravel drive. He walked with the compact deliberation of a man with back trouble. Walt walked alongside and waited to be told what he didn't know.

"Your granddaddy managed to keep the unions out of the creamery during the Depression years but they were back organizing after the War. He wanted some way to show the rank and file he was on their side."

Walt stopped in his tracks. Farley took two more steps and turned to face him. "What?" said Walt. "It was all a set up? Tossing you off the loading dock?"

"From the get go," said Farley. "We lost our farm after Pap was killed at Anzio. Dumbshit volunteered, too old to be drafted. So there I was. A punk kid shovelin' corn and stompin' rats in the silo when Henry Sumner called me up to that big upstairs office. I wasn't lookin' for any factory job. Which he knew. 'Jimmer,' he said to me, 'Jimmer how'd you like to get your pappy's farm back?'" Farley shook his head slowly. "He was a piece of work, your granddaddy."

They walked alongside an irrigation ditch brackish with standing water and corn silk. Walter thought James T. Farley's version of the story pure cornpone.

"Well, I know he hated unions. There's an old family story about Granddad running over some striker's foot when the guy tried to block his car."

The Violin Player

James Farley stood with a slippered foot on the ditch berm and looked out over the remnants of his autumn soybean crop gone to seed. He threw dirt clods at a crow that was pecking at something dead. The crow ignored him.

"He run over his foot all right. He run over his foot and right on up his leg. Crushed half his pelvis. Put him in a wheelchair for life."

"Oh come *on*," said Walt.

"The man's name was Papalapagus or somesuch. This was back about '38 when union fever was running high."

"Then why didn't this person file charges?" demanded Walt.

James Farley cocked his head and pursed his lips. He threw another dirt clod. The crow cawed but did not take wing.

"He was a Greek right off the boat. Henry Sumner wrote the meal ticket for half the goddamn town. You add it up."

Walt felt the blood drain from his face. He squatted on his haunches and fumbled for dirt clods to cover his lightheadedness. This could not be true. His grandfather would not have done anything like this. Ever. Walt took two deep breaths and stood up, spreading his legs out to steady himself.

"So what supposedly happened to this Greek right off the boat?"

James Farley squinted against the rising sun and suppressed a smile. "Henry Sumner promoted him to shipping foreman. Dimitri Papalapagus wheeled himself up and back that loading dock all the livelong day, a reminder to the rest of the boys of what could happen if they stepped out of line. You gonna chunk those?"

Walt looked down to discover that he held a handful of dirt clods. He tossed them into the putrid water of the irrigation ditch one by one as he listened to James T. Farley repeat himself.

"Like I said, your granddaddy was a piece of work."

Chapter 18

Walt had expected to be asked for identification at the Indianapolis office of the Federal Bureau of Investigation. He had not expected to be taken to a windowless room by a buzzcut young agent and asked to consent to a pat down search and an X-ray of his briefcase. He consented. They returned to the reception area where Walt was issued a guest badge. The buzzcut agent placed his palm on a scanner and the door to the inner suite of offices opened with a pneumatic whoosh. He escorted Walt down the corridor to a corner office. The agent opened the office door, said "He's clean" and closed the door behind him.

"I'm special agent O'Connor," said a young and pretty brown-skinned woman with high cheekbones and long black hair who looked anything but Irish. "Are you here to give yourself up?"

Walt's polite smile froze. Had Evanston PD issued a warrant for his arrest? "I just talked to the Chief of Police two days—"

"Just a little joke to break the ice," said Agent O'Connor.

"Oh," said Walt. "Ha ha." Agent O'Connor smiled at him, a smile so perfect it didn't seem real. "You don't look anything like Efrem Zimbalist Junior," said Walt, referring to the star of the old

The Violin Player

FBI television series.

"Who?"

"Never mind."

"Wendy, the receptionist, said you had some new information regarding the murder of your mother, Virginia Sumner."

"Yes I do."

Agent O'Connor came around from behind her desk and led Walt to an overstuffed chair and love seat in a corner of the room. He sat on the love seat, she on the chair. She hiked her skirt in order to cross her legs and leaned forward in a cloud of expensive perfume. "Now," she said, "What can you tell me?"

Walt caught himself staring at her tawny thigh and turned toward a far window murky with drizzle. Another Canadian Clipper had come to call. The radio said scattered snow flurries were possible overnight. Walt felt dark eyes upon him, felt as if he were conducting an assignation in Mata Hari's perfumed chamber. He said, "I need to ask you a question first." Agent O'Connor inclined her head, spilling the silky black hair tucked behind her ears. "Does the FBI have jurisdiction if someone makes a death threat on the internet?"

"Where did the threat originate?"

"The first one apparently came from Chicago."

"The first one?"

Walt soothed his drumming temple with his fingers. Should he tell her about the threat to his wife and risk another press leak? Agent O'Connor's dark eyes searched his face earnestly, tenderly. What the hell, Walt told himself. If you couldn't trust the Federal Bureau of Investigation who could you trust?

"There's been another threat. Where it was issued, we can't tell."

Agent O'Connor scratched her bare knee. "Well, almost any internet communication involves out-of-state server networks so, yes, I would say we have jurisdiction."

"I have to have your personal assurance that the information I give you will not be released to the press."

"You have it."

Walt nodded, drew a long breath and told her everything. That the Evanston PD had prematurely decided on his guilt, that they based this on Walt's supposed financial motivation, that an anonymous cyberstalker posing as an elderly woman had entered his mother's date of death on the family tree website the day before she died and had now targeted his wife in just seven days time, that both he and his wife had million dollar life insurance policies on one another, that his mother's date of death had been posted from a cyber café where he bought coffee using an internet service provider account that was charged to his company in an obvious attempt to implicate him, that his wife's date of death had been posted from a Kinko's near his home for the same reason, that he had been on the road interviewing people who described a strange man doing research on the Sumner family, that he had an artist's sketch of the suspect and several clues left by him at a remote family cemetery, that he had considered going to the media with his sketch but that that would necessitate telling them about the website death threat which would give the story a 'terror in cyberspace' angle that would vault it onto the cover of Time magazine and turn the baying pack of presshounds loose to do the killer's legwork for him just as Walt and his family attempted to disappear before Laura's designated date of death, which was why he decided to bring this newly discovered evidence to the FBI.

"Well," said Agent O'Connor. "That's quite a story. Would you like something to drink?"

"Sure," said Walt, half-expecting her to break out the bourbon

The Violin Player

or blend up a pitcher of margaritas.

"A coke okay?"

"A coke would be great."

"Need a glass?"

"Nope."

"Good," said Agent O'Connor as she returned with two frosty red cans. "I don't have any." They shared a smile as she sat down and hiked her skirt. Walt followed the line of her inner thigh as she readjusted herself in the overstuffed chair. Shouldn't FBI agents be required to wear pantyhose? He removed the artist's pencil sketch from his briefcase and passed it over.

"Good, it's good," she said. "Though the ears are fuzzy. We'd like to see more definition there. Ears are as distinctive as fingerprints." Walt handed her the laminated cards he had found in the Sumner Cemetery. She grimaced at his fingers, held the cards upright between her palms. "Now we'll have to fingerprint you," she said.

"But they were laying in the dirt for weeks or months, rained on, crawling with slugs."

"You would be amazed at what we can recover these days." Agent O'Connor looked at the first card, let it drop to her lap and looked at the second card.

There wasn't a snowball's chance they would find the killer's fingerprints on the laminated cards, thought Walt. But— "Can you remove the plastic lamination without destroying the cards?"

Agent O'Connor eyed Walt from above the edge of the second card. "Probably."

"Because, while I'm sure he wore gloves when he planted those, he's very meticulous, he may *not* have worn gloves when he printed up the cards themselves."

"Before he had them laminated."

"Yes. You may have a perfectly preserved set of fingerprints under that plastic."

"*Excellent*, Mr. Sumner," she said, patting his knee. "You should have been an agent." Walter blushed. Agent O'Connor continued. "Would you say the characterizations on these cards are accurate?"

"So far as I know."

"Why would he leave these?"

"Agent O'Connor I don't know the first thing about this person. However I did find something else." He removed the tiny ziploc bag from his briefcase with his fingernails. "This was under what I believe was the headstone of my great-great-great-great-great grandfather, John Sumner."

Agent O'Connor's dark eyes got big. She bent to examine the black bead. She made cooing sounds. "Could be a Santerian amulet, we just had a seminar on that. Or a Greek worry bead. They're called kamolas or kombolas, something like that. Our ethnoforensic team at Quantico would know." She gave Walt a breathless look. "May I keep this?"

"Well, I have someone I'd like to show it to. Will I get it back?"

"*Of course* you'll get it back. And we can give you a three dimensional portrait to take with you."

"Three D?"

"You'll see." Agent O'Connor placed the ziploc bag in the folds of her skirt. "You said you don't know the first thing about the suspect but that's not strictly true is it? You know he's interested in your family, you know he's hostile to women – these cards, the attack on your mother and the threat against your wife—and you know he considers you important somehow. Why else go to all this trouble? He's trying to win your approval."

The Violin Player

"Oh please."

"Respect, I should have said. He's trying to win your respect," said Agent O'Connor. "This amulet, was it difficult to find? More difficult than the other clues?"

"Y-es," said Walt, thinking back. "It was under an unmarked grave. And buried deeper."

Agent O'Connor's face lit up, making her look all of seventeen. "Which means this—" She held the tip of the ziploc bag between her thumb and forefinger and swung it back and forth like an incense thuridor, "is an important clue."

Walt pondered, squinted, said, "I'm not sure I follow."

"It's your reward," said Agent O'Connor. "For playing the game by his rules. For taking him seriously."

Walt set his can of coke on the table. "Well I don't really have much choice, do I?"

Walt removed the nozzle from his gas tank and replaced it in the slot. Did he want a printed receipt? He pressed NO. The receipt would show up on his credit card statement and he would write it off as business travel. Could you do that? Could you write off expenses incurred while tracking a psychopath who had targeted your family for death?

Walt got behind the wheel and waited his turn to climb on Interstate 65 and head north. 2:14 p.m. Even with Friday traffic he should be back in Bucktown by seven. Laura had said she would wait dinner. Dear Laura. Walter was at a loss to explain his behavior to himself. He had lusted after an FBI agent, he had gotten drunk with three women and kissed one, had dawdled and sightseen and tossed back high octane bourbon while his wife and daughters were held prisoner at the corner of Paulina and Bloomingdale. It was unforgivable.

A honking horn brought him to. The XJR motored up the on-ramp and merged into the slipstream. Walt inserted his Mozart's Greatest Hits CD and let the music transport him where it would.

Somerset, Ohio. Weaving through the dappled sunshine of the picture postcard hamlet nestled in the Appalachian foothills. Perhaps they could move there once this madness was over. Laura could get a job behind the counter of Phanny's Phudge, he would work as a waiter at the Towne & Country Inn. They would buy an old farmhouse on twenty acres and fix it up, raise horses. The girls would love it. Though much of the small town Midwest seemed to be on its last legs, its spirit remained intact. Life in Chicago would certainly never be the same. Even if, *when* the FBI brought this loathsome stalker to heel there would be too many unpleasant memories, too many unasked questions poised on the lips of neighbors and business associates for the Sumner family to continue as before. He was not, Walt was beginning to realize, his grandfather. He did not need or want to succeed at all costs.

Chapter 19

"So I'm in my room at the Royal Coach, getting ready to go out for breakfast, when I notice there's no coffee for the coffee maker," said Walt to Laura as they were sipping coffee after dinner. "I call down to housekeeping and ask that they send some up. When I return to my room after breakfast I find they have left me two green packets. Decaf. I call down again and request some real coffee. Some guy arrives a few minutes later with a red packet, saying, 'Sorry about before, but they didn't tell me what kind you wanted.'" Walt tucked up his knee and turned to face his wife. "Okay, he's right. I didn't specifically request caffeinated coffee. But *wouldn't* you *think*, given the ambiguity of the request, that he would have left one of each?"

"Did you tip him?" said Laura. She had her hair up in a chignon and looked glamorously sexy in a beaded top that hugged her breasts. "When he brought the real coffee?"

"Just five bucks."

Laura did a Groucho with her eyebrows. "Maybe they're not so dumb."

Walt laughed. He had felt like a wayward husband creeping

home in the wee hours when he entered the kitchen from the garage shortly after seven p.m. but had been very pleasantly surprised to find dinner on the stove and the dining room table set with china. The girls had drowned him in hugs and breathless tales of seeing themselves on TV. Laura had kissed him warmly. It was good to be home. Only the occasional flare of a white light behind the drawn curtains disturbed their domestic idyll.

"Have they been driving you crazy, the reporters?" said Walt.

"I just shake my head when they swarm my car in the alley. I almost feel sorry for them. What a stupid way to make a living. Maybe you should make a statement on the front steps or something." Walt said he didn't think that was a good idea. "Then appoint a spokesman or hire a lawyer. Me mouthing 'no comment' behind the window of our shiny new Lincoln Navigator while you're out gallivanting across the country is not winning us any friends out there in TV Land, I promise you!"

Laura leapt up and stormed into the kitchen. Walt got up to follow, then sat back down. He sipped his coffee. Though they did not normally drink coffee after dinner, he was glad of it. It was beginning to look like a long night.

The girls tumbled by, pausing at the base of the stairs, oblivious to Dad now that he had returned safely to the fold. "You go," said Irene. Thea sagged her shoulders and looked bored. She held this pose for a long while then exploded into a tongue-jutting, eye-rolling, ear-wiggling funny face guaranteed to produce merriment within the hardest heart. No response from her little sister.

Irene said, "My turn," and pounced like a bearcat, tickling ribs and armpits furiously while Thea stood stolidly with her eyes closed. No giggle passed her lips. Irene attempted to wrestle her older sister to the ground to attack her weak spot, the soles of her feet. Thea

The Violin Player

swacked her on the ear with an open palm. Hard. Irene looked up in stunned silence before she bent over and bleated in pain.

"Thea!" said Walt.

Laura was back before Walt could climb to his feet. "That's *it*. I've had it! To bed. The both of you!"

Walt put his elbows on the acrylic dining room table. The only thing he could think of to think about was that his devoutly suburban wife had sounded just like a city girl. Her last sentence came out *dabodayas*.

"Tony Sobczak has a suggestion for us," said Walt.

"Who?" said Laura. They were seated on the black leather couch in the third-floor family room. The girls were in bed. The Ten O'clock News reported that a recently freed death row inmate had been arrested in a domestic dispute and the newly-elected Governor denied pressuring state employees to sell tickets to fund-raising events. No mention of the Sumners.

"Tony. The security guy I hired to look out for you while I was gone. I told you about him."

"You did?"

"Of course," said Walt. "Didn't I?"

"I don't remember," said Laura. "And I never noticed anyone 'looking out' for me."

"Good. You're not supposed to."

Laura sat back and examined her husband. "Not *supposed to*. Jesus, Walt, what in the—"

She stopped speaking at the flare of white light outside the window. On the television screen the anchorman introduced a doe-eyed reporter who was standing on the corner of Paulina and Bloomingdale.

John Knoerle

The low-angled camera shot featured the reporter in the foreground and, in the distant background, an eight foot green skull with bulging bloodshot eyes.

There are no lamp posts on the train tracks, thought Walt. The news crew must have rigged a spot lamp to highlight the grotesque green skull that had been spray painted on the wall of the town homes on the far side of the train trestle.

"Heartwarming, isn't it?" said Laura.

"What's that?"

She drained half a glass of wine. "The local media and the neighborhood thugs working together to make the Sumner family look as sinister as possible."

Walt entered Sumner International first thing Monday morning to find Jeffrey Lezak standing in the corridor, cell phone to his ear. "Hey there, Chief," he said. Walt nodded curtly, alarm bells sounding in his head. Jeffrey looked entirely too pleased with himself.

"Did you happen to catch the Friday close on that December contract?" said Jeffrey, referring to his unauthorized $500,000 investment. Walt shook his head. "9.77," said Jeffrey, "Up point twelve since the buy date."

"That's great," said Walt. "Congratulations."

"Oh and Sung Yee is back with us. A big order came in last Thursday. He changed banks was the hang up."

"That's great."

A young trader wearing a goatee and horn rimmed glasses passed them in the corridor. "Welcome back, Mr. Sumner," he said, then turned and aimed his finger at Jeffrey Lezak, mouthing '*You da man.*'

The Violin Player

Walt continued down the hall. "What's on the docket, Hyrametta?"

"You've got some catching up to do," she said, staring up at him.

"Is Marcy in?"

"Haven't seen her." Hyrametta continued to stare. It wasn't a hostile stare as Walt had first imagined. More a challenging look of deep concern. "You lookin' out for yourself?" she said in her churchy baritone.

"Best I know how."

Hyrametta grunted. "You lookin' out for your family?" She closed one eye. "And don't tell me 'best I know how' cause you're a man cain't remember to take his *um*brella in a rain storm. I wanna hear you got some help."

"I do. I did."

"Serious?"

"Serious help."

Hyrametta opened her closed eye. "All right then," she said, dismissing him.

Walt found Marcy sawing logs on the couch when he entered his office, a copy of the *Wisconsin Fluid Milk Review* tented over her face. Walt chose not to disturb her as he went about his morning routine.

The weekly sales figures were superb thanks largely to the return of Sung Yee. The settle price on his $900,000 November contract had edged up. It looked as if Jeffrey Lezak had been right. Dry milk futures had made a bottom. Not that anyone could make a reliable call in the market these days. When commodity futures had been used as a means for farmers and food wholesalers to hedge their risk, a careful analysis of international demand and domestic supply would lead to accurate price predictions more often than not. But with the Merc's introduction of short term options the hot money boys had come to call. The result was wild price fluctuations that no one could foresee.

Walt did a quick check of the GenealoG website. There was no new terror to deal with. Thank God. He was chipping away at his stack of emails when Marcy arose like Frankenstein's monster from the slab, stiff-legged and blinking against the light. "Good morning, sunshine."

"Nnnmmmmff, what?" said Marcy. Her eyes popped open when she recognized her boss. She jumped to her feet and grabbed for her glasses. "Mr. Sumner, shit, I'm sorry, I'm *so* sorry. The whole system went hinky on me last night and I was working late and I just laid down for a *second*."

"Not a problem. Is the system back up and running?"

"Yup. I gave it a little—" Marcy mimed a couple of whacks with an open palm. "Percussive maintenance."

"Sit down. You look exhausted."

"No rest for the wicked," she said, slumping down.

Exhausted was the kindest word that came to mind, thought Walt. Haggard was more accurate. Sunken-cheeked and sallow-skinned.

"When's the last time you took a vacation Marcy?"

"Dunno." She reared her head back and searched the ceiling, then sat up and grinned. "In high school I took a field trip to our nation's capitol!"

Walt tsk'ed. "Just as soon as my family gets through this rough patch you're taking two weeks fully paid." Marcy ping ponged her eyeballs about the room, seemingly panicked at this suggestion. Walt changed the subject.

"Any chance you'd be in the market for a Siamese cat?"

"Siamese, oooo. Regal animals. The Egyptians worshiped them

The Violin Player

as gods."

"So I've heard," said Walt. Laura had informed him the previous evening. Had told him that the ancient Egyptians believed that cats could assume human form and walk around and create all sorts of mischief. She also told him that she thought Twyla knew something and was evil and was somehow involved in the plot against their family.

"We inherited one when my mother died, a female named Twyla. She's about ten years old, eats only boiled shrimp and raw kidney and is driving my wife crazy," said Walt. "I would happily pay a monthly stipend for her care and feeding if you would consider giving her a home." Marcy yawned. "Or find someone who would."

Marcy parked her glasses atop her helmet of hair and used her thumbs to prop open her eyelids. "Well," she said, "I've always had a thing for cats."

"My wife doesn't think much of your suggestion that we substitute a female officer as a decoy," said Walt to Tony Sobczak. They were sitting in Tony's panel van, parked alongside Walsh Park on Marshfield. Walt could hear muffled shouts from the basketball court. It was dark.

"Why's dat?"

"She's afraid that the killer wouldn't fall for it. Or worse, if he did and then discovered the ruse, he would kill one of our daughters as revenge."

"Unless the female o'ccer kilt him first."

"She doesn't want to take the chance," said Walter. "And I agree with her."

"Then you're all going into protective custody."

"She doesn't want to do that either. She's sick of being cooped up and doesn't trust the FBI to keep its mouth shut."

Tony Sobczak shifted his great bovine head from side to side.

Walt looked out the window at a striking young woman in a long coat, walking her Irish Wolfhound after work, plastic bag of dog feces dangling from her wrist.

Tony took out a cigarette and packed it against his thumbnail. "What's your plan?"

"Pack up and disappear."

"Then wait'll the last minute," said Tony. "You go missing too soon and the media'll join the hunt." Walt nodded. "You gotta gun?"

"No."

"Want one?"

"Laura won't permit it around the kids."

Tony smoked and grunted, grunted and smoked. Walt lowered his window and worried about his wife. Tony said, "You had somethin' you wanted to show me."

"Almost forgot," said Walt. He opened his laptop and propped it up on his knees. He slipped the CD that Agent O'Connor had given him into the sliding arm. The black bead materialized on the screen in simulated 3-D.

"It's a hologram," said Walt. "Of that clue from the cemetery I told you about. You can even spin it around." Walt used the joystick to demonstrate. "FBI thought it might be a Greek amulet or something."

Tony studied the screen for a moment and laughed a great noisy phlegm-echoing laugh.

"What's so funny?" said Walt.

"It's a rosary bead."

"A rosary bead?"

"Yeah." Tony looked closer. "It's one of the beads between the

The Violin Player

strings of Hail Mary's. See that length of chain on bot' sides?"

"Yes," said Walt. "So what prayer would this particular bead represent?"

Tony indicated his contempt for the all-knowing G-men and his affluent client by not bothering to remove the cigarette from between his lips, by letting it flap up and down and dribble ashes down his front while he said, "The Our Father. The Our Father is what it would represent."

Chapter 20

"Yes, we figured that out," said Agent O'Connor when Walt called to tell her the amulet was a rosary bead.

"My source says it represents the Our Father."

"We know," said O'Connor tartly.

"Well," said Walt, "Since it was planted in the grave of the family patriarch I assume it means our suspect is a blood relative."

Agent O'Connor mumbled her assent.

"Right. So I combed through our family tree looking for direct male descendants aged thirty-five to forty-five and came up with five possibles. The problem is that I haven't seen any of these men recently, if ever, so I don't know if they fit the suspect description." Walt paused. Agent O'Connor remained silent. "I was hoping that, if I sent you these names, you could use your considerable resources to obtain their physical descriptions—Hello?"

"I'm here. Just calling up your file to refresh my memory." Walt listened to Agent O'Connor typing on her keyboard.

"We didn't pick up any prints or partials on the laminated cards or the ziploc bag other than your own, Mr. Sumner. No luck on the paper inside the laminate either, or what was left of it once we stripped off the plastic. DNA screens also came up blank." Agent O'Connor paused before telling Walt what he already knew. "This guy is very, very careful."

"I'll give you those five names now," said Walt.

"No, you're on a cell phone."

Walt didn't bother asking how she knew. "I can fax them from my office."

"Don't." said Agent O'Connor. "'*The suspect used an internet service provider account that was charged to my company*,'" she said, reading Walt's own words back to him. "This guy is plugged in to you somehow."

"How then?"

"Put the names and everything you know about them on a piece of paper and go to the Post Office and stand in line and send them overnight express."

"The Post Office?"

"Safest way we've found," said Agent O'Connor.

"According to the website my wife's date of death is this Friday."

"I understand."

"We need this information as soon as possible."

"I'm on it." Walt heard a call waiting click on the other end of the line. "Damn, gotta go," said Agent O'Connor.

Walter listened to the silence on his cell phone and felt queasy, felt like an overeager suitor who had just been shown the door. He climbed out of his Jaguar and ascended the steps to his mother's home. A determined young jogger plodded down the sidewalk, her legs bright red from the raw lake wind. Agent O'Connor hadn't offered to provide protective custody or to station agents outside the house, hadn't even asked what his plans were. Walter unlocked the front door to the great gray ghost on Hamilton knowing he was

John Knoerle

on his own, knowing that the Sumner family would have to face down the demon by themselves.

The house smelled like a horse blanket. Walt jacked open two sash windows in the living room. He pushed through the swinging doors to the kitchen. It smelled of gas.

Walt threw on the lights, opened a window and attempted to move the giant stove away from the wall. It was a two man job. He rooted through drawers for a pack of matches. *Le'Toile* read the embossed silver letters on the shiny white cover. His mother's favorite. Salmon en croute with lemon dill sauce, waiters in white gloves, candlelight, crystal, chamber music. For a small town girl from New Castle it must have seemed like heaven. Walt held a lit match to the pilot lights of his mother's stove and felt his eyes grow moist. Nice that she had kept a token of happier times. He watched the pilot lights come to life and snorted at himself. His mother hadn't thrown anything away since the Ford Administration.

Walt climbed the stairs to the master bedroom. The bureau drawers hung open, Virginia's clothing spilling out. He restored order, cursing the Evanston PD, hating beyond reason the twist of fate that had permitted chortling detectives to paw through his mother's underwear drawer. "God!" he said to no one, sitting down on her bedspread, grabbing up a hunk of green silk in each hand, shouting, bellowing, "God fucking dammit to hell!"

Feeling better and not one to wallow in self pity, Walt stood up and searched his mother's closet. A woman who kept twenty year old matchbooks would not have tossed out financial documents. Both his father and grandfather had been generous benefactors to less fortunate family members. He was hoping to find a record of who had received their largesse. And who had not.

The closet smelled of mothballs and old potpourri. Walt clawed

The Violin Player

through his mother's hanging garments and felt his way down the top shelf to the back of the closet. He turned and felt his way back up the other side. Nothing of interest. He started toward the guest bedroom and stopped. There were hatboxes in the closet. His mother hated hats.

The first hatbox contained canceled checks from the account of Mr. and Mrs. Henry Sumner, Jr. The second hatbox contained canceled checks from the account of Henry Senior. Walter lugged them down to the study and set to work with great anticipation. Family researchers prized letters, public journals and private diaries. But they were made of words, inexact, craven, self-serving words. Money told no lies.

The checks painted a flattering portrait of his mother. Concoran Galley, $3250. The Sumner-Cooper Scholarship Fund, $5000. Royal Viking Cruise Lines, $8,689, 'Round the world!' jotted in the memo.

Not so his father. Straightforward bill paying and little else. If he had been a generous benefactor to the less fortunate Henry Jr. hadn't done it by check. There *were* many checks made out to cash. Usually in the amount of $500, 'travel expenses' jotted in the memo. But Henry Jr. had been a sales rep in the Midwest at a time before credit cards were widely accepted. Satisfied, Walt attacked the second hat box. It smelled faintly of cigars.

Walter Sumner was thankful that his mother had ignored his pleas to clean out this fire trap. She had saved checks from his grandfather's account dating back to 1940. Granddad had indeed been a benefactor, dispensing a flurry of hundred dollar checks at Christmas and others scattered throughout the year. Birthdays, Granddad never missed a birthday. There were also larger checks issued to relatives, from five hundred to a thousand dollars. They all had 'gift' noted in the memo. Walt assumed that this was

Granddad's way to remind himself to write off these charitable donations. Or his way to embarrass the recipients. Walt cross checked these gifts against the names of the five direct male descendants in order to determine if any of their families had been bypassed. Two of them had.

The family of James and Sarah Conklin, granddad's first sister, had not received a penny. But why should they? James Conklin had been a successful attorney in Indianapolis. Walt scratched their grandson Thomas Conklin off the list. The other overlooked family was more problematic. They were from a distant branch, the descendants of Travis Sumner, son of John Senior. Travis was the man who became 'a stranger to reason' until he was doused in the waterfall. Why would the descendants of Travis Sumner expect to receive money from a distant Great Uncle? Well, because Granddad had favored other distant relations. Had the gr.gr.gr.grandson of Travis Sumner inherited his insanity?

Walt threw down his pen. *Pathetic*, he said aloud. You have *nothing*. Yet he felt certain that money played a part. Didn't it always?

Walt picked up a stack of the bank blue checks and flashed them with his thumb. Granddad's perfectly rounded almost feminine signature spun by, unwavering in its precision. Was he going about this backwards? Perhaps the aggrieved party had been *receiving* checks, not denied them, and had then been cut off.

Walt rechecked his log. There were no regular payments. None of the families in question had received more than three 'gifts'. He went through Granddad's stack again and discovered a series of monthly checks in the amount of two hundred dollars made out to cash. They began in March of 1951 and abruptly ceased in June of 1953. When he turned them over Walt saw that they had all been cashed at the New Castle Bank and Trust. With no endorsement sig-

The Violin Player

nature. A check to cash did not require an endorsement signature. This was not Granddad's walking around money. He had moved to Chicago in 1949.

The house shuddered, the wind sucked the curtains to the windows. Walt barely noticed. The two hundred dollar checks ceased in 1953. The year Dad quit his attempt to become a professional tennis player, got married and got a real job. Regional sales rep for Dairy Dream.

Well, of course! Granddad had sent the checks to help his son through his lean years. They were made out to cash in order to hide his support of his son's ambition, which Granddad publicly derided. Sure, that was it. But hadn't—? Walt again pored through the checks from '51 to '53. Yes. There were quarterly checks in the amount of one thousand dollars made out to Henry Sumner Jr.

Henry Sumner Sr. was just like his signature—unwavering. All his charitable checks were made out to the recipient with 'gift' noted in the memo. He would not have changed that practice on a whim. Henry Sumner Sr. was not a whimsical man. If his monthly two hundred dollar checks had been intended to help a needy relative they would not have been made out to cash. Dear God. It was not a word that Walt ever dreamed of using in the same sentence with the Sumner family but it smelled like blackmail.

Granddad's checks to cash ended about the time that Dad's 'travel expenses' checks began. Walt tried to imagine what his father could have done that was worthy of blackmail. Growing up he had never heard even a whisper of scandal. An accident while driving drunk? Granddad would have said we'll see you in court and by the way our attorney is the judge's brother. Some trouble at Ball State? Dad wouldn't have cared. You didn't need a college degree to play tennis or work for your father. No, short of rape, assault or murder, of which his easygoing father was completely incapable, the obvious conclusion was that Henry Jr. had fathered an illegitimate child. Of that the old smooth talker was eminently capable.

Walt shot to his feet at a racketing sound from upstairs. Easy, Walter, easy. It's just the wind scraping branches against the windows. The lights flickered momentarily. He lowered himself to the armchair. Maybe blackmail was the wrong word. The checks to cash were probably his family's attempt to do right by the unfortunate young woman that his father had seduced and abandoned. It wasn't blackmail, it was child support.

"Our father." The rosary bead had a double meaning. Walt stared at the twelve page printout of the Sumner family tree. It was worthless in this instance. No wonder the phantom researcher who had filled in so many names, dates and places was angry. GenealoG did not provide any slots for bastards.

Walt felt the now familiar dread spider stepping up his spine. Dread spiked with shame and anger. If his speculation was correct he was no longer the eldest son of Henry Sumner, Jr. He, Walter Sumner, had an older half brother out there somewhere. Racketing around like a fierce lake wind.

Chapter 21

Did you like my self-portrait? The green skull with the high forehead and widely-spaced eyes? I thought it a nice touch. And I enjoyed my time on the train trestle while painting it, watching the Walter-less females scurry about the *palazzo*. They didn't miss him a bit. Why should they? *He's never there!*

But that's not why I called you all here this evening.

Women are *so* fucking incredibly rude. Had you noticed? Especially to other women. We have just returned from an indulgence. Cy's Crab House on North Ashland.

My current female is truly lunchy, as in 'out to'. Fine. Just the way I like 'em. But a chronic case of bipolar disorder does not excuse bad manners in my book. Good manners may just be anger with its hair combed but, hey, *everyone is angry*! You can be incredibly, all-consumingly *angry* and still be polite. Trust me.

Our waitress, our ditzy, eager-to-please, had-been-pretty-before-the-strain-of-raising-two-wildass-kids-with-no-husband-carved-up-her-face-like-a-soapstone waitress was doin' jes fine so far as I was concerned. She didn't blink when I ordered the Shrimp Louie without the shrimp. She said, 'Sir, we serve anyone' when I asked if they served crabs here. She was great!

Then milady started in. 'What's the history of this place?' 'Is this the low calorie Ranch dressing?' 'Are the crab legs shipped fresh or flash frozen?' The waitress, obviously a rookie from the way she followed my lemonade from her tray all the way down to the table with her chin, didn't know how to answer these questions. Her sunny smile got tight and she whiteknuckled her pen till it begged for mercy. *Just a figure of speech. I am aware inanimate objects do not enjoy sentient feeling.* Niels Bohr was right about one thing. *Nothing* likes to be cornered. When you close in on a placid surface you begin to see that it is churning, *roiling*, SHRIEKING with frenzy and violent eruptions. Which is why it's important to practice good manners. You don' wanna narrow that spatial focus.

Hold on. Back in a second.

The female's out like a light. Su-pine on the *so-fa*. I rolled her over on her side so she wouldn't pull a Jimi and choke to death on her own vomit.

Where was I? Oh yeah. *I have seen too much with too fine an instrument.* That's the explanation distilled to its essence. Humans are transparent to me. One wincing, sideways look and I see— 'see', shit, I wish it were that bloodless—I feel, *know*, ABSORB their every doubt, self-delusion, painful hopeless yearning and unspoken fear! It's why I can't stand being near them. *Imagine trying to carry on a casual conversation with someone while watching every drip and gurgle of their internal organs.*

Grim? *You betcha.* Lesser mortals might even feel a wee bit sorry for themselves. But I am essentially an optimist. *Tis true*! I class myself in that rarefied group of experts you hear gassing on NPR who, after spending twenty minutes explaining in exquisite detail why the AIDS crisis in Sub-Saharan Africa will make the

The Violin Player

Holocaust look like a hangnail, turn on a dime and declare, 'But I'm an optimist!' *Why am I an optimist?* Because others before me have understood.

I imagine that the average reader thinks that the murderer in *The Telltale Heart* hears only his own guilt thudding underneath the floorboards. No. No. No. Not so! This is not what the Poe-t meant. The *low, dull, quick sound* the murderer hears is, in fact, the heart itself!

You suppose dipshit has figured me out yet? That I'm more Sumner than he is? He will. He is, though an embarrassment to his wonderfully hard-nosed progenitors, a Sumner after all.

Hey there, *my dear half brother*. Time to step up and take a closer look.

Chapter 22

Six Flags Great America
Gurnee Mills
Welcome to Wisconsin
Mars Cheese Castle
Apple Holler Farm Cookin'

The journey north seemed to pass by as a succession of signs. Walt was fixated on the road, but I looked at each one. I tried to get the girls interested in a road game—a banana split to whoever finds the silliest.

"I won, Mom!" Thea bragged. She spotted the winner just before we reached Sturgeon Bay.

Havegard's Bird Seed Factory Outlet

It was all I could seem to see. Signs. The scenery was a blur. Artists and poets have celebrated the rustic idyll for centuries, but I'll take leafy suburban Winnetka any day of the week. It doesn't reek of cow dung for one thing.

The Violin Player

Willow Road

We sailed right past the sign for Willow Road without a word. Yes, it could be boring, yes, it could be narrow and, yes, I would have given anything to take that exit back to our previous life where we were happy or at least content in our boring and narrow way. Residents of Winnetka do not have a street by the train trestle that the neighbors call Blowjob Alley. Residents of Winnetka do not have giant green skulls peering bloodshot eyeballs into their bedroom windows. Residents of Winnetka do not have to pile their children into a rental car at the break of day and drive north to God knows where, watching the side view mirror to see if they are being 'tailed'.

Waldo, Sheboygan
The American Club, Kohler
Titletown USA

Whoo! That last one just sneaked up on me. Must be the stress. It happens that way sometimes no matter how scrupulously you measure. Stress. Time of day or day of the week. We'd had plenty to eat though. A brown and white plate at the Greystone Castle. Fried perch, waffle fries, deep-fried corn nuggets, sour cream and milky coleslaw. Dairy products and fried foods. The entire state needs a high colonic. Walter hadn't wanted to stop but the Ryder van that kept reappearing in the rear view mirror from Chicago to Milwaukee was long gone and Reenie was hungry and kicking up a fuss. We parked in the sandy lot in back. Walt hadn't permitted us to gather any food from home, or toiletries, or medication. Or jewelry, believe that? He got a bee in his bonnet about a homing device, how a microchip might have been planted in an earring or a shoe heel. *He went through Thea and Irene's things one by one, but I put my foot down when he started in on mine.*

We have been here before. Door County. It's a bucolic getaway for stressed out urbanites, though the shaggy sunburned young men slamming the dice cup on the bar didn't look like tourists. Walt herded us to a table in the back, past the mounted fish and the bags of potato chips clipped to the wall. Past the woodburned plaque.

Free Beer Tomorrow

You could see the channel if you sat up straight. Irene asked why the lake was on both sides. Walter explained the concept of a peninsula, a long strip of land jutting out into a body of water. He had a definite peninsula for the redheaded bartenderess with the curlicue tattoo on her upper arm. When he went back to get us another round she pulled up her sleeve. The Aztec sign for happiness he explained later though I don't remember asking. Can't really blame him. I just haven't felt like it lately.

We did it up right tonight, though. He's snoring contentedly beside me now. Poor thing. This ordeal's aged him ten years. I can't remember the last time he fell asleep before I did. We have a date to pop open a bottle of Cristal at one minute past midnight which is—where's the damn clock in this place? Twenty-three minutes from now.

The Cornerstone—Antiques, Lodging, Conversation
Bea's Ho-Made Pies & Pickles
Cherry Lounge & Lanes—For Sale

Walt asked if I had any interest in running a bowling alley. The girls thought it a wonderful idea. But Wisconsin is not what I have in

The Violin Player

mind. Not today. Not tomorrow. It's a beautiful place. You sense it as soon as you cross the state line. As if the giant glaciers that carved its glittering lakes and fjords took one look at Illinois and turned back. But it's not where I would choose to sing my swan song.

God. Wasted. Just pinched my thigh and couldn't feel a thing. Doesn't make sense. Friday is one of my good days. Must be the late hour. Must be the altitude. Ha ha. Washington Island is flat as a barge. We stood on the dock at North Port and waited for the ferry. I read the logo on the back of the deckhand's jacket and cringed.

Washington Island Ferry, Crossing Death's Door

I read the brochure. The French explorers called the channel Porte des Morte because of the strong currents and sudden squalls. The first sailing ship to navigate the Great Lakes set sail from Washington Island on its maiden voyage and was never seen again.

After the crossing we drove through yellow birch and blue pine until we passed the Bitter's Pub, established 1895. A clump of weathered cottages were huddled next door.

The Bitter End Motel

I, of course, suggested we stay there. Walt pretended not to hear. We stopped at North Star Realty. I stayed in the car with the girls and tried to make light while Walt went inside. Irene was having a gay old time playing hooky but Thea barely spoke. We told her we were escaping the media circus for a few days. She wanted to know why Daddy had searched her things.

Walter returned to the car with the key to this lovely resort home. It has a Roman brick fireplace and an enormous picture window that *faces south across the channel. It's the last house on a private lane. The girls are asleep in an adjoining bedroom. It's very quiet.*

I thought I was going to faint over when we cut the tether, when the ferry edged into the water and I saw, I swear, a jet black cormorant skimming along the waves looking for something to kill and eat. I had grown more and more apprehensive as we made our way up the peninsula, water on both sides, squeezing us in. But then, sitting on the upper deck with the engine thrumming through the soles of my shoes, the lake wind stinging my cheeks, little Reenie shivering on my lap, I felt a great and happy…relief. A freedom. Not freedom from worry so much as freedom from caring. Reenie and I sang and giggled all the way across the channel.

I'm looking out the window at the little rocky beach. The moon is up. The waves are lapping. So peaceful.

Walt showed me the sketch of the suspect when he returned from his trip. The same high forehead, the same widely set eyes. His brother. I should have known. Women are supposed to be good at these things but I haven't been thinking clearly for some time. Shouldn't have put my career on hold to raise the girls maybe. I had hoped to become a child psychologist but ten years of child rearing scratched that itch. You love them, you feed them, you guide them as best you can and they don't pay the least attention. They are who they are.

It has been exhilarating, I must admit. This game of cat and mouse. Fun to be the center of attention for a change. Endearing to see Walt so unsure of himself and fumbling around. He is always such a rock. Not so fun to look into Thea's frightened eyes in the back of the rental car.

Brrr. Cold in here. Shaky cold. Sweaty cold. They say it's beautiful in the wintertime. I keep thinking about that young family we saw in Wendy's. Walt took an off-ramp to see if the Ryder van would

The Violin Player

follow. Nope. We trooped to the bathrooms two by two, passing a young dad, a young mom and a little girl with a ferocious mop of strawberry hair. She was straddling the top of the bench seat like a hobby horse, chattering away while Dad dipped and swirled his fries in a lake of ketchup. Mom sat next to them and sobbed silently into her meaty red hands. That's the way it is with families. Mom is the catch basin, the depository of all sorrow. Thus speaketh Laura Jennifer Sumner to the ticking clock.

My brain is shivering. How is that possible? I need to get up and move around. I need another drink. Eennhhh! My legs are asleep. I had to drag them to the edge of the bed. Is this a trick? Power of suggestion and all that? I tell my toes to flex but they don't listen. Who's in charge here? Step, dammit, step lively now!

I do. I fall to the floor in a heap.

I take inventory. I can hear wind soughing through tree branches, waves lapping, Walter's faint whistling breath. I can smell mold, and piney smoke from the fireplace. I can see the hooked rug upon which I have fallen, dust bunnies under the bed, my eyelashes. I feel only the beating of my heart and taste only the sour bile in the back of my throat. I have been poisoned.

My eyes search for something comforting. Never thought about it till just now. Isn't that funny? You smell what you smell and you hear what you hear but you see only what you choose to see.

I select a small scab on my finger. My left index finger. I gouged a chunk out of it while peeling potatoes. I have always liked my fingers. They're delicate, nicely tapered. The scab is almost healed, pink edges surrounding a tiny red dot.

They will cover it up with body makeup. They will. They will lay me out in my dark gray Donna Karan and cover it up with body makeup. You never see scabs on a corpse.

Chapter 23

Walt felt like Granddad in his later years. Tired. Silent. Parked in a chair on Kay's back patio in a dark suit, watching the kids frolic and the grownups stand around and talk. Kay and Chrissie were fussing over Thea, stroking her hair. Irene was chasing Chrissie's young daughter across the lawn.

"Carly, stop that," snapped Chrissie. Carly stopped so suddenly that Irene ran right into her.

"It's okay, Chrissie," said Walt when he found his voice. "Let them play."

Carly waited for her mother's nod before she took off running. Walt watched his daughter give chase and almost smiled. She had her mother's resilience. It was Thea he was concerned about. She had barely eaten a bite of food in three days and when she did she threw up. He met Thea's haunted look for an instant and turned away. Had she known about her mother's problem? Of course she had. Kids know everything.

Chrissie came over and squatted by Walt's chair. "You did good, sis. Thank you."

Chrissie had come to the rescue. Walter had not even reached

The Violin Player

the bottom of page one of his handwritten five page eulogy when his voice left him and his eyes clouded over. Mourners shifted in their pews and coughed. Then Chrissie marched to the pulpit, braced Walt with an arm strong as a barrel stave and took over. She did a better job with his words than Walt ever could have. She even gave an impromptu remembrance at the end. How Laura, an only child, had often called to commiserate on nights when Walt was working late, embracing Chrissie as the sister she never had.

"Did Laura really call you?"

"Of course she did," said Chrissie. "Once or twice." Walt pushed her away. Chrissie mussed his hair.

Lonely, thought Walt. Laura was lonely. And bored. The kids in school, living in a new neighborhood where everyone worked. He had stayed home with the flu one day, sat by the window wrapped in a blanket. The city was supposed to be a beehive of humanity but the only people he saw on the sidewalk were Mexican maids pushing strollers and an old babushka pulling a two-wheeled shopping cart. Laura fed him aspirin and chicken soup, happy to have his sodden company. Moving to the city had been a mistake. His mistake. A selfish mistake. The Washington Island deputy found a fifth of vodka wrapped in a sweater in Laura's suitcase. After the doctor pronounced her dead. The bottle was half empty.

Walt had taken every precaution he could think of to take. He even had programmed the phone numbers for the local cops, the local doctor, the Flight to Life medical evacuation team and the Wisconsin Poison Control Center into his cell phone. And then he slept through it. His beloved wife Laura's lonely death. Slept right through it, dreaming sweet dreams.

"*You had any of this?*" asked the Deputy, hefting the vodka bottle in his bare hand. Walt said that he had not. The Deputy had

John Knoerle

uncapped the bottle and sniffed.

Walt looked up when he heard Reenie's cry. She had tripped on a sprinkler head and was laying face down on the grass. Walt stirred from his lawn chair. Kay waved him off. She and Chrissie got Irene up on her feet and dusted off. Irene just stood there. Not crying, not moving. Stunned.

"Why do they call you Fifth Avenue Bob?" asked Walt.

Attorney Robert Samuelson got up from his desk to poke at the fire in his fireplace. He was a handsome broad shouldered man with a great deal of hair. His gold cufflinks matched his tie clasp. His office commanded the top floor of a turreted Romanesque brownstone on Lakeshore Drive and reminded Walt of a turn-of-the-century gentleman's club. He charged more per hour than most families made in a week.

"I'm a New Yorker," said Samuelson. "The headhunter who recruited me ten years ago said the second most difficult task she faced was convincing someone to move from New York to Chicago."

Fifth Avenue Bob returned to his desk and reclined in his dimpled red leather throne. Walt picked up his cue. "And the first most difficult task?"

Samuelson's flush of satisfaction rose from the base of his throat to the top of his forehead like the mercury in a thermometer. "Getting him or her to move back!"

Walt smiled and nodded. No wonder this preening cockatoo was so successful with juries, he thought. His self-love was so conspicuous that you couldn't help rooting for him.

"Am I going to be arrested for the murder of my wife?"

"How do you take your coffee?"

The Violin Player

"With cream."

Samuelson placed the order on his intercom. "That depends on the results of the autopsy conducted by the Door County coroner. I would have advised against your granting permission for that by the way."

"I wanted to know why my wife died."

"Of course you did. Perfectly understandable. But if they discover she was poisoned the answer to your question is, yes."

Walt pulled up his socks and stroked his brow and wished for a cigarette. "But I told the Evanston PD about the threat to her life weeks ago."

"The email posting of her date of death."

"Yes."

Samuelson nodded his understanding. "To which they will say you set up a straw man to deflect suspicion."

"But if I planned to poison my wife I wouldn't leave the poison, a bottle of poisoned vodka laying around for the cops to find!"

"Sure you would," said Samuelson, unlacing his hands from behind his head and flattening them on the desk. "That's your out."

A snowy haired black man dressed in livery wheeled in a serving tray. He poured coffee into monogrammed china cups. Walt accepted his with thanks. The old man served Samuelson and shuffled out.

"You set up the straw man and the advance date of death scenario when you killed your mother for her estate," said Fifth Avenue Bob. "That works just fine so, feeling frisky, you do the same for your wife and her million dollar insurance policy. You cover your hind quarters by informing the minions of the law of the threat against your wife, remove her to another jurisdiction ostensibly to avoid this threat and then discover *nimis tardus* that she is a secret tippler and has, despite all your best efforts, brought the fatal elixir along with her!" Samuelson mimed wiping sweat off his brow. "My goodness gracious." He shot his cuffs and continued. "Not to belabor the point—all right I'm belaboring the point—but we had a case in New York, gentleman out sailing on the Sound with his new bride. She's washed overboard while he's below decks, never to be seen again. He collects her life insurance. Couple years later he remarries and, wouldn't you know, same thing happens. No witnesses in either case, no evidence, no corpse."

Fifth Avenue Bob hiked his eyebrows and waited. He looked hurt when Walt stole his punchline. "He's now in jail."

"Life, no parole. *Attica*."

"I need a cigarette," said Walt.

"What brand would you like?" said Samuelson. Walt told him. Samuelson keyed his intercom. "I just want to make plain that, in a case of premeditated murder, motive is all important. Have you filed a claim for your wife's life insurance?"

"Of course not."

"You should."

"But you just said…the guy in New York—"

"The insurance wouldn't be much of a motive if you were to use it to endow a charity in your wife's name," said Samuelson. "Some cause that she cared about."

Walt turned away from Samuelson's thousand-watt stare and held his coffee cup in both hands, embarrassed that he didn't know what causes Laura cared about. She got fat envelopes from some group every so often, return address stickers for Laura and Walter Sumner in seasonal motifs. The…what was it?

"Veterans," said Walt. "She was involved with The Paralyzed Veterans of America."

Fifth Avenue Bob nodded approvingly. "Do it now," he said.

The Violin Player

"But the insurance company won't pay," said Walt. "They'll say they need time to investigate the circumstances of my wife's death and then sit around and wait for me to be convicted."

"Sadly true. They may even encourage your insurance agent to testify that Mr. Sumner seemed particularly eager to get the coverage as soon as possible," said Samuelson, waggling his eyebrows lasciviously. "But that's not the point. We need a witness who, after he says all these terrible things, I can stroll up to and ask, 'And what did Mr. Sumner instruct you to do with this million dollar insurance settlement?'" Samuelson leaned back in his chair. "Send your agent a letter detailing your instructions. Better yet, give it to him in person."

The snowy haired black man reappeared. He peeled off the cellophane, removed the gold foil and popped open the hard pack before he presented Walt with his pack of cigarettes. Walter thanked him and had a déjà vu.

Out on the town with a dazzling Northwestern classmate by the name of Laura Beck. A tony nightspot. Mr. Kelly's, or the Blackhawk Lounge. He'd ordered a pack of cigs and resumed their nuzzling low voiced talk. He glanced over a minute later and the pack was standing upright on a serving platter, one cigarette sticking up, already lit, trailing smoke. It seemed a hundred years ago.

Chapter 24

"You see those lamp posts? Look like they're cast iron?" said Tony Sobczak. Walt looked out the window of Tony's van at the old fashioned mercury lamps that city crews had installed in Walsh Park as part of Mayor Daley's multimillion dollar citywide wrought iron makeover. "Aluminum alloy. You could pick one-a-dose up and throw it across your shoulder."

"Fascinating," said Walt with more sarcasm than he had intended. He liked Tony. But Tony was still a cop at heart. A member of that tight knit fraternity who asked questions, took notes and did nothing. The Evanston PD had prejudged his guilt from the beginning and said as much to the local media. Agent O'Connor had seduced him with sweet talk then dropped him like a hot rock. And the Washington Island Deputy was such a dolt that Walt, in his shock and disorientation, had to instruct him not to handle the vodka bottle with his bare hands.

Tony said, "Heard you hired Fifth Avenue Bob." Walt nodded. "What'd you think of him?"

"He's a putz."

Tony grunted his assent. "A putz who's never lost a capital case

The Violin Player

in twenty years."

"That may well be but, Tony, here's the thing. If we could actually *accomplish* something, say for example, *tracking down* and *apprehending* the man who murdered my wife and mother, then I wouldn't have to be concerned with Robert Samuelson's won-loss record, now would I?"

Tony wheeled his massive head, eyelids narrowed. Walter met his gaze and held it. "Terrible thing about your wife," said Tony. "I feel bad that I couldn'ta did more."

Walt looked away, at the basketball court where Irene was tossing a red kickball at a netless hoop. Thea was guarding her, arms raised. The park was empty on a Monday morning.

"It hasn't sunk in yet. Just before I left the house I started to say 'I'm going down to the park to meet Tony.' Got half the words out." Walt fumbled for the pack of Carltons he had buried in his pants pocket. It was intact, the white filters lined up like mourners in a pew. Tony gave him a light. Walt slumped down so the girls wouldn't see.

"Din't know you smoked."

"I don't." The cigarette was very mild. Walt's head didn't begin to spin until the third puff. "I know who this person is," he said to Tony. "I just don't know his name."

"I can try checking birth records for New Castle and vicinity—"

"They're not computerized, I promise you," said Walt. "You're not going to be able to just pull them up on your screen."

Tony squeezed his eyelids down to a slit. Walt felt almost giddy, felt like a smartass kid poking a stick through the bars at a big black bear in the zoo.

Tony said, "Point I'm trying to make here is that this was an illegitimate kid born to a rich daddy. The name Sumner's not going to show up anywhere in the birth records. Hold on!" he said to the rude reply forming on Walt's lips. "Obvious, I know. Doesn't help us. Nuttin' does. Pregnant unmarried girl in those days was farmed out to a distant relative or packed off to some 'private school'. No questions asked, no records kept."

Tony stuffed his cigarette into the van's overflowing ashtray. Walt took a final drag and did likewise.

"*Na wszyscy nie skrzypce graj*," said Tony. "The violin doesn't play for everybody."

"What in the name of God does that mean?"

"Investigation's like an instrument. Not everybody can play it. On a local b&e you want a beat cop."

"Who plays what?" said Walt.

"Huh?"

"What instrument?"

"Shit, I dunno. Somethin' simple. A drum. Narcotics trafficking you want a DEA agent."

"Who plays what?" said Walt.

Tony sighed, sorry he'd brought it up. "Something big. Piano. But this is family, murder inside the family. Worst there is. I've walked into crime scenes you—" Tony looked through his pockmarked windshield and shook his head. "For an investigation that involves family, family history, you want a family member."

"Who plays what?" said Walt.

Tony smiled thinly. "A violin. You get a gun?"

"No."

Tony pried himself from his bucket seat with a grunt and ranged around in the back of the panel van. Walt heard him key open a lock box. He looked out the window. Irene was hoisting the red ball at the iron hoop over and over, not coming close. Where was Thea? Walt was halfway out the door when he saw her or, more precisely,

The Violin Player

her hair, fanned out on a stone bench as she sat on the concrete and watched her little sister play. Tony squeezed back into his seat with a big shiny gun in his hand.

".357 Magnum, fully loaded, mushroom caps. They go in small, they come out big. No safety. Just point and click." Tony's laugh was more like a wheeze.

"I don't know, Tony—"

"Mr. Sumner, look, this slick suckin' sumbitch is out there walkin' tall, proud of himself. He's gonna try again. He's worked the poison thing twice. He might try something more direct the next time."

Walt took the gun. It felt heavy and wicked and perfectly natural in his hand.

"The serial numbers are burned," said Tony, digging out a smoke. "You found it in the alley."

Chapter 25

The house on Hamilton stood mute testament to the sad state of the Sumner family. Fallen leaves clogged the sidewalk, yellowed advertising circulars were piled ankle deep on the doormat and rubber banded to the doorknob. The lawn was an embarrassment.

Walt shouldered open the front door. The girls scattered to explore the old barn's many nooks and crannies. Walt raised the windows in the living room. Irene removed her head from a hinged box next to the front door and said, "Cool!"

"That's a milk box," said her father. "The milkman used to leave the milk, butter and eggs there every morning. For breakfast," he added to Irene's blank look. "C'mon, we're going to the garage."

"I don't wanna," said Irene. "I don't wanna go to the garage!"

Walt studied his daughter's defiant pie-eyed stare. "All right, stay here. *Don't* go outside and *don't* answer the door."

Irene beamed. Back to happy in record time. Walt kissed his daughter on the crown of her head and entered the sitting room, telling himself that it was okay to leave Irene unattended. The girls were not in any real danger. Not yet. He had checked the GenealoG website. Their dates of death were blank.

The Violin Player

"Thea," said Walt. "The-*a*!" No answer. He pushed through the swinging doors to the kitchen. She was kneeling on a stool, rummaging through canned goods in a cabinet. "Thea?"

"Yes?"

"What are you doing?"

"Nothing."

"Are you hungry?"

"Not really."

"Because if you are hungry we can go out to eat at any place you like."

"I'm not hungry."

"Even Chuck E. Cheese," said Walt brightly, hoping to bait a 'Vomit' or a groan or some, any, response from his elder daughter.

"No thank you," said Thea. She was arranging the cans in the cabinet just so, the bigger ones in back, the smaller ones in front. She puzzled over a small jar.

"That looks nice," said Walt softly. Thea moved the stool over and started in on the next cabinet. "I'll be in the garage if you need me."

The sight of his mother's pearl-gray Lincoln gave Walt a start. It didn't seem as if it should still be there. Someone should have sold it or given it away by now. The executor of his mother's estate. Himself. Walt had searched the house on Hamilton from stem to stern after finding the cancelled checks, but found nothing of note. It was while smoking a cigarette with Tony that the thought had occurred to him. The garage. His father's hideaway. He had never searched the garage.

The fluorescent tube light buzzed to life. Dad's recliner and hubcap ashtray were long gone but his old round-shouldered Philco remained covered with plastic and wedged into a corner. Walt looked around. Oil stained concrete bathed in sickly green light. What moldering sorrows had Henry Jr. been contemplating as he sat here in his Laz-Y-Boy, listening to the radio and smoking himself to death? Walt opened the wide green cabinets above the tool bench.

The first cabinet was filled with trowels, tilling claws and hedge clippers. Yard tools. Implements of torture. Everything looked vaguely sinister to him now.

The second cabinet held cans of paint, brushes, a caulking gun, a hand sander and a power drill with a stiletto bit. Walt imagined placing it against his half brother's forehead and squeezing the trigger, slowly boring in. He moved over to the third cabinet, stopped and turned around. Thea was standing just inside the door.

"What's up buttercup?" Thea shrugged. "Is Reenie okay?"

"She's watching TV," said Thea.

Walt waved her over. She crossed the concrete on stiff unbending legs. "I'm looking for clues. Would you like to help me?" Thea shrugged again. "Thea, as you know, someone has chosen to attack our family. I think, I'm pretty sure, that he's related to us."

"I figured."

"You did?"

Thea nodded. "Is he going to try and kill us?" she asked matter of factly.

Walt cleared his throat. "I don't know, snowflake. I don't know what he's going to do."

The third cabinet was crammed with tennis gear, a wooden racket still in a trapezoidal press, a can of dirty white tennis balls labeled "Semi's '49". Several plaques and trophies, too, from the same era. Walt picked one up. *Henry Sumner Jr., Champion, Chicagoland Seniors Tournament*. The old man had never mentioned it.

Walt handed the trophy to Thea to distract her while he investigated a pile of glossy magazines stacked in the back right corner of

The Violin Player

the cabinet. A secret *Penthouse* collection? No, they were CanneCo annual reports. Walt shook them out one by one. Two thirds of the way through the stack Thea said "Look!" as a black and white photograph see-sawed jaggedly to the concrete floor.

Chapter 26

I understand that dipshit got himself a lawyer. The honorable Robert Samuelson from the legal firm of *Moo, Oink, Baa and Cluck*. He should save his money. He's going to need it.

So. There I was on my Murphy bed, basking in the afterglow and wondering 'Who's next?' when his imperial majesty Ralph the Fat started in again. It wasn't the usual sharp, percussive stamp of the Black Rod. More like a dull thud. I climbed the back stairs dutifully, thinking—I'm always thinking—what kind of perversely inverted world is it where a man of my intelligence and breeding becomes the manservant of a racially inferior Slovak just because he bought a four flat in a Puerto Rican war zone for pocket change twenty-five years ago that's now worth well over half a million because artists looking for cheap loft space discovered Bucktown in the 80's and suburbanites sick of living life inside a carton of homogenized milk espied them and said, '*Hey! If these pink-haired twangle boys can manage not to get tied to a telephone pole, doused with gasoline and set on fire down here then Bucktown must be a wonderful place to enjoy the urban experience*!'

Ralph was on the toilet and couldn't get up. The dull thudding

The Violin Player

was his swollen red feet stomping the bathroom tile. It had to hurt. He has diabetes. I've told him time and again to keep his feet up and always wear his electric booties. Does he listen? *He does not*!

So, one minute Ralph is standing up there on his stoop greeting passersby with a smile and a wave and the next minute he's laying face down on the sidewalk, his yappy little dog dancing the *baile del muerto* around his varnished skull. I let myself out the back door. *I don't get along well with authority figures.*

Hold on—a blonde nymphet is draped over the barsill here at the Mad Bar, exposing the downy hairs on the small of her back. *Chicks today wear pants and tops that don't quite meet in the middle, had you noticed?* Whoops, fun's over. She stood up.

I know what you're thinking. You can understand, maybe even *sympathize* with my dispatch of a snotty old richbitch who patted herself on the back for helping the *less fortunate* with one hand while gorging herself on white truffles at the Captain's table with the other. But why kill a devoted wife and mother of two? It's a valid question and one to which I have devoted a good deal of morbid introspection. Here is my carefully considered response: *Motherhood is a form of mental illness!* What these little peckernecks need is a Dad.

But hold up a second there, Mister Man, you reply. *Walter Sumner is (was) a terrible husband and a worse father!*

Too true. *I*, on the other hand, having experienced firsthand the unanswered questions in the one-way conversations with the empty chair at the head of the table would make an exemplary paterfamilias. I have the answers now—*I do!* I lack only the wide-eyed innocent to ask the questions. *My former ex-wife conspired to thwart my biological imperative without my knowledge. The pharmacy left a message two weeks after her departure. Her monthly*

John Knoerle

prescription for orally ingested baby stoppers was languishing in their bin. I don't believe in adoption. Parenthood requires a blood connection. *And adoption agencies have traditionally been leery of single divorced unemployed sociopathic men.* But I haven't ruled out kidnapping.

I suppose you want all the gory details. How I pulled it off. *Know Your Victim!*

Laura Sumner made a run to a bodega on Western every two days between noon and one. You could set your watch. She queued up with the penny-counting stewbums and the sheetrock-dusted construction workers to buy her 750 ml of 100 proof vodka. I wandered in from time to time to buy a tall boy. *It's a popular misconception that witnesses identify familiar faces. It's the unfamiliar faces they remember.* I selected her D.O.D. with this schedule in mind. I followed her to Western Ave, a doctored bottle in a paper bag hitched to the inside of my trench coat. *I used superglue to rejoin the severed shrink wrap on the neck of the bottle. It had a tiny wrinkle but I was unconcerned. Mrs. Sumner wouldn't be worrying her pretty little head about safety seals when she finally found a solitary moment to pop the cherry.* The dilemma, the predicament, the *Gordian knot* that wanted undoing was how to make the switch without being observed. I considered setting a tiny remote-controlled charge in the pyramid display of Angela's Amber Ale. Press the button at the crucial moment. *Naw.* Too complicated, too many ways to fail. I contemplated greasing the palms of the preteen felons-in-training who hang at the corner of Western and Belden, instructing them to create a distraction when I gave the high sign. Same problem.

So here is what I did. *The toxin was a touch of genius, by the way. It mimics the effects of hypothermia. The extremities shut*

The Violin Player

down one by one, leaving the brain till last. Emily Dickinson nailed it: As freezing persons recollect the snow/First chill—then stupor—then the letting go.

I queued up behind Mrs. Sumner. I stumbled forward—pretending to be jostled by the man in back of me—*bumped* into her and grabbed hold of her bottle to gain my purchase, *knocking* it to the floor. 'Hey, Watch it asshole!' I cried, which turned all eyes to the man behind me.

It was there, on the dirty linoleum in front of the cashier's station, that I made the switch.

Chapter 27

The reception that Walt received at the offices of Sumner International following the death of his wife was different than the reception he received following the death of his mother. There were the same awkward expressions of sympathy but this time no one touched him or made eye contact. Except Hyrametta. She stood up, walked around her desk and crushed him to her ample bosom for all to see. The rest of the staff kept their distance.

Walt wandered the office corridors and the trading floor, drawing darting glances and silencing all discussion. They had all heard the media speculation that Walter Sumner was soon to be arrested for the murders of his wife and mother. He took his time strolling between the banks of networked computer monitors. No one was playing golf, everyone was bent to their task. Walt walked to his office door and turned around. Not a single head popped up. Was this the dirty little secret of success that his professors at the Northwestern School of Business Management had neglected to mention? If James T. Farley's stories were true, it had worked for Granddad. Want your *yee*'s to work like hamsters from dawn till dusk? Make them fear you. Walt opened the door to his office.

The Violin Player

Marcy and Jeffrey Lezak dropped their magazines to the coffee table in unison.

Walt sat down at his desk. "You get the IT system back up and running, bugs worked out?" Marcy nodded so vigorously that her impenetrably kinky hair shifted forward. She shifted it back with a quick, practiced move. A wig. Marcy wore a wig.

"I'm headed out of town for a couple of days and God only knows what happens after that," said Walt. "I'll monitor email and check in when I can. Don't call my cell phone unless it's an emergency." Walt paused. Marcy's expression conveyed deep concern. Jeffrey Lezak's face betrayed a more hopeful outlook. "If you're thinking when the cat's away the mice will play, don't. Either one of you," said Walt to Jeffrey. "We have a well-defined risk management program in place that has been very successful over the long term. Stay within the parameters."

"Mr. Sumner, let me assure you that I—and Marcy—that Marcy and I and *everyone* on staff will do our darndest to keep things moving here in a forwardly direction."

"Thank you, Jeffrey," said Walter. Jeffrey seemed to hesitate. "Is there something more you'd like to tell me?"

"We do have this temporary flow squeeze problem."

"I'm not sure what a flow squeeze problem is, Jeffrey, but it sounds painful."

Marcy smiled. Jeffrey did not. He said, "Sir, our Bank One credit line is maxed out."

"How can that be?"

"Well, we are currently holding positions totaling—" said Jeffrey in a reedy voice that struggled to find a lower timbre, "two point eight million and change in dry milk futures with termination dates from next month to March." Jeffrey shook his head sadly, sagely. "Problem at the moment is that the Merc made a margin call."

"They what?"

"They made a margin call."

"You didn't," said Walt. It was not a question because it was not a possibility.

"I'm afraid so," said Jeffrey.

"You used our line of credit to buy the contract!?"

"Didn't mean to. But a temporary dip in the dry milk price last week pushed us below our maintenance limit." Jeffrey's eyes avoided Walt's fearsome stare. "Hey, I covered it! It's not like I had to liquidate our positions!"

Walter willed calm into his voice. "Jeffrey, as you may have noticed, futures contracts are already leveraged. We put down the earnest money then pay the balance on the settlement date."

"I know but—"

"What you have done, Jeffrey," said Walt Sumner, accused double murderer, "Is to *borrow* money in order to *borrow* money!"

Jeffrey gripped the arms of his wing chair, got up, sat down and crossed his legs tightly. "But my contract's up twelve per cent since the buy date," he squeaked. "With more to come! Even the RM program predicts another ten per cent by year end. I'm thinkin' fifteen per cent easy. If we can just squeeze through this month we're in fat city." He added, "I'll defer my salary if that's what it takes."

Walt had to bite his tongue to keep from saying 'That won't be necessary. You're fired.' He did say, "We're not a brokerage house, Jeffrey, we're not a hedge fund. We're a trading firm. We buy and sell commodities. As you know we generally take delivery upon expiration of the contract. However—" Walt paused long enough for Jeffrey to anticipate what he was going to say. "Sell your $500,000 contract and settle the bank loan."

The Violin Player

"*Now?*" said Jeffrey, horrified.

"This minute."

"*All* of it?"

"All-of-it."

Jeffrey huffed and puffed and squirmed in his seat and even turned to Marcy for help in righting this rank injustice. Marcy removed her glasses and blew on them.

"Right now, Jeffrey," said Walter.

Jeffrey jumped up and stalked off. Walt motioned for Marcy to remain. He tried to deep breathe himself back to sanity. Jeffrey's little adventure would give the State's Attorney another club to beat him over the head with. 'Walter Sumner was a man in dire financial distress, a sole proprietor whose company's credit line had been exhausted at the time of his well-insured wife's death!' Did Jeffrey do this on purpose? Or was he simply one of those people put on this earth to make your life miserable? Walt came to when he heard the music.

Papa Haydn, a string quartet. Marcy had turned on the stereo on the window sill. "Thought you could use some cheering up," she said, gliding about to the sound.

Walt thought of Laura, how she would break into a mock balletic dance whenever she came upon him listening to Mozart. If he was listening to *Don Giovanni* she would join the sopranos at ear-splitting volume.

"Did you want to talk to me, Mr. Sumner?"

"Yes. Absolutely," said Walt.

"Anything in particular that you wanted to say?"

Walt looked up to see Marcy looking down at him. She had been saying something. "Why do you wear a wig?"

"Think of what I save on shampoo! And haircuts!" Marcy

removed her hairpiece and held it in her hands. Her shaved skull was splotched with Eczema. "Throw it in the washing machine every weekend and it's good as new."

Walt watched Marcy replace her wig. "How are you and Twyla getting along?"

"Great! She's a magnificent beast," said Marcy, snugging down her hair and straightening her eyebrows with her little finger. "My roommate's having a bit of a spraying contest with her though."

"I didn't know you had a roommate."

"Men," said Marcy. "And I thought cats were surly and independent." She resumed her waltzing, fluttering her fingers downward, caressing the lacework of stringed notes that billowed from the window sill.

"You know Marcy," said Walt. "You may just be crazy enough."

"To do what?" said Marcy.

"To assume day to day control of Sumner International while I'm gone."

Chapter 28

Walt paused at the front door of Ted and Kay's to say goodbye. He reconsidered his plan when he saw Ted, standing behind Thea in the foyer, place his plump pink hands on her shoulders. She flinched.

"Girls, give your daddy a kiss," said Ted.

Thea did so, if only to escape Ted's clutches. Reenie slunk down and hugged Walt's leg. They loved Kay. She would take good care of them. And Walt didn't really think Ted would do anything untoward. Not at all. Ted was more the type to favor little boys.

"Be good, darling daughters. I'll be back in a couple days." Walt had to peel Irene off his leg before he made his way out the door.

"I'll walk you out," said Kay and followed her brother into the crisp Park Ridge evening.

Kay still had asters blooming along the front walk in late October, pink dahlias thriving in planter boxes under the windows. She was a genius when it came to growing things. It was a crime she had no children. They stopped by the Jaguar at the curb.

"You should have smooth sailing," said Kay, searching the skies. "The weather channel said the low pressure system was hours away."

"I still have to go home and pack," said Walt.

Kay said "Oh" and "How in the name of God do you do it?"

"Do what?"

"Lose the person you love most in all the world and just keep going?"

"You just do," said Walt, shaking out his keys. "You lie to yourself, you stay busy, you concentrate on the task at hand. I still can't believe that Mom is gone. I can't even begin to think about Laura."

Kay took her brother's hand between her own. "Walter you can't just pat me on the head and give me a licorice stick like Dad used to do. I have a right to know what's going on."

"Okay," said Walt. "Okay. But you can't repeat this to anyone, not even Ted." Kay nodded, then bent down to pinch dead blossoms from a rose bush along the curb. "I've been doing some digging, out at the house. I don't have anything nailed down one hundred per cent but it looks as if the murderer is our half brother."

"Good God," said Kay, standing up. She put her hands on her hips. "Of course. That son of a bitch."

"Who? Dad? Did you know? How did you know?"

"What was the first thing Dad did when he came home from a road trip?"

"I don't know. Kiss Mom."

"How?"

Walt shrugged. "On the lips."

"Yes," said Kay. "Like you'd kiss your great Aunt Edna, all puckered up, leaning over so they wouldn't touch. Little tippy taps. I knew he was fooling around even then, I just didn't know I knew."

Walt opened his briefcase carefully so Kay wouldn't glimpse the gun and removed the six by nine black and white photograph.

The picture had been taken in the back yard of the house on

The Violin Player

Hamilton. A lawn party, folks gathered under a canopy, tri-colored bunting, tables groaning with food. Granddad in shirtsleeves and a straw boater and Grandma in a polka dot dress sat in high-backed canvas chairs and stared impassively at the camera. They were flanked by smiling neighbors and family members. In the far left corner Aunt Jeanne, Dad's older sister and only sibling, held hands with dashing flyboy Ronald Edmunds, her future husband. They would disappear off the coast of Nova Scotia in 1951, Ronald at the controls.

Odd. And annoying. How dumb decisions like trying to impress your new bride with your night flying derring-do punished future generations. Aunt Jeanne could have told Walt everything he wanted to know. Had she lived she might even have kept her younger brother on the straight and narrow. In Walt's memory she was the only person that his father ever spoke of without a trace of sarcasm.

Henry Jr. mugged at the camera in the far right corner of the photograph. He looked natty in a cableknit tennis sweater and pleated pants, sunglasses parked atop his head. He had his arm around a handsome young woman with a magnificent head of hair. Walt pointed her out to Kay.

"Do you have any idea who this woman might be?"

Kay blew a steamy breath out her nose. The night was turning cold. "No. No idea."

"I direct your attention to our father's arm. And the young lady's expression." Kay moved under the bell of the street lamp for a better look. She saw that her father was grinning fiercely, that his forearm disappeared down below the young woman's waistline and that the young woman wore a startled look. "Where is his hand do you suppose?" said Walt.

"That son of a bitch," said Kay.

Chapter 29

Walter handed two dollars to the booth attendant and checked his dashboard clock. 10:48 PM. That would put him in Muncie about four in the morning. Didn't matter. He would park in front of Aunt Belle's apartment complex and catch a few winks.

"Thank you sir," said the booth attendant. She said it loudly, as if she were repeating herself. Walt nodded and drove on, across the Skyway. The necklace of diamond lights on the power station blurred by. Walt opened the sunroof and all the windows and pushed the speedometer past ninety. He felt a little better. His mind rolodexed through his card file of pressing concerns and spun to a stop on the least grim. The office. Marcy was supremely unqualified to manage daily operations. But she was the only one he trusted without reservation.

The XJR flashed by the state trooper parked on the shoulder so quickly that Walt had to check his rearview mirror to make sure he had really seen him. He had. The trooper's light bar lit up like New Year's Eve. The road was clear, Walt was scant miles from the Indiana border. What the hell. He pushed the accelerator to the floor and clung to the steering wheel. The Jag's 370 horsepower V8 did,

The Violin Player

effortlessly, what it had been engineered to do. The needle swung past one hundred and twenty miles an hour and the trooper's light bar disappeared from the rearview mirror.

The world got still. The buffeting wind through the windows slackened. The Jag was outracing it. Walt lit the high beams and passed a tarpaulin-covered flatbed in a blink. He took one hand off the wheel and eased the back of his seat down a notch. There, that was better. His Rolodex stopped spinning. He hadn't felt so relaxed in weeks.

Welcome to Indiana, the Crossroads of America.

Damn. Walt slowed to a crawl, sixty-five miles an hour. The Illinois State Trooper couldn't ticket him now. He *could* follow him across the state line, run his plates and inform the media that Walter Sumner was on the lam. Walt took the next off-ramp, a tight corkscrew exit, into the depths of Hammond, Indiana.

He turned south on Indianapolis Boulevard. The sidewalks were busy. His car drew approving gestures and whistles from the clusters of homeboys on the corners. Walt had noticed, when he took his Jag in for service, that a goodly number of his fellow owners were sharply dressed young black men. Walt power locked his doors but kept his windows open. He stopped at a red light. A young man shouted something he couldn't understand and came running up to the passenger's side door. Walt grabbed his briefcase and groped for the gun. The young man's smile faded when he peered inside.

"Shit," he said. "You ain't Artis."

Walt's hand found the butt of the .357. The light turned green. "Sorry to disappoint you," said Walter. The young man leaned on the door and surveyed the Jaguar's interior, looking everywhere but at Walt's hand in the briefcase. Two of his friends walked up behind him. The young man reached in and stroked the passenger's seat with the tips of his fingers. Walt whirred the driver's seatback upright for a better angle. Cars behind him began to honk. The young man's smile was bright white where it wasn't gold.

"Nice leather."

"Calfskin," said Walt and motored across the intersection.

Drug dealers. They were drug dealers. That's what all those gestures and whistles had been about. They sold a commodity on the open market and enjoyed profits if they stayed ahead of the demand curve and suffered losses when they fell behind. A great apprenticeship for future dairy traders. At least they performed a recognizable service. Jeffrey Lezak and the new generation of speculators could take a lesson.

The XJR veered left at a Y-shaped intersection and drove down a dim street of one story brick homes. Walt's Rolodex flipped over another card. Life insurance. He hadn't gone to visit his agent, hadn't instructed him to pay the settlement to the Paralyzed Veterans as Fifth Avenue Bob had told him to do. Such an obvious ploy seemed like the act of a guilty man. Even the cops were smart enough to see that. Weren't they?

Walt and his Jaguar wandered the bungalow belt looking for some sign of the expressway. A squad car crept past and raked them with its alley light. Walt waved. He saw an overpass, turned right and drove under the vaulted six lane span of Interstate 90. No on-ramps, can't get there from here. Walt turned left on Chicago Ave. No rush, he would get there eventually. A mist of rain spritzed his windshield. Walt closed his windows but kept the sunroof open. The rain felt good. His Rolodex flipped over another card.

The media. The circus on Paulina had struck its tents. Walt had naively assumed it was a gesture of deference to his family's grief. Then he saw the lead story on the ten o'clock news. An eleven year

The Violin Player

old girl on the South Side had been raped and murdered. The police were holding two male suspects, one seven years old, one eight. Black preachers led a protest march on City Hall. How could an eight year old boy commit rape they demanded to know. Walt, who had always admired and respected police officers, thought it a very good question.

The Jaguar pulled up next to a tow truck that was idling by the side of the road, the driver busy with paperwork. Walt put the XJR in park and poked his head through the sunroof. That didn't work so he climbed to his feet on top of the calfskin seat. That proved a little squishy so he braced one foot on the center console. The tow truck driver lowered his window.

"Can you tell me how to get to I-90?" It was a perfectly reasonable question. No reason for the tow truck driver to stare at him in such a peculiar manner. "Interstate 90," repeated Walt. The driver gave him directions. Walt thanked him and drove on.

The Jaguar leapt up the on-ramp, excited now, the scent of blood in its nostrils. Ah, but Walter was still in control. He was the driver, the jockey, the pilot, the master of disaster. He knew the road was slick with a ruinous mix of oil and water following the first rain in several days. They might even encounter patches of black ice as the temperature dropped. So, once he took possession of the number one lane, Walt notched the cruise control at a conservative ninety-six miles an hour.

His Rolodex flipped over another card. Walt turned on the radio. His classical station was breaking up so he hit the scan button. The tuner searched out the next FM signal, played it for three seconds and moved on down the line. And so on. His Rolodex flipped over another card.

That bottle. That goddamned fucking bottle was the reason.

Laura told him that she didn't want to go into protective custody because she was sick of being cooped up, that she didn't trust the cops to keep a secret. But that bottle was the reason. Laura wasn't worried about the cops keeping their mouths shut. She was worried that they would search her things and find that bottle. You should have known, Walter. For Christ's sakes you should at least have *suspected*. The flushed cheeks, the mood swings, the early bedtimes, the ducking into the kitchen a dozen times a night. Your half brother knew. Why didn't you?

Walter checked the rearview mirror for approaching headlights. The coast was clear. Walt depressed the accelerator which disengaged the cruise control. The Jaguar breathed a sigh of relief. Walter jerked the reigns at a hundred and ten. His Rolodex flipped over another card. The same card. That same card. He slid Mozart's Greatest Hits into the CD slot, cranked up the volume and waited for the customary relief. Track one did not satisfy. Track two was worse. Track three sounded lightweight and candyass, the music of a talented young man to whom things came far too easily. The situation called for Beethoven, or Gustav Mahler. Walt pushed the XJR to 128 mph. He slowed to fifty. The rain intensified.

His Rolodex remained stuck. That same card. *Lividity*. The word the doctor on Washington Island used. *Lividity*. The puddling of blood in the extremities. Why Laura's lips had been so grotesquely swollen and discolored, a dark grayish blue, when Walter woke up in the rented house on Washington Island, checked the clock, thanked God and rolled over to kiss his wife awake.

Chapter 30

"Good Lord, Walter, you look like you've been drug through a knothole," said Granddad's baby sister when she opened the door at seven o'clock in the morning.

"I ran out of gas," said Walt.

"Come in, come in."

Walter entered Aunt Belle's neat as a pin apartment and said, "I ran out of gas on I-65."

"Oh dear."

"I called information to get the number of a towing service but they said they couldn't recommend one in particular, that I had to ask for a specific towing service by name. So I waited more than two hours with my hood up before a state trooper pulled over."

"You need some coffee," said Aunt Belle, dressed for the day in a navy blue wool skirt, white cotton blouse and pearl earrings. No two-toned jogging outfits or polyester pants suits for Aunt Belle. She escorted Walt to the divan. "Why didn't you call 911?"

Walt frowned. "That's only for emergencies."

"Sit down. Put your feet up. I was just about to make breakfast. Would you like some?"

"Yes," said Walt. "Very much." He got both his feet balanced on the tiny embroidered footstool on the third try.

The smell of crisping bacon woke him up. He stumbled into the kitchen and splashed water on his face. Aunt Belle, in a blue-striped apron, pulled a square pan from the oven, removed the perforated top and set the thick cut bacon on a bed of paper napkins to drain. She spooned some grease from the bottom of the pan into a cast iron skillet and broke in four eggs. Walt was impressed. At eighty-two years old Aunt Belle was still a one-handed egg cracker. She dusted the eggs with pepper and seasoned salt and then spooned hot bacon grease over them until they sputtered on top and got brown lacy edges.

They ate at a formica table in the kitchen. Maxwell House coffee with Meadow Gold half and half, Tropicana orange juice, oven broiled bacon, basted sunnyside eggs and honeydew melon so ripe it looked like cantaloupe. The buttermilk biscuits were Pepperidge Farm but the blackberry jam was as thick and satisfying as only homemade jam can be.

"I didn't expect you for several hours," said Aunt Belle.

"I don't have any hours to spare," said Walt and, chasing egg yolk with a biscuit, "*God* this is good." They ate slowly and in silence. After breakfast they took a second cup of coffee into the parlor. Walt tried to make himself comfortable on the shiny pink divan many years older than himself.

"I apologize for not attending Laura's service, Walter. I don't travel well these last few years."

"That's okay, Aunt Belle."

"I couldn't face another trip to Chicago so soon after Virginia's funeral."

"I understand."

The Violin Player

"Though I didn't know her well, I always found your wife to be very gracious and unassuming. A small town girl at heart."

"Yes," said Walt, the heartless brute who had pried her fingers from the backyard rose trellis. "That's true."

"Would you care to talk about her?"

"Not at the moment," said Walt, smiling an apology and reaching into his briefcase for the black and white six by nine photograph. A thought occurred. Walt left the photograph inside the briefcase. "Aunt Belle, in your opinion, could my mother have had an illegitimate child?"

Aunt Belle's face remained serenely composed. Only a bit too much clatter of cup on saucer betrayed her surprise at the question. Walt asked it because he realized that his preoccupation with the Sumner side of the family had blinded him to a central fact. The killer killed his mother not his father. The blizzard of Sumner family data Walt had downloaded from Alice Langley might have been an elaborate subterfuge to send him off in the wrong direction. Some checks made out to cash were the only tangible evidence Walt had to suggest that the killer was his father's son.

"No," said Aunt Belle. "There is not a great deal you can be sure of at my age but I'm fairly certain that your mother was never pregnant outside of marriage."

"But you're not positive."

"No, Walter, I'm not positive. But Virginia was a very proper young lady in her day and she never to my knowledge took any long trips to visit a distant aunt and I cannot, in any event, imagine a young man at that time risking the wrath of her father."

Walt nodded. Jacob Hanes was a bald compact man who looked like a department store floor walker in his polka dot bow tie and *pince-nez*. In fact he was a Superior Court judge with an Old

Testament faith in the cleansing power of harsh punishment swiftly applied. Walt knew this from family legend. Grandpa Jake had died of cancer when Walt was five. He didn't know how Jacob had gotten along with Granddad though he pictured the two old lions circling each other warily. It was probably not happenstance that, other than a formal wedding photo, there were no pictures in the family albums in which both Henry Senior and Jacob Hanes shared the frame.

"Could my dad have fathered an illegitimate child?"

Aunt Belle cupped her cup of coffee in both hands. Her knuckles were swollen. "This is quite a conversation to be having at this hour of the morning," she said.

"I need to know," said Walt without apology, with something approaching anger. His sainted family elders had known something, had been joined in a conspiracy of silence or at least a willing amnesia that was keeping him from the truth that was methodically exterminating his family. If Aunt Belle was the last conspirator left standing, so be it. She would come clean.

"Well," said Aunt Belle, setting down her coffee cup and pulling at the corners of her collar, "Your father was very popular of course, handsome, well to do, a star athlete. If he wanted to fool around I doubt that he lacked for willing partners. But they had condoms in those days too. We called them rubbers." Aunt Belle gave Walt a knowing, you young people think you invented sex kind of look. "And you have to remember that your father was in an awkward position for a young man. It must have been very difficult for him."

"What do you mean?"

"He was the object of affection," said Aunt Belle. "He was the one pursued. If you got a young lady pregnant in New Castle in those days you married her, plain and simple. Putting a child up for

The Violin Player

adoption simply wasn't done."

"They had abortion in those days," said Walter.

"That's true," said Aunt Belle. "And no young lady would ever have considered aborting a Sumner family heir."

Walt nodded. She was right. He filled in the blanks. Dad would not have entrusted his future to a latex condom. Unless he was so crazy in love that it didn't matter. Which didn't sound like his father. Still. Walt removed the black and white photo from his briefcase and handed it to Aunt Belle.

"Ah," she said, smiling so deeply that the feathered wrinkles in her cheeks squeezed together like bellows. "An Independence Day party. See the bunting? Your grandparents had one every year."

"Do you have any idea who the young woman on the far right might be?" said Walt, stifling a yawn. "The one next to my father."

Aunt Belle struggled to focus, then got up to rummage in the bottom drawer of her walnut secretary. She returned with a square magnifying glass attached to a cord that she looped around her neck. She clicked on a battery powered light inside the glass.

"I used to use this for cross stitching." She studied the photo. "Why that's Jarlene Ward, daughter of my sister Margaret, God rest her soul. She, Maggie, died of malaria on New Year's Eve in, when was it—1932. An hour before midnight. Twenty-six years old."

"Twenty-six, that's terrible," said Walt, struggling upwards through layers of gelatinous exhaustion. The big breakfast had made him drowsy. He had the distinct impression that Aunt Belle said the young woman with the magnificent head of hair was a relative.

"She had five children. Jarlene was the baby. Her Christian name was Jane, I don't know why they called her Jarlene," said Aunt Belle. "Lester Ward, her daddy, Maggie's husband, was a worthless piece of smooth talking white trash if ever there was.

Couldn't hold a job. Or keep the screens patched in the summertime for that matter. We had swarms of mosquitoes thick as wood smoke in those days, before they—"

"Is Jarlene still alive?"

Aunt Belle paused to compose herself in the face of her grandnephew's unaccustomed brusqueness. "I was getting to that," she said. "I know her two older brothers are dead. Her younger brother Caleb moved to Alaska in 1980 to work on the pipeline. But Jarlene, I want to say that she passed away but I honestly don't remember."

Walt tugged the family tree printout from a zippered pocket in his briefcase and paged through to generation number six. *Jane H. Ward, born 17 March, 1933.* Her date of death was blank, as was her date of marriage and list of offspring.

"Caleb Ward died in Fairbanks, Alaska in 1985," said Walt.

Aunt Belle clucked her tongue. "Honest to Pete they were the most unfortunate family."

Walt consulted his printout. Jarlene had a fourth brother, two years her senior. His D.O.D. was also blank. "What do you know about Clovis Ward?"

Walt waited while Aunt Belle shucked the magnifying glass and laboriously wound the cord around its neck. "Cousin Free Gas?"

"If that's Clovis Ward."

"He was an acorn who didn't fall far from the tree," said Aunt Belle, knotting the cord and replacing the magnifying glass in the bottom drawer. She resumed her seat with a sigh. "In and out of jail, married and divorced more times than you can count. The last I heard he was living down in Kentucky."

"Any idea where?"

"I can check," said Aunt Belle.

The Violin Player

"Any idea why Jane, Jarlene, would be in my grandparent's backyard in Evanston so many years ago?" said Walt "Was she attending Northwestern?"

Aunt Belle laughed. "Goodness no, what an idea. No, I felt sorry for the poor thing. She barely knew her mother and her father was a common thief, yet she was just sweet and trusting as she could be." Aunt Belle stopped to drain the dregs from her coffee cup and blot her lips with a napkin. "I prevailed upon brother Henry to take her in for a summer. To expose her to proper manners and good conversation and so forth." She handed Walter the black and white photograph. He returned it to his briefcase. "Was that so wrong?"

"What did Jarlene say when she returned to New Castle?"

"Just that she had the most *wonderful* time imaginable. She was all aglow," said Aunt Belle and folded her hands in her lap. She looked imperious, queenly. Walt didn't care.

"This was what year exactly?"

"Ohh, I guess it would have to be 1950."

"I see," said Walt. Granddad started issuing his mysterious checks to cash in 1951. March of 1951 if memory served. They had all been cashed in New Castle. "Did you stay in touch with her, Jarlene, after she came home?"

Aunt Belle knitted her brow and seemed to concentrate mightily. "Did she move away? I'm usually so good at this." She flicked a hand in front of her face as if shooing flies. "She must have moved away. And then we moved to Muncie after Floyd sold the store and no, to answer your question, I didn't stay in touch with Jarlene."

Walt drummed his fingers against his temple. Floyd didn't sell the hardware store until the early 60's. Walt rummaged in his briefcase one last time.

"Walter, am I to know why you are asking all these questions? Surely you can't think that—" Aunt Belle stopped in midsentence when Walt looked up.

"Yes?" he said. His Great Aunt did not reply. Walt presented her with the pencil sketch of the suspect. "Have you ever seen this person?"

Aunt Belle accepted the sketch gingerly, between thumb and forefinger. She reared back slightly at first glance. She passed it back and said, "No, not to my knowledge. Who is it supposed to be?"

Walt set the sketch down on the coffee table, face up. "It's our murder suspect. A young woman at the Henry County Department of Health gave this description." Walt looked over at Aunt Belle. She was staring down at the expressionless face with the bad toupe. Walt recalled scraping fallen leaves away from the base of a gravestone, finding a laminated card glued to the slab. *Cousin Fucker*.

"I believe this person is my half-brother, Aunt Belle. The bastard son of Henry Sumner Junior and, yes, based upon what you've just told me and some other evidence, Jarlene Ward."

Aunt Belle cocked her hand behind her ear. Walt repeated what he had said. Aunt Belle sat silently in her high-backed chair, knotting a paper napkin in her right hand, her eyes seeking the pencil sketch on the coffee table then darting away. Walt watched and waited. Aunt Belle picked up her cup and set it down. She asked Walt if he would care for more coffee. He declined. She started to speak, then cleared her throat.

"I can't disprove what you are suggesting, of course, but really Walter, heavenly angels, it's just simply, well, it's just…well. As I say, I can't disprove it."

Walter didn't press for details. He didn't ask Aunt Belle whether she had seen Jarlene Ward trailing a ragamuffin little boy

The Violin Player

around town or been implored to carry an urgent message to Henry Jr. She knew. Small town girl goes to the big city to stay with her wealthy relations and their handsome son. She returns with stars in her eyes and nine months later there is a blessed event. Aunt Belle kept track, she knew the year her nephew Caleb moved to Alaska. She knew.

Aunt Belle tossed the napkin she had been worrying on the coffee table. She pointed her chin at the pencil sketch. "It makes no sense!" she fairly shouted. "Why would this supposed half-brother attack your wife and mother? They're not even Sumners!"

Walt found himself unoffended at this brickbat. It was true that his wife and mother were not blood Sumners. Good for them. The most full-blooded Sumner on the family tree was a homicidal maniac.

"I believe that my half-brother is killing my loved ones in order to strike at me," said Walt.

Aunt Belle jerked her feet from the embroidered footstool and tugged at the stocking behind one knee. "Why?" she said irritably.

Walt wiped his hand across his mouth, suddenly so tired he could barely see. What was it that sister Kay had said? Someone shivering in the cold, peering in a lighted window. A fire in the fireplace.

"I'm not sure, Aunt Belle. Maybe he feels left out."

Chapter 31

I miss the parade of sawed-off people walking by my basement window. I enjoyed guessing what their heads looked like. The bedroom window in my new crackerbox overlooks the pebbled roof of a carport. What is this? *Los Angeles*?

Met the girls not so long ago. Up close and personal. They like to walk down to Walsh Park after school and pretend to play hoops with a silly red kickball.

They stood and watched as I swished hook shots and drained jumpers from the top of the key with my well-scuffed official NBA leather b-ball. *I'm a Hoosier, I know hoops.* I challenged them to a game of two-on-one, *right-handed. I'm a southpaw.* Thea politely declined, but the younger one—they call her Reenie—was raring to go.

I went easy on them. Thea couldn't throw a pea in the Pacific, but she was good at lay-ups. And Reenie was a whirling dervish on defense, registering three steals. I eeked out a 21-16 victory.

Afterwards I put little Reenie on my shoulders and let her toss up a few. Thea got hinky about this but her little sister had a blast. I set her down after that, thanked them for the game and dribbled

The Violin Player

on down the block.

I didn't much care for the older one. Thea. Too snotty and standoffish. *Too much like me!* But that little one, little Reenie, *wowsers*. The resolutely cantankerous wilderness-taming Sumner spirit is alive and well in that little peckerneck.

All she needs is a loving, guiding hand.

Chapter 32

Walt awoke to a sharp insistent sound. He turned. Someone was rapping on his car window. He saw only a gloved hand and the top half of a man's face. The face was saying something. Walt found his keys and lowered the window.

"You okay buddy?" Walt nodded, sitting up straight. The man was in a wheelchair. "I'm with IDOT. I was through here a few hours back and got worried when I saw you was still here." Walt checked his dashboard clock. 1:21 p.m. He had been passed out at an I-65 rest area since ten o'clock that morning. "There's a four hour maximum stay," said the man, peering over the windowsill. He winked. "But I'll never tell."

"Thanks," said Walt. "I'm glad you woke me."

The man wheeled off with a wave. Walt checked his briefcase. The gun and the fat manila envelope were still there. He felt his eyelids sliding south. His hand brushed the pack of cigarettes in his pants pocket. Remembering that a smoke used to get him going in the morning, he fished one out. He pushed in the lighter and thought about what Aunt Belle had said about Jarlene? 'I *want* to say that she passed away'. No doubt. 'But I *honestly* don't remember.' Years of

The Violin Player

experience in the business world had taught Walt to distrust any statement that began with 'To tell you the truth' or 'Honestly'.

He lit the cigarette and inhaled deeply. He searched around for the ashtray and slid it open, christened its surface with a spray of ash. Aunt Belle had found an address for Jarlene's brother Clovis Ward. 178 Snow Creek Road, Clay City. Walt turned on his navigation system and programmed in Clay City, Kentucky.

Walt searched the small screen. Clay City was located about fifty miles southeast of Lexington, on the edge of the Daniel Boone National Forest. Appalachia. Walt pictured Clovis in overalls and bare feet, chawing tabaccy on the steps of a tar paper shack.

The drive would take about four hours. Best if he got a hotel room in Lexington, showered and changed clothes. He wanted to look crisp and authoritative when he confronted his first cousin once removed. Walt snuffed the cigarette in the ashtray and plodded to the men's room.

The Jaguar crept up on an enormous white warehouse on I-65 south of Columbus, Indiana. Though they hummed along at high speed the warehouse kept its distance. *Wal-Mart Distribution Center* said the sign. It looked twice the size of Ford's River Rouge assembly plant and was ringed by at least a hundred tractor trailers. That's what we do in America now, thought Walt, depressing the accelerator. We don't make things, we distribute them. The XJR settled in at eighty-five miles per hour. Walt took a breath and tried to think things through.

What had Jarlene Ward done when she returned to New Castle and realized that she was pregnant? Called Dad. Who said what? Have an abortion? She obviously hadn't done that. Steered her towards some out-of-state baby farm where young women of means repaired to dispose of their embarrassment to childless couples? Maybe. Walt knew such places existed despite his Great Aunt's insistence that adoption in that era simply wasn't done. That would help explain why his half brother had waited forty years to seek his revenge. He had been adopted by dirt farmers who used him as an indentured servant only to find out, years later, that his real daddy was rich.

All of which did not explain Granddad's mysterious checks to cash. And Aunt Belle's description of Jarlene as all aglow. Granddad never gave money outside the family and a lovesick young girl would not have abandoned her one indisputable claim on Henry Jr. Jarlene may have left New Castle for a time. But she almost certainly kept the kid.

Then why, if his half brother was raised by Jarlene and presumably knew his father's name, was he lashing out now? Maybe he *hadn't* known his father's name. Maybe that was the quid pro quo. The Sumner family provides a regular cash stipend. Jarlene tells her son that daddy was a good for nothing who died in prison. Youngblood does some research later in life and discovers the truth. Or Mom finally comes clean. Or, worse, the killer knew everything all along and had executed Henry Jr., his father, *their* father, and God only knew who else. Dad *had* died of a stroke.

Walt passed a lumbering livestock hauler, pink hog snouts pressed to the half-moon vents. Off to the slaughterhouse. None of it mattered, Walt told himself. Not really, not now. All that mattered at the moment was running this sick son of a bitch to ground.

The Violin Player

The XJR jounced across the cantilevered bridge that spanned the broad and placid Ohio River. Walt read the sign and thought there had to be something more compelling to say about the home of Henry Clay, bluegrass billionaires, bourbon distilleries and Transylvania University. *Welcome to Kentucky, Where Education Pays.*

Louisville beckoned from the riverbank. A phalanx of modern hotels and office buildings faced north, their backs turned resolutely on the old downtown. Walt passed a white sedan with the Orkin Pest Control logo painted on its side. He looked over. Four Orkin men in starched uniform shirts were joined in uproarious laughter. Walt smiled, then turned his thoughts to the task at hand.

How to approach Clovis Ward. As the son of the man who had seduced and abandoned Clovis' sister Walt did not expect a warm reception. He would ask politely for Jarlene's whereabouts. And that of her son. If that didn't work he would offer Clovis money. If that didn't work, well, he would do what he had to do. Assuming Clovis was in town. The XJR swung left onto I-71 as Walt picked up his cell phone and searched his pockets. He dialed the number that Aunt Belle had given him.

"Yeah, whozsat?" said a male voice in a spray of sibilance. He has a cleft palate, thought Walt. Or cheap false teeth.

"Whozsat already?!"

Walt pushed the kill button on his cell phone. Clovis Ward was in town.

Walt drove the Newtown Pike to Main Street and checked into a Radisson Hotel in Lexington. He basked in the amenities of a $90 room. Internet hookup, mini-bar, coffee maker, lotion, shampoo, two bars of French milled soap, four pillows on a king size bed. He plugged in his laptop and checked email. The sales figures that Marcy had posted were exceptional. And annoying. A quick check of the Merc's closing quotes on dry milk futures was more so. Sumner International was doing just fine without him. He typed in the web address for GenealoG and clicked through to his family tree page, his pulse thudding in his ears. His D.O.D. and that of his daughters was blank.

Walt selected a drink from the mini-bar. Bourbon, in honor of Kentucky. The tiny bottle had a red wax seal. Cute. But a pain to open. He took a swig, and placed a call.

Sister Kay said that everything was hunky dory. Walt asked to speak to Thea. Kay thought she was asleep. Walt asked Kay to wake her up. He wound the phone cord into knots until he heard his daughter's voice. "Daddy?"

"How's my girl?"

Thea yawned in his ear.

"What are you doing in bed so early?"

"I was tired."

"Is Reenie okay?"

"She's watching videos."

"But is she okay?"

"Sure. I guess."

"Are you okay?"

"I'm bored. I miss school."

"You can go back soon, I promise."

Walt listened to his daughter's breathing. Thea spoke first. "Are *you* okay?"

"Absolutely. I'm in Lexington, Kentucky. Horse country. Prettiest place you ever seen." Thea yawned. "We'll come visit real soon."

"Are you finding out anything?"

The Violin Player

"Yes," said Walt, having a deju vu, back on the Bob Evans' pay phone between the restrooms, reporting on the progress of his investigation. "Yes, I'm getting closer. Definitely."

"Is he related to us? You said before you thought he was related to us."

"He is," said Walt. Thea said, "I miss Mom. A lot."

"I do too, snowflake. I do too."

Thea, who never cried, who had not shed tears since she was a toddler, began to sob and hung up. Walt cradled the receiver against his cheek. He held it in his hand and looked at it and wondered how he was ever to work his way through all these many layers of grief. Grief at the untimely death of his mother. His wife. And the innocence of his daughters.

Chapter 33

Clay City was not much more than a T-junction of highways 11 and 15. Walt passed six gas stations, a drive-in tobacco outlet, a general store and a shiny new red and white Dairy Queen. Walt parked his Jaguar next to the rusted pickups out front of the Wagon Wheel Restaurant and Bingo Parlor.

No bingo tonight. Just four leathery old men muttering over cold cups of coffee. Their heads popped up when Walt entered in his pinstripe suit. He approached their table to ask directions, then realized that one of them might well be Clovis himself.

"Evening, gents. My name is Walter Sumner and I'm here looking for Clovis Ward." No one raised their hand. "I understand he lives near here, on Snow Creek Road." The men stared at their coffee cups. "I'm not a lawyer, a cop or a process server. Just a cousin who's come all the way from Chicago."

The men turned to the youngest of their group, a man who needed two chairs to support his girth. He had a bowl of food in front of him. Soupbeans and cornbread. $1.79 a serving according to the corkboard menu on the back wall. "I hate to be the one to tell you 'is,'" he drawled, removing his tractor cap solemnly. "But Clovis

The Violin Player

turned to shit and the hogs ate him."

Walt smiled along with the laughter. They were very playful here in Kentucky. Walt had grabbed a quick bite at a restaurant across the street from the Radisson before he drove the fifty miles to Clay City. After he finished eating he got up and asked a waiter to point him towards the men's room. The young man, unspeaking, stepped behind him and turned Walt's shoulders in the proper direction.

"That was jes' too good to pass up," said the man on two chairs. Walt agreed that it was a good one. The man gave him directions to Snow Creek Road. "But Clovis'll likely be up at Keeneland 'bout now," said another man.

"No sir, he won't either," said a third man. "Trotters stopped runnin' last week."

"But they got off track betting up 'ere now," said the second man.

A fourth man shook his head so vehemently that his eyeglasses slid down his nose. "Clovis don't bet OTB on harness racing," he croaked in a voice just above a whisper. "Says they don't post the odds in a timely fashion. Said it right here at this table."

Walt thanked the men for their help and left them to their dispute. He motored south through town as he had been instructed, crossing the overpass above a four lane highway. That explained the six gas stations. Snow Creek Road was half a mile further. He turned right at The Gift Shack and climbed the hill. His image of a tar paper shack in Possum Holler was wide of the mark. Clovis lived in a tidy white frame house with dark red shutters that matched the trim on the front porch. Moths fluttered about the porch lamp. Walt killed the headlamps and pulled into the driveway. Lights were on inside the house. It looked as if Cousin Free Gas, the pony-playing son of smooth-talking Lester Ward and tragic Great Aunt Margaret, was home.

John Knoerle

Walt grabbed his briefcase and walked to the front door. He knocked three times, bruising his knuckles. The door was made of steel. A dog started to bark. A big dog, coming closer. He knocked again. The dog howled with bloodlust and raked his nails against the floor. Walt detected motion behind the peephole. He heard a voice. The dog's howl lowered to a chesty growl. Walt heard the voice more clearly.

"Whozsat?"

"It's Walter Sumner, Mr. Ward. I need to speak with you."

"Who?"

"Wal-ter Sum-ner."

The dead bolt turned and the door opened an inch against the chain lock. A watery gray eye and a black dog snout presented themselves in the crack. "How'd you come to git here?"

"I'm sorry?"

"Who sent ya?"

"No one sent me. I got your address from Belle Jenkins, your aunt."

The watery gray eye blinked. The door closed. Walt bided his time, assuming that the hushed commands and the dog whimpering meant that the *Hound of the Baskervilles* was being led away. Chained to a stout tree hopefully. A smiling Clovis Ward opened the door a minute later and put his hand out. Walt shook it. It was soft.

"So you're Henry Sumner's boy?"

"I am that."

"Heard a lot about ya. C'mon in. Sorry about Hector. He's the suspicious type." Clovis closed the steel door. "Ah'd offer you some sippin' whiskey but this is a dry county." Clovis cackled and walked into the kitchen.

Walt ran his eyes around the room. It was piled high with racing

The Violin Player

forms and dusty magazines. *Argosy. Soldier of Fortune. Gent.* There were no family photos anywhere that Walt could see. A computer screen glowed from a back bedroom. Did everybody have one now? Walt shifted over to get a better look. Some sort of spreadsheet, red numbers in the balance column. Clovis returned with glass tumblers and a porcelain figurine of a confederate officer. He set down the glasses, unscrewed the soldier's hat and poured.

"Cheers."

"Cheers."

Clovis quaffed his two fingers of bourbon standing up. Walt took a sip and sat down on a plaid couch. "You want a beer back? Hold on." Clovis returned dangling two cans from a six pack necklace. Walt accepted his without thanks and sized up Clovis Ward. Whippet thin, twitchy, an angular face framed by sideburns and long greasy hair with wispy tails eddied up in back. No sign of a cleft palate or false teeth. Walt wondered why Clovis seemed so pleased to see him.

"I seen on the TV about your troubles up 'ere. Sorry to hear it," said Clovis.

Walt was sorry to hear that Clovis was sorry. It blew his cover story. That he wanted to contact Jarlene and her son to flesh out details of his family research. Time for plan B. "Thank you for your concern. In fact, that's why I'm here."

"Oh yeah?" said Clovis. He popped his beer, scraped the spray off his brown and blue print polyester shirt and dried his hand on the seat of his pants. "To do what?"

"To ask your help in tracking down the killer," said Walt.

"Well sure," said Clovis, plunking himself down on the lip of an old hickory rocker and planting his feet on the floor to keep from sliding off. "Do anything I can."

John Knoerle

Walt smiled without showing any teeth. "You can tell me how to contact your sister Jarlene."

"Well now that would be a job o' work," said Clovis, sitting back on the rocker and resting his hush puppies on the skids. "She died in a car crash in Fairbanks, Alaska. My brother Caleb was at the wheel. 'Bout fifteen years ago now."

Walt didn't believe a word of what Clovis said but he did admire it. It was a skillful lie, wrapped in truth, told without hesitation. Walt waited to see if Clovis would ask what possible connection Jarlene might have to Walt's search for the killer. Clovis did not.

"That's unfortunate," said Walt. "How about her son? Seen him around lately?" That stopped ol' Clovis a-rockin' in his rockin' chair. He pulled at his lips and his eyes got slippery. "Save your breath," said Walt. "I know all about him."

"Don't care if you do or don't!" said Clovis. "You and yer family got no call to come up here and high hat me and mine. None at all." Clovis snatched a strand of hair from the corner of his mouth.

"I apologize," said Walt coldly. "I was hoping you'd help me to locate him. Jarlene's son."

Clovis responded by sucking at his beer, noisily. Walt removed the fat manila envelope from his briefcase, tore it open and tossed the bank bound stack of one hundred newly minted hundred dollar bills on the coffee table with a satisfying *whump*. Clovis rocked forward in his chair, his tongue thrashing around like the tail of a just-swallowed newt. "Jesus," he said. "Jesus God."

"Any idea where he might be?" said Walt.

Clovis shook his head. "Plain don't know, dammit. Haven't talked to Henry in twenty years. But sit tight."

Clovis bounced up and darted into the back bedroom. Walter followed his movements and sought the butt of the .357 in his

The Violin Player

briefcase. The big dog barked and scratched against a closed door. Clovis returned with a stack of envelopes bound in twine. He dropped them on the coffee table next to the ten thousand dollars. Walt removed his hand from the briefcase.

The envelopes were vellum, cracked and brittle with age. Walt recognized his father's handwriting. This was why Clovis was so pleased to see him.

"Thought you might be interested," said Clovis, hovering.

Walt looked up, then looked over to the rocking chair. Clovis took his seat. "In what?" said Walt.

"Love letters from your Daddy to Jarlene," said Clovis, leaning forward, tracing his bony fingers lightly along the stack. "Plus a few from her to him that got sent back. Later on."

Walt used the index finger of his left hand to pull up on the paper band that bound the crisp brick of hundreds. He wet the index finger of his right hand, slipped it under the band and extracted one bill. He placed it atop the stack of letters. Clovis snorted. Walt split the paper band with the index finger of his left hand. The top layer of the brick of hundreds fanned out nicely. "Tell me where to find your sister and the rest is yours," said Walt. "I know she's not dead."

Walt did not know any such thing. But he was playing the game by his half brother's rules. And his half-brother had left Jarlene Ward's D.O.D. conspicuously blank.

Clovis swirled his beer around in its can, set it down, ran his hands through his greasy hair, shot his legs out and wiggled his feet inside his hush puppies. Walt could almost hear the fleshy gears grinding. "Git yourself another beer," said Clovis at long last.

"I already have one," said Walt.

"Then git another one," said Clovis crossly, staring off. "In the Frigidaire."

John Knoerle

Walt kicked off his shoes and flopped down on the bed of his Lexington hotel room. The covers had been turned down. He jumped up and got a bottled water from the mini bar, grabbed another bourbon while he was at it. Why not? He had earned it. He had tracked down his second cousin, Jarlene Ward.

Walt had done as he was told, and had gone to the kitchen for another beer. The refrigerator was plastered with local flyers. *Lions Club 12th Annual Casino Nite, Come One, Come All. Powell County School District—All You Can Eat Pancake Supper!* He saw a taped-on note, smudged with fingerprints. *J* and a local phone number were written on it. He'd dialed the number from the wall phone. The Mount Sterling Convalescent Home answered. He asked for Jarlene Ward and was told she had retired for the evening.

Walt sat up, determined not to fall asleep on top of the bedspread with all his clothes on. He struggled out of his suit jacket and threw it at a chair. There. Walt stared at a sprinkler head in the cottage cheese ceiling and thought about what Clovis had revealed in passing. A long ago conversation with his mother came to mind. She was signing printed invitations to a party. His job was to lick the stamps.

'Granddad's name is Henry, Dad's name is Henry, you even sign your name *Mrs. Henry Sumner.* Why is my name Walter?'

His mother said something about a fresh start or that name's old fashioned or somesuch as she worked her way through the pile. All Walt remembered for certain is that her answer hadn't satisfied.

Clovis Ward said he hadn't talked to Henry in twenty years. Henry. His homicidal half brother's name was Henry.

Chapter 34

Is manic depression contagious? I ask because I, *me*, Mr. *Accentuate-the-Positive-and-E-liminate-the-Negative*, have spent the last two days in bed hypnotized by the wheeling shadows of the ceiling fan. The fan is moving in the counterclockwise sucking the summer heat to the ceiling mode. Ditto the female.

I let myself into the house on Paulina and Bloomingdale, to see how the other half lives. *Madre de Dios*! At least Judas got thirty pieces of silver. Probably got a wild weekend in Babylon out of the deal before he hanged himself.

Walter J. Sumner has sold his soul for a four-story cell block with wall hangings. Not a scrap of individuality in the place. The *kitchen*, that cozy center of family life where our ancestors gathered round a cook stove fired with corn cobs, had all the charm of an operating room. And who snuggles up in front of the tube on a *black leather* couch. Even the girls' rooms were sterile.

I'm old enough to remember when the wealthy were a breed apart, refined style setters and revered benefactors who *trod upon the common berm but dwelt not in this earthly realm*. Now they're just rich. Ma and Pa Kettle with a bank balance and a host of decorators and consultants telling them what to buy and where to put it cuz they're so busy chasing after it and so bereft of historical perspective once they acquire it, that they have no idea what it is they now possess. Money = Power = Freedom.

I ax you now, is there a less free free man on the planet than Walter J. Sumner? Youth is wasted on the young and wealth is wasted on the rich and I've got to dig down deep into my fathomless reserves and summon the energy to climb out of these grimy sheets.

I have important work to do.

Chapter 35

Mount Sterling, Kentucky was a beguiling blend of foursquare Midwestern simplicity and pillared antebellum extravagance thirty-five miles west of Lexington. Stately homes built by slaves from bricks they mortared with mud and horsehair had been lovingly restored and converted to museums and bed and breakfasts. It was called *Mount* Sterling because the town had been constructed on and around a very large Indian burial mound. So said the waitress at the coffee shop. 'But the settlers didn't know it was a burial mound at the time,' she added quickly. Walt nodded his understanding and finished his breakfast. He was not about to pass judgement. There was quite enough moth-eaten guilt being parceled out and passed around.

Walt turned right on Richmond Street after passing a row of hill mounted Historic Homes. The neighborhood went downhill as the Jaguar climbed. Shingled one-stories, modular pre-fabs and a boarded-up cottage, blackened smoke around its windows. The Mount Sterling Convalescent Home was a two-story, tan brick building set back from the street. It looked efficient, charmless and relatively new. No doubt a feather in the cap of the local congressman.

John Knoerle

The Jaguar parked in the empty visitors section. Walt made his way to the front entrance. Framed pictures of President Clinton and Congressman Fielding on the wall behind the entry desk confirmed that the place was government run. This presented a problem. Walt had planned to offer to pay for Jarlene's accommodations in exchange for information, but the good Congressman had already seen to that. Time for Plan B. Whatever that was.

The young black woman behind the desk had a gravity-defying ziggurat of shellacked hair and a wonderfully welcoming smile. Walt gave her a phony name and said he was a long lost nephew of Jarlene Ward who just happened to be passing through town and thought he would stop by for a visit. The young orderly picked up the house phone.

"I'd really like to surprise her," said Walt. "Go knock on her door and present myself."

The orderly shook her head. "No sir, cain't do that. Jarlene got to give her permission and, well, Annie mightn't like it." Her voice was quite musical but her words came in short bursts as if she had trouble breathing.

"Annie?"

"Annie's her roommate up on two."

"Oh," said Walt. It hadn't occurred to him that Jarlene might share a room. He had hoped to see her living quarters, maybe search for an address book while she was in the bathroom. Old people spent a lot of time in the bathroom. "Then just tell Jarlene I'm here." The orderly did so on the phone, repeating the information twice.

"What medical problem does she suffer from?" asked Walt.

"She senile," said the orderly. Walt thought that odd. According to the family tree Jarlene Ward was only sixty-seven years old. "Does she have many visitors?"

The Violin Player

"Her brother once't in a while."

"No one else?" The young woman shrugged. "Any phone calls?"

"You'll have to ax her about that," she said, backing up a step.

"I'm just concerned about her is all," said Walt gamely, mustering a smile.

The orderly excused herself and went through a door behind the desk. Walt chided himself for overplaying his hand. He stood in front of the entry desk and prayed that Jarlene would appear before some bespeckled senior bureaucrat emerged from the back office asking questions and demanding identification.

A short time later, Jarlene did. Walt recognized her from the black and white photograph. Her hair was much shorter but still thick and curly and only streaked with white. He had expected to find a haggard old woman beaten down by life but Jarlene Ward's face was smooth and pink with health. She offered a tenuous smile and blinked at Walt as if she were not yet fully awake. Once she had him in focus she uttered a small cry and lost her balance.

Walt leapt forward to brace her just as the dreaded senior bureaucrat emerged from the back office, the young orderly right behind. They swarmed Jarlene in a flurry of good heavens and dear me's as Walt stepped back. Short, he thought. Why are senior bureaucrats always short? When the young orderly had Jarlene firmly in hand the senior bureaucrat turned his attention to the tall and sinister interloper.

"And you are who again exactly?" Walt repeated his phony name. "And the purpose of your visit would be?"

"To visit his dear lonely aunt, Mr. Saunders," said Jarlene, shaking off the young orderly's arm. The milky vagueness in her eyes was gone. "I get so few visitors. Please don't send him away."

The senior bureaucrat relented mutteringly and escorted Walt and

John Knoerle

Jarlene to a couch by the front entrance. He admonished Walt to keep the visit brief as Jarlene tired easily. Jarlene leaned over to Walt once the senior bureaucrat was gone. "She's partial to Junior Mints."

"Who's that?"

Jarlene nodded toward the desk. "Lateesha."

Not two minutes later Lateesha headed down the corridor. "You see," said Jarlene, standing up. She gestured for Walt to follow. They slipped out the front door like third graders cutting class.

"Won't they call the police?" said Walt. "When they see you're missing."

"Is that your Fleetwood?"

"Actually it's a Jaguar. Would you like to go for a drive?"

Jarlene walked over and stood by the passenger's side door. Walt helped her in, then ran around and jumped behind the wheel. He kept his eyes trained on the rear view mirror as he backed up. No arm waving red faced bureaucrats emerged.

"They like to act protective of me in front of folks," said Jarlene, struggling with her seat belt. "But they don't really care."

The XJR motored down the long drive while Walt asked if there was anywhere in particular that Jarlene would like to go. She studied his profile. "You look like a younger him."

"My father?"

"The big guy."

"My grandfather?"

Jarlene snagged her seat buckle into place and asked if he had a radio. The XJR turned left on Richmond Street. Walt pushed his Mozart CD into the slot, hit the preset button that caused the passenger's seatback to whir into a reclining position and punched the button that unpeeled the sunroof to reveal the sun-splashed autumn color. "Well now," said Jarlene, looking up. "Well now."

The Violin Player

They took a right on Main Street, away from the row of Historic Homes and towards downtown. Walt lowered Jarlene's window. She drew back as the glass disappeared then thrust her head out the window like the family dog. They passed a new tan brick building set back from the road. The Mt. Sterling Library and Research Center. Congressman Fielding had been a busy boy. They passed the twin-steepled First Presbyterian Church and a Greco-Roman building with great Doric columns called the Presbyterian Post. They passed Nina's Place and Myrna's Too. *Needlepoint. Rubber Stamps.*

Walter eyed the instrument panel. Range, 420 miles. He could turn left on Highway 460, zip up to I-64, turn right on I-65 at Louisville and arrive home in Chicago without once stopping to refuel. Why not? Why should his half brother hold all the cards? If Henry cared about anything other than his own skin it would be the woman sitting in the passenger's seat, bathing her face in the balmy Kentucky breeze and waving gaily to passersby. Walt could use her as a bargaining chip, or bait to lure the killer out of hiding or—

"Turn here," said Jarlene. The Jaguar swung left on Broadway and bumped along the brick pavement that ringed the Montgomery County Courthouse. Long haired young men in T-shirts smoked cigarettes on the Courthouse steps, waiting their turn. "Stop," said Jarlene. The XJR found the curb.

Jarlene was out the door by the time Walt unhitched his seat belt. He joined her in front of a raised-letter metal plaque commemorating the Battle of Mount Sterling. Three hundred Confederate cavalrymen captured the town from the Union Army in 1863, taking 438 prisoners. Jarlene reached up and touched her hand to the plaque.

"Did you have an ancestor who died here?" asked Walter.

"Kentucky was not a member of the Confederacy," said Jarlene. "Most people don't know that. Kentucky didn't want any

John Knoerle

part of a war between the States." Jarlene patted the plaque and smiled ruefully. "So Kentucky was attacked by both sides."

Walt made a sympathetic noise. Jarlene sounded as if she were commenting on her own life in some way. She looked around at the Courthouse and the handsome vintage buildings that lined the cobbled square. "Can we go to Rio's?"

Rio's Steakhouse and Lounge was located on the outskirts of town. The sign on the door said they opened at eleven a.m. The dashboard clock read 10:28. Walt suggested that they go across the street to McDonald's. Jarlene said the food at the Convalescent Home was tasteless due to lack of seasoning. Walt took this to mean she wanted to wait for Rio's to open. She wasn't senile, he decided. She simply didn't process information in a linear fashion. Walt lowered the volume on the CD.

"Jarlene, I know what happened. I know that my father seduced you when you visited Evanston as a young girl and left you with child and that is simply unforgivable. But I ask that you please accept my sincere apology and that of my family."

Jarlene did not respond. Walt sat back and gave her time. A young woman in waitress garb crossed the parking lot and did a doubletake at the fancy car. "Eleven o'clock?"

"Yes," said Walt. "They open at eleven."

Jarlene pulled the hem of her skirt down over her knees and started to speak in a strangled voice. She coughed demurely and began again.

"They had two kitchens, I'll never forget that. There was this big party in the back yard and I went looking for your father because the photographer wanted to take a group picture and I went through a wrong door into a whole other kitchen with all these sweaty people in white uniforms. They were so upset I was afraid they might strike

The Violin Player

me!" Jarlene lowered her voice. "They were drinking."

"*No*," said Walt.

"Yes they were." Jarlene caught Walt's grin and giggled. "Don't make fun of an old woman. And don't apologize." Jarlene paused to conduct a brief conversation with herself. She continued aloud. "I would like to say that, other than the birth of my son, that summer in Evanston was my whole life. We went sailing on the lake under a full moon, your father and I. We ate oysters, we went skinny dipping off the pier at dawn after an all night party. And we exchanged looks across the dinner table that might have scorched the wallpaper right off the wall. Even the big guy noticed. Don't apologize, don't blame your father. Blame God."

Jarlene licked her lips as if parched. Walt offered her a half-drunk bottle of Evian, saying, "I've already—" She grabbed it and drank thirstily. "We were in a church. I'm sure you know it. The church that looks like a cathedral."

Walt knew it. The First Presbyterian, site of two very recent family funerals.

"It was my second day there. Your father and I were seated next to one another when someone arrived late and the usher seated him in our pew. I had noticed Henry of course. He was quite good looking but he was, oh what would you say? What we used to call a wiseacre. We all had to squeeze down to make room for the newcomer and my hand brushed against Henry's wrist and, well, I almost fainted. I almost did! Henry felt it too. I started taking these quick gulps of air and Henry slipped his hand inside mine and we started breathing together, deep and peaceful, all the while pretending to listen to the homily and squeezing each other's hands for all we were worth. And why would that have happened inside a church unless it was sanctified?"

John Knoerle

Walt said he didn't know the answer to that question. He dug in his briefcase and removed the stack of letters bound in twine. "Your brother found these and thought you ought to have them," said Walt, adding, "I didn't read them."

Jarlene placed the letters on the floor mat by her feet. "What time is it now?"

"Ten thirty-nine."

"Good." The car stereo played *Divertimento Number One* for the second time that morning.

"We were going to run away to Paris. Henry was going to play the European tennis circuit. I was going to raise our baby and cheer him on from the, what do they call it?"

"The player's box," said Walt. "What happened?"

"What always happens to young dreams," said Jarlene.

"Did my father and grandfather provide you with any financial support?"

Jarlene screwed the cap back on the empty water bottle with exquisite care. "Is my son in some kind of trouble?"

Walt ignored the question. Two could play at this game. "Did my father and grandfather provide you with any financial support?"

"Not for many years now."

"How many?"

"Many."

This answer did not square with Walt's investigation. Dad's checks to cash continued long past the days when he was a traveling sales rep who needed a full money clip. Walter had added them up. From the beginning of his career in 1953 until his death in 1995 his father had written checks to cash that totaled over a million dollars. Walter studied Jarlene's face for signs of duplicity. She looked guileless as a seraph.

The Violin Player

"Did your son know who his father was?"

"He wouldn't eat meat," said Jarlene. "Just wouldn't eat it. He didn't like dairy foods either, they made him sick. He kept alive on popcorn and cornmeal mush. And green vegetables. He'd eat a stalk of raw broccoli the way another child ate an ice cream cone. They just crucified him at school." Jarlene paused to make a quick sign of the cross. "We were Catholics, Catholics in New Castle. He was frail, he didn't have a daddy at home and he was the smartest boy in class. Scary smart. I walked him to school every morning but I could see them hanging on the fence, the other boys, waiting for him." Jarlene leaned forward and traced a finger along the Jaguar's walnut trim. "He knew who his father was."

Walt felt a twinge of sympathy for his half-brother and a clutch of fury at their common sire. Dad had to know the fate awaiting a bastard child in small town Indiana in the 1950's. Checks to cash did not begin to pay the debt.

"Jarlene, I have a crazy idea that I would like you to seriously consider."

"What time is it now?"

"Ten fifty-two." She nodded. "Jarlene, you said that they don't really care about you at the Convalescent Home so I'm wondering if you might consider moving to Chicago to live with my two daughters and myself – hear me out – we have a lovely home in a nice neighborhood, my sisters are nearby and my girls could use some looking after. What do you say?"

Walt thought this a brilliant proposal. He would swathe Jarlene in luxury and true affection while holding her as a trump card against his murderous half-brother. It was a clear win-win. Why then did Jarlene appear so agitated?

"What about your wife?" she sputtered.

"She passed away."

"What about your mother? I know that Henry died. But what about Virginia Hanes? You said your sisters but not your mother."

"My mother is gone too."

Jarlene muttered something and looked out the window. She said, "Is my son in some kind of trouble?"

She must know, thought Walt. Not the particulars, but she knows what her son is capable of. She hadn't asked the obvious question. How did your wife and mother die?

"No he's not in any trouble," said Walt. "In fact, I've got some great news. When my mother died recently the money in my grandfather's trust was released for distribution. Now the trust doesn't mention your son by name but then it doesn't mention any of his grandchildren by name. It simply says that the money should be distributed *in stirpes*."

"What does that mean?" said Jarlene. "Those words."

"It means in the line of descent. Your son is a direct descendant of Henry Sumner Sr. and hence entitled to his share of twelve million dollars."

This was a bald-faced lie of course. But a good one, Jarlene was all ears. The trust did specify Walt and his sisters by name. Didn't it? Walt remembered their names being listed in one of the inheritance documents but that may have been his mother's will. The only thing he recalled about the trust with certainty was that the instrument mandated distribution to male issue in double shares to that of female issue. Good *God*.

"What would his share be?" said Jarlene.

"Who's that?" said Walt.

"My son."

"Henry, you mean."

The Violin Player

"Yes," said Jarlene, barely audible. "Henry."

"About four million dollars," said Walt, his brain doing back flips. What he'd just said might actually be *true*. "But I haven't been able to find him to give him the good news. Do you have any idea where he is?"

Jarlene said she didn't know. Just like that. Didn't know and wished she did. He hadn't visited her in years though he called every Mother's day and every once in a while at Christmas. He was very busy, had done very well for himself, working as a lab technician. He was living somewhere in Ohio the last time he called but he liked to move around and never stayed anywhere for very long. He did say something about having a job opportunity in Chicago.

Walt made a final attempt to smoke her out. "That's unfortunate. I'm sorry to hear you've lost touch because probate on the estate, on the trust and the inheritance, closes at the end of this month."

Jarlene watched a car park in the parking lot.

"Hey, it's eleven o'clock," said Walt. "Do you want to go in?"

"I'm tired now," said Jarlene.

The Jaguar proceeded down Maysville Street in a swirl of colored leaves to the strains of *Eine Kleine Nachtmusik*. Jarlene was curled up in the calfskin seat. Walter whirred her seat back into the fully recumbent position. She did not stir. He felt a wave of strong emotion wash over him. Tenderness mixed with grief mixed with something else. Envy. That was it. He wished that he too had his life behind him and could return to the rest home and eat a bland lunch and stare at the television for a few hours before being tucked into clean sheets with hospital corners because he also was very, very tired.

Chapter 36

Walt called Marcy as he drove west toward Lexington. She gave him a good report. Jeffrey was behaving himself, sales figures were solid, prices on their myriad futures contracts were generally firming up. The market had achieved a *breakaway gap* in her opinion. Walt was amused and impressed in equal measure. Marcy had been studying up.

He called Kay. The girls were doing fine and eating well though Thea would only speak when spoken to. She hadn't seen anything in the local media about the case. Walt told her to make a dinner reservation at Gibson's, home of hand-rubbed Kobe beef and three pound live Maine lobsters, to celebrate his return.

"What time?" she asked.

"I should be back about seven."

Walt disconnected, wondering what he was celebrating. The only thing of immediate importance he had learned in three days was that his half-brother worked as a lab tech and probably lived in Chicago.

Walt called FBI agent O'Connor in Indianapolis and left the information about Henry on her voice mail. He realized that he hadn't

The Violin Player

informed her of another recent development and added, "By the way, the suspect is my half-brother. The son of my father, born 1927, died 1995, and Jarlene Ward, born 1933." That would get her attention.

What now? The clock was ticking. The results of Laura's autopsy were due any day. Results that would almost certainly lead to his arrest. The XJR sped westward on I-64.

The young man behind the coffee bar was very entertaining. The cyber café in Lexington was empty at one-thirty in the afternoon so the highly-caffeinated multiply-pierced youngster greeted Walt like a long lost friend. Finding that his customer was from out of town he endeavored to put him in the know.

Did Walt realize that Lexington was the money laundering capital of the world? Hadn't Walt noticed all those big banks and fancy restaurants amid the conspicuous absence of any industry to support them? Dead simple. Saudi oil sheiks and Indonesian cabinet ministers, under cover of diplomatic immunity, arrived in their private jets *ostensibly* to bid on million dollar breeding stallions but *in truth* to swap trunks filled with gold bars for hard currency at a very favorable exchange rate and no questions asked. Fort Knox was right up the road. And the limestone caverns that run for miles beneath the city? Walt did not *for one second* want to know what went on down there.

Walt excused himself after his second latte and plugged in his laptop at a wobbly corner table. Wizz.net apparently deemed Lexington worthy of service. He got on line without difficulty and spent an hour answering email. His Asian customers, accustomed to his constant attention, left terse messages in broken English. 'You are still in dairy busyness, OK?' Walt begged their indulgence while he dealt with the unexpected passing of his wife. This they would understand. They were much like Granddad, his Asian customers. Cold-heartedly ruthless about everything but family.

Walt accessed GenealoG.com and stared at their home page till his head swam. He hadn't checked the family tree site for almost twenty-four hours. He clicked his way through the maze. The dates of death for Walter, Thea and Irene Sumner were blank. Same for Kay and Ted and Chris, Chrissie and Carly. Walt resumed breathing, then climbed back up the tree. Generation #6. Jarlene Ward's D.O.D. was also blank. All right. Of course. He checked the family tree page of Clovis Ward just in case.

Oh shit. What's today? *Hey*, somebody! What's today's date?

The Jaguar raced down four lane Highway 402, passing a convoy of rumbling dark green dump trucks in a blur, swallowing the fifty miles in thirty minutes. Walt had called Clovis' number and let the phone ring a dozen times. He'd called 911. He identified himself to the male dispatcher and said that Clovis Ward of 178 Snow Creek Road, Clay City, was in imminent danger, that a man had targeted him for death that very day.

"What man?"

"His name is Henry, last name might be Ward."

"And how do you know this?"

Walt had paused to consider. He had already given his real name. If he told the dispatcher about the D.O.D. posting and that Henry had already carried out two such previous threats the dispatcher might put two and two together and get on the horn to CNN. Too bad. A man's life was at stake. Walt explained everything in plain English. The dispatcher had no idea what he was talking about but

The Violin Player

promised to alert the Powell County Sheriff's Department. The XJR angled over for the Clay City exit, slowed for the stop sign by the Shell station and tore on up the hill.

Clovis Ward's white frame house drowsed peacefully in the afternoon sun. The front door was shut, the curtains closed. There were no vehicles in the driveway and the door to the detached single car garage was closed. The XJR parked on a turnout. Walter stuffed the .357 inside his belt and walked the hundred yards back to the house, cursing himself for not checking the website earlier.

How in the name of God had Henry learned of his visit to Clovis so quickly? Walt felt sure he hadn't been followed. Had Jarlene called her son to tell him about her visitor, tell him of the letters that Clovis had handed over? That had to be it. Even if Mr. Scary Smart had some high tech way to monitor Walt's cell phone calls he wouldn't have learned anything. Except that Walt had called Clovis to make sure he was home. And that Walt had made a call from the vicinity of the Mount Sterling Convalescent Home the next day. Headed home and ready to celebrate. Christ.

Walt crept up to the front porch and listened. Nothing. He rapped on the steel door and listened some more. No big dog skittered across the wood floor, barking its head off. He took out his handkerchief and tried the door knob. It opened. Walt removed the handgun from his belt.

A big German Shepherd lay stiffly on its side on the kitchen floor, legs extended. Clovis was sitting in the living room in his old hickory rocker, his back to the door.

"Clovis?"

Clovis did not respond. Walt crossed the threshold and closed the door behind him. He circled around the plaid couch, sniffing the air for the telltale stench. A breeze billowed the curtains of the back bedroom window. The house smelled clean and crisp as an apple. Walt turned to face the rocking chair and caught his breath.

Clovis sat with his eyes closed, his hush puppies on the floor and his hands firmly gripping the armrests. His skin was a pale and frosty blue. Walt edged closer. Clovis' eyelids were shut tight. The tips of his eyelashes glistened with refracted sun. Ice. His eyelashes were tipped with ice. Walt moved two steps closer and stopped.

CPR would not be necessary. Clovis did not exhibit the lividity, the puddling of blood in the extremities that Walter had witnessed firsthand with Laura. There were no signs of struggle, no bloody wounds, no outward evidence of trauma of any kind. But Clovis Ward was just as dead as it was possible to be.

Walt leaned forward and squinted. A button had been pinned to the breast pocket of Clovis' brown and blue print polyester shirt. It bore a saying that Walt had seen before, on gag t-shirts in tourist town gift shops. *I only do what the voices tell me.*

Chapter 37

The county mounties were surprisingly reverent in the presence of the dead body, thought Tony Sobczak as he stood in Clovis Ward's living room at approximately 2200 hours. In Chicago the victim would have been dubbed the corpsicle by now. Of course the body had thawed out some. The eyes had popped open and reddish purge fluids were trickling from the nose and mouth. The morgue crew was outside, waiting on a forensic team from Lexington.

"Any ideas?" said the Sheriff of Powell County, a short self-possessed man whose eyebrows met in the middle.

"One or two," said Tony with more confidence than he felt. He had blustered his way this far by citing his eighteen years on the job with the Chicago PD including six years homicide. But he had never stumbled on a homicide quite like this one.

Tony had recruited a buddy to fly him down to Clay City in his twin-engine Beechcraft following the call from the law offices of Robert Samuelson. The secretary, with some distaste, had explained that their client Walter Sumner was in custody in Kentucky facing a charge of homicide and had used his allotted phone call to contact his attorney. Unfortunately, Mr. Samuelson was giving the keynote address at a legal conference in Bali at the moment so Mr. Sumner had requested that she contact Mr. Sobczak and request his immediate assistance.

"Try this on for size," said Tony. "The killer shows up on the doorstep with some cock and bull story, just passing through, thought I'd stop by. He's known to the victim but not trusted. That's why the land shark wasn't chained up."

"Land shark?" said the moon faced young deputy who caught the call, found the body and arrested Walter Sumner at the scene. The Sheriff grinned.

"The German Shepherd," said Tony. "They discuss matters of mutual interest. The killer finds out what he wants to know and goes to the fridge on the pretense of getting the victim another beer, you see the empty under the chair. The dog follows him. He hasn't figured on the dog. So he keeps up a line of bullshit to cover the noise as he pulls on his rubber gloves and searches for a blunt instrument. He finds a hammer in a drawer, clonks the dog a good one and races back to the rocking chair before the victim can react."

The Sheriff's long eyebrow formed a thoughtful *S*. Tony continued. "He downs out the vic from behind with a rag soaked in chloroform. He now has the place to himself. He injects the victim, and the dog, with whatever he injects them with, picks up after himself and pins that little button on the victim's shirt pocket as a parting joke."

The moon faced deputy shook his head. "Dun't make sense. Why not just clonk the victim if he means to kill him? Why mess with chloroform and injections and all that?"

Tony shook out a cigarette and chewed on the filter to calm himself. He hated rookies. "Because the killer wanted to screw up the time of death calculation. I wasn't here when your ME took the body's liver temperature but I'm guessing his charts indicated the

The Violin Player

victim died a couple decades before he was born," said Tony. "That's why the killer messed with chloroform and injections and all that."

"Then why not do it the same way twice?" said the rookie. "Why not chloroform the dog?"

"And get his arm chewed off?"

"Then why not clonk the victim to subdue him? Killer's already got the blunt instrument in hand."

"Good point," said Tony. "'Cept he went to a lot of trouble to kill the victim in this way. The killer didn't want to ruin the effect by bashing in the skull." The rocking chair creaked backward ever so slightly. The thawing process was causing the leg muscles to lengthen and expand. Tony shook his head in grudging admiration. "He considers this a work of art."

The Sheriff said, "Makes some sense. But I don't see as it clears your client necessarily."

"No it don't, necessarily," said Tony with a sympathetic touch of drawl. He loved the way these boys talked. "But I'm guessin' that if your deputy found a vial of chloroform and a set of works in Mr. Sumner's jacket pocket you wouldn't be wasting your time talking to a broken down old ex-cop from Chicago." Tony took the Sheriff's silence as a yes. "Mr. Sumner was concerned for the victim's life. He had good reason to be here."

"Going through things in the back room?" snapped the deputy.

"You'll have to ask him about that," said Tony.

"Already did."

Tony got quiet. He had spoken to Walt in his holding cell, told him to keep his yap shut. But there was no telling how much he had volunteered, and Fifth-Avenue Bob was sunning himself halfway around the world. Typical. There was never a lawyer around when you needed one.

"Seems your client paid a coupla visits to Clovis Ward," said the deputy. He looked to the Sheriff for the okay before he continued. "Some ole boys down at the Wagon Wheel let us know they met a well-dressed man from Chicago last evening. Axin' directions to Snow Creek Road."

Tony bit clean through his cigarette and growled, "So he drives all the way from Chicago to grease Clovis Ward, slips into town under cover of night then walks into a public place to ask directions?" Tony nodded toward the rocking chair. Clovis' hands were relaxing their grip on the armrests. "This wasn't a spur of the moment decision to kill after a heated argument." Everyone in the room turned to look at the dead body with the shiny white-turning-to-pink skin and watery eyes. Clovis Ward looked as if he were about to spring to his feet. "This is about as premeditated as it gets."

The Sheriff addressed Tony in his silky drawl. "Y'all said that the killer wanted to screw with the calculation of the time of death."

"Yes I did," said Tony.

The Sheriff folded his arms across his chest. "But you didn't say why the killer would want to do that."

"Well, it's obvious, isn't it?" said Tony.

"Not to me," said the Sheriff.

Tony realized he should have taken his own advice and shut his own yap. He should not have, just to show up a dumbass rookie, brought up the time of death.

"Well, the killer wanted to erase the time line. You don't know when the vic died, you don't have a case."

The deputy started to say something. The Sheriff silenced him with a look. "We'll figger out when he died. Maybe not to the minute but we'll narrow it down some. Ah'm not worryin' about that too terribly." The Sheriff scratched the tip of his nose. "We

The Violin Player

know something about your Mr. Sumner by now a'course. Death of his wife, death of his mother, possible motive of personal gain in each case. But poor ol' Clovis here din't have a pot to piss in. Hard to figger how he fits in 'less it's blackmail."

One of the morgue crew poked her head in the door. "The team from Lexington just pulled up."

"Give us a minute," said the Sheriff. He looked up at Tony with the equanimity of a man accustomed to commanding others twice his size. "We know, that is we strongly *suspect* that Mr. Sumner paid a visit to Clovis Ward last evenin'. Could be the killer knew that too. Are you sayin', *suggestin'* the killer wanted to mess with the time of death so that Mr. Sumner would be implicated?"

"I'm not saying anything," said Tony Sobczak stonily. "I'm not his lawyer."

"Course you're not," said the Sheriff with a friendly pat. "Just askin' your opinion."

He looked up at Tony and waited. Footsteps thudded on the front porch. Idiot, said Tony to himself. Andy of Mayberry is just awaitin' on you to say those magic words so he can nod like he believes it then rush back to the station house and call the DA. Cops hated lame excuses. And on the universal roll call of lame excuses 'I was framed' ranked number one. It was Walter Sumner's piss poor luck that in his case it happened to be true.

"I think it's possible," said Tony Sobczak.

"I hear ya," said the Sheriff, nodding his head.

"What do you call ten thousand lawyers at the bottom of Lake Michigan?" said Captain Davidson, head of the Evanston PD homicide division.

John Knoerle

"A start," said Detective Lieutenant Bjork impatiently.

Davidson did a deadpan take to Chief of Police Franklin H. Reeder. "I gotta get some new material." The Chief spun his hand like a stage manager.

"Awright, awright," said Davidson. "Here's the up-to-the-minute." Davidson wore a path in the beryl blue carpeting of the office of the Chief of Police as he spoke. "The Cook County State's Attorney took about two seconds to say he'd decided to file against Walter Sumner for the murder of his mother once he got the 'asphyxia brought on by pancuronium intoxication' results for Laura Sumner from the Door County Coroner. Yay for our team. So we conference call the Door County DA. We explain that we caught it first, that we've got the resources *and* the hot shot experts like Bjork here with the training and experience that make their opinions not only admissible in court but practically bulletproof, blah blah blah blah dee frickin' *blah*."

Davidson paused to tuck his tie inside his belt. "Does the Door County DA agree to give us first bite at the apple? He does not. He says Door County personnel have logged a lot of overtime on this case and he'll have to get back to us after careful consideration which is lawyerspeak for 'Now that our wealthy pillar of the community suspect has topped the charts by freeze-drying his uncle on the same day our autopsy report indicates he also poisoned his wife which corroborates the suspicion that he also poisoned his mumsy-wumsy, there is no way short of prolonged torture we're gonna give up this career-maker to a bunch of arrogant Illinoyance like you guys.'"

Davidson stopped pacing and parked himself on a window sill. Bjork said, "Wisconsin doesn't have the death penalty."

"I pointed that out," said Davidson. "Fucking dinks are proud of it!"

The Violin Player

Chief Reeder asked if Captain Davidson had talked to Powell County, Kentucky. Davidson said that he had. Walter Sumner was being held while the DA determined if they had enough to arraign. The Chief tapped his desk and cleared his throat.

"If Powell County decides to file charges we will face the same situation down there. Even if they don't we're in a turf war with Door County. I don't hold with turf wars. They make us look stupid. We can try to cobble together a multijurisdictional task force and waste a lot of time and money trying to one up and outguess one another—" Bjork and Davidson listened with rapt attention. This was the longest speech the Chief had made since his swearing in ceremony. "Or we can put our personal agendas on hold and call in the one agency set up to deal with separate homicides in different states."

"Not—?" said Davidson. The Chief nodded grimly. Captain Davidson and Detective Lieutenant Bjork groaned as one.

Chapter 38

I finally figured out why Moms breast fed me till junior high. As a Catholic she wouldn't use birth control. But she didn't want Henry Jr. to knock her up again on one of his little 'visits'. Solution: *lactation prevents ovulation.*

We did our best to avoid each other, Junior and I. Moms would say she was working a double at Krogers and come bumbling in after midnight. I would hear the tires crunch on the gravel, the car radio click off, the smothered conversation spiked with boozy laughs. He talked his way in the door one night. Junior. Guess he hadn't gotten all he wanted at the No Tell Motel and wanted to anoint our tabernacle. I stumbled to the bathroom and came *blazingly* awake when I bumped into Henry Jr. at the bathroom door. He was naked. *And he smelled of fish.*

Good Night Nurse! What a moment of clarity for a painfully sensitive young boy that was! This, the man who campaigned to have me scraped from my mother's womb *and might well have succeeded had Moms not been afraid our old gasbag minister would spill the beans and instead sought the counsel of New Castle's one and only Catholic priest who did not mince words when it came to*

Violin Player

the sanctity of the zygote, and this, this…man, Henry Sumner Jr.—*My Father*—looked at me like I was a towel boy at his tennis club, said excuse me and bare-assed himself down the hall.

Guess you've heard about Clovis by now. You'd have to be buried at the bottom of a corn crib not to. In the wobble-jawed words of Richard Nixon, *let me say this about that*. Never lie to a psychopath! *I thought I'd made that perfectly clear.* I was an Eagle Scout with twenty-one merit badges. I arrived prepared. But I would have been just as happy to leave Uncle Free Gas just as I found him.

'I hear Walter Sumner paid a visit to the nursing home. The day after he visited you.'

'How you come to know that?'

'I'm well-connected.'

'Well I don't know if he did or he didn't but I admit I might've screwed the pooch. He went to git us a beer and he might've seen her phone number on the Frigidaire.'

'But you didn't tell him where she was.'

'God as my witness I didn't tell him.'

'Then why did he give you a big wad of cash?'

'Who says?'

'I say.'

'You always was a smartass know-it-all. I sold him his daddy's love letters to your ma.'

'What about Ma's love letters to Henry? The later ones? All those adoring tear-stained tomes on lavender stationary addressed to his highness marked return to sender and returned unopened. I would *Most Definitely* not want Walter Sumner to read those.'

'I u'nerstand.'

'May I see them?'

'Nawp. Jarlene asked me to burn 'em years ago. Which I did.'

Clovis Ward hadn't spent fifty years on the grift for nothing. He knew I wouldn't call Moms and upset her by asking if it were true. *I observe the matrilineal dictate of the fourth commandment.* Clovis pled ignorance about Walter's visit to the nursing home yet was readyfreddy with an excuse when I braced him. *I made an educated guess about the wad of cash.* He was, as we used to say in New Castle, slicker'n deer guts on a doorknob.

So I did him. Did his dog too. *Enjoyed that.* I had entertained all sorts of grisly scenarios. I wanted him to look just so for my dear half-brother. I considered bludgeoning him into a clotted pulp and casting him adrift in a lake of blood. But it just wasn't *me* somehow. But *en vivo* embalming with a femoral infusion of a cooled 4% solution of glutaraldehyde that causes a massive crosslinking of proteins which results in uncontrolled wormy twitching and produces accelerated rigor mortis, *that* was a thing of beauty. *Even symbolic, doncha know*. Killing him then making him come back to life. Sweet. *Curled up time.*

I did learn one valuable lesson from this experience. I don't particularly enjoy the hands-on process of killing a fellow human being. It's tedious, sweaty work.

It's the death part that turns me on.

Chapter 39

Laura had done a remarkable job with these children thought Kay as she watched Irene, sprawled on the rug in the den, sounding out words in her first grade reader. They washed their hands before meals, said please and thank you, and brushed their teeth twice a day without prompting. "Reenie, hon, where's your sister?"

"Upstairs," said Irene without looking up, digging her toes into the weave of the hand-loomed rug. Kay climbed the stairs to the guest bedroom. Both beds were made, pillows plumped. A bedraggled oversized teddy bear with a torn ear sat on Irene's bed. No stuffed animals for Thea, just a hardcover book on the nightstand. Such a mature young girl.

Kay crossed to the bathroom door and heard running water. It was almost bedtime. Thea showered in the morning. She knocked. "Thea?" She knocked again. "Thea, are you okay?" The water ran. Kay tried the knob. The door was locked. She knocked again, loudly. "Thea?" The water ran.

Kay threw her weight against the door. It didn't budge. She ran into the bedroom and rummaged through drawers. She found a purple bobby pin with a neon bug at one end. She used the other end to poke at the hole in the door knob, thinking, saying out loud, "Enough! No more. Not one more thing!"

The bathroom door popped open. There was no steam. Kay had expected to find steam. She stepped inside and stood stock still. Thea had not drowned or slipped and broken her neck. Kay could see her through the sliding glass door. She stood under a torrent of water in a sodden nightgown, her head bowed, arms wrapped around herself, shivering violently. Kay slid open the shower door and shut the faucet.

She helped Thea from the tub, wrapped her in a bath towel and sat her down on the toilet. Ted and Irene now stood in the doorway. Kay told them that there was no cause for concern and closed the door. She returned to the toilet and bent to one knee. "Thea, sweetheart, what in the world?"

Thea peeled a hank of pasted hair off one eye and dripped water on the ceramic tile. She said something through her chattering teeth that Kay couldn't understand.

Walt concluded that incarceration was probably a great deal like retirement. Plenty of time to spend examining your past life and where you had gone wrong.

He was confined in isolation. The larger holding cells on either side resembled impromptu house parties where young rowdies got together every evening to top each other's war stories amidst great hilarity. Even the jailers joined in. Walter was not included. He was a forlorn fearsome figure in an orange jumpsuit and three day's growth to be stared at by jailers and inmates alike. Which was fine. It gave him time to think. And sleep. Despite the constant din and clang of the Powell County Courthouse holding pen he slept fourteen

The Violin Player

hours a day. He couldn't remember the last time he had felt so rested. He would have to get himself arrested more often.

Tony had assured him that Robert Samuelson had cut short his Balinese getaway and would arrive soon. Were it not for Walt's concern for his daughters he would have told Fifth Avenue Bob to take his time, work on his tan. A high-priced trial attorney should always have a tan.

What time had it gotten to be? The jailers had confiscated his watch. They had wanted to take his wedding ring as well but Walt explained that it no longer came off. It twirled easily on his finger now. He would have to talk himself into eating. One of those servings of powdered eggs and cold grits, or the baloney sandwiches on white bread without a speck of mustard or mayonnaise. Was it possible to be that hungry?

Walt put his feet up on his bunk and cradled his hands behind his head. His neck was hairy, disgustingly so. Laura used to shave his neck in the bathtub on Sunday mornings. It was one of their rituals. He had been a terrible husband. The division of labor that worked in his Grandfather's day—you run the family, I'll run the business—worked no longer. Probably never had. Bottom line, if he hadn't spent ten years of eighty hour weeks trying to live up to the expectations of a dead man he would still have a living breathing loving wife. Walt felt the familiar tug of drowsiness. He slid down the bunk until his feet dangled.

"On your feet Mr. Sumter," said the moon faced young deputy who had arrested him. "We need to get you showered up."

Walt bent over and tugged at the cuffs of his cotton drawstring pants, drawing a nervous glance from the young deputy at the wheel of the squad car. Walt pulled up his socks as best he could in handcuffs. His clothing had been taken into evidence so the deputy had pawed through jail castoffs in order to attire Walt for the reunion with his daughters. The deputy had seemed both insulted and impressed at the orders from above. 'We got a visiting area at the jail, tables you can sit around. It's nice, it's clean. You with the CIA?'

They pulled into the parking lot of a motel. Two jet black war wagons with smoked windows and whip antennas sat parked at the far end of the lot. The deputy turned right and parked between them. "Y'all have fun," he sneered as he keyed open the cuffs. Two men in dark suits pulled Walt from the vehicle and escorted him into the room at the end of the one-story structure. Another dark-suited man entered the adjoining room.

Walt was patted down and deposited on the end of the bed. One of his dark-suited escorts returned to the doorway and began speaking into a transmitter that Walt could not see. The second man said, "There are toiletries in the bathroom. If you want to shave."

Walt took the hint. He didn't want to frighten his daughters. He had let his beard grow once before, on a five-day fishing trip to Quebec. When he returned Thea and Irene shrank from him as if he were Pierre the Mad North Woodsman.

The second man stood and watched Walt lather his face. He seemed neither interested nor disinterested, friendly nor unfriendly. Who were these guys? FBI? State cops? Operatives of some clandestine intragovernmental agency? Walt wondered if Fifth Avenue Bob had pulled strings to make it possible for him to visit his daughters in civilian clothes in a neutral setting. If so he was worth every centime of his outlandish fees.

Walt finished shaving and toweled off. The dark-suited man gestured toward the room. Walt sat on the edge of the bed and dried

The Violin Player

his moist palms on his knees. The dark-suited man watched the door. "They just pulled up," he said. "Won't be a minute."

Walt wondered how he could know that. He wasn't wearing a visible earpiece. Perhaps the government implanted microchips in these shadowy operatives to network their brain waves. Why not? It made as much sense as anything else that had happened in the last year. Few months. However long it had been.

Came a knock at the door. The first dark-suited man swung it open and admitted Thea and Irene. Walt caught a quick glimpse of Kay in the slanty sun. She waved. Both dark-suited men stepped out and closed the door behind them. Walt tried to blink his daughters into focus. After the burst of sunlight they stood against the drawn blackout curtains as one dimensional silhouettes, cardboard cutouts of little girls from long ago.

Walt rose and held out his arms. Reenie ran to him. Thea walked. Reenie hugged his waist furiously. Thea stood to the other side and allowed her head to be stroked. No one spoke. This went on for a wonderfully long period of time.

Irene stood back and said, "This lady was touching me!"

"What?"

"She was searching you, dufus brain," said Thea.

"She wasn't searching me, *dufus brain*."

"She *was*. To see if you had a *gun*."

"Girls please," said Walt. "Don't do this. Not now. We've got to stick together."

"Thea took a shower with her clothes on."

"Did not."

"I *saw* you."

"Did you do that Thea?" said her father. Thea looked away. Walter pined for his wife. Laura would know how to untangle this chaos. He felt lightheaded and sat down heavily on the end of the bed. His daughters eyed him warily. "We'll get through this," he said weakly. "We will. We'll get through this and move to a horse farm in Ohio where you can feed the chickens and gallop over the pastures and we'll sit around the fire at night and tell stories and—"

The cold eyes of his daughters stopped him. He'd not previously informed them of his plan to flee the city. They had endured quite enough upheaval lately. He was screwing up this reunion royally. A knock at the door. "You've got one minute," said a male voice.

"Are Kay and Ted taking good care of you?" The girls said that they were. A sickening thought occurred. "What were you wearing in the shower Thea?"

"I did-ent—"

"Her nightgown," said Reenie. "I *saw* her."

"Why Thea? Did something bad happen to you in your nightgown? At Kay and Ted's."

Thea gave him a look far older than her years. A look that said I know what you're suggesting and shame on you for even thinking it.

"Then tell me why, snowflake." Thea hesitated. "I worry about a lot of things, including this little knucklehead," said Walt, mussing Reenie's hair. "But I've never had to worry about you."

Thea kept still for the longest time. Walt ticked off precious seconds waiting for her to speak.

"I saw Mom," she said. "Not like in dreams but like...*seeing* her. She was looking right at me. Out the window at Auntie Kay's. On the other side of the street. She was wearing her purple sweater."

Thea sat down on the bed next to her father. Irene snuggled up on the other side with eyes wide and ears open. The door leaked light. "Not yet!" bellowed Walter. The door closed. "We're listening Thea."

The Violin Player

"I didn't know what to do. So I looked away and then I looked back and then she was gone." Thea leaned her cheek ever so lightly against the crown of her father's shoulder. "I thought that I might be going cuckoo so I went under the shower and made it real cold and real hard and I stood there for a long time until Aunt Kay came and got me. And then I was fine. I was fine just like our uncle in that stupid story."

Walt had no earthly idea what to say. He hugged his daughters to himself and waited for the door to open. When it did Walt knew that it wasn't Fifth Avenue Bob who had made this precious reunion possible.

Chapter 40

"My wife was *murdered*," said Walter Sumner. "I called to tell you that her date of death had been posted, I sent you a list of possibles, I gave you a sketch of the suspect, I turned to you and your agency for help and you did exactly nothing!"

FBI Special Agent O'Connor said, "That's not true."

"Bullshit! You didn't even know a rosary bead when you saw one."

Agent O'Connor's dark eyes flashed. Walt knew what she wanted to say. 'Neither did you dumbshit.' Her not saying it calmed him down. It was difficult to stay angry with a beautiful woman who had allowed him to see his daughters and who sat in a chair so close to his bed in a cheap motel room and absent-mindedly scratched the bare brown skin above her knee.

"We ran a check of your list of possibles but none of them matched the physical description," said Agent O'Connor. "I ran the suspect sketch through our database personally without success. We did a global search for a birth certificate for Henry Ward and got zip."

"You're not going to find a birth certificate."

The Violin Player

"Same with Selective Service and Social Security. So far as we're able to determine Henry Ward does not exist."

"He exists."

"I believe you Walter but it would be nice to have a photo, a document, *something*," said Agent O'Connor. "We could interview his mother."

"Don't drag her into this. I'll get you something."

"I understand your frustration, Walter."

She leaned over and touched his wrist. On the smooth hairless inside part. Walt moved his arm away but her hand was already gone, had flitted away unseen, leaving only the silken heat of her fingertips.

"My lawyer would tell me not to speak to you. If he ever bothers to show up."

"Of course he would. He's a lawyer." Agent O'Connor selected a wan smile from her considerable repertoire. Lip-biting, tentative.

Walt looked away. "I'll tell you whatever you want to know on one condition."

"What's that?"

"That you assign someone to monitor the Sumner family page on the GenealoG website. Hourly."

"Done," said Agent O'Connor. "But why not have someone at your office do it?"

"I don't trust that they wouldn't screw it up."

Agent O'Connor studied Walt as if he had said something profound. "You're a heroic manager aren't you?"

"A what?"

"Unable to delegate, fingers in every pie."

"I suppose."

"I can relate. I'm exactly the same way." Agent O'Connor gave him her insouciant grin. Asymmetrical, dimpled. "And I have an even better idea," she said. "Let's put a trap on the website. If somebody posts a date of death we can trace it back to the transmission site."

"I don't know," said Walt, weakly.

"You look pale," said Agent O'Connor. "Have you eaten?" Walt shook his head. Agent O'Connor tucked her chin to her breast. "We need two turkey and swiss subs with everything and a side of coleslaw. There's a Subway around the corner. Oh," she said and winked at Walt. "And two cokes."

Just the mention of food revived Walt enough to continue. "Thank you," he said. "For all…this."

"I think the taxpayers can afford a forty-two dollar motel room." She smiled conspiratorially, eyebrows arched, lips compressed. "The sandwiches are on me."

"I don't like the trap on the website for two reasons," said Walt, thinking this woman was wasting her talent in law enforcement, thinking she could be pulling down seven figures in the sales division of some Fortune 50. "First, my tech expert tells me that an email posting usually takes several minutes to wend its way through the pipeline. The killer always sends them from a public place, he's not gonna sit around and wait to be apprehended." Walt paused to think it over. "The second reason is that, sick as it may seem, the website's my only line of communication to him. My homicidal half brother. If he detects a trap on the site he might pull the plug."

"I disagree," said Agent O'Connor. "He's not going to quit the game now."

Walt straightened his spine against the headboard. "I'm in jail, I'm facing multiple counts of first degree murder. What more could he want?"

The Violin Player

"Even if you're convicted and sentenced to death it would be at least ten years till you're executed," said Agent O'Connor.

Walter made a defeated guttural sound at the back of his throat. He bowed his head. Agent O'Connor crooked her neck and leaned in. When Walt looked up her eyes were perpendicular to his own. "Then why bother to frame me if he means to kill me?"

"To humiliate you," said Agent O'Connor. "To strip you naked before he runs you through." She sprang to her feet suddenly. She kicked off her shoes and dusted the shag carpeting with her bare feet. "Or—I hadn't thought of this before but it raises some fascinating possibilities—*what if* the point of his elaborate frame job is to stage an attack on you and your daughters and make it look like a guilty man's murder-suicide? He skates, case closed."

"What?" said Walt. "I kill my daughters, then myself?" Agent O'Connor bobbed her head. "How in name of God's he gonna pull that off?"

Agent O'Connor stilled her enthusiasm and made meaningful eye contact. "We're just speculating here, Walter. No need to get upset." She strode up and down at the foot of the bed. "*Or*—God this is good—what if he's been setting us law enforcement types up all along? What if the point of this elaborate frame job is to convince us law enforcement types that you're guilty as sin?"

"Well obviously."

"Yes of course," said Agent O'Connor, on the move again, shoving chairs out of her way. "But what does *our* presumption of *your* guilt get the killer? Nothing." She grinned at some private joke. "And when the killer posts your date of death and you turn to the local authorities for protection that's exactly what you'll get. Nothing. No protection. The killer strikes as promised, leaves his calling card and disappears. Do you see it?"

"See *what?*"

"How it gratifies his every fantasy," said Agent O'Connor, black eyes blazing. "He wreaks vengeance on the Sumner family, he humiliates the law enforcement community and he assumes mythic status in the annals of crime!"

Walter Sumner was rendered speechless. Agent O'Connor lacked only pom poms and a fight song in her cheerleading routine for Henry the master criminal. Was everyone in law enforcement insane? The last place Walter would turn for protection were the local cops with their petty rivalries and their press leaks. He would take Tony Sobczak over any ten of them. If he were truly up against it he would take his daughters to Shanghai and let his homicidal half-brother try his luck against Sung Yee's cadre of stone-eyed bodyguards.

Henry knew all of this as well. Or most of it. Henry wasn't stupid. Which made Agent O'Connor's lurid theories the purest pap. Except what she'd said about Henry wanting to strip Walt naked before he ran him through. Whatever sick game Henry was playing he would want it to end in a blaze of glory.

Walt stared into the middle distance. He felt like the unsuspecting victim of a natural disaster. He had seen their stories on cable television. 'They just stood there,' the few plucky survivors would always say of the victims when the twister touched down out of nowhere. 'They just stood there and waited to die.' Walt understood completely. But he had his daughters to protect. At least he had the FBI in his corner. That was a hopeful sign.

"Food's here," said Agent O'Connor, going to the door. She returned with a big white bag.

"You left me alone with Thea and Irene," said Walt. "So I'm assuming you don't consider me a suspect." Agent O'Connor's face

The Violin Player

went blank as a table napkin. "If you considered me a suspect you wouldn't have left me alone with them."

Agent O'Connor hauled up paper-wrapped submarine sandwiches from the big white bag. "What makes you think you were alone?"

Chapter 41

The moon faced young deputy had been correct. The outdoor visiting area adjacent to the County Courthouse holding pen was nice and clean. It even had picnic tables. Walt basked in the fresh air and intermittent sunshine and felt halfway restored. Fifth Avenue Bob had arrived bearing gifts in preparation for Walt's arraignment. A suitcase of clean clothes packed by sister Kay and a Marshall Field's gift bag filled with herbal soap, fluffy towels and three choices of cologne. He had even remembered Walter's brand of cigarettes. This was Kentucky. Ashtrays were provided.

Samuelson conferred with his associate, an anorexic blonde woman who looked twenty-five years old under cloud cover and forty-five when the sun broke through. He put one well-shod foot up on the picnic bench and spoke in his full round attorney voice. He was very tan.

"What did Agent O'Connor ask after you told her you were searching Clovis Ward's files for phone records?"

"She asked if I had given Clovis some money. In cash," said Walt. "I thought about denying it. I realized that she might assume it was an extortion payment of some kind and that's what I came back to search for in Clovis' file drawers but that doesn't make any kind of sense under the circumstances."

"What did you tell her?"

"I told her I gave Clovis Ward $10,000 in cash in exchange for the location of his sister, Jarlene Ward." Walt looked from one incredulous stare to the other. The blonde woman shook her head and looked away. Robert Samuelson summoned an expression of grim confidence.

"Walter, rather than doing a line by line Q and A, why don't you just recreate the conversation as best you can."

"All right," said Walter. This would not be a problem. He remembered Agent O'Connor's velvety interrogation in the motel room quite vividly. "She asked if Clovis Ward was blackmailing me. I said no. She asked when I gave Clovis the $10,000. I said the night before I found his body. She asked if I visited Jarlene Ward. I said yes. She asked where I got a gun with no serial numbers." Walt paused while the blonde woman, writing furiously on a legal pad, flipped over a page. "I told her what Tony Sobczak told me to say, that I found it in the alley behind my house. She asked me how my business was faring. I told her we've had better years but that, recently, things were looking up."

Walt paused. There was more to say but he wanted to see how he was going over so far. Samuelson's expression of grim confidence was now simply grim. His anorexic associate bummed a cigarette from Walt's pack and wandered away, talking to herself between puffs. Walt didn't understand. What he had just recounted to his attorneys was not self-incriminating. Not really. If these two resplendently attired nitwits didn't see that they were out of a job.

"It's not the end of the world," said Robert Samuelson gamely. "The gun with the burned numbers may be the worst element. It shatters the whole solid citizen, innocent victim caught in a web of terror thing."

"I think it's the ten grand," said his associate, waving her cigarette around like a Fourth of July sparkler. "It gives him motive and opportunity in all three cases."

"But it makes no sense!" said Walter. "Either I killed Clovis Ward over a blackmail threat or I paid him. I wouldn't do both."

"Here's what the other side will say," said Samuelson. "You paid Clovis to put him at ease, get him to lower his guard. Clovis goes to the back room to stash the cash. While he's gone, you kill his dog. When he returns, you kill him. You search for the money, can't find it. You're rattled, keyed up. You hear a noise, panic and take off. Fearing the cash will be traced back to you, you steel your nerves and return to retrieve it the next day."

Fifth Avenue Bob thumbed his eyes and stretched his arms over his head. Jet lag, thought Walt. He knew the feeling. If he felt charitable, which he did not, he would chalk up his high-priced attorney's glaring idiocy to an eighteen hour flight across the International Dateline. "I called 911 to alert them to the threat. From *my car*. On the way back to Clovis Ward's house!"

"So you said," said Robert Samuelson, shrugging the shoulders of his charcoal gray suit back into alignment. "Problem is that none of the 911 dispatchers have any such recollection."

"Oh come *on*!" said Walt, so loud that birds flew. He lowered his voice. "I *talked* to him, the dispatcher. I did! Why would that Sheriff's deputy have come to investigate if I didn't call it in?"

Samuelson deferred to his associate. "The Powell County Sheriff's Office says they received an anonymous tip." She paged back on her legal pad and read from her notes. "A passing motorist who declined to give his name, quote, in case it's nothing, close

The Violin Player

quote, reported seeing, quote, a stranger attempting to gain entry to 178 Snow Creek Road, close quote."

"And the 911 dispatch crew on the day shift," said Samuelson, "are all female."

Walt lowered his gaze from the plangent concern of his high-priced legal team. He saw handcuff abrasions and grimy fingernails in need of trimming. He looked up and saw a ten foot chain-link fence topped with razor wire. He looked right and saw his keeper, a leonine black deputy, standing ten feet away. One hand resting on his nightstick, the other on his gun butt, a cryptic smile greasing his lips. Walter closed his eyes. Where was Laura? She had always been his translator in social situations. She always understood the droll asides and the obscure references. She would know how to make sense of this. Laura was always in on the joke.

Chapter 42

Tony Sobczak was pleased to see that the man behind the counter of Hi-Time Liquors on Western looked Middle Eastern. Arab merchants respected authority. The shopkeeper became very still as he approached. "How ya doin? I'm Sergeant Sobczak. Got a minute?" Unlike the military, the Chicago PD said your rank retired when you did but screw them.

"Yes?" said the shopkeeper. He was light-skinned. Lebanese, maybe.

"I'm conducting a felony investigation."

"Yes?" said the shopkeeper, sad-eyed, looking over Tony's shoulder at his customers heading for the door.

Tony handed him a photostat of the suspect sketch that Walt had given him. "Seen this guy in here the last few weeks?"

The man waited until the last of his customers filed out before he studied the picture. "I don't know."

"*I don't know*'s not what we're lookin' for here, Mister—?"

"Zarmin."

"Mister Zarmin. We need a definite yes or a definite no. Look again." Mr. Zarmin looked again. "Think back about ten days. He

The Violin Player

was prolly wearing a long coat and might've had on a hat or dark glasses or bot'." The man looked hard at the sketch. "He might've created some sort of disturbance."

Mr. Zarmin squinted and grimaced and shuffled his feet around the floor. He shook his head. "I don't remember him."

Tony grumbled and pulled a photo of Laura Sumner from his raincoat pocket. "Maybe this'll help."

This was a last resort. Mr. Zarmin had to know Mrs. Sumner from her frequent visits and had likely seen her picture in the paper. The Door County cops had said only that Laura Sumner was poisoned. They hadn't said how. If Mr. Zarmin put two and two together he might clam up. Understandable. Selling poison hooch was bad for business.

Mr. Zarmin said that he knew the nice lady. Tony placed the suspect sketch over her photo. "Could be this guy was in here the same time. Following her around, next to her in line."

Mr. Zarmin asked to see the picture of the lady again. Tony showed it to him briefly and returned it to the bottom of the deck. Mr. Zarmin's pupils dilated. "Isn't that the lady who—"

"Not your problem right now," said Tony. He leaned his great head forward and slid the photostat across the countertop until it curled up against the shopkeeper's belly. "Your problem right now is to decide if you ever saw this man in this store in physical proximity of the woman."

Mr. Zarmin's eyes were spinning like cherries in a slot machine. Tony lowered his voice to a volcanic rumble, "Thursday, eleven days ago, about one in the afternoon."

An elderly customer limped in the door, turned around and limped out. Mr. Zarmin took the sketch and laid his hand across the top of the suspect's brow. The Budwesier clock behind the counter ticked off several seconds. "His hair was not so long."

"But he was here."

"Yes."

"The same time as the woman."

"Yes."

"Good," said Tony. "That's real good. What'd he do?"

"Please?"

"When he was in here. What'd he do?"

Mr. Zarmin unhinged his neck and tick-tocked his chin back and forth. Could be he was a fair-skinned Indian or Paki. They were the only ones who did that thing with their chin.

"It was lunch hour, very busy." The shopkeeper put his finger on the photostat. "This man, he was standing behind the nice lady in the line. Then, right away, he falls down! Right on the floor!" Tony nodded encouragement. "He shouted swear words to the man behind him who, I think, did not touch him one bit."

Tony waited to see if Mr. Zarmin had any more to say before he popped the question. "D'you get a look? Lean over the counter or get a look in the security mirrors to see what our boy was doing down there on the floor?"

"No, no. How could I do so? I reached across the counter only to protect the nice lady who was my customer, to protect her from fighting."

"Was there fighting?"

"No fighting, cursing."

"And you don't have a closed circuit camera system."

"No, no."

"Get one," said Tony wearily. This was going to take some work. "What happened after the subject, the man with the short hair fell to the floor?"

The Violin Player

"There was cursing—"

"*After* the cursing. Did the lady pay for her purchase?"

"Oh yes. Of course."

"Did the man with the short hair pay?"

"No, no. He went out."

"Was he carrying anything?" Mr. Zarmin shrugged. "What about the guy he shouted at? The guy behind him in line. What'd he do?"

"I think that he paid his money."

"Did he say anything?"

"Oh yes."

"What did he say?"

The shopkeeper tapped his finger on the photostat. "He said that this man was crazy."

Tony pressed his belly against the counter. "The man who said that. Is he a regular?" Mr. Zarmin unhinged his neck and tick-tocked his chin. Tony had never figured out what that chin thing meant exactly. "Is that a yes or no?"

Chapter 43

"Why are we here?" said Judge Harold Macallan, a fierce-looking man with bushy eyebrows, a beaked nose and yellow teeth. "Your boy's never gonna hit the sidewalk anyway."

"I don't believe that's true." Robert Samuelson kept his voice low and his manner easy. This was not a man he could intimidate. Though a couple oblique glances at the judge's chambers couldn't hurt. They were better suited to an assistant bank manager. "I'd be happy to explain."

The Judge smiled encouragement. The heavy-set District Attorney made himself as comfortable as he could in a straight-back chair. Go ahead hotshot, their eyes said. Dazzle us.

They were holding a bail review hearing following the arraignment of Walter Sumner in the Powell County, Kentucky courtroom of Justice Harold Macallan. As was customary in murder cases bond had been denied. Judge Macallan's 'sidewalk' comment referred to Illinois' supposed warrant. If issued, Walter Sumner would be served immediately after he was released on bail from the Powell County Jail, resulting in his reincarceration pending extradition proceedings.

The Violin Player

"Contrary to press reports, the Cook County State's Attorney is not currently planning to seek a warrant for Walter Sumner's arrest. And no, it's not just a desire to let you gents do all the heavy lifting." Samuelson allowed the judge and the DA to ponder the implications of that statement, *Just* being the operative word. He continued.

"I spoke to the Cook County State's Attorney yesterday, in his office. It was a lengthy and very colorful conversation but we came to the same conclusion. Illinois' case against Walter Sumner is weak. They have a personal gain motive, which also applies to Walter's siblings and in-laws, and little else. No weapon, no witnesses, nothing to place him at the scene. And he has an alibi. Phone records corroborate his assertion that he was, tragically, on the phone to his mother at the time of her death." Samuelson anticipated their objection. "The poison could have been planted at any time? Not true. The final coroner's report indicates that the toxin was dissolved in a solution of highly concentrated sugars and polyphenolic compounds, otherwise known as port wine. The killer put it in Virginia Sumner's wine glass."

"How do we know that?" said Macallan in a deep-voweled Scottish burr. "They test the bottle it came from?"

"No sir." Fifth Avenue Bob took a dramatic pause. Judge Macallan told him to get on with it. "We know that the poison was in the glass and not the bottle because the Sumner family *consumed* the remainder of the bottle drinking a toast to Virginia Sumner during a memorial ceremony following her funeral." Judge Macallan ran a knuckle across his nostrils and sniffed. Robert Samuelson said, "My client could not have—"

"How do we know it was him on the line?" said Macallan.

"That's just what the State's Attorney wanted to know!" said

Samuelson happily, thinking that the judge would be flattered to be included in such august company.

"Mr. Samuelson, I don't give a roaring shit in hell *what* the State's Attorney wanted to know, what he was wearing or how he takes his coffee. Just answer the question as asked."

"Yes sir."

"How do we know that Walter Sumner didn't have someone in his household place the call to his mother in order to afford him an alibi while he administered the poison?"

"We don't," said Samuelson. "Not positively."

Judge Macallan chewed on his tongue, determined to puzzle it out. Robert Samuelson and the District Attorney waited. "The wife's dead," said Macallan. Samuelson nodded. "Any kids?"

"Two," said Samuelson.

Judge Macallan shook his head. "The chickenshit."

Fifth Avenue Bob assumed the epithet referred to the Cook County State's Attorney. He had decided to decline prosecution because it would require him to allege that a loving mother of two, now deceased and unable to defend herself, conspired with her husband to commit murder.

Robert Samuelson straightened his tie and shot his cuffs. "You've got some minor twists and turns along the way but that phone call is the six car pileup the prosecution can't get past."

The District Attorney spoke up. "What about Door County?"

"I believe Wisconsin will follow Illinois' lead," said Samuelson.

"Why? They've got oppor*tun*ity and *motive*," snarled Macallan, his accent growing more pronounced.

"A two legged stool," replied Samuelson. "They need the common plan or scheme exception to make it stand up. If Illinois doesn't

The Violin Player

establish the conduct that shows a pattern—Walter Sumner murdering close family members for personal gain—Door County's case is one lamb chop short of a mixed grill."

The District Attorney chortled. Judge Macallan lowered his head, pronging his bushy eyebrows. "They can *use* uncharged conduct to do that."

"They can," said Samuelson. "They can they could they might they should. But I would make it abundantly clear to the good burghers of Door County that the Cook County State's Attorney, despite his eagerness to nail a rich white pelt to the wall in the face of all the controversy about his overzealous prosecutions of black death row inmates, had not found Walter Sumner's conduct actionable."

Robert Samuelson sat back, pleased with his summation. Judge Macallan's broken capillaries shone road-map purple on his florid cheeks. "Mr. Samuelson," he growled, "Your opinion of other jurisdiction's prosecutorial strategies has no bearing on my judicial responsibilities in this venue."

Fifth Avenue Bob almost laughed out loud. 'Judicial responsibilities in this venue'? It was a *bail review hearing*. Despite Macallan's bluff and bluster Samuelson thought he had this hayseed worried. The official criteria for granting bond were considerations of flight risk and danger to the community. The unofficial criteria was, could this defendant beat the rap and turn around to file a massive false imprisonment lawsuit that a poor rural Kentucky county could ill afford to lose.

Time to get up, Robert. Time to get up out of this straight-back chair, shake off the jet lag and earn your keep.

"Walter Sumner is not a flight risk, your honor. He has deep roots in the Midwest, a successful business of long standing, and substantial liquid assets including his million dollar home." Robert

Samuelson made a quick calculation and plunged ahead, knowing his candor would buy him credibility. "Though it's *true* that Mr. Sumner's business requires him to travel overseas from time to time he will gladly surrender his passport to your honor until this matter is adjudicated."

Judge Macallan did not immediately object to this idea. Robert Samuelson rebuttoned his double breasted jacket, stepped back and addressed both men.

"Is Mr. Sumner a danger to the community? Well, indulge me for a moment if you would. I'd like to try something. Let's imagine that every allegation against my client in every jurisdiction is true. He, Walter Sumner, successful entrepreneur and father of two, is in reality a cunning master criminal. He's grown tired of the daily grind that last year alone netted him an income of over eight hundred thousand dollars and has decided instead to exterminate his loved ones for fun and profit." Samuelson cupped his hands like a parentheses. "I'll get to Clovis Ward in a second. So, Walter Sumner is sailing along, enjoying his new life of crime when the long arm of the law finally reaches out and grabs him in Clay City. Put yourself in his place. What do you do now? Continue your homicidal rampage for personal gain?" Samuelson cupped his hands again. "For the sake of argument I'm assuming that Walter Sumner executed Clovis Ward because Clovis threatened to expose him."

Fifth Avenue Bob paused. He had the full attention of the judge and the DA. He resumed.

"These are not heat of the moment crimes, gentlemen. They are carefully planned executions undertaken by a perpetrator with rational motives and every expectation of escaping arrest if, for the sake of our hypothesis, we agree that the date of death postings on the internet and the assertion of the existence of an unknown and

The Violin Player

unstable half brother are elaborate fictions designed to lead our guardians of public safety down the garden path. Where does he go from here, our cunning master criminal if released on bail? It seems plain to me that he is severely constrained by his present circumstances and will comport himself like a model citizen, if for no other reason than he has no alternative."

Robert Samuelson, finding that he had parked a haunch saucily on the Judge's desk, returned to his chair to await the magistrate's decision.

"You want to say anything Jimmy?" said Judge Macallan.

The District Attorney, who was busy picking at the laces of the shoe crossed atop his knee, said, "The defendant lives outside the territorial jurisdiction of the court."

Robert Samuelson removed a document from his briefcase. "My client has signed an affidavit forswearing his right to any and all extradition procedures by and for the Commonwealth of Kentucky." Samuelson handed the paper to Judge Macallan. "It's notarized by your court clerk."

"Don't miss a trick do you?"

"Just doing my job, your honor."

The Judge read the document aloud. The District Attorney said it sounded all right. Judge Macallan raised his shoulders and lowered his beak. He looked like a prehistoric bird of prey. Fifth Avenue Bob masked his face in indifference and breathed through his nose.

"Bail is set in the amount of one million dollars."

Robert Samuelson did his best to look pained at the amount.

Chapter 44

"What's that big salt shaker thing?" said Reenie from the back seat as the XJR shushed north on Highway 3. A black thunderhead on the horizon spilled rain like a torn feed sack. Walt waited, expecting Thea to put her baby sister in the know. She did not. His daughters were city girls.

"It's a grain silo, silly goof. Though they use them mostly for corn silage around here."

"What's corn silage?" said Reenie.

"It's a kind of fodder made of ground up corn. Pigs and cows eat it in the wintertime. Because in the wintertime there's no grass in the pasture."

"Horses eat carrots," said Reenie.

"That's right, they do," said her father.

"Can we listen to some music?" said Thea.

"Sure."

Thea rummaged in her knapsack and removed a compact disc. Boyz II Men. She placed it in the changer arm with shaky fingers and breathed sharply through her nose until the richly textured acappella singing commenced. She heaved an audible sigh, scooted back

The Violin Player

in the bucket seat and closed her eyes. Walt tweaked up the volume and let the Jaguar and the music carry them across the rain gray prairie.

New Castle did not make a favorable first impression. Driving down Broad Street Irene said what both girls were thinking. "You used to live here?"

"Yep," said Walt. "So did Grandpa Henry and Grandma Ginny. And their mom and dad and aunts and uncles and cousins and everyone."

Walt drove past the Courthouse Square and parked across the street from the Henry County Department of Health. He looked around for Rita's blue Corsica. The coast was clear.

They trooped up the absurdly long steep staircase and stood in front of the counter with the sign that said Vital Statistics. Mrs. Cantwell looked up from her desk. She had to have heard the latest developments by now. It was everywhere.

"Look who's here!" said Mrs. Cantwell. Reenie stood on tiptoe to see over the counter. "And who, pray tell, are these handsome young women?"

Walter introduced his daughters and asked them to sit and wait while he discussed some important business. Mrs. Cantwell ushered the girls next door to the Health Department waiting room and found them some books to read. She led Walter back behind the counter and into the Xerox room. She closed the door. "What can I do to help?"

Walt explained that he was searching for his half-brother Henry Ward, born circa 1951 to Jarlene Ward at an unknown location though he had attended school in New Castle. "The FBI says they couldn't find a birth certificate or any other record to indicate that he really exists. I was hoping you could."

"What kind of documentation do you need?"

"Anything," said Walt. "But a picture, some kind of documented picture like a newspaper photo would be best."

"Go look after your daughters," said Mrs. Cantwell and went away.

Reenie was playing leap frog with a small boy in the waiting room, his mother grateful for the distraction. Thea was reading a pamphlet on sexually transmitted diseases. Walt sat down in a plastic scoop chair and nodded to the mother of the boy. A very pregnant teen hobbled in on swollen ankles and placed her paperwork on the counter.

Walt and his daughters waited there with the other charity cases for the better part of an hour before Mrs. Cantwell called Walter's name from the other side of the counter.

"This is all I could find," she said in the Xerox room. "No birth record, nothing in the newspaper, nothing in the census tracts, church records, police files, not even a class picture. Just this."

She opened the 1968 Walter Chrysler Memorial High School yearbook. Walter saw team pictures of the lesser sports. Lacrosse. Tennis. Track and field. In the lower left-hand corner a husky farm boy prepared to put the shot. In the upper righthand corner a gaunt young runner broke through the tape with an exultant upturned face. *School Record in the Mile.* The caption under the picture identified the record setter as Henry Ward.

Walt felt a rush of relief and triumph and hope flood his veins. Not to mention profound gratitude and something approaching awe. This woman was a marvel. "I can't even begin to thank you."

"Then don't," said Mrs. Cantwell. She pushed the yearbook

The Violin Player

across the counter. "I only ask that you return it when you're done."

"I will."

"Do you *promise*?"

Walt returned her smile. "I promise." He looked again at the yearbook picture. His half-brother had a nickname. The caption read, *Henry 'Three Locks' Ward, doing what he does best*. Mrs. Cantwell could offer no explanation.

Walt sent the girls off to the bathroom before the long drive home. He bent down to the drinking fountain in the entryway and heard a very out-of-breath woman say, "I saw your car."

"Rita."

"I was just driving over to pay my phone bill or I wouldn't even have seen it. Your car. It's parked out front. That is your car isn't it?"

"Yes. Yes it is." Walter and Rita stood and looked at one another. "You changed your hairstyle."

"Do you like it?" said Rita, cupping a hand around the stiff and shiny blonde globe atop her head. "That palm tree look was out of date. Are these your baby girls?"

"They are."

Rita was on them in a blink. "Hey there punkin', what's your name? Irene! Well isn't that *ironic*. My granny's an Irene too! And who's that shy one behind you there? Thea? That's a Spanish name in'it?"

Rita kept this up all the way down the long steep staircase, out the door and across the street. Walt took out his car keys. "You guys hungry?" said Rita. "Chi Chi's is open for lunch till two."

Walt said nothing. He felt as if he had already squared this circle. He had gone with Rita to the sketch artist and bought her lunch afterwards and thanked her profusely after that. But Walter was one down where Rita was concerned. He might need her to testify about the curly haired man with the sick sense of humor. So Walter didn't refuse her invitation to lunch at Chi Chi's. He let Thea do it.

"Well then next time you're in town we've got a date, the four of us. And you girls don't forget, there's a light at the end of the rainbow!"

Thea and Irene climbed into the car. Walt extended his hand.

"Now now, we're not gonna have any of that," said Rita, wrapping him up in a steaming hug. Walt was surprised at how comforting it felt. Rita was a good hugger.

Walter extricated himself after a time and climbed behind the wheel of the XJR. His daughters were enormously silent beside and behind him as he took a right on Vine Street.

Walt followed the shadow of the pole sign down the off-ramp. The girls were asleep. He turned right at the stop sign and parked in the lot. "French fries anyone?" Thea's eyelids fluttered. "Hot apple pie for dessert?" Reenie stirred in the back seat. The girls blinked themselves awake and the tattered remains of the Sumner family straggled into the world's most successful franchise restaurant for a meal of reliable mediocrity.

Walt got five dollars change from the cashier and watched his daughters through the window as he fed the pay phone. Marcy wasn't in the office at 5:30. He called her home.

"Yeah?" said a brusque male voice.

Walt hesitated. A roommate. Marcy said she had a roommate. "Is Marcy there?"

"She's zz'ed out," said the man.

"Oh," said Walt. "Is she sick?"

The roommate didn't answer right away. He seemed distracted.

The Violin Player

"Who is this?"

"Her boss, Walter Sumner. It's important that I see her as soon as possible."

"Tell me where she needs to be and at what time," said the man, suddenly polite.

"At the office. Say seven p.m."

"Seven o'clock, office. Any message?"

"Not really," said Walt, bemused at the transformation. Being an accused serial killer was apparently all it took to win the respect of the younger generation. Walt heard a familiar yowl. "Is that Twyla?"

"Who?"

"Twyla. A spoiled rotten Siamese that I browbeat Marcy into adopting. She's—"

"You *beat* her?"

"No, no—"

"S'not cool to beat women, man."

"You misunderstood what—"

"They'll lock you up in a heartbeat. Trust me."

Walt heard a rustling sound on the other end of the line. "Hello?"

"Yeah, I'm here. You say something?"

"Just have Marcy meet me at the office at seven."

"Gotcha covered," said the man and hung up.

Walter held the receiver in his hand and observed his daughters through the restaurant window. Thea was tormenting her baby sister, using her long spindly arm to dangle the last french fry above her mouth, catching drizzles of ketchup with her tongue. Reenie solved this problem by jumping up on the table to snatch the prize.

Forget Somerset, Ohio thought Walt. Let's just settle here,

wherever we are. Northern Indiana somewhere. The people huddled around the white tables on the yellow chairs looked like solid down-to-earth folks. They would make good neighbors. People he could talk and joke with on a daily basis. Because the rest of the world had obviously gone berserk.

Chapter 45

Robert Samuelson felt so inordinately proud of himself when he arrived home in Chicago that he went directly to the Johnston and Murphy store on Michigan Avenue and spent a fifteen hundred dollars on three pairs of shoes. A pair of cordovan loafers with black tassels, a pair of cap-toed Spanish leather oxfords and a pair of handmade black wingtips with a cushioned insole and latticed leather uppers that allowed the foot to breathe. He had earned his keep.

His little chat with the Cook County State's Attorney had torpedoed Powell County's case. Yes, the defendant had been apprehended at the scene in possession of an unregistered firearm, had admitted to visiting the victim the night before his death and giving him ten thousand dollars and, according to the local authorities, the defendant had not contacted them at any time prior to his arrest. No wonder the Powell County District Attorney half-slept through the bail review hearing. He had big city rich boy Walt Sumner dead to rights.

Save for one minor detail. The key to all cases of premeditated homicide. Motivation. Why would a multi-millionaire risk a murder rap to recover ten thousand bucks?

'Because Clovis Ward had knowledge of Walter Sumner's

involvement in the murders of his wife and mother and the ten grand was hush money.'

Howsomever, dear Mister DA, crusty old Judge Macallan here has ruled the blackmail theory unfairly prejudicial since the defendant has not been charged in the murders of his wife and mother!

Fifth Avenue Bob was happily composing headlines—*Brilliant Barrister Works His Magic* in the Trib, *Silk Suited Shyster Slickers Hayseeds* in the *Sun-Times*—when he arrived at his turreted office on Lakeshore Drive. Those stuffed shirts at the Columbia Law Review might even feel compelled to give a brassy old alum some ink. Then Robert Samuelson saw the phone message chit his secretary had left on his desk. From the Door County District Attorney. The Urgent box was triple checked.

Marcy was waiting in the foyer of Sumner International, bright-eyed and bushy-tailed. Walter introduced her to his daughters. She shook their hands formally and said she was very pleased to meet them. In Walt's experience there were two types of women. Those who preferred cats and those who preferred children. Marcy, like his mother, unlike his wife, was a woman who preferred cats.

"Go bug those guys," said Walt to the girls, pointing them toward the graveyard crew on the trading floor. "Tell 'em you're the boss' daughters. They'll like that." Reenie tore off, Thea slowfooted after her with eye-rolling forbearance. Marcy followed Walt to his office.

Walter seated himself on the couch by the window. Marcy remained standing. "I was surprised to find you were at home when I called this afternoon," he said. "Are you ill?"

"Mentally, yes. Physically, no."

"What else is new?"

The Violin Player

Marcy balled her fists at her side and seemed to gather herself to say something. Then she took two quick steps and sat down on the far side of the couch, her right knee pumping like a piston.

"Has Jeffrey Lezak elbowed you aside in my absence?" She did not respond. "I'm sorry, Marcy. I should never have put you in this position."

Marcy burst into tears. Walt moved to comfort her but she leapt to her feet, produced a tissue from somewhere, dabbed, sniffled and said, "There. Now I'm better. What did you want to see me about?"

Walt gave her a moment. "I need your technical expertise. I need to know if my cell phone calls could have been monitored."

"Anything that's broadcast can be monitored."

"So cell phone calls aren't encrypted, scrambled in some way?"

"Digital ones are," said Marcy. "But not your old diesel-powered piece of shit."

"Could my cell calls have been intercepted? Rerouted to a different number without my knowledge?"

Marcy said, "Hmmm. Well, the thing about cell phones that ungeeks don't get is that they're really computer terminals. Computer terminals connected to this humongo network. They can be programmed to do all kinds of stuff."

"Such as reroute numbers?" said Walt.

"Such as link to your PC and track other users as they move from cell to cell. Send a signal that turns your phone on when another user makes a call. You can even…no, that wouldn't work…well, anything's possible with phone phreaks but I don't see how…unless…Got your cell phone with you?" Walt handed it over.

"I'll need a screwdriver," said Marcy, walking off.

"But we're on a roll!" said Jeffrey Lezak when Walt Sumner told him to bank the balance when the current contracts cleared. "We've turned around the whole year in the last three weeks!"

"A job well done, Jeffrey. Which your bonus will reflect. But I need to keep all my personal options open."

Walt girded himself for another outburst. Jeffrey's reply was soft spoken. "If I may adventure an opinion here, sir, I think you might be putting your carts before the horse. You're concerned, no question, you're concerned about legal matters impending before the courts. You're taking steps. *My* concern is that by taking money off the table right about now we'd be flying the pink flag to our vendors, our customers and our competition."

Jeffrey continued. "I didn't have the privilege of making the acquaintance of your grandfather, Mr. Sumner. But from the scuttlebutt I've heard around town he was one tough stand-up s.o.b. with no quit in him."

Walter was surprised that Jeffrey was aware of, much less had formed an opinion about, Henry Sumner Sr. "And you think that I'm betraying the legacy of my grandfather by, what was it, *flying the pink flag?*"

Jeffrey Lezak ignored the sarcasm. Or didn't recognize it. "I think he would say for you to keep doin' it right if it takes all night. And don't let the bastards get you down."

Walter looked his operations manager up and down. Granddad would have liked this guy. Might even have seen himself reflected in the naked ambition, relentless drive and the complete breathtaking absence of self-doubt. Walter, who had walked into the office this evening intending to fire him, said, "That, Jeffrey, is exactly what my grandfather would have said."

"So can we—"

The Violin Player

"Yes."

"Awright!"

Walt climbed to his feet. "Just stay within the parameters of the system."

He wandered off to find Marcy, his last words ringing hollowly in his ears. The risk management system he had toiled for so many years to perfect was obsolete. There was an x factor in today's market that he couldn't quantify. It was time to get out.

"*Ta da*," said Marcy, standing in the corridor outside her office. She was holding something aloft between her thumb and forefinger.

"What is it?" asked Walt.

"A retransmitter. And don't look in there," she said, closing the door on the chaos of her office.

"What does it do?"

"It acts as a relay. I'm not the world's leading expert on this stuff but I believe it can be programmed to rebroadcast the original signal in specific numerical sequences using VLSI circuitry."

"In English please, Marcy."

"You dial one number on your cell phone and Senor Module, " Marcy waggled the tiny component back and forth— "*steals* the signal and *re-routes* it to another number."

Walt cast his mind back, to his call to the cops as he was speeding down the highway towards Snow Creek Road. It made sense. There was no other explanation. His phone had been programmed to dial another number if and when Walter dialed 911. The dimwit dispatcher with the good ole boy accent had been his homicidal half-brother. "So you found this thing inside my cell phone, correct?"

Marcy met his gaze with pupils so dilated they squeezed her irises into rims. "Yes sir, I did!"

"Let me see it." Marcy fumbled the hand off. Walt bent down

and picked it up. "Could this thing have the number, the *re-routed* number still inside it?"

"Sure," said Marcy. "Unless it was programmed to erase itself once it was activated."

Of course, thought Walt. Mister Scary Smart wouldn't make it that easy. Marcy appeared anxious to go, knotting her fingers and twisting her feet. "Are you okay, Marcy?"

"Absolutely!" she said, her clogs punishing the carpet fiber. "Why would you ask that?"

"You seem…wound up."

"Double espressos have that effect on me," she said breezily.

"How's Twyla doing?"

"Well, she's an ancient Egyptian goddess living amongst peons. We're doing the best we can."

"We?"

"My roommate. You talked to him."

"Yes. Strange fellow."

Marcy smiled with the left half of her face. "Roommates always are."

Walt wanted to ask her more questions. Are you involved with this guy? Does he abuse you? Are you on drugs? But he didn't believe he would get a straight answer. It was an odd feeling to feel about someone you trusted without reservation. There was one question he had to ask. "Marcy, do you have any idea how this module came to be inside my cell phone?"

Marcy staggered as if she'd just been slapped, her face drawn in horror. "Ye gods, no, what a question, *no*, of course not, I can't believe you'd…no, no, no, a thousand times no!"

Walt wanted to believe her. It was a convincing performance, spontaneous and heartfelt. His Nokia handheld spent most of its

The Violin Player

time in the console of his XJR. Henry Ward could have gotten his hands on it any number of times. "It's all right Marcy," said Walt. "I believe you."

Marcy shot forward and gave Walt a quick embrace. Her sweat smelled feral.

Chapter 46

Life plops such ripe plums on your plate when you least expect them. Me, kicking the cat around the crackerbox, pondering the imponderables when, *egads*! shithead materializes from the ether. Awright, awright. I *admit* my legendary impulse control betrayed me momentarily. I shun't of called attention to myself by jookin' him. That was not the proper thing to do under the circumstances. But I do *so* weary of being perfectly proper at all times. It's important to kick up your heels once in a while!

I'm feeling guilty, can you tell?

For such a wussypie he has a very manly voice, my dear half brother. I almost felt sorry for him, trying *so hard* to sound in control. I knew a crazed cokehead, dipsomaniac, pill-popping club musician name of Woodrow who could do that *with authority*. The more his brain boiled with peach flake, peach schnapps and nembutol the purer his noun declensions, subject-verb agreement and insightful observations about life. Woodrow maintained this proud tradition until the day he died at 27 of an overdose. *And no, I didn't kill him.* Tried to save him in fact. He was a man worth saving.

I posted Clovis Ward's date of death after he died.

The Violin Player

I *stoopidly* thought that administering CPR on a barroom floor with several of our dusky brethren a-hootin' and a-hollerin' in the background would flip the switch for a young man who had ingested *wayyyyy* too much yin for his corresponding yang.

Is that cheating? Not technically. I never actually said the dates of death would be a priori.

Sad, quick, too short? *Sho nuf.* But the point is that he took *action*. He could've died a retired high school custodian. He could've been a Trappist monk and lived forever. But he wanted to leave an *ineradicable stain* on his little corner of the universe before he 'tunneled through to the new dimension' as the quantum mechanics like to say.

I performed the en vivo embalming so that the time of death would be difficult to determine, maintaining the illusion of my space-time omnipotence. I sinned in spirit. Mea culpa, mea culpa, mea maxima culpa.

So he took action.

Action is what poor and obscure people take to make themselves known to the wider world. Action is universal. There are no proper verbs.

Chapter 47

Mr. Zarmin seemed to enjoy having a cop hanging around his store. He didn't have to worry about getting robbed. And he had someone to bitch to about the government. Why should his property taxes double just because a bunch of yoopies had moved into the neighborhood? They chased out his regulars, gutted their four flats into single family homes and would rather drive five miles to Treasure Island than walk across Western Avenue for a six pack. He had tried. He had cases of Goose Island and Sierra Nevada Pale Ale turning to malt in the storeroom. And then the Wirtz cartel tacks on another twelve percent *on top* of the state's liquor tax increase. This is America?

It's Chicago, Tony Sobczak had said, listening to Mr. Zarmin's complaints with half an ear while profiling male customers for height, weight, age and facial composition. It was just like old times. A boring stakeout with a grousing partner.

Mr. Zarmin wasn't kidding about his business. After the parade of after-shift nail-slammers shambled off with their twelve packs of Old Style, Hi-Time Liquors was a tomb. The peewees on the corner of Western and Belden would send an older brother in once in

The Violin Player

a while to score a forty of malt liquor. A broken nosed local name of Pietro came in every night and counted out nine ones for a quart of paint thinner. That was about it.

And why does the state keep raising the tax on cigarettes, Mr. Zarmin wanted to know. They make three times as much on a carton as the poor shopkeeper and then all the time telling the peoples they shouldn't smoke! Then they tax their own tax hike with the sales tax! Is crazy, no?

Tony didn't disagree. There was no love lost between Tony Sobczak and the mullahs of the great bureaucracy. He had quit the department after being yanked off the street to hold the hands of a buncha widows in da Mare's neighborhood CAPS program. Tony Sobczak hadn't signed on to be a social worker.

The Budweiser clock read 5:46. The witness in question was a construction worker. He wasn't coming tonight. Mr. Zarmin brought Tupperware dishes from home that he microwaved in the back office, filling the store with the smell of curry. Tony told the shopkeeper to go have his dinner. "Then I'll hit the road."

Tony took his position behind the register. He had been at Hi-Time Liquor for four days running and had learned the prices. He used a calculator to figure change. He was atoning for his sins.

Tony Sobczak and a part timer from Irving Park Investigations had security detail on the day before Laura Sumner died. Tony had parked his van at the corner of Paulina and Bloomingdale and covered the front perimeter. The part timer parked in the alley to cover the back. Laura Sumner was sequestered inside. Tony and the part timer 10-5'ed on the radio every so often but Tony should have known better than to trust a minimum wage new hire. Or a drunk.

Tony had followed Laura Sumner to Hi-Time Liquors twice before, at two day intervals. Seen her return to her car with a plump brown bag. That was her business. It was too far from the Date of Death to be a threat. But he should have known she wouldn't change her pattern. Addicts don't change their pattern just because their life is threatened. Laura Sumner knew her keepers were out there. She would have been standing at the back window, peering through a crack in the curtains, waiting for the part timer to sneak off for a burger or fall asleep. When Tony heard about the half-drunk bottle of vodka in Door County he knew what had happened.

Shit. First guy in the door. Never failed. The subject always appeared when your partner was elsewhere. He looked Eastern European. Could be Romanian with all that black hair. He matched the height, weight, age and facial composition. But Tony needed a positive ID from Mr. Zarmin.

The man grabbed a bottle of brandy and approached the register. Tony didn't want to spook him by shouting for the owner. Think of something, genius.

The black-haired man set his bottle down on the counter. Tony squeezed out a smile. The man reached for his wallet and said, "Could be you are looking for me." He plunked down a twenty.

Tony said only, "Could be." He made change from the twenty and placed it on the counter. The man didn't reach for it. The Budweiser clock ticked off seven or eight seconds.

"I believe that you are a police officer," said the black-haired man. Tony did not respond. "I believe also that I am a witness."

"Witness to what?"

"To a thing that happened here. In this—" The man gestured at his surroundings.

"The English word is *store*."

The man smiled with bad teeth. "In Belarus we call it a *tanny krama*."

The Violin Player

A White Russian. Of course. Hoe scrapers with attitude. Conquered by Poland eighty years ago and still pissed about it. "What thing did you witness?"

"I think that you know," said the man.

Tony summoned his big voice from the base of his diaphragm. "I don't know shit about shit, Pedro. *You're* the witness. You tell me."

The man lowered his head but did not back away. After a time he looked up. "I was here, with the lady who is dead. I saw the man switch the bag with her. When he fell down."

Tony grunted. "And how'd you come to know I was looking for you?"

The man shrugged. "At my job I hear that a policeman is at the Hi-Time. On the…how do you say it?"

"Stakeout."

Again with the bad teeth. "Yes. The stake-out."

Tony squinted. This was all too easy. Third party witnesses never came forward after the fact. The Belorussian wanted something. Tony asked the sixty-four thousand dollar question. "Will you repeat what you just told me in a court of law?"

The black-haired man wig-wagged his brainbone back and forth in some sort of V pattern. Friggin' immigrants. Someone ought to teach them basic American head gestures. A nod means yes, a shake means no. Tony waited, watching him.

"I haf a problem about that," said the man.

Chapter 48

Walter Sumner and his daughters were ambushed as the XJR crept down the alley in the dark of night. The Jaguar was not designed for stealth. When he turned off the headlamps the automatic sensor turned them right back on. It wouldn't have mattered. The media had his home surrounded. A legion of cameramen swarmed in front to block the way, blinding Walter with their lights.

Walt lowered his window as he opened his garage door. The shouted questions dovetailed into one long polysyllable. Walt repeated what Fifth Avenue Bob had told him to say. "I'm sorry but I can't comment on a pending court case. Please contact my attorney."

A reporter asked Thea a question and thrust her microphone through the window. Walt gunned the engine and Thea keyed the remote control. The reporter jumped back and the cameramen scattered as the XJR shot through the lowering door, leaving the moiling rabble howling outside the castle walls.

Stepping into the dim glow of the night light stopped them cold. The kitchen mocked Laura's homey touches. All that green slate and stainless steel refused to be domesticated. "Well," said Walt heartily. "What an adventure. You guys hungry? I can heat up some soup."

The Violin Player

The girls said no thank you in subdued voices. The kitchen reminded them of their mother.

"Alrighty then. Let's get unpacked and get some lights on and get some life back in this place!"

Thea and Irene took his instructions to heart, going room to room and floor to floor, clicking on lights against the darkness. Walt watched their progress. Jeffrey Lezak was correct. The Sumner's were tough stand-up s.o.b.'s with no quit in them. It was time that Walter remembered who he was. He climbed to the fourth floor master bedroom and placed a call.

"Walter, I was just about to call you. We need to—"

"Before we get down to cases, Robert, I have a brilliant suggestion."

Fifth-Avenue Bob said that he was always open to brilliant suggestions. Walter said that he had acquired a yearbook picture of his phantom half-brother and that, rather than giving it to the cops to bury in a file drawer, he wanted to reveal the picture in an exclusive one-to-one interview with a TV reporter.

"We can show the pencil sketch too, feature that. We need to seize the initiative Robert."

"I don't disagree with you Walter."

"But—"

"Even the fish wouldn't get caught if it kept its mouth shut."

"You can prep me Robert. And you'll be present of course. At the interview."

"On camera?"

Walt had anticipated this question. Humans were so depressingly predictable. "No, Robert. Nothing looks more damning than some schmuck pleading his innocence with trembling lips while holding hands with his high priced attorney."

Robert Samuelson laughed. "We wouldn't have to hold hands."

"You'll sit right across from me Robert. We'll work out some hand signals. Hell, you can hold up cue cards!"

Samuelson manufactured another laugh. Walt knew he didn't approve. It was risky. And it took the spotlight away from Fifth Avenue Bob. Well screw him and the horse he rode in on. Walter Sumner was signing the checks.

"Do you know anyone at WGN News?"

"Y-es," said Samuelson.

"Oh and good news. My systems analyst found a switching module in my cell phone. It re-routed my call when I dialed 911 in Powell County."

"They'll say you installed it yourself."

"The module?"

"We could introduce it into evidence but a conspiracy theory's like a house of cards," said Samuelson. "You don't want to pile it up too high."

"Back up a couple of steps."

Fifth Avenue Bob assumed his lawyerly baritone. "It has been my experience that people, that is to say jury members, believe that life is basically a series of random unrelated events over which they have no control. Which is why I used the house of cards analogy. A house of cards—"

"Has no foundation just as a conspiracy theory has no foundation in the minds of the jurors," said Walter. "Got it. Which is all the more reason to *build* that foundation by introducing Henry Ward to the jury pool. Which is why I mentioned WGN. It's carried on cable in Powell County."

Walt looked up to see that Thea was unpacking his suitcase, hauling mounds of dirty laundry to the hamper, assuming the role of primary caregiver. It was a sight of such poignancy that it would have rendered him speechless under normal circumstances. But there were no longer any normal circumstances. "So why were you just about to call me?"

Robert Samuelson said, "A judge in Door County in the sovereign state of Wisconsin has issued a warrant for your arrest. The DA requests that you waive extradition and surrender yourself in Sturgeon Bay."

"Jesus H. Christ!" said Walt. "Can you stall them?"

"A day or two."

"Call your contact at WGN and set something up for tomorrow. They can ask anything they want, no preconditions."

"Walter—"

"Except one. I want the interview broadcast live, no edits. From my home."

"My God, man, they haven't done that since Edward R. Murrow. Maybe on a Sunday morning show—"

"I want it on the nightly news."

"Walter, I say again—"

"It's an *exclusive* Robert. You can swing it. Work your magic and call me back. Tonight." Robert Samuelson muttered something unintelligible and Walter hung up.

Chapter 49

An enormous craggy-faced man in a gray raincoat pinned the hydraulic door open with one arm, spilling late afternoon sun. He looked around. This has to be the guy, thought Robert Samuelson. He waved from a back booth. The man rumbled in, running his palm along the bar rail as he walked. "Tony Sobczak?"

Tony nodded and said, "You need to switch sides."

"Geez, I hope things aren't as bad as that," said Fifth Avenue Bob, smiling up at the looming figure. Tony looked down upon the attorney without expression. He pointed. "I need you to sit over there."

Robert Samuelson got up and switched sides. The red leather booth gave out a great *whoosh* as Tony Sobczak sat down facing the door. He looked around. "This used to be a two-calls-a-night hellhole."

"Really," said Samuelson. Club Lucky looked as if it had been a well-kept Italian restaurant forever, from the hammered tin ceiling down to the speckled red, black and green linoleum. "Great martinis here. What can I get you?"

"I don't drink on the job," said Tony, eyeing Samuelson's frosty

The Violin Player

Ketel One with the pinkish swirl of Chambord.

"It may look like a nancy drink but it packs a mean punch." Tony Sobczak did not reply. Robert Samuelson pushed the drink aside. "So, what have you got for me?"

"A witness," said Tony, patting the pockets of his raincoat. "A witness who was in line to buy booze at Hi-Time Liquors on Western." Tony dredged up an empty cigarette pack and crumpled it. "A witness who says he saw a man matching the description of our suspect fall to the ground and knock the bagged purchase of the customer at the head of the line to the floor." Tony patted his shirt and pants pockets. "The customer had just purchased a fifth of hundred proof vodka. Witness 1 clearly witnessed Suspect 1 switch bags with the customer without her knowledge." Tony turned to the young woman behind the bar. "You got any Old Golds?"

"Excuse me?" she said.

"Old Gold cigarettes." Tony prowed his chin toward the wooden cigarette box on the wall by the front window. *For a treat, Old Gold.*

"Oh, that's an antique," said the barkeep cheerily. "I've got Marlboros."

Fifth Avenue Bob said, "And the customer at the head of the line was Laura Sumner?"

"Vic-1. Both the witness and the owner ID'ed her. She was a regular."

"Did anyone else see this switch get made?"

"Don't know. Doubt it."

"The owner?"

"He was at the register. S-1 was on the floor."

Robert Samuelson jabbed a thumb under his cheekbone and worked it into his jaw muscle. This was entirely too good to be true. "I take it there's a problem."

293

"You got any gum?" said Tony Sobczak.

"I've got some Tic-Tacs." Tony nodded. Samuelson handed him the pack.

"He's an illegal immigrant from Belarus. Wants a green card before he testifies." Tony emptied the pack into his palm.

"Tough shit," said Samuelson. "We'll subpoena him." Tony tossed the Tic-tacs into his mouth and crunched them contemplatively. "You promise anything?"

Tony shook his head. When he opened his mouth to speak his teeth were green. "He lost his wife and kid back there. He's not interested in going back."

"Political persecution?" said Samuelson.

"Chernobyl," said Tony. "We sub him without a green card and the INS deports him no matter what he says."

Robert Samuelson cursed long and colorfully. Tony Sobczak chewed and swallowed. "You know anyone?" said Samuelson.

"I got a guy," said Tony.

A large party stepped down from the dining room and tripped past, talking and laughing. An elderly woman stopped at a glass bowl filled with after dinner mints. She spooned several into a cocktail napkin, wrapped them up and placed the napkin in her purse. Samuelson waited until she shuffled off.

"How much?"

"I'll let you know," said Tony, standing up.

Tony Sobczak ran his hand along the wooden bar rail again on the way out. He stopped and poked a thick finger at something and grunted in satisfaction. He left without a backward look, the spring-loaded door scissoring to a close behind him. Robert Samuelson walked over to the bar and looked to see. There was a cylindrical notch in the varnished wood. A bullet hole.

Chapter 50

Walt felt a bead of sweat slither down the thick orange makeup on his forehead and dangle from his eyebrow. It evaporated in the heat of the spot lamps. The sound tech wouldn't allow him to open the windows. The fire in the fireplace had been a mistake.

Irene kicked her patent leather mary janes in delight as the makeup girl sponged her face with foundation. Thea had dressed her baby sister in a plaid jumper and a Peter Pan collar blouse and brushed her hair till it shone like a new penny. She looked perfect.

Thea edged into the living room. She wore a knee-length navy blue dress, blue and gold cloisonne earrings and had her hair pulled back severely from her face. She looked like an investment banker.

"You look beautiful, snowflake. So grown up," said Walt. "But let's loosen your hair up a little—"

"Daddy *don't!*"

The room got quiet. WGN reporter Matarina Jones, who was huddled with Fifth Avenue Bob, craned her swanlike neck to see. Thea turned on her heel and stalked off. Walt followed her, ears burning, hearing what they all were thinking. *Figures,* the accused killer's also a child abuser.

John Knoerle

Thea ran into the bathroom. Walt stopped the door with his foot. She leaned against the sink and hugged herself and stared at the floor. Walt's anger left him. Thea had a serious case of stage fright. Come to that, so did her father.

"Scary huh?" Thea gave him a tiny nod. Walt searched his memory for a high-minded quote, something inspirational about overcoming obstacles. But all that came to mind was one of Granddad's crude epigrams. "All those people out there, all those strangers might seem intimidating but they don't know us do they? They don't know our family. In fact," said Walter, "they don't know shit from apple butter."

Thea giggled. Her father never used bad language. Walt smiled and said, "You'd look prettier with your hair down."

"They've been teasing this thing since the top of the hour," said Chrissie.

"They said it was coming up next."

"They've been saying that for thirty minutes."

"No," replied Kay patiently. "They said 'coming up' before. This last break they said 'coming up next'."

Chrissie stood up, hitched at her pantyhose and sat down. "God this is nervewracking."

"Here we go," said Kay as the WGN anchorman introduced the segment. The Sumner sisters watched the artful crossfade to Walter and the girls seated on the hearth in a firelit tableaux. "Ohhh," said Kay. "They look like a Christmas card."

"They look hot," said Chrissie.

Walter introduced himself. The girls introduced themselves and gave their ages, their grade and the name of their school. They all

The Violin Player

stood up and the girls filed out.

"Touch them Walter," said Kay. Walter smoothed Thea's long hair as she passed. "Good," said Kay. "That's good."

Walter took a seat on the white couch across from the reporter in the Queen Anne chair.

"How is your business, Mr. Sumner?" said the poised and elegant black lady.

"Quite good at the moment," said Walter, smiling at the camera. The red light blinked off. He could hear the camera behind him whir.

Matarina Jones looked plumb puzzled at this comment, knitting her brow, checking her notes, tapping a pencil on her legal pad. "I ask because Bank One reports that, as of two weeks ago, your company's credit line was maxed out."

"Well—"

Matarina Jones wasn't finished. The camera behind Walt continued to whir. "That was just prior to your wife's death."

The sound tech shook his head violently as Walt readjusted his tie, disturbing the lavaliere mike. Walter blinked sweat from his eyes and ignored Matarina Jones' crooked eyebrow and his attorney's gesticulations and addressed himself directly to the dispassionate convex eye.

"Why doesn't he say something?" asked Chrissie. Walter's face filled the screen. "He's crying!"

"He's sweating," said Kay.

"I grew up in a perfect family," said Walter to the camera. "Or so I thought. As it turns out my grandfather mistreated his employees.

And my father, God rest his soul, impregnated a young girl. His cousin."

"*Cousin?*" said Chrissie.

"Be *quiet*," said Kay.

"You're not answering my question, Mister Sumner," said Matarina Jones.

"You didn't ask a question, you made a statement," replied Walter. The camera whirred. Walter took his time. "I did not kill my mother. I did not kill my wife. I did not kill Clovis Ward. But I know who did. His name is Henry Ward. He's my father's illegitimate son." The camera continued to whir. Matarina Jones cleared her throat noisily. The red light blinked off.

"And you know this how?" she said.

Walter had thought long and hard about how to answer this question. He was surprised he had to answer it at all. The media had yet to pounce on the terror in cyberspace angle. Didn't they know about it? Didn't they have informants and confidential sources?

"I know this because both my mother's and my wife's dates of death were posted on our family GenealoG webpage before they died," said Walter, unveiling the secret he had fought to keep, opening the door to copycat postings, cutting the cord to his homicidal half brother.

"You didn't tell me this?" said Chrissie. "How could you not tell me this?"

Kay did not reply. Walter and the reporter were arguing back and forth, something about a line of credit. The perspective shifted. A

The Violin Player

broader camera angle that showed both combatants. Walter, "You agreed to show the picture." Matarina Jones, throwing up her hands. "Fine."

A camera zoomed in on an easel that held an open book. A black and white photo came woozily into focus. A young runner bursting through tape at the finish line.

"That's him?" said Chrissie. "That's our *brother*?"

"I guess so," said Kay.

She hadn't seen the picture before. And didn't see the point of showing it now. No one in the viewing audience would recognize Henry Ward from a thirty year old photograph. And the image was anything but sinister. The skinny boy bursting through the tape had his arms outstretched and his face upturned. The camera zoomed in for a massive close-up. Henry Ward's expression was pure joy.

Walter felt his opportunity slipping away. Matarina Jones was not keeping to his timetable. He had accused his half brother of murder. She was supposed to ask him follow-up questions, which would lead Walter to recount his investigation, which would lead to an opening for Walter to reveal the pencil sketch of Henry Ward.

But Matarina Jones kept hammering away at the drawdown in Sumner International's line of credit. She wanted to make the most of the new nugget of information she had unearthed despite Walter's repeated assurance that it meant nothing.

Matarina Jones put a finger to her chin, smiled and said, "Why would this Henry Ward person want to harm your family?" Fifth Avenue Bob nodded his encouragement. Go for it.

"I assume he feels he was treated shabbily by my family," said Walter to the camera. "Which he was. My father abandoned him to a life of poverty, though he did provide some covert financial support." Walt addressed himself to Matarina Jones. In repose her face looked glum, morose. "My father was a busy man. Growing up I barely saw him except on weekends. But I always knew that he loved me. And, what may be even more important for a young boy, I knew that he was proud of me. Henry Ward never knew any such thing."

"It's possible he's watching this interview," said Matarina Jones. "Is there anything you would like to say to him?"

"Stop killing members of my family," said Walter.

"No apology on behalf of your family?"

"Henry Ward murdered my mother and my wife. I don't believe an apology is appropriate."

Robert Samuelson shook his fingers as if they'd just been singed. Walter Sumner didn't get this game. Matarina Jones had served up a softball question. Wasn't he supposed to park it in the upper decks? The rhythmic pulsing of her temples said no he was not. Walter braced himself for a high hard one, amazed that he had been able to think these thoughts in the few seconds it took Matarina Jones to glare at him. Time slowed down when you were broadcast live.

"What lessons have you learned from this ordeal?" said Matarina Jones, nice as pie.

Clever, thought Walt. Not a beanball but a slider just off the plate. He asked a question to buy time. "Can my daughters join me? I'd like them to hear this."

Walt called out their names before the reporter could respond. The girls peeped around the hall corner. Walt waved them over and they sat on either side of him on the plump white couch. A boom mike operator took up a position behind them.

"I don't know how to answer your question, Matarina," said

The Violin Player

Walt. "Except to say that, before this happened, I considered myself a good family man. I was faithful to my wife, I provided for my family and I attended all my daughter's dance recitals and soccer matches."

Thea swacked her father on the arm.

Walt grinned. "Almost all. But I didn't know the first thing about the importance of family." Walt paused to let the camera creep closer. "Not until now."

Matarina Jones gave Walter a small and very elegant nod. Fifth Avenue Bob gave him two thumbs up. But Walter wasn't through. He plucked the pencil sketch of his homicidal half brother from between the cushions of the couch and held it up to the camera with both hands. "I guess in some sick and twisted way I have this man to thank for that."

Chrissie screwed up her face and said, "Why are psychos always skinny, you ever notice that? The Psycho Killer Diet, there's a best seller for you."

Kay mumbled something in reply. The pencil sketch on the TV screen filled in a blank that Kay had noticed growing up. Walter resembled Granddad in his thick-necked stolidity. Chrissie was her mother's clone. Kay took after poor forgotten Grandma Sumner. But not a one of them looked like their handsome father. Not really. But the thin-faced man in the pencil sketch had Henry Jr. stamped all over him, right down to the furrowed smirk line at the corner of his mouth.

"Aren't the kids of cousins supposed to be retards?" said Chrissie. "How could a retard do all this—?"

Kay shushed her sister. The interview had concluded. The WGN anchorman was saying something about further developments. The station cut to an outdoor shot, a familiar ebony inlaid door. It was bathed in white light. The door opened. Walter Sumner stepped out and squinted, his hands manacled behind his back.

Chapter 51

For the life of me I don't understand why all you habitual TV watchers constantly complain that *THERE'S NOTHING ON*. In the preceding half hour I have enjoyed *The African-American Roundtable* with a group of middle-aged black folks whose dashikis and canary yellow headdresses could not camouflage the implacable faceplates they'd developed after many soul-stultifying years as paper shufflers at the Triple A and conductors on the Metra honkie hauler to the northern suburbs; a public access program entitled VEGAN *FOR LIFE!* that ought to be mandatory viewing for patrons of Chicago's many fabled steakhouses featuring, as it did, full color photos of the lower intestines of meat-eating dead people with impacted bowels; and, oh yes, an interview on WGN.

Weeellllll now, ladies and germs. Well now indeed and couldda knocked me over with a feather! Family secrets flung open like a *Hustler* centerfold. I expected better of you, my dear half brother. You said yourself that family was all-important.

I do understand and appreciate your choice of words. I *do*. Your father's *first* son would have been preferable to your father's *illegitimate* son but at least you didn't use the '*b*' word. And that question about an apology? *Give me a fat fucking break!!* You were right. We are *decades* past an apology.

The character sketch? Didn't look a thing like me. Besides, I am *wayyyyyy* off the grid. I was born at a baby farm in the Ozarks, so my dear mama sez. *No birth certificate was ever issued*. Hence no social security number and hence no draft board call to go kill slopes in Southeast Asia. I have always enjoyed my non-existence.

Exposing my little Date of Death *billets doux* at GenealoG.com? Bound to happen.

So what, you might ask, am I so *ferociously hauled up about that I can barely see straight?*

Picture this. A nodule, a piece of cartilage, a chicken knuckle that the garbage disposal keeps spitting back no matter how many times you grind it. I know I said before that I wanted to travel back in time. *But, brace yourself, I lied*! Not there. Most assertatatively *not* there.

Still muddy? Here's a better analogy: The Big Bang proudly unfurled four lovely dimensions for all to see. Height, width, depth and time. But there are, allegedly, other curled-up spatial dimensions. Other 'resonant vibrational string patterns' having themselves a hellacious good time out of view of adult supervision cuz they're so danged hard to see, *a hundred billion billion times smaller than a nucleus*.

So here's the question: Why do the seriously misguided new generation of physicists assume that *time* is the wallflower at this brannigan? The shy kid wedged in the corner watching the other dimensions spherically gyrate on the universal dance floor? Why should muons, taus and quarks have all the fun? Why not a parallel dimension of curled up *time*, spinning round and round, returning to the same previous place again and again and again and again and again?

The Violin Player

Which pretty much describes my life to a T.

A tip of the Hatlo hat to you, my dear half-brother, for tracking down the one public photograph of myself in all the world. Took me a second to recognize who it was. *I was so happy then.* But that caption. *Tanto yerro*! Ixnay on the *Aptioncay*! They saw it. WGN is the flagship station of Tribune Broadcasting, carried by some 12,000 cable providers in forty-nine states. They saw it. It was legible. Henry "*Three Locks*" Ward, *doing what he does best*. It is now captured on videotape. It will soon be digitized and will then spin around and around and around the ethernet forever and pitch me back, most unwilling and unfortunately, to the same, previous, time.

Did you do this on *purpose*, my dear half-brother? Did you use your ill-gotten wealth and power to ransack my miserable youth and re-broadcast my shame and humiliation for the prurient pleasure of my big-assed, corn-fed tormentors? If you did know, you shouldn't have. If you didn't know, you should have.

So-no-mo', bro. No more frolicsome parlor tricks, no more Mr. Nice Guy.

The game, she is over.

Chapter 52

"I thought you hated the media with a passion?" said Walter from the back seat of the unmarked car.

"I do," said Detective Bjork. Detective Hernandez was riding shotgun. His job was to blast the thousand watt alley light at the betacams whenever a news van pulled up alongside as they headed north on Lake Shore Drive. "And you can bet your ass that Matarina Jones hates me back. Now that she's a cop whore." Bjork goosed the siren at a slow moving car in the number one lane. The driver signaled and changed lanes. "She wanted details of our investigation. I asked why and pressed it. She told me about your interview. Time, date and place."

"So you felt the need to fill her in," said Walt.

"Yeah," said Bjork, checking the rear view mirror. "I felt the need." Hernandez laughed.

Walter said, "It was my understanding that my attorney and the Door County DA were working something out."

"Guess the DA changed his mind," said Bjork.

Walt got the picture. Bjork had called the Door County DA to inform him that his suspect was stalling so that he could make his

The Violin Player

case on national television. The warrant for the arrest of Walter Sumner in the death of Laura Sumner would not have been long in coming.

"And explain again about my daughters." The unmarked car cut across three lanes of traffic as Lake Shore Drive curved west at Devon. Horns blared as the caravan of news vans followed.

Detective Hernandez said, "The DCFS matron will remain with them at the house until one of your sisters can be contacted."

Sisters, thought Walt. Where were his sisters? Why hadn't he told them about the interview? That's right, he had. They had seen his arrest broadcast live. They would be racing towards the intersection of Paulina and Bloomingdale at this very moment.

"And what happens if my sisters don't show up?"

Detective Hernandez sighed and rubbed his head. "Then your daughters will be taken to DCFS headquarters where they will be held overnight."

"A nice place is it? DCFS headquarters?" said Walter. Thea had been remarkably stoic when Bjork and Hernandez marched upstairs and took her father into custody. She was steeled up and ready for anything. But Reenie had freaked out.

"Not really," said Bjork.

Walt paused to clear his throat. "Then you had better pray to God, Detective Bjork, that my sisters show up."

Chapter 53

Thea hugged Reenie and Reenie hugged Thea. Reenie didn't mind. Reenie would hug anything. Reenie would hug a big slobbery dog at the dog run at Walsh Park until the dog growled and the owner came running. Reenie was a touchy feely kind of girl.

It was dark. Black dark. They had night lights in every room at home. And in the hallways and on the stairs. They came on automatically when the sun went down. When it was yucky out sometimes the night lights would snicker on and off as the clouds passed by. It was never this dark at home.

Ooomph! Oh great. Oh cool. Reenie hadn't cried the whole time. She's pretty brave, Reenie is. But Thea could have told them what would happen if Reenie went on a car trip without taking a pit stop. She would pee her pants at the first bump in the road.

Reenie cried a little and tried to say something behind the green tape that covered her mouth. Her voice came out her nose. Thea made noises out her nose too and squeezed her arms tighter around her baby sister.

The Violin Player

The tangible prospect of a life in prison had not previously occurred to him. Not until the jailer closed the iron door and Walter Sumner turned around to survey his four by eight foot greenish yellow isolation cell. There were no windows and no bars. Just a peep slot in the iron door and a wider food tray slot further down. The light bulb in the ceiling was recessed and covered by plexiglass. The steel toilet reminded him of an Asian squat hole. No seat. Walter attempted to fight his sense of black despair with righteous indignation but failed to summon any. What good was anger in the present circumstance?

He scanned the graffiti etched walls to see gang tags and a detailed depiction of female genitalia. And two complete sentences. Someone had a sense of humor. Someone with an education and a lot of time on his hands. *Do not tip staff. Gratuities are included in cost of service.*

Funny. Walter spread out the rolled-up mattress and struggled to make himself comfortable on a steel mesh cot even shorter than the one in Powell County. If he ever awoke from this nightmare he would go out and buy himself one of those absurdly expensive Swedish mattresses that Laura had tried to talk him into. Four times the number of springs as a conventional bed, three different spring modules, three different support zones for your shoulders, torso and legs. They *had* been amazingly comfortable. And they could afford it. Five thousand dollars was a small price to pay to make your wife happy. But stodgy old Walt Sumner had said no.

Walter wallowed in sorrow and contrition for another thirty seconds before he shook himself like a wet dog and set to work.

The question he had never answered was this. Why was Henry Ward lashing out now? Jarlene said that Henry had known the identity of his father since childhood. She said Henry Jr. had not provided her with financial support for many years. Yet Dad had continued to write substantial checks to cash until the day he died. No doubt extortion payments to his illegitimate offspring. But there was a much bigger prize at stake. Granddad's trust.

Walter had re-read the instrument. The trust had not specified the remaindermen by name. The twelve million dollars was to pass *in stirpes* to direct issue. Granddad knew about bastard Henry, could have excluded him. But bastard Henry was a blood Sumner so bastard Henry was in the trust.

However, the trust had a codicil that was added later, shortly before Granddad's death. His signature had been very shaky. The codicil granted either Henry Sumner Jr. or Virginia Sumner, whichever was the last surviving, the power of special appointment for the payment, transfer and distribution of the trust estate. This was almost certainly Mother's doing. She knew she would outlive her husband. And she knew her husband had been giving money to his bastard son. Virginia's last will and testament stipulated that proceeds from the trust go to her issue exclusively.

Walter was supposed to meet with his mother on the night she died. She had wanted to discuss her finances. Walter hadn't understood why at the time but knew better now. Her finances were a mess. She called later to re-schedule, citing a conflict. She called again the afternoon before her death and left a message. Her charity board meeting had been postponed and could he still come on short notice? That was why Walter was on the phone to his mother when her heart exploded. To tell her that he was tired and that Laura already had dinner on the stove.

Henry must have known about their scheduled meeting somehow. That's why he planned Virginia's death when he did. He didn't know the meeting had been postponed. That eliminated a phone

The Violin Player

tap. Mother didn't keep a calendar in the ordinary sense. The house on Hamilton was her calendar. She left herself sticky notes on the roll-top, on the bathroom mirror, on the clock of the Tappan range. Wherever she happened to be when the appointment was made. Henry must have seen a sticky note and planned accordingly. How? What was Henry Ward doing inside the house on Hamilton?

If he had come to shake down Virginia it would have been five years earlier, after Dad died. And Virginia would have laughed in his face. Was he searching for a copy of the trust? Mom kept a copy in the roll-top desk. If he found it he would have seen the codicil. What an emotional roller coaster that would have been. From Sumner family heir back to unacknowledged nonperson in one dispassionate compound sentence.

Payback? If Henry Ward wanted revenge he could have killed Virginia and gotten away with it. Hell, he already *had*. The initial corner's report ruled that she died of natural causes. Without the premature date of death posting that would have been that.

Walter had listened to a lot of country and western music on his travels through the lower Midwest. There was one bit of deep-voiced lyric that stuck with him. Something about being crazy but not insane.

Henry Ward had systematically blackmailed Dad for many years. He had devised an elaborate scheme to implicate Walter in the death of Virginia. When Walt called his mother instead of visiting her on the appointed date Henry simply built a better mousetrap. When Door County didn't pay immediate dividends he did it again in Clay City.

But Henry Ward had not kept within the parameters on that one. He had no compelling reason to kill Clovis Ward. Clovis revealing the whereabouts of Jarlene Ward didn't put Henry in any jeopardy.

And Walter would be charged with the murder of his wife once the autopsy results came in. Killing Clovis Ward had been pure hubris, crazy but not insane. Like planting the clues in the Sumner Cemetery. Just showing off. And in so doing Henry Ward had let the mask slip ever so slightly.

Both Laura and Agent O'Connor had tried to convince Walt that his half brother was a raging psychopath. But there was a telling detail at the crime scene that didn't jibe with that diagnosis. The little button pinned to Clovis Ward's brown and blue print polyester shirt. The saying Walt had seen on tourist town t-shirts. *I only do what the voices tell me.*

Too cute by half.

Self-referential irony was something Walter knew well from the younger generation at work. They used it to hold themselves above the plodding reality of their day to day. Walter found it reassuring that his half brother was also a practitioner. Irony was a weak person's defense mechanism. Irony never won a war.

Walt sat up at the metallic ka-*chung* of a slamming iron door. He was being held in the basement of the Evanston PD headquarters on Elmwood. He had been afforded no phone call, issued no jumpsuit. Just made to surrender his valuables, belt and shoelaces and locked away in his pinstripe suit. Fifth Avenue Bob would track him down. He wouldn't fall for that 'Sorry, we lost his paperwork' line that they always used on TV cop shows. He would show up soon. Walter lay back down on the steel mesh cot.

So. Kay would keep the girls snug and safe at home tomorrow. She would keep their hands and minds busy to the point of exhaustion. Tony Sobczak would guard the perimeter. So.

Why was he lashing out now? Henry Ward had not killed his father, their father, anymore than he would have strangled the gold-

The Violin Player

en goose. But Henry Jr. had been dead almost five years. A long time for Henry to do without that money from home. Once Virginia refused to continue the extortion payments Henry would not have waited five years to investigate the trust. He would have searched the house on Hamilton until he found it. And the codicil.

What, then? How did Henry Ward know about Walt's scheduled meeting with his mother and why did he do what he did about it?

Henry Ward. Wrong name, Walter. Your homicidal half brother thinks his rightful name is *Henry Sumner III*. And what does a proud scion of the Sumner dynasty aspire to do? Emulate his forebears. Make his own way in the world. Turn a profit.

How? What scheme had he been hatching these last five years? How did framing Walter Sumner for the murder of his mother do Henry Ward any good at all?

Thea thought Reenie was losing it big time. She did this little whoop shriek every time they hit a pothole which was a lot. They were in a not so good part of town now. Lots of holes in the road and lots of sirens going by. They had seen a movie about this on the Lifetime channel that Mom used to watch when Dad was coming home late and would always end up crying. At the movie, not Dad.

This woman was kidnapped, *wife*napped by her abusive husband who punched her out and threw her in the trunk. The woman woke up and listened for sounds about where they were going and she heard a bell at a train crossing and called 911 on her super teeny cell phone that she had stuck in her bra. But that was on TV.

Thea tried to shush her sister through the green tape. They were having a fight in the front of the car. The same loud swear words over and over. Thea and Reenie, bound together, rolled into the spare tire when the car stopped all of a sudden and bumped against something hard. Maybe it was the curb. The man was wearing the woman's hair when he opened up the trunk. The man they had played basketball with at Walsh Park.

His voice was soft, kidding like. "Pardon all the sturm und drang, liebchens. Just a little domestic dispute." The man had a big shiny knife in his hand. "My point is simply that one is even better than two." He leaned his face in to look at them. "So who's it going to be?"

Reenie cried herself into hiccups.

54

Walt was asleep on his back with his forearm across his eyes when the iron door opened. Had Fifth Avenue Bob tracked him down? Someone kicked his cot and told him to get up. Walt blinked two slender figures into focus. Detective Bjork and someone else behind. A woman.

"*Up* asshole," said Bjork. "Your lady friend wants to talk to you." Bjork's blue-white cheeks were singed with pink. Walt sat up. Bjork turned to the woman and said, "This is goddamned stupid and against regs."

"So you've said," said Agent O'Connor. Bjork muttered a four letter word for female and slammed the slam lock door behind him. Agent O'Connor withdrew an extra large coffee from a Starbucks bag and said, "Charming gentleman." Walt hobbled to the sink and splashed cold water on his face.

When Walt turned around she was seated on one end of the cot. Two extra large lattes, stirring sticks and several packets of sugar and sweet'n'low sat on the Starbucks bag that she had smoothed out to act as a serving tray. Agent O'Connor patted her hand on the cot and gave him her happy homemaker smile. Cheeks up, chin down. Walt bit his lip to make sure he wasn't dreaming.

"The Cook County State's Attorney wants to see my complete report this morning."

Walt remained standing. Cook County?

"Don't you want your coffee?"

"Not right now," said Walter. He didn't need it. He was suddenly, clangingly, awake.

"You really stirred it up with your performance on television last night."

"It wasn't a 'performance'."

Agent O'Connor didn't bother to contradict him. "This morning's *Tribune* has an editorial questioning the...how did they put it...the *suitability* of giving the celebrity treatment to an accused murderer. The tableaux in front of the fireplace, the use of your daughters."

The Tribune Corporation owned WGN. The corporate parent was scolding its own child in print. "What does this have to do with my extradition hearing?"

"Sugar?"

"No thanks." Walt accepted the coffee that Agent O'Connor held out to him.

"The State's Attorney didn't take me into his confidence."

Walt took a sip, inhaled the sweetly bitter taste and said, "Guess."

"Well—" said Agent O'Connor. "I don't think you're going to Wisconsin anytime soon. The state with physical custody of the suspect has priority."

"But Cook County has no case!"

"It doesn't much matter to the State's Attorney at this point. You forced his hand."

The Violin Player

One step forward and two steps back, thought Walt. His attempt to seize the initiative had come back to bite him. Robert Samuelson had talked Powell County into granting bail. Cook County wouldn't make the same mistake. The only thing Walt knew for certain about high profile court cases was that they took forever. Even if he were acquitted in all three jurisdictions he could be held without bond till his daughters were in high school. Walter braced himself against the steel sink.

"I've developed a theory that explains everything."

Agent O'Connor lapped at her milk foam mustache with a curled pink tongue. "I'm all ears."

The cell floor was damp. Walt sat down on the cot to put on his shoes and heard himself speaking. Explaining about the scheduled meeting with his mother, the codicil in the trust, how Henry Ward was crazy but not insane, how Henry Ward's motive was nothing more demented than gathering a tidy nest egg for his golden years. "You said once that 'this guy's plugged into you'. Remember?"

Agent O'Connor nodded.

"He knew where I went for coffee, he knew my company's credit card number, etcetera, etcetera. Well, I think I know who the plug is." Agent O'Connor raised her eyebrows, furrowing her brow. "My operations manager, Jeffrey Lezak. He's made a big unauthorized trade while I was out of town and when I said I wanted to back off a bit and bank some money he groused and grumbled and talked me out if it. I know, I know. So what, big deal. Even if he's stealing me blind he doesn't need Henry Ward. And he couldn't steal me blind if he wanted to. My clearing house handles the settlement of futures contracts and I outsource my payroll."

"So this Jeffrey Lezak couldn't possibly be stealing from you and even if he was he wouldn't need help from Henry Ward." Agent

John Knoerle

O'Connor looked at her watch. "My report's due in fifty minutes."

"But he is stealing from me," said Walt.

"Forty-nine minutes," said Agent O'Connor.

Walt stood up and clonked around the cell in his shoestring-less wingtips. "Henry Ward and Jeffrey Lezak are shadow trading dairy commodities based on insider information. Jeffrey Lezak informs Henry Ward just before Sumner International buys a contract and Henry Ward purchases a call option, an option to buy a futures contract, that mirrors ours."

Walter stood back and waited for Agent O'Connor to react to this bombshell. Agent O'Connor scratched her nose. He pressed on.

"Options have smaller margin requirements than futures contracts so you don't need a big pile of dough to play *and* you can trade them intraday, get in, get out and count your profits. It's called 'scalping'. But as an employee of a trading firm Jeffrey Lezak's brokerage accounts are subject to review by the NFA, the industry watchdog. *Which is why* Jeffrey Lezak needs Henry Ward. To do the deals."

Agent O'Connor said, "Assuming I understood a word of what you just said, how do you prove it?"

"Get a year to date graph of the price of dry milk futures, that's our primary product. Overlay it with Sumner International's major purchases for the same period of time. I *guarantee* you will see the price tick up just before our contracts are executed. Henry Ward is one reason that Sumner International's had such a subpar year."

"You said on TV your company was doing better in recent weeks."

"Yes," said Walt, grinning darkly. Lips flattened, nostrils flared. "Henry Ward was apparently too busy stalking and murdering family members to tend to business."

"I don't see it," said Agent O'Connor. "If Henry Ward's about money why close up shop to go on a three state murder spree?"

The Violin Player

"Because he knew that, given time and no distractions, I'd catch on eventually," said Walter. "Now that I'm locked away he'll really go to town."

Agent O'Connor folded her arms across her chest.

"Okay, you're right," said Walter. "The shadow trading's about more than money. It's about Henry Ward beating me at my own game. Demonstrating he's the best, the brightest and the first born."

Agent O'Connor nodded and patted the cot with the flat of her hand. Walt took a seat. "I had you pegged as a classic bifurcated personality—did you know that? For most of your performance last night I was more convinced than ever."

Walter, who thought he was beyond surprise, found that he was not. "You thought *I* was Henry Ward?"

"Yep."

"What? How?"

Agent O'Connor hitched up a knee and turned to face him across the cot, exposing miles of silken inner thigh. Walter averted his eyes, saw the detailed depiction of female genitalia over her left shoulder, looked away.

"I thought you had a great well of anger inside you that you cover up with good manners. But I treasured you." She brushed Walt's forearm with her fingertips. "Even at the federal level we don't get many smart criminals. Yet here you were, this soft spoken model citizen who had devised this brilliant self-correcting system. Send the date of death posting from your local coffee bar, charge it to your company credit card, no problem. It was your phantom half brother, not you."

"So what was all that bullshit in the motel room?" said Walt. "About the killer's scheme to humiliate law enforcement and stage a murder-suicide and all that?"

"I was baiting you," said Agent O'Connor. "Baiting Henry. Trying to draw him out."

Walter looked at Agent O'Connor, at her big dark eyes shimmering with moist heat and deep concern. He had assumed that she was this way with all men. A beautiful woman who used her sexuality as a negotiating tool. But there was much more going on here. She wanted him to be Henry. It excited her.

"I'm sorry to disappoint you," said Walter. "But I'm just me. Stodgy old Walt Sumner."

Agent O'Connor faced away. "I think I believe you," she said pensively. "There was a moment in your interview last night, when you were giving us all that googaw about what a great family man you were. Your older daughter—"

"Thea."

"Thea. Pretty name. There was a moment when Thea smacked you on the shoulder to contradict you," said Agent O'Connor. "That was spontaneous, off the script. A true ob-com control freak would have flinched, hesitated, frozen up for a second. *Something*. He would not have laughed so easily right away. That didn't fit the profile." Agent O'Connor slurped up the remains of her extra large latte and put her knees together. The spell was broken. They were brother and sister now.

"Will you tell the State's Attorney this?" said Walt. "Put it in your report?"

"I'll render my professional opinion," said Agent O'Connor, dangling a black shoe from the tip of her toes.

"Will you do me a favor?" asked Walt.

"Maybe."

"Will you call my sister Kay and check on my daughters?"

"Sure," said Agent O'Connor. "As soon as I finish my report."

Chapter 55

"I'm sorry Mister Samuelson," said the male secretary. "But the State's Attorney is going to have to reschedule."

"And why is that?" said Fifth Avenue Bob with his hair combed, shoes shined, and a very jumpy Belorussian at his side.

"He has an emergency meeting," said the male secretary.

"With whom?" said Samuelson. "And don't tell me you can't divulge that information or you're not at liberty to say because Mister Meldakov and I have taken time out from our busy schedules to keep this appointment which you yourself confirmed personally just yesterday."

"I'm sorry, Mister Samuelson, but I'm not at liberty to say."

"I *told* you not to tell me that," said Fifth Avenue Bob, trying to keep a stern face while performing this stupid Borscht Belt routine. He ranged around for a clue. The empty limo parked out front on California Avenue. It had out of state plates. Kentucky? Wisconsin? "Is he in conference with—"

The male secretary pushed past him to greet a newcomer. Robert Samuelson turned to see. Well, they weren't Kentucky plates. The Powell County District Attorney had just arrived.

Which meant the Door County DA was already inside.

Fifth Avenue Bob dragged his Belorussian witness back to the bank of elevators. "We are done, yes?" said Mr. Meldakov.

They climbed into an elevator car. "We're past done," said Samuelson, trying to suss it out. The three DA's were having a war council, a war council to decide how best to draw and quarter Walt Sumner. The Cook County State's Attorney had joined the battle after the Tribune editorial. Give me a guilty client every time, thought Samuelson. Guilty clients know the drill. Admit nothing, deny everything, demand proof.

The Belorussian squeezed into a corner as the car filled up with cops and lawyers. He looked as if he were about to soil himself. Samuelson gave him a smile and a reassuring pat and wondered why the Powell County DA had made the trip. It was to his benefit to let the other jurisdictions go first, to let them establish the motive that his case lacked. Not that reason's slender voice had much chance of being heard over the clamor of a highly publicized three state pissing contest.

The elevator door opened at the lobby level. Robert Samuelson instructed Mr. Meldakov to take a different exit door, not wanting some stray camera crew to ambush him and his secret witness on the steps of the criminal courts building. No good could come of that. The Belorussian hesitated, then fell in step directly behind Samuelson and followed him out the door.

A TV news van was packing up at the curb. Samuelson stopped dead. He shouldn't have done that. He should have continued walking because the Belorussian piled into him, a crew member looked up and sharp-eyed little Jessica Reynoso was on him before Samuelson took three steps down the stairs.

"Who's your dark-haired friend?" Jessica wanted to know.

The Violin Player

Samuelson shook her off. "How much for an exclusive interview?"

Robert Samuelson smirked and said, "Ten dollars, cash."

Jessica Reynoso bummed a ten from a crew member and held it out to him. Fifth Avenue Bob's brain began to churn.

Why not? It might be a back door into the war council. His client was facing protracted terms of pre-trial confinement as the three states took their turns. If Samuelson could scare Wisconsin off with the Belorussian, Illinois might reconsider, which would leave Kentucky standing alone at the circle jerk when the lights came on, dick in hand. Fifth Avenue Bob hooked Mr. Meldakov around the elbow and reached for his comb with his free hand.

Walter Sumner lay uneasily on the steel mesh cot in his greenish yellow cell in the basement of the Evanston PD. He realized that he had made an assumption based on personal prejudice. He had told Agent O'Connor that Jeffrey Lezak had access to personal and business information that he could have used to implicate his boss. Which was true. It was also true of most of the employees of Sumner International. Laura had laughed at his suggestion that Jeffrey might be the culprit. No, he had imagined her laughing. Didn't matter. He knew his wife. And she was an excellent judge of character.

Walt got up and stuck his mouth under the faucet of the steel sink for a drink of water. He ducked his head under the stream and ran his hands through his hair and scrubbed behind his ears and hummed a little tune and distracted himself as long as possible. He sat down on the cot and dripped water on the concrete floor. It cost approximately $40,000 per annum to incarcerate the average inmate, he had read somewhere. That came to over $100 per day.

What were they doing with all that money? Even his $25 a night motel room had towels. Walt shook his hands dry.

Laura had never cared for Marcy, said she wasn't all there. Walt assumed his wife was naturally jealous of a woman with whom he spent so much time. But Laura knew that Marcy was not a rival. *She's not all there*, Laura had said. Where, exactly, was she?

Marcy knew where Walt went for coffee, knew the business account numbers, knew where Walt traveled and when, knew or could find out when significant trades were about to be executed, even had access to his cell phone. She had discovered the rerouting module, true, but Walt had forced her hand there. And what a great opportunity to deflect suspicion. Look what I found Mr. Sumner! Walter had known right then and there, seen the guilty terror in Marcy's dilated pupils and had pushed the recognition away.

And then there was Twyla. It always came back to Twyla.

The night he returned home from his trip to Ohio, Laura told him that the ancient Egyptians believed that cats could assume human form and walk around and make all kinds of mischief. She'd said that Twyla knew something and was evil and involved in the plot against their family. Laura had been drunk at the time, biblically drunk, talking in parables drunk. And trying desperately to communicate something that she herself didn't understand.

Walt didn't put much stock in evil omens and presentiments. Still, there they were. Laura's words of warning, ringing in his ears. Twyla knew something and was involved in the plot. Cats can assume human form and make all kinds of mischief.

Well shit, he said aloud, startling himself. It did make a kind of loopy sense. The killer didn't need to break into the house on Hamilton to find a sticky note. Walt's date with Virginia had been on his day planner at work. Laura had been speaking about Marcy.

The Violin Player

Marcy was Twyla in human form.

Virginia ran into the kitchen, said Twyla had knocked a pot off the stove, returned to their conversation and promptly expired. The next thing Walt knew he was calling Marcy from a pay phone in northwest Indiana and listening to Twyla yowling in the background as he spoke to Marcy's roommate. Is that Twyla, Walt had said. Marcy's roommate said *who*? As if you wouldn't know the name of an ancient Egyptian goddess of an extremely demanding Siamese cat with whom you shared your living quarters.

He was taunting Walter with his lie. The entire conversation had been a taunt. Marcy had made a pact with the devil. Her roommate was Henry Ward.

Chapter 56

Agent O'Connor struggled to complete her report amidst the growing tumult outside the interrogation room she had commandeered. What the hell was going on? She finished, encrypted the report, copied it from her laptop to her handheld and uplinked to the bird from the basement of the Evanston PD, annoyed that she was twenty minutes late. She packed up and followed the flow of cops and jailers to a subterranean day room with a TV that hung from the ceiling by chains.

The eminent Robert Samuelson was holding forth on the steps of the criminal courts building at 26th and California. The mop-haired guy standing next to him looked ready to bolt. Agent O'Connor couldn't hear what Samuelson was saying over the buzz of reaction in the room. Detective Bjork passed by, saying, sneering, "Your boyfriend'll be loving this."

Agent O'Connor snagged him by the wrist. Hard. He spun around and squared up. He was a little guy, not much bigger than herself. But taut and bristly. A marathoner or a hundred mile road biker. The kind of opponent who if you didn't put him down in the first pass would scrap and slug and bite until he wore you down, his cop and jailer buddies cheering him on. Agent O'Connor stepped out of her shoes. She set herself, legs apart, hands curled lightly on her thighs. "Lose the gun," she said.

Detective Bjork put his hands on his hips and smirked. They always did that, thought Agent O'Connor. Men, when you called them out, put their hands on their hips. "You called me a very ugly name, detective."

Bjork shrugged and stirred his hands, "If I said something—"

"I'm not interested in an apology," said Agent O'Connor. "Lose the gun."

Detective Bjork laughed and shook his head. He removed the Glock from his shoulder holster and handed it to a nearby cop. Agent O'Connor shot forward as he turned back, hooked her left hand behind Bjork's shirt collar, drove her right forearm into his windpipe and threw him down. She jerked on his collar just before impact so that the back of Bjork's skull made only a gentle *squonk* on the concrete floor. She unhooked her hand and planted a knee in his solar plexus, churning up a curl of spittle. Bjork swung wildly with both arms, his eyes half shut. Agent O'Connor parried one blow and ducked another. Bjork's pale blue eyes popped open to see her raise up, cock her arm and flatten her hand, preparing to drive the heel of her palm into his nasal cavity.

"All right," he sputtered, turning his head away. "I give."

"Smart boy," said Agent O'Connor brightly for all to hear. She sprang to her feet and hunted up her shoes. "Now get the prisoner."

Detective Bjork led Walter Sumner into the day room just after Mr. Meldakov began to tell his story to the camera. Bjork was behaving himself. The prisoner's hands were cuffed in front. Bjork

John Knoerle

handed Walter Sumner to Agent O'Connor and slinked away, not joining his cohorts, bested in combat by a girl.

Walter asked who the mop-haired guy on TV was. Agent O'Connor filled him in.

"I knew someone would come forward after I showed that sketch on WGN."

"Actually," said Agent O'Connor, "according to Samuelson some guy you hired dug him up. Tony something."

"Tony Sobczak," said Walt. Of course. The American free enterprise system was alive and well. In what other nation could you select a yellow pages' ad at random and contract with a vendor to save your life?

The man with the mop of black hair finished speaking and the young Hispanic interviewer wrapped up the report. The crowd of cops and jailers began to disperse, looking everywhere but Walt's direction.

"Don't get yourself too excited," said Agent O'Connor to Walt's beaming mug. "Prosecutors in three states have got the boiler stoked and the wheels turning. They're not going to throttle back based on one witness."

Walt's smile dimmed. Not at Agent O'Connor's comment but at something taking place in the front of the room, on the television suspended from the ceiling by chains. A long-haired crew member in scruffy attire handed the reporter something. The reporter pushed the something back at him. He refused to take it and darted away. The camera crept in for a closer look. The something was a cell phone which the reporter held to her ear. She listened, holding her microphone in her other hand. The cops and jailers stopped and turned around, curious as to why the idiot box was suddenly silent.

The reporter said brief words into the cell phone, searched the unseen others arrayed in front of her for guidance and found none.

The Violin Player

She was a cub reporter on her own.

"We have a man on the phone, a person," she coughed, moving the mike away. She swung the mike back into position in mid-sentence. "...murders and claims to know things that only the killer would know." She paused. She yanked an earpiece from her ear, held it up and mouthed the words *I-can't-hear-shit*. This was followed by another pause. "Okay," said the reporter, "I don't know if this is legal or whatever but here goes."

She placed her microphone directly on the mouthpiece of the flip phone. A shriek of feedback rang the television speaker in the dayroom. The long-haired man reappeared, removed the foam windscreen from the mike, duct taped the mike to the phone's earpiece and handed it back to the reporter. Jessica Reynoso stood on the steps of the criminal courts building, holding the contraption with both hands.

"Hell-oooo, testing, testing, testing," said a fey male voice. "Oh, duddums, we're on the air!"

Walter Sumner recognized the voice. It was he. A different tone and accent this time. But it was definitely he.

"The truth is so refreshing, in'it? said the sing-song voice. "Like a quick dip in a glacial lake. You see so little of it in public life these days. Which is why I was so inspired by Walter Sumner's declaration on the boob tube last evening. 'I didn't kill my mother, I didn't kill my wife and I didn't kill Clovis Ward.' He is 1000% correct. *He* didn't. *I* did. I'll even tell you how. Now, all you DeVry graduate lab rats from Cook, Door and Powell counties, get your number two pencils ready because I'm only going to say this once."

Agent O'Connor turned to Walt as Henry Ward rattled off the chemical components of his lethal cocktails, her big dark eyes as wide as they would go. She said you believe this, or this is unreal, words to that effect. Walt wasn't listening. He was thinking this was all wrong. Henry Ward wouldn't throw in the towel just because one witness had stepped forward. He didn't know that Walt had sniffed out his shadow trading scheme. So far as Henry Ward knew he had won the game hands down.

Walter felt a great and cold and dreadful stillness gather within him. He turned to Agent O'Connor. She was watching the reporter standing stupidly on the steps of the criminal courts building, listening to Henry Ward lecture the medical examiners on their shoddy work. "You see," she said, "He *does* want to humiliate law enforcement."

"Did you call about my daughters?"

Agent O'Connor made a face and said she plain forgot. Walter turned his stony stare to the television screen and waited for the other shoe to drop.

"So in conclusion, ladies and germs, I urge the jackbooted bluecoats to let the poor sap go. He's suffered enough. Isn't that right, sweetheart?"

Walter had lost all sensation in his extremities so he didn't feel Agent O'Connor's hand clutch his. There was a pause and a shuffling sound and whispered instructions.

Then Reenie said, "Daddy?"

Chapter 57

Was it still night? No, there was light down by her feet. Thea tried to sit up and bumped her head on something squishy. Her arm hurt where the man had stuck the needle. She laid back down and tried to think her way through the gunkiness in her head. Reenie. Car trunk. The creepy man with the woman's hair. Her eyelids slowly closed.

"Shit, double shit and times that too!"

Thea opened her eyes. The voice was close. There was a sound of stuff being tossed around.

"Ain't got *no* shit here today. Jes…ain't…*got it*."

Thea crawled further into her dark space, feeling around. It was a box, a cardboard box with a soggy top.

"Well now hey. Looky heah."

The man was talking to himself. Laughing to himself now in a crazy kind of way. Thea tried to curl herself into a ball but her legs went all wopperjod and the cardboard box flattened out sideways, shutting out the light. She lay still and didn't breathe. She listened for the man's voice to keep talking to himself but she didn't hear anything.

John Knoerle

The box tilted upright all of a sudden and a fierce bearded black face appeared at the far end of the tunnel. Thea remembered what her mother had taught her and screamed as loud as she could. The man hauled up the long box and tossed it away, spilling Thea out the other end.

"Whatchou hollering for girl?"

Thea looked up at him. He was big and old and he had a bent rusty knife in his hand. Thea screamed her lungs empty. The man shook his head. "Cain't nobody hear you up here."

The Evanston PD tried to make amends. Chief of Police Franklin H. Reeder issued an immediate certificate of release and instructed three units to give the former prisoner and Agent O'Connor a code three escort back down Lake Shore Drive. He even shook Walt's reluctant hand and said his department stood ready to help in any way it could. Detectives Bjork and Hernandez were nowhere to be seen.

The Evanston PD units switched their sirens from the cruising down the highway cadence to a more urgent snarl. The onlookers scattered and the camera crews swarmed. The caravan of squad cars brodied to a stop in a V formation at the corner of Paulina and Bloomingdale. Agent O'Connor pulled her unmarked car into the slot. The uniformed officers fanned out to keep the crowd at bay. Walter informed Agent O'Connor that he didn't have his keys.

The media vultures and curiosity seekers circled the unmarked car, shouting questions and voicing support. A woman held a hand lettered placard denouncing the death penalty. A young man climbed up on the rear bumper which got Agent O'Connor out the door. When the uniformed officers started in on the front door the

The Violin Player

crowd surged off to watch the fun.

Walt felt stoned, woozy, felt like he was trapped in a tape loop of that Led Zepplin song they always played at frat parties where the psychedelic instrumental whorled around and around and around and left you dazed and faintly nauseous. He watched the cops batter down his brass fixtured ebony inlaid mahogany door, thinking there wouldn't be any need to replace it. He didn't have anything left worth stealing.

The uniformed officers ran back to the unmarked car, formed a ring around Walt and hustled him through the chaos. Agent O'Connor followed, talking to her shoulder. A man tried to follow them inside. The trailing cop shoved him back so forcefully that he flew off the steps, skidded across the grass on his rear end and came to a rest against the boxwood bushes by the wrought iron fence. It was almost funny.

"It's okay," said Walter. "He works for me."

"You g'wan stop or not? Cuz I got other things need doin'. Whole entire case of alligator pears back there, most of 'em green."

Thea nodded her head. She couldn't say yes because the man had his big stinky hand clamped across her mouth. They were on a side street with no people and no cars and a lot of big square buildings with For Sale or Lease signs tacked on.

"I'm gonna turn you loose here in a second and if you get to screamin' I'm gonna turn right around and leave you be on the twenny-six hundred block of South Hoyne." The man removed his hand. Thea wiped her lips and didn't scream. "Attagirl. Now, we're g'wan walk on up here to Blue Island and flag a cruiser. They just like cabs in the Loop round here. One every minute," said the man and cackled as he walked.

Thea didn't know what he was laughing about exactly but she decided he wasn't crazy. His bent rusty knife was in a leather sheath on his belt.

"That's a box cutter," said the man off her look. "These warehouses are down to three day weeks, one's still open. I come by off days to make sure they don't forget nuthin', you know what I'm sayin'?" He winked down at Thea. "That's what *I'm* doin' up here." They walked on towards Blue Island Avenue.

"My name is Thea Sumner."

"Please to meecha. My Christian name is Theodore." A pick up truck drove past, the back piled high with rusty junk. The driver looked at them and looked again.

"My father was taken away to jail," said Thea. "And my sister and I were kidnapped by a lady who works in his office and the man who killed my mom and grandmom. He's related to us."

Theodore stopped walking and looked down with one eye closed. "Cross your heart and hope to die?" Thea crossed her heart. "And I figgered my family for screwed up," said Theodore in a low voice, moving again, two blocks from Blue Island Avenue. "Where's your sister now?"

"She's still being kidnapped," said Thea. "They put us in the trunk of the car and she got so scared she wet her pants."

Theodore snorted and spat in the gutter. "You a good runner are ya?"

"I'm an *excellent* runner," said Thea.

"Then whatchou walking for?" said Theodore, loping on ahead.

Chapter 58

The whorling chaos at the corner of Paulina and Bloomingdale moved indoors as FBI telecommunications specialists arrived to tap Walt's phones, a senior DCFS bigwig appeared to apologize for the 'mixup', Fifth Avenue Bob entertained the media at the broken door and Jeffrey Lezak dogged Walter from room to room until he finally cornered him in the master bedroom.

"I think Marcy may be involved in all this," said Jeffrey breathlessly. "I think she may be insider trading."

"Tell me something I don't know," said Walter, stripping off his clothes.

"You *know*?"

"She *signed* for my children," said Walt in his boxer shorts. "Just signed for them like a parcel. She told the DCFS lady she would wait with the girls till my sisters arrived and the dumb bitch gave her a form to sign and got home in time for supper!"

"Holy cow," said Jeffrey, following his boss into the master bath. Walt yanked on the fixture and waited for hot water. "I walked in on her, Marcy," said Jeffrey. "Just to ask a question and she had the day's program trades on her screen for some reason and she acted all guilty like and turned off the screen and like *yelled* at me!"

Walt tested the water with his hand. "When was this?"

"Two days ago." Walt nodded and stepped out of his boxer shorts and into the stream. "What should I do?" sang Jeffrey over the pebbled opaque shower door.

He stood on the tan and gold bathroom rug and watched his employer soap himself. Walt slid the door open and said, "You're in charge now, Jeffrey. Get back to work."

A montage of conflicting emotions flickered across Jeffrey Lezak's boyish face. Prideful glee at his new authority, guilt at feeling this feeling while his employer faced a life or death crisis, rank embarrassment at the circumstances of the moment. He started to extend his hand. Walt slid the door shut. Jeffrey wandered off. Walter turned the water all the way cold. Travis Sumner was right. It cleared the mind.

Busted. Walter had asked Marcy pointed questions about the transmitter module in his cell phone. Jeffrey had found her examining the day's trades. Marcy thought she'd been busted. That was good. It explained things. Why she and Henry had kidnapped Thea and Irene. Why Henry Ward called the TV reporter. You can't negotiate a ransom with a prison inmate.

Negotiate. There was hope. Henry was planning to negotiate.

Reenie had sounded okay, considering. Terrified, but not drugged or beaten up. He had only heard the one word from Reenie but it was enough. He had not heard any words from Thea. Not one. Walter turned the faucet fixture to the left until the water was scalding hot. It felt good.

"Walter," said a misty figure from the other side. He slid the shower door open a crack. "Jesus, you're beet red," said Agent O'Connor. She pushed the door aside and shut the faucet. Walt

The Violin Player

jumped back. "Get some clothes on. We've got work to do," she said and was gone.

Walt dressed in chinos and his last clean polo shirt, folded with great care, the top button buttoned as always. He took cold comfort in Laura's absence. Happy she wasn't here to suffer this torturous unknowing. Agent O'Connor breezed in as he was pulling on his socks.

"We've got the phone tap in place. We need to talk about—"

"Not here," said Walt. "Not in my bedroom."

Walt slipped on his topsiders and marched Agent O'Connor out the door, thinking that it didn't feel much different being a victim than it did being the accused. Either way you were livestock, livestock they could walk right in on and take no note of your nakedness.

Theodore was a good runner for an old man, thought Thea. He kind of galloped like a horse, one leg stretched out full, the other leg hitching along behind. She had to put her head down and run like crazy to catch up. They were closing in on Blue Island Avenue when Theodore pulled up and she raced past. Thea slowed down and turned around, jogging backward like they did in soccer drills.

"G'wan, g'wan," said Theodore, shooing her forward, making a big show of gasping for air and dragging his short leg. "I'll catch up."

Thea almost tripped on some railroad tracks that were sunk in the pavement. Theodore wasn't catching up. He was looking around for something and talking to himself. Cars and trucks whizzed by on Blue Island Avenue. Thea jogged back towards Theodore.

"G'wan out to the corner," he said.

"I'm scared to."

"I got my eye out," he said. "I won't let nobody snatch you."

"What are you looking for?"

"A place to hide," said Theodore. "Me and John Law got some unfinished bidness."

"What is it?" said Thea.

Theodore snorted, looked away and pulled at the bottom of his raggedy coat that was the color of pea soup and smelled like it too. "That what they teach you up there in Lake Forest? To ax rude questions about people's bidness?"

"We don't live in Lake Forest."

"Cuz in Back o' the Yards rude questions can get you hurt."

Thea didn't think that Theodore was really angry at her. He was looking every which way and what, saying his words to the world. "I'm sorry," she said. "I apologize."

"The charges ain't nothin' 'bout nothin'. Blues round here leave me be," said Theodore. "Cept you being who you are they might throw me in the back seat and get on that computer they got now."

Thea stopped her mouth from speaking. Theodore might get insulted if she said her father would give him a reward. And he wouldn't care about being a hero, an old man like him. What did old people care about? Well, Gramma Ginny had a saying she always used to say.

"Okay, I'll go by myself," said Thea to Theodore. "But it's neither right nor proper."

Thea turned away and walked towards the corner of South Hoyne and Blue Island Avenue. She heard Theodore stumping along behind her, spitting and cursing.

Walter opened the sunroof and turned on the dome light. He told Agent O'Connor about Jeffrey catching Marcy in the act of

The Violin Player

abetting insider trading. They were seated in the XJR in the darkened garage at his suggestion. FBI agents were sweeping the house for listening devices.

"Good," said Agent O'Connor. "That means this is definitely a kidnapping."

"What else?" said Walt.

"I was afraid it might be some grisly *coup de grace*, game over."

"No!" said Walter, both a statement and a plea. "No, I've been thinking about it. This is about money. This is. The market would have kicked Henry's ass, even with the inside dope. He would have gotten greedy and full of himself and pushed his luck. Then Marcy gets busted and he goes back to doing what he does best. Shaking down the Sumner family."

Walter gripped the steering wheel. Agent O'Connor cupped her hands and breathed into them as if it were cold in the garage. Perhaps it was, Walt couldn't tell.

"*Elotes!*" called the pushcart vendor passing in the alley. *Elotes!*"

One of the FBI techs ducked his head into the garage and gave Agent O'Connor the all clear.

"We can go in," she said to Walt.

"In a minute. I need to ask you a question."

"All right."

Walt gripped the walnut and leather steering wheel and stared through the windshield. "What does it mean that we didn't hear Thea on the phone call?"

"I'm not sure," said Agent O'Connor. "We've been monitoring the website. Your daughters' Dates of Death are blank."

Walt nodded. "I think he's done with that game."

"Let's go in," said Agent O'Connor.

Walt continued to stare through the windshield, hands on the steering wheel.

"Walter?"

"I don't think I could stand it. I've survived the murder of my wife and Mother and I love Reenie heart and soul. It's not that. I'd swap my life for hers in an instant. It's just that, if I lost Thea—if I lost Thea I don't believe I could stand it. I really don't." Walter did not look to Agent O'Connor for her reply. It would be difficult enough just to listen. "I know you don't *know* what Thea not being on the phone call means, but what do you *think*?"

"I don't know!" she said and slapped him a stinging shot to the shoulder. Walt turned to face her. Agent O'Connor had her jaws set and her brow lowered. "You're about to be the point man in a hostage negotiation so stop crying in your beer and try to concentrate!"

"Okay," said Walter. What else could he say? She was right.

Kay was waiting in the kitchen when Walt entered from the garage. She started towards him and stopped, a *what have we here* expression on her face. Walt introduced Kay to the special agent. Agent O'Connor offered her hand. Kay shook it with her fingertips. Walt thought about explaining that he and the special agent had been discussing the case and not making out in the back seat as Kay's reared back look seemed to suggest. He said, "Nice of you to put in an appearance."

"Let go of my elbow, Walter," said Kay as they marched upstairs. Walter did not. "I did everything I could. I raced down here when I saw them arrest you. I rang the doorbell for *hours*. I called the—"

"Never mind," said Walt and gave his sister a clumsy hug as he banged into the spare bedroom he used as an office. "We'll discuss

The Violin Player

it later. What I need from you right now, forgive me, is food."

"Of course," said Kay. "How are you holding up?"

"Fine."

"Are you going to talk to them?" she asked, canting her head toward the media clamor outside.

"Why should I?"

"To show him you're in charge. That he hasn't won," said Kay. "You know he's watching."

"Not yet," said Walter and pointed to his open mouth.

Kay said, "Yes sahib," and returned to the kitchen.

Walt slumped into his desk chair. Slumped in his desk chair and grabbed pen and paper and tried to concentrate on the most important task he would ever face. More sirens yelped outside followed by more crowd hubbub, whorling chaos and giddiness. The giddiness was what got to him. What didn't they understand? Two young innocents had been kidnapped by a psychopath. How does that make you giddy?

Pressure Points wrote Walt on the notepad.

Undercapitalized—Henry Ward would not have emerged from his dark cave of total control unless he needed money.

Protective of his mother—Clovis Ward sold Jarlene Ward's whereabouts. And her love letters. Clovis Ward was murdered.

"Three Locks"—Henry Ward had been bullied by his peers. The nickname below the yearbook picture was almost certainly pejorative.

Not much leverage in that list, thought Walt. He would happily exchange his money for his daughters but it wouldn't be that simple. Henry Ward wouldn't risk the conventional money for hostages exchange. Law enforcement was involved. Henry Ward had involved them. He would probably propose some electronic funds transfer to an offshore account and trust me on getting your daughters back.

That would not be acceptable. Walter Sumner was not going to trust Henry Ward.

And your BATNA is what, Walter? Your best alternative to a negotiated agreement is the *death* of your *daughters*. Make a counter proposal, baffle him with bullshit, stall as long as possible in hopes the FBI whizz kids can trace the call but don't count on it, Walter. Henry Ward hadn't come this far to be that stupid.

And Thea. Walter straightened his spine to keep his shoulders from slumping. Don't go there. This guy's a customer now. He's on your turf and knows it. Henry Ward wouldn't…dispose of Thea and then expect you to sit down and do a deal. Henry's crazy, not insane. He doesn't need to prove he's capable of violence. He's already demonstrated that quite convincingly.

What if…what if Henry did it deliberately? Excluded Thea from the first phone call so that you'd go crazy with dark imaginings and be a soft touch when he called with the ransom demand and put Thea on the line? *Of course.* That was it!

Walt bolted out of the room to shout the good news. Thea was still alive! The house was quiet. The third floor was empty, the second floor was empty, the first floor contained only one FBI tech in headphones. There was no crowd of media at the broken door.

"What's going on?" Walt shouted. The man in the headphones didn't hear him.

Walt started for the front door, made a u-turn and checked the kitchen. Water boiling on the stove, a sheaf of pasta, a handful of mushrooms, a bell pepper on the cutting board and no Kay. The portable TV snagged his eye.

It was shoved discreetly under the beveled glass cabinets. Laura

The Violin Player

had liked to keep one eye on the local news while she prepared dinner. Someone on the small screen was speaking to reporters at the corner of Paulina and Bloomingdale. Someone short. *Thea*!

The phone rang. Walt picked it up by reflex. "Got a minute?" said a soft malevolent voice that he had come to know.

Chapter 59

Tony rumbled into the dining room as Walter began his second retelling of his conversation with Henry Ward. Kay was tending to Thea upstairs, Chrissie had arrived and taken over the kitchen duties, and a grumbling Robert Samuelson had been dispatched to make certain that the homeless man who had rescued Thea did not spend the night behind bars.

Walter's audience consisted of Lieutenant John Skowron and two of his sergeants from the Chicago Police Department's 14th District Tactical Team, Special Agent O'Connor, and a gaggle of shamefaced FBI phone phreaks who had abandoned their posts to witness Thea's arrival and had not captured the ransom call on tape. The geek in the headphones was still doing something at a portable workstation in the living room.

"Got here quick as I could," said Tony. Walt nodded, very happy to see him.

Thea had still been Thea. Her clothes filthy, her face a little flushed but clear eyed and self contained after her ordeal. She hadn't wanted to be hugged. She described a boxy green Volvo with the letters HV on the license plate. Lt. Skowron issued an APB for the car.

The Violin Player

Tony Sobczak took a seat at the far end of the see through acrylic dining room table. Walt introduced him to the assembled and began again. An FBI sound tech recorded him on mini disc and the 14th District sergeants made notes in their department-issue blue pads.

"Henry Ward told me to raise five million by close of business tomorrow. I told him it would take at least another day. He said he was looking at a printout of my portfolio and that stocks and bonds were very negotiable. I said cash and checks are negotiable, stocks and bonds are liquid. I offered him four million and an additional four million for his mother. He asked why such a generous offer. I said to atone for my father's, *our* father's misbehavior. I said four million was his fair share of our grandfather's trust and that I was, in effect, donating my share to his mother. He asked how long it would take to raise the eight million. I said seventy-two hours because some of the trust holdings were overseas. He paused and said, 'Moms can have two, I want the other six.' I said I wouldn't hand over ten cents until I was assured that my daughter was alive and well. He said, 'Of course, Walter, of course.'"

"Did you hear anything in the background when he paused?" said Lt. Skowron. "Low flying planes, highway traffic, kids in a school yard?"

"I heard a television," said Walt.

"You're sure it wasn't a radio? Maybe a police scanner?" said the Lieutenant.

"It sounded like a television," said Walt. "A news report."

Lt. Skowron nodded his close cropped head as if Walt had just imparted a great pearl of wisdom. "Any idea what station? What reporter?"

Agent O'Connor said, "What possible difference could that make?"

"If we know who he's watching we might get the reporter to invite a personal call." said Skowron. "These guys always want their fifteen minutes of fame."

"This isn't a domestic snatch'n'book, Lieutenant," said Agent O'Connor.

"I have no idea what station or what reporter," said Walter to no one.

"Agent O'Connor," said Lt. Skowron, "I've been working kidnaps since Christ was a corporal. I know what works."

"And I've been working this case for weeks, Lieutenant, I know that—"

Walter tuned out. He considered slamming his hand on the table and telling these overgrown high schoolers to take it outside but he was locked in now and didn't want the bother. He traded looks with Tony Sobczak. They stood up and walked into the kitchen.

"Kay's obviously never seen *The Godfather*," said Chrissie without looking up, whisking a thick and aromatic red sauce around a skillet at high heat. Walter smelled something meaty splitting and blistering inside the oven. "If we're going to the mattresses we're going to need all the fatty protein we can get. Has Thea eaten?"

"I don't think she should have anything until the doctor examines her," said Walt.

"Good thinking," said Chrissie. "Now go away and let me work."

Tony and Walter convened in the laundry room off the kitchen. The washing machine shuddered backwards as Tony leaned his girth against it. "Anything about the terms of exchange?"

"He wouldn't say," said Walt. "Just gave me the three days to raise the cash."

"You talk to your daughter?"

The Violin Player

"Yes."

"She sound okay?"

"Not really," said Walt, squinting against the harsh light in the little room. "I told her that Thea made it home safely and she started to cry."

Tony grunted and shook his head. He asked where Thea had been found. Walt said the South Side. Tony said he needed the address. Walt said the cops would know. Tony scratched his thumb against his cheek. "Was the TV up real loud?"

"Not very."

"You hear anything else in the background?" Tony held up his hand before Walt could say no. "Take your time," he said. "I'll go take a leak."

Walt attempted to replay the phone conversation in his head. All he could hear was Henry Ward's dead flat voice, a voice without antecedents. Henry had not been playing a part this time, no accents or ironic attitude, no Eddie Haskell toadyism. He was himself. A bloodless phantom, more an abstraction than a human being. Walter had tried to convince himself that his half brother was a spineless poseur who would cave in if challenged. But the man on the other end of the phone line had been terrifying.

Tony returned to the laundry room, licking a telltale spot of red sauce from the corner of his mouth. Walt said, "I came up empty." Tony nodded and hinged his sacrum against the washing machine in such a way that it didn't slide backward. Walter asked him a question. "Assuming I fulfill every detail of my agreement with Henry Ward is there any chance I'll get my daughter back alive?"

Tony said a quiet, "Not likely."

"He spared Thea," said Walt, hyperventilating, seeing starbursts before his eyes from hunger, exhaustion and rimy fear.

"That was his down payment. His earnest money."

"Meaning what?" said Walter. Tony's craggy visage returned the question. Walter knew exactly what he meant.

The safe return of Thea meant that Walter had to complete the transaction with Henry no matter how ludicrous the terms and conditions. *Transfer six million dollars to an offshore account and I'll tell you where she is. Airdrop a ton of gold bullion on a desert island and your daughter will be returned in thirty days.* Walter was not in a strong negotiating position. If he did not comply he would spend the remainder of his miserable life wondering if there was one chance in a billion that Henry might actually have done as he promised. This was Henry's endgame, his way to strip Walt naked before he ran him through. Take his wealth then kill his daughter. Walter took a big draught of air and exhaled to his ankles. His vision cleared.

"I understand," said Walter. "That's why I offered him an extra three million. To buy another day."

The men left the laundry room to find the combined forces of the Federal Bureau of Investigation and the Chicago Police Department lined up in front of the stove like stewbums at the Rescue Mission. They shifted over to make room for the head of the household. Chrissie handed Walter a sausage hero covered in marinara sauce and grated provolone. It looked grotesque, bloody. He handed his plate to Tony and got himself a glass of milk.

The headphone-wearing FBI sound tech entered the kitchen without his headphones. He planted his feet and did a very poor job of attempting not to appear immensely pleased with himself. He cleared his throat, twice. The troops, jostling in the food line and raiding the refrigerator for soft drinks, ignored him. Crestfallen, he spun around and went back out. Walter snagged

The Violin Player

Tony with a look and followed.

They found the sound tech on the second floor, at his work station in the living room, headphones back in place, clicking around a laptop screen atop a stack of signal processing components. Walter tapped him on the shoulder. The sound tech removed his headphones. He said he had your bad news, your good news, your bad news and your good news.

The bad news was that the ransom call came from a cellular phone, much more difficult to trace than a land line. The good news was that he had managed to hop from cell to cell to cell to trace the call to Indianapolis, Indiana. The bad news was that the cell phone number from which the ransom call supposedly originated was registered to the FBI. *Yuk yuk*. The good news was that he had managed to record the last 45 seconds of Henry Ward's phone call on his software program.

"Why didn't you mention this earlier?" said Walt.

The sound tech's eyebrows danced around his forehead. "I had some work to do first," he said. "I eq'ed out the frequency range of the human voice, one hundred to four thousand hertz, compressed everything else, notch filtered out transmission hum, made a new sound file from that EDL and came up with this."

He clicked the sound file that was displayed on the laptop screen. The plug-in speakers played a muddle of pink noise punctuated with a faint, high pitched sound that repeated itself at short intervals. Walter noted the procession of graphic spikes on the sound file. "What is it?"

"Not sure yet," said the sound tech.

Tony asked the sound tech to play it again. Walt thought he recognized the sound this time. "Shit," he said, "Isn't that—"

"What?" said the sound tech eagerly.

"Never mind," said Walt. It wasn't the most convincing response but Walter found it difficult to improvise with Tony's big hammy hand on the back of his belt hoisting him halfway off the floor.

"Good work," said Walt to the sound tech and followed Tony upstairs to the third floor family room. Tony paused at the top of the stairs to catch his breath. "I thought it sounded like a truck's back-up beeper," said Walt.

Tony nodded. "What's your plan of attack?"

"Liquidate my assets, do some background research and call Henry's mother and invite her up. I want her to answer the phone the next time he calls." Tony nodded his approval. "What are you up to?" said Walt.

"Nuttin' yet."

Walt sighed. "Tony, stop hiding behind that blue wall of bullshit and *talk to me*."

Tony combed sweat off his brow with a forefinger and said, "I gotta thought about the back up beeper."

"Based on what?"

"It beeps the whole time and gets louder at the end." Tony unclipped a pager from his belt and handed it to Walt. "You gotta picture of the female?"

"Marcy? Umm, *yes*. In our annual report. Hold on." Walt fetched a copy from his office.

Tony shoved the Sumner International Annual Report in his coat pocket, said he would be in touch, and thudded down the stairs, leaving his employer two stories above the Chicago PD-FBI task force and one story below his middle sister and elder daughter. Walter looked past the black leather couch and pictured his living wife. Next to the large screen TV, swaying on her high heels after their dinner at

The Violin Player

the Mid America Club. Their last night out.

She wore her red suit and gold necklace, her eyes were shiny bright, she was grinning madly, drunk as a lord. He understood it now, too late to make a difference. She was unhappy. Alone, neglected, shoved aside. It was why they so seldom made love. It was animal rutting to her. Sex with a stranger. The worst of it was that he had been so preoccupied with precautions and paranoia in the last few days of her life that he had never told her of his renewed devotion, his plan to simplify their life and start anew. Laura had died unhappy. That was the worst of the worst of it. Walter walked down the hall to his office and closed the door.

"Mrs. Cantwell this is Walter Sumner calling."

"Mr. Sumner, gracious me, what a time you've had!"

"I have a problem," said Walter.

Mrs. Cantwell said, "What can I do to help?"

"As you may recall the yearbook picture that you uncovered indicated a nickname in the caption. Henry 'Three Locks' Ward. There must be some members of that '68 track team still in town. I was hoping you could find out what 'Three Locks' means."

"I'd be happy to try," said Mrs. Cantwell. She coughed dryly.

The yearbook. Where the hell was it? "Hold on a second," said Walt and searched his bookcase. It wasn't there. When was the last time he had seen it? Propped up on the easel for the camera close up. Walt told Mrs. Cantwell he would call right back and went downstairs to search the living room. Where in the hell? The WGN crew wouldn't have taken it but…but Marcy had been in the house. Marcy had been in the house with instructions to seize the girls and the only known photo of Henry Ward.

Walter called back and apologized. Mrs. Cantwell told him to tend to more important matters. She would find another copy somewhere and track down the members of the track team. Walt thanked her. Should he caution her not to breathe a word of this to anyone? No. Mrs. Cantwell would already know that.

Walter called the number for the Mount Sterling Convalescent Home and braced himself for a battle with a short senior bureaucrat. The young black girl answered the phone. Walt recognized her lilting asthmatic voice. He asked to speak to Jarlene Ward. "Hold on a sec." Could it possibly be this easy?

No it could not. An officious male voice said, "Who is calling please?"

There was one advantage to being the victim and not the accused. You could use your real name. "Walter Sumner is calling."

"And your interest in speaking to Mrs. Ward is what?"

"None of your business," said Walt pleasantly.

"Are you a member of the media?"

"No, I'm not."

"Are you in fact *the* Walter Sumner?"

"Yes."

"How do I know that for certain?"

"I'm in the book, the 773 area code. Call me back," said Walt, not hanging up.

The bureaucrat said, "Jarlene Ward is previously occupied."

"Doing what?"

"None of your business."

"Touché," said Walt. "But here's the deal. I've got the national media parked outside my house. They haven't had time to dig Jarlene out of the bag just yet but one word from me and they'll be swarming all over the Mount Sterling Convalescent Home." The bureaucrat put him on hold. Walt listened to an instrumental version of *Moon River* from beginning to end.

The Violin Player

"Hello?"

"Jarlene?"

"Hello?"

"Jarlene, this is Walter Sumner calling. Hello? *Jarlene, this is Walter Sumner calling.*"

"Why are you shouting, Walter?"

"I'm sorry. I wasn't sure you could hear me."

"I can hear you now."

"Good. How are you getting along?"

"Fine. The residents are looking at your lovely home in the rec room."

"On the television," said Walt.

"In Chicago," said Jarlene. "They're waiting for you to come out and say something."

Walter said that he didn't know what to say. Jarlene said that they'd been waiting a long time. Walter asked Jarlene if she wouldn't rather be with family members right now. Jarlene said she had no family and hung up the phone.

Shit! Now what? If Henry Ward cared about anyone other than himself it was his mother. If anyone could make him promise not to harm his half niece it was she. Calling again seemed pointless. Jarlene had said they were waiting for him to make a statement on TV. Could he make a direct appeal to her on camera? No, Henry would see it. She had to be asked in person and he couldn't leave the house.

Walter cursed and muttered as he climbed one flight of stairs. "It's me," he said, tapping on the door to Thea's bedroom.

"Come in."

Walt entered and immediately felt like an intruder. The female doctor—when had she arrived?—shot him a frosty look, Kay remained silent and Thea hurriedly buttoned her blouse to cover her bony chest. Unlike her baby sister Thea was rigorously, almost morbidly, modest.

"How's the patient?"

"Dehydrated," snapped the doctor. "Exhausted, hungry and suffering a mild case of shock. But her vitals are fine and there are no signs of sexual abuse."

Walt stopped breathing. Sexual abuse? "Thea, did Henry try to—"

"No."

"Did the homeless man, the one who—"

"Not *even*," said Thea. "Gawd."

"Then why, Doctor, would you subject a ten year old girl to an…intrusive examination if—"

"It's the law. She was *abducted*." The Doctor and Walter glared at one another in instant enmity. "She's not to have anything stronger than chicken broth till I get the results of her blood panel."

"When will that be?" demanded Walt.

"Tomorrow at the earliest," said the doctor. She packed up her valise and stalked out of the room.

Kay cast a look at her brother looking at his elder daughter who was staring at her feet. Kay squeezed Walt's hand on the way out.

"I'm sorry snowflake."

"Don't say that," said Thea. "You're not supposed to apologize if you did-ent do anything wrong."

"I'm sorry anyway."

"Is Theodore in jail?"

"The homeless man?" Thea nodded. Walter assured her that they would do whatever it took to keep Theodore out of jail.

"He would-ent tell me why the police were after him."

The Violin Player

"I'm sure it's nothing serious."

"But you don't *know*."

Walter sat on the bed. "Sure I do. Theodore is a good person. He placed himself at risk to give me back my daughter." Thea fiddled with the buttons on her blouse and avoided her father's eyes. She had tape marks around her wrists and mouth. Walter clenched his gut and tried to keep his tone light. "Do you remember the eight most powerful words in the world?"

Thea sing songed, "I have a problem. I need your help."

"Well," said Walter, "My problem is those stupid TV reporters. They want someone to talk to and I just can't bring myself to face them right now."

Thea tucked her chin and looked up. "Me?"

"Absolutely. You can tell them what happened. And how much you miss your sister," said Walt, hoping the sight of a wan innocent pleading for her younger sister's return might bring a certain someone to their senses. Not Henry, Henry's partner in crime. Marcy. "You do miss your sister, don't you?"

Thea did not do as she'd been bidden, did not hold up her thumb and forefinger half an inch apart. Thea was not in the mood for jokes. "We'll get Reenie back," he whispered.

Thea didn't challenge her father's statement. Thea didn't say anything at all. Walter kissed the crown of her head and returned to his office.

Chapter 60

The FBI team had set up camp in the living room. Some of the faces had changed. Fewer shaggy phone phreaks, more buzz cut data miners, most under thirty, mostly male and all working laptops or handhelds. Walt passed by them unseen.

Lt. Skowron, the two sergeants and assorted personnel from the 14th Division had commandeered the dining room. They were listening to police calls on stand up radios and fretting over an enormous city map spread out on the acrylic table.

Walter, having spent two hours liquidating the fortune it had taken the Sumner family three generations to acquire, joined them. They asked him questions about Marcy. What did she drive? Walt said she didn't. Where was she from? Walter thought Moline, Illinois. Who were her friends? Walt wasn't sure she had any. The Lieutenant told one of the sergeants to run South Side car thefts for the last 24 hours.

Walt asked if they had any progress to report. Lieutenant Skowron said absolutely. While the Feebs were busy playing video games the 14th Division Tactical Team had used its God given common sense to determine that the background noise on the ransom

The Violin Player

call was a truck's back up beeper. The Lieutenant pointed to a crudely circled area on the city map, an area on the South Side. "There are a lot of abandoned warehouses near the point of your daughter's drop off. They could be holed up in one of them."

"But I heard a TV in the background," said Walt, seating himself at the head of the dining room table.

"Could be a battery operated portable," said the Lieutenant, seating himself at the opposite end.

"So the back up beeper you heard is what?"

The Lieutenant enunciated his syllables in the manner used to address the feeble minded. "It's a delivery truck."

Walter nodded. "So, you're concentrating your investigation on the South Side based on the theory that your heard a delivery truck at an abandoned warehouse. Do I have that right?"

The Lieutenant held his head very still. The short hairs that fringed his baldness probed the air like plant cilia. None of his subordinates laughed, tittered or guffawed. Satisfied, he explained. "Not all the warehouses are abandoned, Mr. Sumner."

"Of course," said Walt.

He rose from his seat at the head of the table. The Lieutenant rose with him. "You guys are the experts. But from what I know about Henry Ward he's ten times too smart to hide out in an area's he's already marked." Walter walked into the kitchen for another glass of milk.

Kay was glued to the television on the counter. She pointed him toward the small screen. Chrissie and Thea were being interviewed by a silver maned reporter that Walt recognized from the network news. Chrissie did most of the talking, patting and squeezing Thea for emphasis. Thea played along, pulling a long face, mustering a brave smile. "They're perfect together," said Walt.

"Aren't they though," said Kay.

Walter felt a strange agitation just above his hip. His hand stumbled upon the pager clipped to his belt. Was this how they worked? Walter had never worn a pager before. It displayed a phone number in the 312 area code. Downtown. "You have your phone with you?"

"In my purse." Walter took Kay's purse into the laundry room.

"'Lo," said Tony on the first ring. The sound was scratchy, traffic in the background. A pay phone.

"Got your page."

"I think I found 'em" said Tony. "Car's not in the lot, but the motel clerk ID'ed the female. Marcy."

"Jesus, how did you—"

"She checked in last night. Clerk didn't see anyone wit' her. Figures Henry'd be layin' low. I told the clerk I was working a divorce case and keep it under his hat."

"God bless you Tony."

"Thank me later. Right now you got a decision to make."

"What's that?"

"You gonna invite the cops and feds to the party? Or not?"

"Not," said Walt.

"I agree." said Tony. "The media'd be up their ass. Problem is I can't handle it myself, not with two inside and a little one to look after. And I got nobody on staff who's worth a shit."

"Could you and I handle it?"

"I dunno. You know how to use a handgun?"

"Absolutely," lied Walter.

"I only got the one vest though."

"I don't care."

Tony's dubious grunt crackled and broke up. "You willin' to do violence against this guy?"

The Violin Player

"Of course," said Walt. "Why do you ask?"

"That's the other reason we don't need badges," said Tony. "Could be he's got your daughter stashed somewhere. He's been smart so far. Thing of it is, once he's got, he ain't gonna divulge her location no matter how long the cops sweat him. That's how he wins."

Holding out while Reenie dies of dehydration in some abandoned room, thought Walt. "Yes, I am extremely willing to do violence against this guy."

"Be quick," said Tony and gave the address.

Agent O'Connor was waiting in the kitchen when Walt stepped out of the laundry room.

You don't have to tell her anything, Walter. She said herself that kidnappings are unique, the only crime where the victim is in charge of the investigation. But you could use some help. Would Agent O'Conor come alone? Would she look the other way if he had to drag his half brother into the bathroom and hold his head in the toilet? Walter believed she would. He cocked his head toward the laundry room.

"Room 116, nobody in or out" said Tony when Agent O'Connor pulled up to the curb in Laura's Lincoln. Walter climbed out from the back seat where he'd hidden himself. They were on a side street off Mannheim Road, a boulevard of cheap motels south of O'Hare.

Walter introduced the ex-cop to the special agent. She stuck out her hand. Tony's paw ate it whole. Agent O'Connor said, "What's the plan?"

Tony shrugged. "Bust the door, get to the kid quick as possible. Shoot if you have to."

"Any other exit points?"

"Bathroom window in the back, real narrow."

"I might fit."

"I'd rather have you going in," said Tony. "No crossfire fuck-ups that way."

"What if they grab the girl and barricade the bathroom door?"

Tony grunted, seeing her point. The kid could get croaked in the time it took to bust through. "Better take a look first."

Agent O'Connor quick walked down the alley. The Meridian Motel was one story, set back from Mannheim Road, the parking lot out front. Tony kept his eyes on room number 116. Lights were on behind the curtains.

"O'Connor's okay," said Walter. "She'll play ball."

"It's your show," said Tony.

They waited a long time. People came and went in the parking lot, cars and trucks fought it out at the intersection, the sky turned purple. Tony smoked a cigarette and looked at his watch. Walt wanted to ask Tony how he tracked down the hideout so quickly but Tony didn't appear to be in a conversational mood.

Agent O'Connor returned jangling a pass key. "Thought this would help," she said brightly. "And I can definitely squeeze through the bathroom window."

Tony took another look at room number 116. Three guns in a small space was one gun too many. Tony handed Walt his Mag Light instead. "We good to go?"

"Standard tactics say wait till later," said Agent O'Connor. "After they've gone to bed."

Tony ground his back molars. Reporters, cops, grifters, and down-on-their-luck PI's looking to get famous were scouring the city block by block. And Tony Sobczak had never seen a long stakeout prior to a forced entry that had gone according to plan.

The Violin Player

Even scabbed over old pros, given enough time to think about it, got crazy as a rat in a coffee can. But it wasn't his call. "Chief?"

"If my daughter's on the other side of that door," said Walter, "I want her now."

Tony and Agent O'Connor checked their weapons. "How long you need?" said Tony.

"Two minutes," said Agent O'Connor.

"Be better if you jimmied the window 'stead of bustin' it. In case they got the little one in the bathtub."

Agent O'Connor took the shim that Tony handed her and walked down the alleyway. Tony ticked two minutes off his watch.

Chapter 61

Hannigan Brannigan Bippety Bee
Hannigan Brannigan what'll it be?

Rude? Did I actually vent my spleen on the pristine pages of this august journal to say that women were *rude*? Would that that was all they were. Lady Macbeth unsheathed her dagger of deceit and betrayal and now all the perfumes of Arabia cannot sweeten this little hand!

It's true that I came up short in the midget war. Failed to take into account the downbrain subcortical dopaminergic bullpucky that drives so much of modern day life in this modern day world on the crest of the New Millenium. *I ran out of drugs and Marcy sobered up.*

Poor timing on my part.

"Omigod! What've we done? What've *you* done? Why is there a bound and gagged little girl in the bathtub??? We can't do this. *I* can't do this! Why did I ever even *talk* to you?"

Well, because my devastating charm is exceeded only by my exquisitely sculpted form and figure *and* I could tell you were

The Violin Player

enamored of your boss man who never gave you a second look *and I reminded you of him in some intriguingly ambiguous way.*

Hannigan Brannigan Bippety Bee
Hannigan Brannigan what'll it be?

The idiots on the idiot box that Marcy insisted on watching round the clock persist in portraying me as a master criminal. *No es la verdad*! I don't recall Professor Moriarity humping down Mannheim to the bus stop in the early dawn with a duffel bag full of sedated kidnap victim slung over his shoulder. They say Chicago is the city that asks no questions but somebody forgot to tell that to the owl-eyed old fart waiting at the stop. 'Whatcha got there?' *The de-limbed torso of your loving wife* is what I wanted to say to him. *Laundry* was what I did say. And that, my friend, is what is known as impulse control.

Hannigan Brannigan Bippety Bee
Hannigan Brannigan what'll it be?

Algeria is perhaps not the first name that comes to mind when one ponders a luxurious retirement. There is the ongoing civil war that has cost many thousands of lives, most of them women and children hacked to death in their beds with long knives and shovels *Shovels?* by fanatical Islamists who swoop down from the hills in the pre-dawn hours. But that's in the *South*. You don't have to wear a *chador* in Algiers. You can even sit on the veranda overlooking the *Mediterranean* and swill champagne if that's your idea of a good time. Leave your dirty glass wherever you like. It will be whisked away by a mute staff of blue-skinned Berbers in starched white tunics, whispering about the palazzo on silken slippers.

I *explained* all of this. I explained it again. I started to explain it a third time when Marcy shushed me out to hear the lead story on the Early Bird News.

Poor timing on her part.

Hannigan Brannigan Bippety Bee
Hannigan Brannigan what'll it be?

Do you have *any* idea where this mercilessly insistent piece of doggerel comes from? Neither do I. It has been loop-de-looping around my cranial cortex nonstop for the past 48 hours. Here it comes again.

Hannigan Brannigan Bippety Bee
Hannigan Brannigan what'll it be?

I feel like HAL in *2001*. The scene where Keir Dullea removes the supercomputer's golden think pods one by one and HAL starts to regress into imbecility, reciting nursery rhymes for the amusement of his homo sapienic masters.

Hannigan Brannigan Bippety Bee
Hannigan Brannigan what'll it be?

I find this latest development decidedly unsettling—

Chapter 62

Marcia Anne Huber had no known family in the Chicago area so Walter was called upon to make the official identification at the Cook County Morgue. Death seemed to agree with her. She looked as pretty and peaceful as Walter had ever seen her. Only the purple ligature marks on her neck marred the placid picture. The poor dumb brilliant lost soul. Walter turned to the heavyset young man in the rubber apron. "That is she."

The young man walked him down the granite footstep-echoing corridor to the rear exit. "Do you know how she was strangled?" said Walt just to be saying something. The young man mumbled something that the stony hall swallowed up. "Excuse me?"

"With a cord," said the young man. "Electrical cord. Flesh was pinched up into the gap."

"The gap?"

"Between the plus and minus wire. Cord from an iron maybe."

"Maybe," said Walt. But it wasn't. The Meridian Motel did not provide such amenities. Didn't even provide a bedside clock or radio. Every detail of that squalid room was etched on Walt's brain-plate The only plug-in appliance was the TV. Henry Ward had strangled Marcy to death with the cord to the television set.

Henry had plugged the TV back in. They found Marcy 'watching' the coverage of the investigation from the motel room's only chair. Walter had hoped, at one point, a million years ago, that Henry might be dissuaded by a plea from his mother or a threat to reveal an embarrassment from his past. But emotional appeals were not going to dissuade Henry Ward. Money might. A bullet would be even better.

Dear God. Had Reenie watched her die?

"Sir?"

Walt realized that he had stopped walking and was staring at his shoes. They needed shining. He resumed walking, bracing himself for the wolf pack in the parking lot. The media frenzy surrounding the case had metastasized into full blown hysteria. Oddly, blessedly, a new figure had stepped into the spotlight. Tony Sobczak. The press couldn't get enough of him, a no bullshit Chicago character with cigarette ashes spilling down his front. They loved his account of tracking down the hideout.

Tony had been a garbageman in younger years. When they worked a T-shaped alley they would back the business end of the truck down the stem of the T, the back up beeper blaring, and park at the top of the T so as not to waste time negotiating the narrow turn. The back up beeper had grown louder during the ransom call. It figured the kidnappers would hole up in a cheap motel. All Tony had to do was find one located near the top of a T alley that had garbage pick up on Wednesday afternoons.

It was a superb piece of detective work that netted them precisely nothing. Police divers found a boxy green Volvo with the letters HV in the license plate at the bottom of a dredging pond three blocks from the Meridian Motel. There were no reports of car thefts

The Violin Player

in the area, no taxi driver had picked up a fare answering the description of Henry Ward, no one at the Meridian Motel had seen or heard anything. Henry and Irene had disappeared.

They came to the end of the corridor. The young man deactivated the exit alarm and put his hand on the push bar. "You ready to do this?"

"Give me a second," said Walt. He made himself presentable as he chased after a stray thought buzzing around the back of his brain. The young man took off his hair net and straightened his rubber apron. What was it? Oh yes. Twyla. If she was still alive Walter needed to rescue her from Marcy's apartment. And she would still be alive. Twyla would outlive them all. "I'm ready," said Walter.

"You want me to run interference?" said the young man.

"Please."

The Jaguar XJR came to a full stop at the bottom of the Armitage off-ramp of the Kennedy Expressway. The news vans queued up behind. The weather had turned. The WBBM forecast called for snow flurries mixed with freezing rain, sleet and a chance of hail. The XJR's wipers scraped feathery snow flakes off the windshield. Walt signaled for a left turn, looked both ways and gave the great beast its head. They tore across the intersection and up the on-ramp and back onto the Kennedy before the trailing news van could cancel its turn signal.

The traffic was light at 1:34 p.m. The Jag veered across three lanes of traffic and entered the northbound express lanes at Diversey. Speed 94 mph, bearing N-NW, outside temperature 34 degrees. No news vans in the rear view mirror. Freedom.

Lt. Skowron and the Chicago PD were proceeding from the

modus operandi premise. Henry Ward had holed up in a cheap motel once and would do so again. Walt had thought this idiotic and said so. Henry Ward would know that every flophouse clerk in the Midwest had seen his pencil sketch by now.

Agent O'Connor and the FBI were proceeding from the home is the place where when you show up they have to take you in premise. Walt had pointed out that Henry's only immediate family member lived in a maximum security rest home. Agent O'Connor had given him her trying not to gloat smile before announcing that Henry Ward had been a married man.

The FBI had run a data sweep on all white male lab techs in the target age range who had been employed in Chicagoland the last three years. They ran a screen for those no longer employed and got seven hits. They scrambled agents from five districts for follow up interviews.

The XJR settled back to 84 mph and glided, effortlessly, in and out of the lesser vehicles in the express lanes. That was the thing, thought Walt. The cops and the FBI were trying way too hard. Some guy at Harris Labs says he attended the wedding of co-worker Henry King, a dead ringer for Henry Ward. Henry King's 401-k plan listed a Melissa Benson as co-beneficiary, last known address Chesterfield, Missouri.

So what? Any woman unfortunate enough to have married Henry Ward would not take him back now. Any woman unfortunate enough to have married Henry Ward would be long dead. Would the fact that Henry had been married in the recent past somehow explain the five year gap between Dad's death and Henry's reign of terror? Explain why Henry was lashing out now? Had the break up of his marriage finally snapped the twig? Maybe, but who cared?

The XJR exited the express lanes, veered across three lanes to

The Violin Player

the Montrose off-ramp and stopped at a stop sign. A gust of wind tunneled the feathery snow. The Jag turned left.

Montrose Avenue was lined with corner taverns, mom and pop retail and two-story yellow-brick post-war apartment buildings. A pleasant, well kept blue collar neighborhood. Not a place in which you would expect a highly-paid young IT executive to live. Walter had paid Marcy a very generous salary. Hadn't he? It had been generous to begin with but she had never asked for a raise that he could remember. Is that what had turned her against him? All she had to do was say I need more money. All Laura had to do was say I need you to spend more time with the family. He wasn't heartless, he was a sole proprietor. Up to his ass in alligators every working day!

Walt turned right on Meade and told himself to stop sniveling. He was monomaniacal about his business because it made life simple. He wore blinders because he liked the view. It was time now to look around and salvage what he could. Including a spoiled rotten Siamese name of Twyla the cat.

Marcy's apartment building was bigger than the others in the neighborhood and evidently designed by committee. It incorporated all the architectural flourishes of the period. A vertical strip of glass brick above the front entrance, two toned aluminum awnings over the boxy windows, fake flagstone cornices made of molded plastic, and big chunks of decorative volcanic rock affixed to either side of the yellow brick façade.

Walter parallel parked on Meade, buttoned up his suit and approached the added on glass and brick portico. He could tell it was added on because the brick was a darker shade of yellow. There was an inside security door and a buzz box for the tenants. M. Huber was unit #215. Walt buzzed the adjacent units until he got a voice on the intercom. A young woman in unit #212. K. Jagovik.

John Knoerle

"This is Walter Sumner. I was Marcy Huber's employer."

No response.

"I'm concerned about Marcy's cat, Twyla. She's a blonde Siamese with a black face. Have you seen her?"

A long pause. "Not today."

"But recently?"

"Ye-es."

"Any chance you could buzz me into the building? I'd like to look for her. I know you don't know me from Adam but you may have seen me on television. Does your apartment face the street?"

"Ye-es."

"Then I'll go out and stand on the sidewalk so you can see that I really am who I say I am. Okay?"

Another long pause. "I guess."

Walt walked out to the sidewalk and turned to face the apartment building. He stood and looked up into the feathery snow that settled on his eyelashes like mist. He thought he saw a slight parting of curtains. He waved, feeling a strange and solitary peace steal over him. The peace of selfless detachment, the peace of cosmic absurdity understood, the peace of a forty-four year old man whose lifelong quest to bend fate to his iron will had led him here. Standing outside an architectural embarrassment of an apartment building in a flurry of late autumn snow performing an anonymous audition for the coveted role of himself.

Walt went back inside the glass and brick portico and waited. The glass security door buzzed open.

Walt searched the first floor for signs of Twyla and knocked on doors. Nobody home. He climbed the stairs to the second floor. The plaid carpeting was frayed, fat jagged tire marks on the pale green walls. Someone had a mountain bike. He walked down the hall, passing unit #212. He called out his thanks to K. Jagovik. The door did not open. Units #213 and #214 did not answer his knock. Walt softened his step as he approached #215, the corner unit, facing the alley. The door was sealed with an orange crime scene sticker.

The cops had searched Marcy's apartment after the kidnapping. The TV news repeatedly aired the tape of officers hauling out boxes of evidence. But the Chicago PD was now casing cash-only motels. And the FBI was off searching for Henry Ward's 'home'.

Henry Ward's home. If Henry Ward could be said to have a home, wasn't #215 it? Could this be his homicidal half brother's final laughing up his sleeve irony? Hiding in plain sight while the authorities were off chasing their tails? Walt pressed his ear against the door, listened, heard nothing. He tried the knob. Locked.

The Henry Ward express was off the rails, that much was obvious. Marcy had derailed it. Killing her may have been part of Henry's plan, but not so soon. Not before the big payoff, not while he was safely hunkered down in the Meridian Motel, many miles from the South Side warehouse district, in the opposite direction of his apparent line of flight. He couldn't check into another motel without risking exposure. The cops had no reports of a carjacking, no reports of a stolen car near the motel. Marcy didn't own a car, Henry Ward would be hard pressed to rent one. He would have been on foot. On foot and looking for a place to hide. Someplace he could get to by cab, bus or El.

And Reenie? Tony thought she might be stashed at a separate location, but that didn't make sense. Henry knew that Walter wouldn't accept the terms of exchange without hearing Reenie's voice. Not without hearing 'Daddy I'm *okay*.' Wherever Henry had gotten to he had brought Reenie with him.

Walter pressed his ear to the door once again. No sound. Laura said these types always have delusions of grandeur. If the express was finally off the rails, if this was Henry Ward's last stand, he wouldn't risk staging it in the corner unit of an eyesore of an apartment building in Old Irving Park. Henry Ward would select a more appropriate setting. The ancestral home. The place where he had been conceived. The house on Hamilton.

Walter regarded the locked door. Twyla wasn't inside. The cops had searched the apartment and sealed it tight. If Twyla was still around one of the neighbors had taken her in. Or she was scrounging for scraps in the alleyway. How the mighty had fallen.

Henry Ward wasn't inside unit #215 either. If past was prologue, if you could study a human being and plot their future behaviour on a graph like the price of dry milk. He used to know people, Walter did. Not so well as Laura maybe but he could size them up and figure out what was important to them and what was not. Come to find out he didn't know shit from apple butter. Not about his grandfather, his father or his wife.

Don't assume, Walter. Take another look. He pressed his ear to the door a third time. He looked again at the orange crime scene sticker. It was slightly wrinkled. Pasted hard against the door but not quite flush against the jamb. The door had been opened.

Walt raced back to the XJR and grabbed his cell phone and began to dial. Dumb, Walter. Not a good idea to call for help on the phone that Henry Ward had used to track you through four states. He looked around. Whatever happened to pay phones? There used to be a pay phone on every corner. He saw a tavern on the corner of Montrose and Meade. He walked south, feeling in his pants pockets for change.

The feathery snow melted under a blanket of low scudding clouds, shiny and silver green like fish scales. The WBBM forecast called for freezing rain, sleet and a chance of hail. But then people

The Violin Player

said all kinds of things. Walt unbuttoned his suit jacket as the temperature climbed five degrees in five seconds.

The corner tavern was dim. One customer playing video poker in the back and a barkeep from another era, gin blossom cheeks, tufts of hair in his ears, a starched white apron cinched up high on his belly. There was a pay phone near the front door. Walt called Tony's pager and left the pay phone number. He took a stool at the bar and ordered a beer and waited. The barkeep asked if he wanted a glass with that. If he recognized Walt or thought it unusual that a well dressed man was pumping nickels into a pay phone in a dim bar in the early afternoon he gave no sign.

You're trying way too hard, Walter. It's right in front of you. He told himself to relax and let all the pieces fall into place like the notes in one of Wolfgang's perfect concertos. Walter waited, tapped his foot, nursed his glass of beer. But the composition didn't come together. There was a piece missing.

Walt twisted around on his barstool and looked at the pay phone. Where the hell was Tony? He always called back instantly. Should he call the cops? They'd come barreling up in ten units with the news vans right behind. And Agent O'Connor was off chasing ghosts in Chesterfield, Missouri. Walt regarded himself in the barroom mirror and wondered if Henry had a gun. He hadn't used one so far. He didn't seem like the gun type. He preferred poison. Henry had injected Thea with a sedative to knock her out. God only knew what he was doing to little Reenie.

A trap door yawed open at the back of Walter Sumner's brain. A trap door above a teeming pit of unspeakable horrors. He ordered a double Jack Daniels neat and chased it with his beer. The missing piece fell into place.

The Meridian Motel was Henry's safe harbor. If Marcy came to her senses and threatened to call the cops Henry could have tied her up or downed her out with drugs. He didn't need to strangle her with a television cord and take off running. Not forty-eight hours before payday. This wasn't about money anymore. If Reenie was still alive she was being held by a madman. Henry Ward was no longer crazy. Henry Ward was insane.

Walter ticked sixty seconds off his watch. No call from Tony. He put a fifty dollar bill and his business card on the bar and said, "If I'm not back here in twenty minutes, call the cops."

The barkeep nodded as if this happened every day.

Walt raced back to the XJR and popped the trunk. He stripped off the gray carpeting and yanked out the spare tire. Underneath was a two foot black steel rod used to crank the jack. Walt picked it up and smacked it against his palm. The Jaguar people thought of everything. The crank rod had a rubberized grip.

Walt entered the portico, removed his suit jacket and used it to muffle the sound of busting the glass security door. He marched up the stairs at a deliberate pace, following his own footprints contoured in melted snow. Secondary considerations crowded him as he made his way down the second floor corridor. What if this? Shouldn't you that? He kept them at bay by beating time with the steel crank rod and repeating *It's only a door, Walter.*

He stopped in front of unit #215. He pressed his ear against the door one last time and heard only the faint hum of forced air heat. The door did not have a dead bolt, just the standard front door lockset. Walt reared back and kicked two inches above the latch. The door flew open and a slender man sat bolt upright from a couch that had no cushions.

Chapter 63

Walt paused in the doorway for half a second. To get his bearings. To look for Reenie. To see if he was staring down the barrel of a gun. Henry Ward used that half second to levitate off the couch and snake his boneless body over the armrest and disappear down the hall.

Walt pursued him, cursing himself for his hesitation. He found three doors off a short L-shaped hall. All closed. Henry Ward was about to murder Reenie behind one of them. *Think Asshole*! The far left door. A bedroom with a back window.

The knob did not turn. Walt threw his weight against the door in a fury and flew into the room, lost his balance and fell to his hands and knees on the nylon carpeting. The door had not been latched.

He jumped to his feet. What he didn't see gave Walt Sumner hope. Henry Ward was not laying in ambush with an automatic weapon. Reenie's body did not lay crumpled in a heap. What Walter did see caused him to vault up and over the bed and raise the steel crank rod high over his head.

Henry Ward was backing out of the window, climbing out onto

a fire escape ladder he had hooked over the sill. Walter reached out the window and snagged Henry by the collar of his shirt.

Henry sank his teeth into the meat of Walter's palm. Walter spread his legs to brace himself, leaned out the window, *smacked* Henry Ward upside the head with the crank rod and hauled him into the apartment.

Henry Ward lay face down on the floor, unmoving. He's playing possum, thought Walt. He hadn't hit him hard enough to knock him out. He thumped Henry a good one. No response. Walter hit him again, targeting the tip of the tailbone. Henry Ward groaned. Walter knelt both knees on the small of Henry's back, placed the crank rod behind Henry's neck, leaned his weight against it and said, "Where is my daughter?"

Henry Ward coughed and sputtered against the floor. Walter eased the pressure enough for him to speak. Henry Ward turned his head to one side and said, mildly, "Which one?"

Walter pushed hard against the steel rod. Henry Ward grimaced but made no sound. Walter released the pressure and asked again. "Where is my daughter?"

Henry Ward took several quick choppy breaths, sniffed the air and said, "Have we been drinking?"

Walter stood up and yanked Henry to his feet.

Their gaze met in a wall mirror, the two half brothers. Walter had a moment's fear, had to will himself not to look away. Recent events had hardened his heart and steeled his nerve but Henry Ward had a forty year head start. Henry turned his colorless red-rimmed orbs from Walter to himself, looking his reflection up and down. "Remind you of anyone, do I?"

Yes, Henry Ward looked like a hollowed out reincarnation of his father, their father, our father. *So fucking what?* Walter hobbled

The Violin Player

him with a swack to the knee and marched him through the apartment. Henry limped ahead, passive as a rag doll.

Reenie wasn't under the bed. She wasn't in the closet. She wasn't in the other bedroom, the bathroom, the living room coat closet or the armoire. Neither was anything else. The Chicago PD had stripped the place bare.

She *has* to be here, thought Walt. He hooked his left arm around Henry's neck and squeezed his throat into the crook of the elbow. Henry struggled to say something. Walter eased the pressure. "I have a secret in my refrigerator," hissed Henry Ward.

Walter tightened his choke hold and dragged Henry into the kitchen by his heels. Was he, Walter Sumner, capable of murder? If the grisly image taking shape in his mind were true, yes he was.

"Open it!"

He stood Henry Ward in front of the refrigerator. Henry Ward made melodramatic gagging noises. Walter shoved him forward and did the deed himself. Reenie's dead blue-lipped body was not curled up inside. Walter clutched Henry Ward tight as a lover and whispered in his ear, "Where is my daughter, Henry?"

Walter relaxed his grip. Henry Ward hacked and hawed his voice box back into order. "I love it when you call me Henry."

Walter dragged him back, searching the kitchen drawers for an implement of torture. A knife. Or a cheese grater. But the Chicago PD had been there before him. Walter paused before the kitchen sink. He bent Henry forward, threw switches until the garbage disposal started its angry hungry hum, threw down his crank rod, grabbed Henry Ward's right hand and forced it downward.

This got his demented half brother's attention. Henry's back arched, his right hand flattened over the hole, his left hand tugged at the back of Walt's hair, his heels kicked at Walt's shins, his teeth gnashed at nothing. Walt tightened his choke hold. Henry Ward's flailings grew weaker.

Walt concentrated all his pent up fury and sorrow on the task at hand. Grinding his half brother's right hand into hamburger. Did human appendages have a primal intelligence independent of the brain? Henry Ward was convulsing from lack of oxygen yet his right hand strenuously resisted. It knew perfectly well that it didn't want to be plunged into those churning blades.

Walter kept at it, forcing Henry's hand through the orifice, past the rubber flanges and just above the blades. He eased up on Henry's windpipe. They were in an odd configuration, the two half brothers. Bent sideways over the sink, legs twined, front to back as tight as they could go. Henry sucked air in ragged gasps. Walter kept Henry's right hand in place and repeated the question.

"Where is my daughter?"

When Henry Ward got his breath he said, "She's under the sink, dickhead."

It happened in half a second. Less than. Walter didn't feel a thing. He had been distracted by Henry's remark. Relaxed his vigilance maybe. Wanted to search the one space in the apartment capable of hiding his daughter that he had overlooked.

Walter recognized three troubling signs. The first one was the razor blade in Henry Ward's left hand. A one-sided blade, the type used to scrape stickers off car windshields. The second troubling sign was that Henry Ward was running away. The third troubling sign was that Walter couldn't see well enough to pursue him, could barely see his hand in front of his face for the torrent of blood spilling over his eyebrows.

Chapter 64

"Why did you shoot him in the back?" said Matarina Jones, a great deal of furrowed concern contorting her elegant features.

Tony Sobczak took his time answering. Cameras whirred. They were seated across a desk at his office. Tony had removed the sign in the front window and tacked it up on the wall behind him. Irving Park Investigations—Security, Surveillance, Secrecy.

"Because I was behind him at the time."

Matarina Jones managed to appear both amused and disapproving. Tony continued, "Henry Ward was running down the stairs, saw me and turned tail. I had reason to believe my client was on the second floor and that the suspect meant to do him grievous harm. Years of experience in police pursuit told me I was not going to win a footrace." Tony paused. Matarina grinned. "So I fired my handgun."

"And killed him with one shot."

Tony shrugged.

"And how is your client? Mister Sumner?"

"He's gonna be fine."

"And his younger daughter?"

"She'll be fine too."

John Knoerle

"What are their plans? The Sumner family."

Tony patted himself for cigarettes. "To start over."

Matarina Jones said, "Whose your friend there?"

"Her name's Twyla. I'm cat sitting."

"She seems to like you."

"Naw," said Tony Sobczak, eyeing the formerly plump Siamese making herself comfortable in his lap. "She just likes to piss me off."

Chapter 65

Walter Sumner stood at the counter and caught his breath after climbing the absurdly long steep staircase of the Henry County Department of Health. "I have something that belongs to you," he said.

Mrs. Cantwell looked up from her desk. She smiled a bright smile when she recognized him, frowned with concern when she saw the thick ocherous bandage taped to his right temple.

"You remember Thea and Irene don't you?"

"Of course, of course," said Mrs. Cantwell, crossing to the counter. "Welcome back young ladies."

The girls said thank you very much, almost in unison. They had been like that since the end of the ordeal. Inseparable, and walking on eggshells polite.

"Do you like computer games? Because I have a few on my i-MAC that you might find interesting." She ushered Thea and Irene to her desk. "I'll get you a second chair."

"That's okay," said Thea, seating her baby sister on her lap. They selected a game without argument and played quietly. Mrs. Cantwell watched them for a long moment. When she returned to the counter her cool green eyes were moist. "Remarkable children."

Walt just smiled. "The cops found the yearbook," he said, and placed it on the counter.

"Would you like to sit down?"

"No thanks. We've been on the road for hours. It feels good to stand."

Mrs. Cantwell lowered her voice. "How is the little one? Irene?"

"Amazingly well, considering. She was heavily sedated most of the time. Which is a blessing."

Mrs. Cantwell nodded. She knew about Marcy's strangulation in the motel room. Everyone in America knew about Marcy's strangulation in the motel room except Reenie, and Walter intended to keep it that way as long as possible. He tapped the leather-bound Walter Chrysler High School yearbook. "The cops found it taped to the back of a wall mirror in the apartment where Henry Ward was hiding out. I'm wondering why."

Walt didn't need to remind Mrs. Cantwell of his previous request or ask if she had been successful. If it were humanly possible to find out what he wanted to know Mrs. Cantwell would have done so.

She removed her glasses and cleaned them with a tissue, "Well, I don't believe he kept it out of any fond feelings for his high school peers. I was able to contact a member of the '68 track team. Chuck Hancie, he lives in Millville down the road. The reason they nicknamed Henry Ward 'Three Locks' was that, well—" Her cheeks colored slightly. "Apparently he had a pathological fear of nudity."

"I beg your pardon?"

The girls paused in the middle of their game, curious as to why the adults were speaking in hushed tones. Mrs. Cantwell paused until they grew bored and resumed their game. "Chuck Hancie said that Henry would arrive early for practice in order to change alone and would never shower afterwards, would walk home in his sweaty track clothes in fair weather and foul."

"But why the nickname?" said Walt.

"Well because," said Mrs. Cantwell. She was reluctant to say this. Walter waited. "Because Henry would place an extra combination lock on either side of his locker in order to keep other team members at a distance. So he wouldn't, as Chuck so colorfully phrased it, 'risk bumpin' into a big ol' bare butt.'"

Walter almost laughed out loud. That was it? Henry's terrible secret? A childish trick to protect his obsessive modesty? "But if the other boys knew about these locks, well, you can imagine what teenage boys would do."

"They didn't figure it out at first," said Mrs. Cantwell. "Then someone caught on and they started to taunt him, mercilessly. They gave him the nickname 'Three Locks'."

Mrs. Cantwell turned to make sure the girls weren't eavesdropping. She drew a breath. "And one day, apparently, some of the older boys stripped him naked and dumped him out on the field where the football team, and the cheerleading squad, were practicing."

"Jesus."

"They wouldn't let him back in the locker room," said Mrs. Cantwell. "He had to run all the way home in that condition."

Walter opened the yearbook to the bookmarked page. Henry Ward, face skyward, arms thrown open, crossing the finish line, 'doing what he does best'.

Walter, who had felt nothing but relief at the news of his demented half brother's death, had in fact experienced a dark and carnal glee, shook his head and said, "The poor sad son-of-a-bitch."

Mrs. Cantwell pressed her lips together.

LUCIUS BEEBE MEMORIAL LIBRARY

3 1392 00382 1554

FICTION
Knoerle

BEEBE LIBRARY
345 MAIN STREET
WAKEFIELD, MA 01880
(781) 246-6334
wakefieldlibrary@noblenet.org

DEMCO